# SILK & SILVER

### BY
## ANDREW SHIELDS

SILK AND SILVER
Copyright © 2018 by Andrew Shields

Cover art by John Harper

https://shieldsuppublishing.wordpress.com/

ISBN: 978-1-7327586-1-2 (paperback)
      978-1-7327586-2-9 (hardback)

# FOREWORD

When I first created the *Blades in the Dark* roleplaying game, it was a only tiny seed — a core concept expressed with some evocative language on a few pieces of paper and a vision for where I wanted to go. It was through the act of play — the actual game at the table with that first group of players — that the seed was nurtured and took root. Roleplaying games are all about collaboration at their heart. Each game experience is the product of many minds working together with a shared creative vision to bring the material to life at the table. The same was true for the development of the RPG book. I expressed my vision for the book as best I could in words and art, and my collaborators — the professionals who lended their expertise as well as the amateurs who shared feedback from playtesting — helped refine it into its final form. The entire journey of the game was one of collaboration — the product of intense creative teamwork.

And now, with this novel, the collaborative process has reached its apex. In this book, Andrew has achieved something truly magical: something that is wholly his own original work, while at the same time being a celebration of *Blades in the Dark*. Everything is here, from the amazing details he's added to every aspect of the setting of Doskvol, to the touching, human stories he's given to the characters, to the exciting series of daring scores that they pull off — which perfectly express the promise of the systems of the roleplaying game. This is no mere love letter to what I created. I built the anvil and stoked the fire, but Andrew has drafted and forged his own blade here, and it is a keen one. To see everything come to life in Andrew's writing is a great joy for me, not only as a collaborator along the way, but also as a lover of great fantasy adventure stories. I'm excited for you to experience this world and these wonderful characters, and to fall in love the way I have.

*John Harper*
*Seattle, WA*
*2018*

# ━━ CHAPTER ONE ━━

*So the sky broke, and the dead walked, and the sea turned to ink, and immortal demons surfaced from their depths. Still there were children to feed. Still there was need of the public, and the public good, with leaders to aim the works of humanity so that individuals might contribute to the survival of all.*

*Humanity is really only a few stories anyway; tales of love, and revenge, and struggle. The cycles of exaltation and ruin play out across every life, no matter how strange the background may become. We have had eight centuries to prove humanity can become accustomed to anything.*

*- From "Historical Ruminations of the Fall and Subsequent Taxation," by Aletha Sventon*

## SILKSHORE. ANKHAYAT PARK. 51ST SURAN, 847

"Must we meet on Doomsday?" asked the slender woman, her smile skewed wry. A sudden gust of wind lay across the deck of the motionless ship, and the two figures standing at the rail tightened their grip.

"I like the drama of it," replied the much younger man at her side, looking out over the dark waters that flowed past, echoing the dark sky overhead. "Also the tradition. You know how nostalgic I am."

"You never boarded a Leviathan hunting ship in your life,"

sighed the woman, shaking her head. "Tell me, Kreeger, what are you nostalgic for?"

"Hope, maybe," he said. "I once had the sense that I would penetrate the ranks, rise to some sort of standing, make something of myself." He looked down. "Now I feel like this ship."

The massive Leviathan hunting ship had been shorn into thirds decades ago. Now staircases rose from the park's walkways to the aft of the ship. It was built into the shore, but the deck still retained its dizzying height, almost fifty feet above the water of the river. Now it was a scenic lookout. Half a mile downriver, at the other end of the park, the prow of the Doomsday jutted out into the river for those looking forward rather than back.

"Oh, Kreeger," the woman said, reassuringly patting his shoulder, "you're too young to know what time can yet do to you."

"I imagine that's calculated to make me feel better," Kreeger reflected. He looked over at the woman. "It's not working, Nebs. You are terrible at this."

"Well most of my descendants aren't whiners like you," she shot back, baring her teeth in something like a smile. "You've got your job with the Ministry, and enough money to keep your husband in those fancy shirts he likes, and in the next few years you'll likely advance enough to move to a better neighborhood." She shrugged. "This is as good as it gets. You are firmly embedded in the establishment." Her jaw flexed. "You're as safe as we make you."

"And I'm grateful," Kreeger added quickly. "I am." He looked out across the dark rippling current, watching its silent rush towards the ocean.

"You're restless," Nebs sighed.

"There are so many opportunities out there," Kreeger murmured, eyes fixed on the river. "Just upstream, there's a gondolier station that's gotten sloppy with how they handle their contraband. One night's work would net more profit than three months with the Ministry." He glanced over at Nebs. "You heard about the hit on the Grinders tonight, right? The Skovlanders are getting bolder, moving into this territory, threatening everything we've built—"

Nebs put her hand on his forearm, and he abruptly quieted. She sighed.

"Kreeger, when I was about your age, my grandfather had a talk with me," she said, something distant in her voice as she looked out at the opposite shore, glittering in the dimness. "He told me that our family's work with the Hive was expensive, certainly. They keep most of the profits. But the return on that investment," she added with a shake of her head, "is a kind of stability you can't get elsewise in this city. You buy stability. Your loyalty earns you protection. It may not be glamorous," she admitted. "Don't imagine I was propelled out of bed each day by the prospect of calculating value and exchange rates on silk bales and moderating the flow through standard, gray, and black markets." She sighed. "But I got old enough to have this talk with you, and I think we both know that wouldn't have happened if I had let my greed get to me, my ambition overrule my senses." She paused. "Yesterday I played with grandchildren that would not exist were I to be swept up in ambition like yours."

He savored an ironic smile. "That's your pitch? Keep your head down so you can be a grandpa?"

"That's my wisdom, you snide little smartass," she retorted, a smile nudging her indignation.

"To hell with grandchildren," Kreeger said, sharp.

"There you have it," Nebs said as she rolled her eyes. "To hell with them indeed. Come on, buy your aunt some fishstick and lime."

"Why am I buying?" Kreeger shot back, arching an eyebrow.

"You think my wisdom is free?" Nebs responded, raising both eyebrows. "You come to the temple of the elders, you pay your supplication fee." She threaded her arm through the crook of his elbow. "I want a cheese cup too."

They turned away from the stern majesty of the river, heading towards the stairs. "It's good to see you, Nebs," he said with half a smile.

"I know," she agreed. "Somebody has to keep your pretty head on straight."

"Aw, you think I'm pretty?" he grinned.

"Don't push it," she sniffed.

They strolled down the long staircase to the park, once again surrounded by the dim glow of the lights that lay over the deep shadows of the greens and statues. "I think the fish cart was over this way," Kreeger said. He looked over at Nebs. "I used to come here with Styles. I don't know if you heard, but he joined a crew. They call him Piccolo. He's actually doing something—"

"Styles is crazy," Nebs said with a dismissive wave of the hand. "He'll be dead in a year. Or less."

## SILKSHORE. BASEMENT OF THE RIVER STALLIONS TOWER LAIR. 51ST SURAN

The heavy door battered open, and the young woman groaned as she staggered to a chair and collapsed into it. The young man behind her was shoved in to the room, but he gracefully recovered his balance and pivoted to scowl at the big man that followed him in.

"You fool," the last one in growled as he slammed the door. "You idiot."

"My leg," the woman said, her voice tight as she gripped her leg with both hands and hauled it up on a chair. A fresh welter of blood oozed from the nasty gashes on her calf and shin.

"Stay put," the big man snapped, jabbing his finger towards the young man across the table. He turned to the woman, kneeling at her side and examining the wound. "This isn't good, Red," he muttered.

"I know that," she responded, her jaw locked to keep the pain in. "Just get that damn boot off." She squeezed her eyes shut.

"Need some help, Saint?" asked the other man.

"Yes!" Saint shouted at him. "Yes I do! I need some competent scoundrels who can follow an order from time to time and not screw around! But I don't have that, do I?"

"I said I was sorry!"

Saint rose to his feet. "Might as well make yourself useful now, Piccolo. Get some water over here, some clean towels, and the sewing kit." His forehead creased. "We have to clean this out as best we can."

Piccolo scowled, and crossed the musty basement to the covered bucket of water by the wash basin. "Why are we down here in the basement, anyway?" he asked. "And where's Gapjaw?"

"I wasn't about to haul her up the stairs like this," Saint growled as he worked the clothing out of Red's wounds.

"What about Gapjaw? And the Hammer?" Piccolo put the basin down with a clatter, and flicked the towel off his forearm. "I figured they'd be back by now. We took the long way around."

"Now you care about your fellow scoundrels?" Saint gritted out as he dampened the towel. "Fine time to start." He looked Red in the eye. "This is going to hurt."

"Dig in, old man," she hissed, something like rage in her eyes. She raised a leather glove, and bit it hard. He nodded, then turned his attention to the task. She leaned back with a muffled roar, veins pressing against the skin of her neck, her tendons taut. She gripped the chair, every muscle tense as the gray towel darkened with her blood and the big man leaning over her leg probed for debris in the wounds.

Piccolo tugged his leather cap off and ran his hand through his thin dark hair, his eyes seeming even bigger against the backdrop of greasy warpaint he'd rubbed over his face earlier. He did not even realize he was pacing. It seemed like forever before Saint rose up away from the bloody work.

"Rest now," he said, putting his hand on Red's sweaty forehead. "I'll get to the stitches in a minute." He turned his attention to Piccolo.

"Cause I figured Gapjaw and the Hammer would be back by now," Piccolo explained.

"We got separated," Saint muttered. "When the plan went south. We were on the way to the exit, we had passed the check point. You were supposed to be headed out through the tunnel. Why were you on the roof?"

"I found a back way that led up, and I figured it would go to a treasure room. Things were going smooth, so I checked it out," Piccolo shrugged. "I got to the top of the ladder and found a room with no windows and a bunch of paperwork, it was all in Skovic. I put a bunch of it in a bag, figured I'd round out our payday," he said with a crooked grin.

"Yeah, that's what you thought," Saint said, expressionless. "Then what actually happened?"

"I didn't see the alarm on the exit," Piccolo replied, frowning. "I got up to the watch platform, and there was this girl charging at me." He winced, gingerly moving his arm. "She was faster than I thought. Came right in with a knife, didn't even ask any questions. Got a good look at me, and got the bag with the paperwork, and I figured she would make trouble for us."

"A girl," Saint agreed. "She was sixteen years old. Only been in

9

town three months. She'd actually been hiding in that secret area you found. Her name was Asdis."

"Really?" Piccolo said, uncomfortable. "So, you knew her?"

"By reputation only," Saint shrugged. He stared into Piccolo's eyes. "She was Hutton's niece, just in from Skovlan."

"Heh," Piccolo blurted. "Like, Hutton, the man in charge of the Grinders? The head man?" He tried to smile, but his lips wouldn't twist that way.

"The same," Saint agreed. "The second you triggered that tower alarm, the whole warehouse compound went on lockdown and they released their pouncer wolves. Did you stick around to see that?" he demanded. "Wolves with damned bat wings who can leap and swoop. Yes. Dragged the Hammer right off the wagon. Red managed to shoot two of them off him, we believe he probably got out through the sewers. But we didn't get the wagon out." He paused. "So, no payday, and a blood feud started with the headman of the Grinders." He cocked his head to the side. "And the pouncers damn near tore Red's leg off before we got away. I got to crack a jaw hinge to get her leg out of a death grip. This here? This is what lucky looks like, we were lucky to get away after the alarm almost caught us all in a death trap."

"Where—where's Gapjaw?" Piccolo asked, glancing around the basement room again, avoiding eye contact with Red. She stared at him, containing her fury.

"Gapjaw was following orders, securing the exit strategy," Saint said through his teeth. "Gapjaw understood the importance of the mission. How if we stuck to the plan we would get everyone out and nobody would get killed, and we wouldn't trigger an avalanche of pissed off Skovlanders to bury us where we stand."

"Hey, when you recruited me, you weren't all bloodless about some Skov crew," Piccolo retorted. "You said the River Stallions were dead hard."

"We are," Saint replied, eyebrows raised, voice level. "But you choose your battles, or you pay the price. You put us in crosshairs we didn't want to fill."

"Well things change," Piccolo yelled. "You wanted me because I know what to do when things go sideways. I don't fold up when the plan falls apart. So I won't stand here and take your abuse. I was looking for a better payday, and it didn't go as expected. That's—"

"Enough!" Saint roared. "You will stay here in this basement where we can keep an eye on you. I'll talk to Hutton. I get to tell him I've got his niece's killer in custody." He glowered at Piccolo. "We'll work something out."

Piccolo stared at him for a long moment. "Yeah," he said, "to hell with that and to hell with you." He pivoted, bounding to the door, and yanking it open.

He was half ready for the hand that darted in, snatching at his coat. His reflexes pulled him back and to the side, so the hand snatched at the sleeve of his coat. He twisted, tugging hard, and the figure standing in the doorway was yanked into the doorjamb with a meaty smack. In a single smooth motion Piccolo was hopping up to throw his whole body weight into a stamping kick that slammed into the ambushing man's knee, twisting his weight sideways and propelling it again into the doorway.

The big man's grip faltered, and his silhouette only inhabited half the doorway; Piccolo darted into the gap as Saint dragged his pistol out and fired, the crashing explosion filling the room with a gust of smoke. The shot went wide, and the big man in the doorway struggled to rise as Piccolo raced up the stairs.

"He's quick," the big man admitted, limping into the room and leaning heavily on the back of a chair.

"After him!" Saint demanded.

"Not a chance," the big man said, shaking his square head. "You've seen the lad run. The only way I'd catch him is if he was ready for me to." He pulled a chair out, and fell heavily into it, tenderly rubbing at his knee. "He's not much of a fighter," he grunted, "but he plays dirty and remembers old wounds." His smile was almost fond, revealing several missing teeth.

Saint stared at him for a long moment. "That little shit is loose," he snapped, "and he knows I was ready to kill him. He knows us, our faces and names and methods. He gets out, we've got problems."

"Then we've got problems," Gapjaw sighed, dragging the dusty bottle of rum to himself and sloshing it up for a swig. "Not our finest day." He drew a long knife from his belt, studying the blade. "The Hammer will find his way home," he murmured reflectively. "We will work something out with the Grinders, one way or another. Politics." His smile was almost a sneer as he jabbed the knife into the table.

"Saint," said Red, her face pale and her eyes dark. "We need to call in the rest of the crew and deal with this. Like, immediately."

Saint nodded, then picked up the dusty rum bottle and drained it in three swallows.

"Better get to work," he agreed.

## SILKSHORE. VEYLES TEA SHOP. 52$^{ND}$ SURAN

Kreeger shouldered through the heavy door, strolling through the bustle of the tea shop. He nodded to the server at the podium, and headed up the narrow stairs unchallenged. Smiling to himself, he settled at the table overlooking the street—his table. Across the street, a massive clock face was built into the wall of a bookstore, and the susurration of its inner workings was almost audible even at this range.

The upstairs server was at his elbow in a moment, providing the crisped mushroom cap lightly buttered with a pinch of salted bacon shavings, chilled goat milk, and a copy of the Shore Doings paper.

"Thank you, Edward," Kreeger said absently as he picked up the paper, snapping it open, enjoying the familiar smell of curing ink and pulp paper.

The table jostled, and Kreeger's fingers folded the top half of the paper down as he glared at the man who slid into place across from him.

"Styles?" Kreeger blurted, shocked by the other man's appearance. Styles had done his best to rub the greasepaint camouflage off, but his clothes were still rumpled and stained, and he looked a step worse off than homeless. The wild look in his eyes did not help.

"Hey cuz," Styles grinned, a touch manic. "I was hoping we could talk." He stared significantly at Edward as the server glanced over towards the bouncer.

Kreeger waved them back, and frowned intently at Styles. "You're going to get us both kicked out if you don't keep it down and then promise to leave when you've had your say."

"Sure, sure, great," Styles grinned painfully. "So what's up?"

"This is not how small talk happens," Kreeger said, severe. "Why are you here."

"I've had it with the River Stallions," Styles scowled. "Ungrateful bastards. I thought they were the real deal, but they're all talk, and they're never going to get a real payday. Not like what I was promised." He tugged the plate with Kreeger's mushroom cap in range, picking the cap up with his fingers and wincing at the heat, undeterred from taking a bite. He squinted at Kreeger. "I remembered all those talks we had, along the river. All your awesome plans."

"For future reference," Kreeger said, "you take a bath, put on some decent clothes, and set up a meeting to talk to someone to invite them to do business." A mirthless laugh escaped. "And bring a gift, you idiot."

"No, that's how you do it, because you're all fancy with the plans and the manipulation," Styles objected as he waved the mushroom cap energetically. "I come across as sincere because it's important to me to really have this talk, man, right when I have the moment of truth, because it's too important to wait!"

"You think—you think your impulse shows you the way to go? That the first idea is best and you just leap at whatever opportunity dangles in front of you? Are you a thinblooded hagfish?" Kreeger demanded.

Styles blinked, taking another big bite out of the mushroom cap, rapidly chewing, unsure of whether he was supposed to answer.

Kreeger glanced over at the server, who was dutifully ignoring the conversation, then he sighed. "Look, I can get you a job at the Ministry. Somewhere to live until you can pull yourself together."

"Are you serious? You think I'd settle?" Styles managed to choke out around the cap. "Hell no."

"You get your pride I guess, but I'm out my breakfast to support it," Kreeger retorted. "You want mystique, glory, easy money, but that's not how it works. If you want a reason to believe you'll have retirement to look forward to, your crazy underworld antics must stop."

Styles paused, then put the mushroom cap down. "You were eight, I was six. I walked along the beam and collected four griefer bird eggs. Then I threw them, one at a time, down the smoke stack of that parked steamer. Those griefer birds harassed that crew until they left port." He paused. "Age sixteen, I stole Officer Laramye's brass-buttoned hat. I still have that hidden away in my secret stash," he said, "because it was then that I realized I had a gift. All I am ever going to be good at is taking stuff away from people, stuff they want to keep. And don't you think I forgot the time we stole those peaches from Salvari's radiant orchard. I told you we couldn't do it because there were spiders, those big venomous fist-sized orb spiders. What did you say?" Styles stared Kreeger right in the eye.

Kreeger watched him for a long moment. "I said there was no point unless there were spiders."

"Damn straight," Styles said with a firm nod. "I will never forget how delicious those peaches were. But even more delicious was how you used the spiders you caught. Professer Frywell. Those bullies that were always hanging around the end of the block, and their leader, what was his name?"

"Daikinaro," Kreeger mumbled, frowning slightly.

"Right, Daikinaro. Trying to have his make-out session in the alley, and you just dumped the rest of the basket down there. I think he might still be running."

"And our family had to move to avoid the fuss, if you remember," Kreeger objected.

"I don't care," Styles said earnestly. He rose to his feet, planting his fists, leaning over at Kreeger. "When you woke up this morning you didn't give a damn about today and you weren't who you really are. Maybe you can live with that today, but it's gonna suck if you follow this path another ten years."

"Care to order something, sir?" the server asked, standing at Styles' elbow, implacable. The bouncer loomed in the not-too-distant background.

"I'm going," Styles replied, flexing his arm as though shaking off a grip. "You, I'll be in touch," he said, pointing at Kreeger. "Tonight." He pivoted and stalked out, the bouncer close behind.

"Would you like another cap?" the server asked Kreeger, polite.

"No thank you, that's fine," Kreeger said with a wave. He adjusted himself in his seat, uncomfortable, and looked out the window. He was confronted with the massive clock face across the street.

Lit from behind, its numbers and face ornate, the clock was ringed with symbols of the three seasons. The hands moved in a cunning frame that showcased the months of the year as well as the hours of the day. Time within time within time, nested in lockstep, whirling on, the teeth of the clock's cogs as inexorable and impersonal as a glacier that carved a path over rock. Time and gravity, doing their work, and Kreeger felt lines bloom across his flesh and deepen as he sat in the same chair where he had been coming for the last eight years of working in his current position in the Ministry. He felt the eyes of the future upon him, perhaps of himself in twenty years looking back at this moment, wondering if it could have been different.

"I'm as safe as they can make me," he murmured.

As something valuable, he had never felt more locked up.

## SILKSHORE. CHIMEWATER CLOSE. 52ND SURAN

Fog was beginning to rise from the water as Kreeger climbed out of the gondola. He crossed the quay with long strides, lost in thought, and he glanced up at the windows of his narrow row house. Only candle light. His face set, and he rounded the stone fence post and bounded up the stairs to the heavy door, entering his house.

Following the light, he found his way to the den, where the floor-length windows were thrown open to the balcony, and the light rain that was mustering the energy to fall across the river breathed its first drops. A tall man stood framed in the doorway, watching the river's mood.

"Rutherford," Kreeger said with something like relief. "I don't know what I'm doing with my life."

The tall man turned, the small smile that always lurked in his features strengthening, even as the sadness that was always in his eyes did not change. "Seems anti-climactic to ask how work went today," he said. He crossed to the desk, and poured out a measure of spore wine into a cut crystal tumbler, which Kreeger swept up and downed immediately. "Trouble at the office?"

"My idiot cousin," Kreeger breathed out through his teeth.

"Styles."

"I really only have the one," Kreeger sighed. "He thought he was a tough guy, and joined a crew, and now he's on the run. I'm sure they're probably trying to kill him. He didn't even bother washing off his war paint before he tracked me down. He wants me to start a gang so he can keep at it."

Rutherford resumed his post looking out over the river. "And you question your life choices?"

"I want you to tell me this whole thing is preposterous," Kreeger said, scowling at his tumbler.

"This whole thing is preposterous," Rutherford agreed.

"I've got security with the Ministry, and with the Hive, and with a little patience I have all the opportunity I've ever wanted." Kreeger cocked his head to the side, looking over at Rutherford.

"I know you're restless," Rutherford said quietly, still watching the river. "You of all people know this is not the answer."

"Exactly," Kreeger nodded. "Exactly."

"I was thinking about that," Rutherford continued, turning. He stopped abruptly, eyes widening. Then he scowled. "What are you doing here?"

Kreeger scrambled to his feet, pivoting to face the intruder who stood in the doorway to the den. "You had better start talking," he snapped, fear galvanizing to anger.

The intruder had round shoulders and a square head, almost bow legged, slightly misshapen by scars and pain pressed in over time. His stringy hair was combed back, and his clothes looked worse than they smelled. His smile revealed missing teeth. "Hello, my name is Gapjaw. I happen to know you had a visitor today," he said, his accent gravelly. He extended his hands to the sides, utterly failing to put his audience at ease. "I just need to know where he is."

"So you can kill him," Kreeger stated, irritation flowing through him. "Of course."

Gaptooth blinked and squinted in a moment of thought. "Well it's unlikely we will be the ones to kill him," he said.

"It doesn't matter," Kreeger yelled with a wild gesture. "You'll get nothing from me, so get out!"

"I am trying very hard to be friendly," Gaptooth said slowly.

"I retired from the Bluecoats, did you know that?" Rutherford asked. "I think it's time you left." He reached behind one of the curtains flanking the doorway that framed him, and he pulled out a baton. Gaptooth frowned, but did not move. "No?" Rutherford continued. He reached behind the curtain on the other side, and produced a pistol. "Get out." Steel entered his voice and eyes as he squared off with the home invader.

"Some days I'm just not cut out for friendly," Gaptooth shrugged. He took a long step back and pivoted, taking cover in the door frame as Rutherford lined up and fired. The bullet plowed through the wood paneling, blowing a chunk out. Kreeger scrambled to the side, forearm thrown up over his face as debris sprayed back from the hit and smoke from the discharge billowed into the room.

Unfazed, Gaptooth squinted into the room, brandishing a pistol of his own. Rutherford's eyes widened as Gaptooth pulled the trigger, and the shattering crash of gunfire in a confined space was deafening, almost covering up the wet slap of torn flesh as the bullet punched into Rutherford's gut.

Kreeger's inarticulate scream tore loose as Rutherford was hurled back to rebound from the den's balcony railing, clattering down on his knees and elbows on the floor, weapons scattering.

"That's the trouble with trying to be friendly," Gapjaw sighed; Kreeger vaguely registered his words over the ringing in his ears. "Nobody tends to vouch for you after an exchange of gunfire. So, to hell with it."

Ignoring the home intruder, Kreeger scrambled across the room to roll Rutherford over. Rutherford's eyes were glazed with fear and pain, and a certain weariness that never had left them. He clutched his gut with both hands as the swamp of gore spread under the paisley of his silk shirt, wiping out the pattern. "K-Kreeger," Rutherford managed through nerveless lips. "Damned cold in here."

"You are going to be alright!" Kreeger shouted at him, furious. "You just hold on because everything is going to be alright!"

"Probably not," Gapjaw retorted. He had taken a bottle in each hand from the bar, and was liberally splashing alcohol around the den. "I don't need him anyway, Piccolo talked to you, right?"

"Bastard!" yelled a voice from the dark hallway. Light caught along the glittering flat of the knife as it twirled from the dimness, slapping into Gapjaw's shoulder. The big man gasped and stumbled, dropping the wine bottles as another knife slashed out and smacked into his bicep. He fumbled for his pistol as two more throwing blades came at him, and he chose to dodge instead of return fire. Scrambling behind the loveseat, he swore loudly.

"See how you like it!" shouted a hoarse voice as a black-clad figure tumbled into the room in an acrobatic dive, popping up with the bar as cover, snatching a bottle from the tabletop with minimal exposure. Piccolo slung the bottle sidearm, and it burst on the wall behind where Gapjaw was taking cover, raining glass and liquor down on the fighting man.

Kreeger ruthlessly tucked himself under one of Rutherford's long arms and hauled at him, brutally forcing him to half rise as he clutched at his ruptured gut. Rutherford cried out in pain, distracting Gapjaw, but before Gapjaw could act, Piccolo had pulled out a pack of matches and struck them against the grain of the bar; fire bloomed along the pack of redheads, and Piccolo tossed them sidearm at the welter of alcohol stains.

Gapjaw scrambled as fast as he could, but the flames carried on the fumes, and in moments he was on fire. Howling, he leaped to his feet and charged for the balcony, as Piccolo rose to his feet and rapid-fire hurled throwing blades at the man-comet that blazed out of the room, banging into and over the balcony rail. It was a survivable fall that ended at the river's edge.

"Help me!" Kreeger roared, and Piccolo forgot about Gapjaw. The skinny young man dipped under Rutherford's other arm, and together the three of them staggered out of the flaming room.

They stumbled down the front steps, Rutherford crying out at every step. They paused to lean against the wall, and Kreeger slapped at Piccolo's shirt to get his attention.

"Get us a gondola," he gasped. "We gotta move." Piccolo nodded curtly, springing down the steps and around the corner.

"This—it's intolerable," Rutherford hissed between his teeth. "I love you, Kreeger," he said as tears squeezed out the corner of his eyes.

"Don't you get mushy on me now," Kreeger said with real fear. "You're going to survive this and we'll have a good laugh about how my idiot cousin rewrote my life one day."

"Maybe not so funny," Rutherford suggested, one eyebrow raising. Then he slumped forward, unconscious.

Then Piccolo was back, and they dragged Rutherford onto the gondola, and as they cruised the busy canal they could see the rapid spread of the fire as Kreeger's life burned.

"If Rutherford dies," Kreeger said evenly, watching his burning house, "I will kill you and I will kill your crew."

"What if he lives?" Piccolo asked meekly.

Kreeger was quiet for a long moment. "If he lives, then I can take the long view."

As the gondola slid away on the dark water, Piccolo decided

that was going to have to be comfort enough.

# ━ CHAPTER TWO ━

*They say the Imperial calendar's six months were named for lands and people lost when the world broke. Such "oral tradition" is gossip that serves the occult interests of buskers and confidence artists. They can pretend there are ways to know more about the past, and if you believe that, then you're a step closer to believing the other messages read in entrails, tea leaves, and fire-cracked bone. If you ask me, it's equally likely the calendar is named after the Immortal Emperor's first six concubines. Regardless, it is best not to contemplate the weight of the dead that entire lost lands imply. We've dead enough close to home without borrowing whole civilizations of ghosts.*

*- Lord Selvuria Anderos,*
*Personal Correspondence*

## SILKSHORE. MASTER MARKET, UNDER THE BOLDWAY
## CANAL STREETS. 52ND SURAN

"It's almost dawn," the petulant man said, raising the lantern. "Are you nearly finished?"

The underside of the arch was dappled by strange reflections, the luminescence from the lantern rebounding from unsteady water to touch on stone. The narrow canal skiff was nosed up to the lowered grating blocking the waterway off from the tunnel, and a hooded figure stood balanced in the craft, carefully painting on the metal of the grating. Two more hooded figures stood on the ledge on the far side of the water, painting on the wall with visually confusing patterns, and on the near side, one hooded figure stoked the fire in the brass bowl at the center of the ritual markings in chalk. The other hooded figure turned to face the man with the lantern.

"This is not ditch digging," she said in a low, smooth voice. "This is art, captain. There is expression, and nuance, and a certain instinct in play. These things reward the time lavished upon them."

"You said you'd be done by dawn," the man frowned, raising his lantern and squinting at the woman.

She leaned in closer, and a peculiar spicy low-tide rankness flowed from her. "The suspense," she murmured. "What will happen?" The luminescence of the lantern caught her pale eyes, and the pupils did not dilate further as the light hit them. She stared at him, and he took a step back.

"See to it then," he sniffed, and he pivoted, striding back down the tunnel walkway to where several others waited uneasily in the shadows.

"Mistress," one of the hooded figures said to her. "We have prepared the forms. You may anchor them, and we will support."

"Bring the rat," she murmured. The adept lifted a box, opening it with care and reaching in.

Meanwhile the Mistress stood facing the arcane patterns on the wall and grating, her eyes slitted. She breathed, pulling the world inside her body, and exhaled out traces from everything inside her that blood touched. She flexed her eyes, and in the momentary blur she saw past mere bouncing light to the more sturdy truth beneath it. Hooking her thumbs on her hood and pushing it back, she touched the shell and bone mask up on her forehead, and slid it down over her eyes. The mask had no eye holes, and needed none; the side touching her flesh was patterned to focus light away and pull the Veil taut and thin. She felt the delicate bone against her temples, felt the silent hiss of seconds pouring across the barrier between the living and the memory, felt the Ghost Field responding to her blood before she even reached out to grasp it.

She clamped the bladed thimble over her thumb, and reached her hand out to the side. Her dutiful assistant put the drugged rat in her hand; she felt its weight, felt its sluggish attempt at fear, felt its cherry-pit heart ramping up as fast as it could go. She held the life in her hands, and breathed out again. Her life force touched on the painted sigils and runes, filling them out, racing through them to trace for just a moment their shapes and patterns. She pulled her consciousness close to those patterns, bowing the Veil so she stood in the center as the arcane formulae stretched around her. Under the mask, her forehead creased and her breathing shivered as she touched her life energy to the patterns and pulled them into a sphere around herself, centered on her hands, centered on the pathetic and fearful life she held.

She slid the knife thimble forward, into the back of the rat's skull, and it died swiftly with little pain. Its death made a shallow impression on the Veil, just the tiniest dimple as life slid out, but she was prepared. At the bottom of the tiny and almost imperceptible divot on the Veil, the Mistress forced the sigils into place, touching on a pinhole in the Mirror where life had slid through it.

The merest touch, an insubstantial trace of etheric energy twisted through the prepared sigils and runes. The Mistress felt herself smile as the tracework carried energy like an irrigation system carried water, filling out and almost imperceptibly warping the Veil, touching death energies through the complex net her adepts had prepared.

She felt the body and blood of her assistant at her side, deferential, patient. "What is it," she murmured in Hadrathi, the ancient language liquid and peculiar in her mouth.

"We have the other sacrifices," he replied, also in Hadrathi. "We prepared this ritual to sustain with the cat, stringing the entrails across the gate, and we have two more rats if you wish to strengthen the bond."

"You are prepared, as I asked," she breathed. "There will be no more sacrifices. This is good spellwork and it will hold." She directed her mask at her adept, and rearranged its connection to the Veil so she could see through the thin bone that was no longer in front of her eyes. "Collect our payment from Hutch," she nodded. "Maybe I'm wrong, but I have the feeling he will come up short." The sardonic smile below the mask was twisted by a feeling that wasn't humor.

Her assistant hesitated fractionally, then nodded, turning to the figures around the camp table further down the tunnel. He approached, his slippers quiet on the rough stone.

"You're Neap, right?" one of the grizzled men asked, squinting.

"Yes," the assistant nodded. "I serve the Mistress of Tides. She has completed the ritual."

"Was it successful?" the guard asked, glancing over at the captain, who stood with his back to the exchange.

"Yes, it will do what you require. Deflect attention from this entrance to the sewers, and... discourage ghosts," he said.

"Ghost-proof!" snapped the leader, pivoting to face Neap. "The deal was that your precious Mistress would make this tunnel ghost proof."

"Her work speaks for itself," Neap said quietly. "May I please have the payment she was promised?"

"I don't think I like your attitude," the captain said, squinting at Neap. "Evans, give him his box."

The guard aimed a worried glance at the captain, but he did as he was told. He picked up the chest and put it on the table. Neap tilted the lid open looking inside dispassionately.

"This is less than we agreed upon," he murmured. He looked the captain in the eye. "A third less. Were we unclear, Captain Hutch?"

Hutch's face contracted into a frown. "Are you sassing me, boy?" he growled. "This is Gray Cloak territory, and your precious Mistress is getting a chance to work for the Gray Cloaks. Her craftsmanship and her loyalty need testing before she gets full rates, but if she passes muster, she'll have work. Oho, she'll have work!" he said, almost a shout as he squared his shoulders.

"That will be fine," the Mistress murmured from behind Hutch. He twitched with startlement, but recovered fast. "You'll need these," she added, holding up three amulets.

"How does it work?" Hutch demanded.

"There is a light on the embankment above the concealed entrance," the Mistress murmured. "The one wearing the amulet must look at that light, focus on it, try to match its frequency. When the light shifts to orange, then the one with the amulet will be aligned, and the door will be visible and usable."

"Just three amulets?" Hutch scowled.

The Mistress watched him for a long moment. "Just three."

While Hutch was engaged with the Mistress, Neap picked up the box with payment. That refocused Hutch around to the adept. "Oh, are we leaving?"

"It's almost dawn, as you said," the Mistress said, inclining her head. Neap was on his way, and she stepped around Hutch as though he was inconsequential.

Two of the other adepts were cranking the wheel around to raise the gate, and the other one was already in the shallow boat. With grace born of long experience with small boats on the canals, the Mistress of Tides stepped into the boat, joined by the rest of her adepts. They drifted out into the canal, and only Neap looked back. The grating rattled down behind them, and they were beneath the troubled darkness of Doskvol's rumpled sky once again.

As one adept poled the skiff down the canal, the Mistress of Tides faced Neap, sitting in the skiff. "That was closer than I'd like," she admitted, her voice low. "Even now, Hutch is weighing whether we're worth the risk our knowledge brings."

"What would you have me do, Mistress?" Neap asked.

She frowned. "I need you to take a message to a friend."

## BARROWCLEFT. BELDERAN ESTATE. 52ND SURAN

"Barrowcleft is barely even in the city," the adept frowned, peering into the sepia brown fog outside the carriage window as they jolted along.

"Keep that idea to yourself," Neap said with a grimace. "Pay attention, Slack. You're here because of the ever-present possibility something could happen to me, and the Mistress needs you to get word out here. We don't write this down. Just remember it all. If you have an impulse to antagonize this man, suppress it. You hear me?" Neap said, serious.

"Yes sir," Slack nodded. "Sure. Kiss up to the old man."

"Ideally you say nothing," Neap retorted. "This is about professional courtesy." He eyed the Slack, across from him in the cramped confines of the coach. "Just look spooky and mysterious, alright?" he said with a crooked grin.

"My specialty," Slack replied with a grin, reminding Neap just how young the adept was.

The carriage slowed, clattering over a transition from the road to a courtyard, the sounds of the wheels reverberating from the face of a building. The goat pulling the coat let out a deep-chested bleat as the carriage driver slowed and diverted the coach. Neap and Slack stepped out of the carriage onto the cobbles of the yard. Before them, in the brown haze, a low and wide building loomed. Even though it had two and a half stories, the massive structure still seemed squat compared to the overbuilt towers in the space-starved city core.

A servant approached. "May I take your coat?" he asked politely.

"No thank you," Neap murmured, making a hand sign that caught the servant's eye. The servant nodded, leading them into the spacious foyer and down a hallway to a room filled with a tight spiral staircase. The servant bowed to them, and the two adepts finished the climb alone.

The long attic had no skylights, but it was awash in a textured and varied glow. At the top of the stairs, a miniature weeping willow tree raised about four feet up from its ornate planter, then spilled its wands down all the way to the floor. Each wand was studded with nodules like seeds that released a red-tinged purple light. Behind the willow, a trellis connected the floor to the center pole of the attic ceiling, and it was wrapped in a lush rose bush, the roses an impossible soft black. Woven among the thorny vines was a pale and waxy vine that robbed its viewer of night vision without returning much light.

The adepts took in the long attic, noting a fish pond built into the far end where a chimney once stood. A glorious trailing bush overflowed the stone banks, glowing from within the pool as well as its rim. Along one side of the attic, work tables and gardening supplies stood next to a squat electroplasmic condensation array and the tools of the alchemical trade. A tall, thin man stood with his back to the adepts, his hands busy with a waist-tall planter filled with rich earth.

"Thank you for agreeing to see us, Sir Belderan," Neap said politely. "I bring word from the Mistress of Tides."

"She never bores me," the thin man mused, and he put down his trowel, turning to face the adepts. A wry smile tugged at his features. "Neap, my good man. And a new friend."

"I wanted you to meet Slack," Neap said with a nod. "The Mistress of Tides vouches for him."

"Very good. Please join me," Belderan said, crossing the attic to small open space with a round rug in the center and several chairs and small tables, a lowering screen of plants surrounding the private spot. "Tea?"

"Please, for both of us," Neap replied without even looking over at Slack. Belderan lifted a cover from a prepared tea set that was still steaming, and he wasted no time or motion in preparing the tea, pouring it in to the cups, measuring out flavors without asking. The adepts seated themselves, picking up the paper-thin bone of the teacups, careful in their movements. Belderan watched them for a moment, then he sat down, cup in hand.

"You may speak freely," he said, quiet.

"The Gray Cloaks have a new fortified underground base under Silkshore, in the Master Market area. Their second in command, Hutch, hired the Mistress to cloak one of their entrances along the Boldway canal. They underpaid. The Mistress of Tides wanted you to know."

"Sensible," Belderan shrugged. "They are quite possibly short-sighted enough they'd rather kill your Mistress than trust her. You are wise to bring this information to me. Just in case." He sipped his tea. "Your Mistress of Tides, she's a cut above. You must know that. Her talents are wasted on this sort of warding work for ignorant thugs." He cocked his head to the side, regarding Neap. "She could really do something with her ability."

"Indeed," said Neap with a nod. "We lack your big picture, however. Even with us supporting her, the Mistress is vulnerable. You cannot both change the world and tread carefully. Not if you're living out a mortal's lifespan," he shrugged. "The Mistress chooses to tread carefully. The world will look after itself, as it always has done." He paused. "If you had some work, on the other hand, I imagine she'd be interested."

Belderan chuckled. "I don't think she could afford me as a fixer." His smile widened. "And when she comes into her own, it's possible I won't be able to afford her."

Neap hid his expression in the teacup for a long sip.

### BARROWCLEFT. BELDERAN ESTATE. 52ND SURAN (LATER)

The grouchy goat dragged the jolting wagon into the courtyard as the butler strode out. "No more guests today, I'm afraid," the butler called out as he approached. "Sir Belderan is—" He paused, and blinked. "Master Kreeger?"

"I'm sorry to hear my uncle is busy," Kreeger replied, his smile bleak. "It is urgent."

"By all means," the butler replied, "Let's get you inside."

Kreeger and Styles hopped down from the buckboard of the wagon. "Anderson," Kreeger said quietly, "I need a stretcher." He nodded towards the blankets concealing the contents of the narrow wagon. Anderson nodded, heading back to the house. Kreeger turned to Styles.

"So how is this going to go down," Kreeger demanded.

"Just like you said," Styles said quickly. "You do the talking, and I back you up, without talking. If I am asked direct questions, keep the responses simple, no explanations."

"Good," Kreeger nodded. He looked over to where Anderson led another servant out of the house, hustling with a stretcher. Kreeger pulled the blanket back, revealing Rutherford's chalk-white features and blue lips. He checked for a pulse, and found a thready faint beat.

"Hold on," Kreeger murmured to Rutherford. Then the four men got Rutherford's unresponsive body onto the stretcher, and he was carried into the house as Kreeger led Styles in the back way, and up the stairs to the attic.

Belderan was waiting for them, his hands clasped behind his back and his chin elevated just enough that he looked down his nose at the younger generation. Kreeger stopped a respectable distance away.

"Uncle," he said quietly. "Thank you for seeing us."

"And for the medical care, if that man is not already dead," Belderan added. "Either way, you've brought stains to my house that will be difficult to scrub out, so you had better have some payment to offer."

"My payment requires us to expand our business together," Kreeger replied. "I would like some letters of recommendation. It looks like I may be at least temporarily resigning from my Ministry position." He paused. "My house is still burning," he said with a slight shrug.

"What can you offer?" Belderan asked, expressionless.

"I have a path that we can follow that ends with you as the

curator of the High Six gardens," Kreeger replied, intensity bound in his quiet voice. "That's right, the gardens in direct view of the highest apertures of the Red Lantern temple."

Belderan's eyebrow raised. "Intriguing," he said. "I will hear you out, on the condition that you acquire the services of the Mistress of Tides to assist with the plan." He turned his back on Kreeger, strolling back towards the pool end of the attic. "Of course I will care for the injured man that you brought, I would not allow anyone to die of injuries out of greed or spite."

"It's Rutherford," Kreeger said, and he clamped his mouth shut.

Belderan stopped, and turned, genuine concern in his eyes. "Oh, Kreeger, I'm so sorry," he said. "I didn't realize. You know we'll do everything we can for him."

"Yes, uncle," Kreeger said as he nodded. "That's why we came here."

Belderan's attitude visibly softened. "Kreeger, you know you're always—you can come here any time you need to, and I'll do my best to take care of you."

"And me too, and I appreciate it," Styles said earnestly.

"Sure, Styles," Belderan said. He approached Kreeger. "Shelter you've got. But I want you to think hard before you start business in Silkshore." He shook his head. "That you must earn." He raised one eyebrow. "If for no other reason than to pay me for the conversation I'll eventually have with Nebs."

"So is there anything you can give me on this 'Mistress of Tides' person? Contacts, references, description, anything?" Kreeger asked.

"Nothing, you have to do it yourself," Kreeger shrugged. "That's part of the price." He paused. "You don't have to start anything until we've got Rutherford stable and on the mend," he said.

"I feel differently," Kreeger said, something chilly under his tone. He turned to the willow, and snapped off a sprig that was a couple inches along. "Thanks for this. Meet me in two days, at the Diving Bell, at the hour of Thread," Kreeger added. He nodded, setting himself. "We'll see about the plan at that point." Turning, he left the attic, padding down the crooked stairs.

"I do like him," Belderan confided in Styles.

"Sure, me too, he's great," Styles shrugged. "So, you got anything to eat?"

Belderan regarded him. "Now that we're alone, I have questions," he said in a quiet voice that did nothing to put Styles at his ease. "What happened at the house."

Styles shifted uncomfortably. "I contacted Kreeger in the morning, and told him I'd be back that night, then I went to stake out his house. A cutter from the River Stallion crew was on my trail, and must have found out about Kreeger and where he lives. When Kreeger got home, the cutter followed him in, and once I heard gunfire I intervened and chased the guy off."

"Like you don't know his name, he was on your crew," Belderan said, cold.

"Gapjaw," Styles replied quickly.

"That barely hurt, right?" Belderan said with a dangerous smile. "Now you're going to tell me why the River Stallions aren't your friends anymore. All of it," he warned.

Styles swallowed hard, and nodded.

## SILKSHORE. MASTER MARKET, ZEPHYR STREET UNDERBRIDGE STALLS. 53RD SURAN

Neap regarded the various blotchy and swirled jars and bottles in the underbridge stall. The darkness behind the makeshift countertop was loaded with shelves and cages, with a disconcerting undertone of grunts, squeals, and shifting limbs.

"Dere ya go, fresh harvested ta yer ladyship's exactin standards," the wrinkled old man said as he peered through his spectacles at a jar of freshly harvested amber fluid.

"We're paying extra for the thornflower extract in the diet," Neap reminded the merchant.

"You can trust me," the merchant grinned, showcasing his remaining teeth. His grin faltered. "No really, you can, she knows how to find me," he explained. "I'm too old to run and too pretty to die." He bolstered his grin, and Neap looked over his shoulder at the ten pound venomous mole squatting in its cage radiating contempt. He nodded to himself.

"Excellent. See you later," he said, and he turned away.

He found himself squared off with a young man in a long coat, looking at him directly.

"Can I help you?" Neap asked coolly, sliding his hands into his sleeves to touch on the hafts of his wrist knives.

"I bring a message from Sir Belderan," the stranger replied. "This is the only signal he would send." The stranger opened his coat to reveal the glowing sprig from the radiant willow.

"Intriguing," Neap nodded.

"Can you arrange a meeting?" the stranger asked.

"Yes. The Mistress of Tides will either appear if she trusts your message, or send a representative if she does not. Moor in the third tunnel accessing the canal under the Sluice Den at the hour of Smoke."

"You can tell her it is Kreeger that seeks a meeting," the stranger said. Then he turned, vanishing into the crowd.

Troubled, Neap went his own way.

## SILKSHORE. MASTER MARKET, UNDER THE SLUICE DEN. 53ᴿᴰ SURAN. THE HOUR OF SMOKE

Kreeger sat in the shallow, narrow skiff. The bowline was tied to the footing of the stone quay, and sound whispered and twisted as it bounced between the shiftless water and the stone arch overhead. Above, the claustrophobic niches of gambling and whoring establishments that riddled the Sluice Den did brisk business, and there was steady traffic along the waterways and gantry walks except for the area around the center arch, furthest from both sides of the bridge.

Opening his hand, Kreeger relaxed as much as he could, and he was gratified to see only a faint tremor shivering his fingers. Adrenaline pulsed, low but poisonous, keeping his blood spiced. His mind whirled in slow motion, pushing away all the thoughts that screamed at the edge of his mind.

The slow and gentle rock of the skiff shifted rhythm, then stopped altogether, as though the boat was beached. Showtime. Kreeger stood in the boat, his stance firm, and he extended his hands out to the sides so he would look as non-threatening as possible. Shadows crossed the far end of the tunnel, and a skiff turned in, one cloaked figure poling the boat along and the other cloaked figure standing in the prow. A forever minute passed, and the skiffs were in easy conversational range.

"Thank you for coming," Kreeger said. "Are you the Mistress of Tides?"

"Yes," the cowled woman replied. "My agent gave me your name, but we're far enough into the darkness that aliases serve best." She paused. "Do you have one?"

"Not yet, if you'll excuse the oversight," Kreeger replied.

"It is best not to choose your own, or it will bring only shame. I looked into you, as you would expect. May I suggest the name Sanction?"

"I like it," Sanction grinned. "I feel more ready than ever to get down to business."

"You represent the Trellis?" the Mistress of Tides verified.

"I will, if I can persuade you to come to the table," Sanction said with a nod. "The prize is stewardship of the High Six gardens."

The Mistress of Tides cocked her head to the side. "Those are under control of the Circle of Flame," she murmured. "Specifically, the Selwythe House, who have ties to the Circle, and I believe their delegate in charge of security and management is Lord Mora." She paused. "They are out of our league," she said. "Scholars and mystics, nobles with bottomless war chests, spies everywhere." She shook her head. "Challenging them is unwise."

"For you it would be," Sanction agreed. "Or for me. Or even for Trellis. But with a whole crew, and a plan? They won't see us coming, because they're busy with their own internal politics. Right?" he said, pressing. "You know a lot about Silkshore, that's one of the reasons we need you. And they keep such a close eye on each other, an outsider can take them by surprise and get away with something."

"Maybe," she admitted.

"My plan needs your gifts," Sanction said. "Not an adept, or a physicar, or a witch. I need a proper Whisper. One who knows the ritual forms." He shrugged. "That's you."

"If I did choose to move against the Circle, that could end my association with the local gondoliers," the Mistress of Tides said.

"But if we succeed, maybe we'll all have a new alliance and allegiance to make up for it," Sanction said.

She paused. "I need to think about this."

"Of course," Sanction agreed. "We will discuss the plan tomorrow night, in the Diving Bell, in the hour of Thread." He bit his lip. "Or, if you don't come, we'll have a lovely dinner, and go our separate ways."

"What makes you think I would even consider such a terrible risk?" the Mistress asked.

Sanction regarded her for a long moment. "Discontent is pernicious," he murmured. "Sometimes getting by isn't good enough. Sometimes we reach a point where we can no longer tolerate people taking things from us unchecked. Sometimes, every now and then, we need to insist on having our own way." His rueful smile was a grimace. "For that, you need people who have your back."

"I have my acolytes," the Mistress pointed out.

"Yes," Sanction nodded. "Maybe this opportunity isn't for you." He paused. "Think about it. Tomorrow night, the Diving Bell, in the hour of Thread." He felt her release whatever had held his boat in place, and he quickly untied the boat and cast off from the quay. "I will see you later," he said quietly, and he poled his craft to the far end of the tunnel and out into a canal.

By the time he reached the canal, the Mistress of Tides was long gone.

## BARROWCLEFT. BELDERAN ESTATE. 54TH SURAN. THE THIRD HOUR

The pale man stirred, and slowly opened one eye. "Kreeger," he murmured, lips motionless and throat chapped.

"Don't try to speak," Kreeger said, the smile on his face paining him. He gripped Rutherford's cool hand, pulling it up to his chest. "You're safe." He cocked his head to the side. "The bullet is out. You've had some obscenely expensive restorative agents applied to you in a variety of distasteful ways. Now do what's good for you—shut up and let your body do the work."

"Dja do somethin stupid?" Rutherford managed.

"We can argue all you like when you get your strength back," Kreeger replied softly, using his thumb to push a sweat-matted lock of hair from Rutherford's forehead. Then Rutherford slept again. Kreeger squeezed his hand, and rose from the bedside. He adjusted the blankets, then returned to the hallway.

"It's a fair question," Belderan shrugged.

"You know the Mistress of Tides called you Trellis?" Kreeger said.

"This is not my first dip into the far side of the law," Belderan shrugged. "She give you a name?"

"Sanction," Kreeger replied. "I guess she figured out I work for the Ministry."

Belderan regarded his nephew for a long moment. "You wanted this," he stated.

"No, not at this cost," Kreeger protested. "Rutherford shot, my house, burned. And I don't want to go to the authorities, because if I do then I cannot easily regain freedom to put things right without a little too much supervision." His expression hardened. "Maybe they think one or all of us died. We don't know if Gapjaw made it back alive."

"He did," Belderan shrugged, "and the River Stallions have had their hands full dealing with the Grinders. Because our little Piccolo killed their leader's niece."

"Of course he did," Kreeger sighed.

"And now you're playing a hole card you've kept in case you needed something from me, so you can get set up in the city." Lit from behind, Belderan was hard to read.

"The Ministry was the path of least resistance," Kreeger shrugged. "I was never going to make a difference. I could do nothing but watch as the dirty Skovs clog up our city's streets. Aristocrats, doing whatever they want, because they bought the courts and the Bluecoats. It's—galling."

"You are an arrogant son of a bitch," Belderan said, shaking his head.

"An easy judgement from an aristocrat," Kreeger retorted. "You believe those powers lie with you."

Belderan heaved a deep sigh. "Someday, my dear nephew, I'll fill you in on what you may miss out on now that you've jumped the rails and plowed your train out to the Deadlands." His smile was audibly wry. "For tonight, get some rest. We've got a big day tomorrow."

Kreeger watched him go, then turned and headed out of the house, to the stable. Pushing through the sally port, he saw the lantern at the far end of the building, and he approached. Glowing grubs climbed over each other and around the glass, dully exploring their confinement in the lantern's glass. Kreeger crossed his arms, regarding Styles. The lanky young thief was shirtless, hunched over his kit, sharpening some knives.

"Sounds like Belderan got a more complete account of your situation than I did," he said.

"He's scarier than you. And richer. Has a more mysterious past," Styles pointed out, beginning to track the points on his fingers. "He's like a radiant plant expert, he has more servants, better hair—"

"I kind of regret saving you," Kreeger said reflectively.

"Saving me?" Styles scoffed. "I chased Gapjaw off. Looked after your husband while you were running around in town."

"Seriously," Kreeger said, his smile fading.

"I know, really, I know," Styles said earnestly as he rose, putting his kit aside. "I'm grateful," he said, his eyes sincere. "And... man, I'm sorry."

"For what it's worth," Kreeger said after a moment, "Looks like I won't kill you straight off. Rutherford looks like he's going to pull through. So you can start thinking ahead to all the chances you're going to have to make it up to me. Destroying my life and all."

There was an element of relief in Styles' features as he shrugged. "Whatever you say, old man," he grinned.

"Starting tomorrow." Kreeger headed to the bunk in the back of the stable, and Styles watched him go.

"Starting tomorrow," Styles echoed, and he pivoted, tossing a knife with a flick of the wrist. It thudded deep into the compressed fungal panel of the barn wall. Styles turned to the lantern, and pushed the tube down into the shield, and the barn was buried in shadow.

# CHAPTER THREE

*Grasping human minds need to have names to hold on to, or they cannot handle certain ideas. If you name a hill, an island, a street, a building, then you can talk about it with precision even in the abstract, even when the subject is not present. Therefore it should tell you something about the Akorosian character that they number each hour after dawn, but name each hour after dusk. Six hours from dawn to noon, six more till dusk. Six from dusk to midnight, and another six from midnight to dawn. Neighborhood public towers ring chimes on the hours, day and night.*

*Honor, Song, Silver, Thread, Flame, Pearls (Midnight), Silk, Wine, Ash, Coal, Chains, Smoke. In this next chapter, we will unpack the origin and occult significance of each.*

*- From "Everyday Codes: The Meaning Behind the Symbols" by Sir Whycaster*

## SILKSHORE. THE DIVING BELL. 55TH SURAN. THE HOUR OF THREAD

The gong's reverberation was unearthly and beautiful, filling the tall restaurant. Sanction slid his reservation to the Master of the House, who graciously consulted it. Sanction's eyes wandered the four story teardrop of glass that held the diving pool; the teardrop was about twenty feet across and eighty feet deep, smooth glass surrounded by the ramps and balconies where the patrons enjoyed their food and the show.

"This way, please," the Master of the House gestured politely, and he led Sanction down the first ramp as the musicians at the bottom of the tank began their peculiar dirge. The musicians were clustered around a many-limbed anemone-like structure that had air tubes protruding from it, sending up glittering strings of bubbles. From time to time, a musician would lean over and draw heavily on the air. Rigid inflatable vests protected them from the worst of the pressure in the tank. Masks and vests were further decorated with bits of carapace and crab armor, to make half-human musicians of the artificial depths.

The instruments themselves were mostly percussion; gongs, hollow drums, chimes. Sanction noticed a couple stringed instruments adapted to work in the pressure of the bottom of the tank; one began an unearthly wail that sounded like a distant kind of longing.

They rounded the third balcony deep before finding an alcove with a massive slate tabletop. It was etched and inlaid with the primitive map of an early leviathan hunter ship, trying to mark the passage of the giant demons under the sea while keeping an eye on the tides, winds, and underwater constellations. Enough practical information made an abstract pattern that leaked more desperation than information. The Master of the House bowed to Trellis, who was already seated, and he withdrew.

"You always did like being early," Sanction said as he seated himself.

"That's no mystery," Trellis shrugged, looking elegant and perfectly at home in his brocade jacket and precisely tied cravat. "Who has more power? The one who repeats the information, or the one who gets the repeated information?" He chuckled. "I took the liberty of ordering."

"Of course you did," Sanction shrugged. "Where is Piccolo?"

"One level up," Trellis sighed. "He wanted to watch the lady jump in."

Above, there was a silver plume of force down through the surface of the water, and a scantily clad woman dove deep. The percussion took on a syncopated roll, almost a strut, and she twisted deeper against the pressure of the water using her whole body. Her hands curled out against the deep, sliding along her sides as her torso flexed and her legs twisted, her muscle and sinew rejecting the buoyancy of her form as she almost glided along the side of the tank, legs propelling her deeper.

Spheres with tiny quantities of quicksilver floated lazily at different depths, and she reached the limit of her strength and air, straining down, and snagged one. With practiced ease, she pivoted to point up towards the distant surface, and her legs scissored together to send her lunging upward, the bubbles of her breath slithering around her as they could not keep pace. There was some scattered applause from patrons; a good dive.

"I'll have to keep the speeches short tonight," Sanction sighed, "or we won't be able to keep Piccolo's attention."

Trellis regarded him for a moment. "I don't see charts, blueprints, reference materials, anything like that," he observed.

"We're here for broad strokes," Sanction shrugged. "The real work of fleshing it out begins after we decide to do it." He looked Trellis in the eye. "That's the hardest part."

"If you say so," Trellis shrugged, his eyes returning to the silver strings of air twirling up in the tank.

Piccolo strolled down the ramp, a big smile on his slightly gawky features. "I like it when the ladies jump in," he explained. "And look! I told you I wouldn't be last!" he said to Trellis, not even trying to conceal the triumph in his voice.

"I suppose you've outwitted me," Trellis smiled, something distant in his eyes. "Savor the moment."

"For the record," Sanction added, "no one likes to hear 'I told you so.' No one in the history of ever. In case you didn't know that."

"Well, nobody likes being wrong," Piccolo retorted. "Do you figure the Mistress of Tides will come?"

"She will," Sanction shrugged casually.

"Oh no," Piccolo grinned, glancing over at Trellis, sly. "This might be one of those moments where somebody clever is all wrong and doesn't want to hear about it." He grinned.

"It's like he can't hear," Sanction said to Trellis.

"Or doesn't care," Trellis shrugged in return. "Some people just can't take a hint."

"A hint is just trying to make somebody else carry the load for you," Piccolo snorted. "You want something, better ask for it."

"Good point," Sanction nodded. "Shut up."

There was a moment of silence, then all three of them chuckled. Sanction turned in his chair, then rose as the Mistress of Tides descended the ramp with a waiter at her side. Behind her were two adepts, wearing pressed and glittering robes in the dim restaurant.

Trellis and Piccolo rose also, and the three men bowed to the Mistress of Tides as she took her seat at the table, her two acolytes stepping back to the servant position near the table.

"Thank you for coming," Sanction said, earnest. He looked over at her acolytes. "Only two?"

She watched him for a moment through the gauze of her teal and gray veil. "They serve the gondoliers," she murmured. "If I act on my own, outside the interest of the gondoliers, only these two will follow me."

Sanction nodded. "Very well. Now that we're all here, it's time to talk about the plan."

"Not yet," Trellis said quietly. "After food."

Sanction paused, and almost squinted at the older man, then he nodded. "Very well. Business after the feast."

"For such business as this," Trellis nodded, "we have quite a feast."

For a long moment there was little use for small talk, so they were relieved when a muscular man with a trident, a loose robe, and a tiara in his hair plunged into the tank. He dove deep, showing off his cable-like muscles and his collection of tattoos before snagging a deep mercury buoy and pivoting to return to the surface. Polite applause rippled through the restaurant.

Then the feast arrived. The Platter of Last Visions, with infused eyeballs separated into sweet and savory flavors. The never-here/long-gone platter, with eggs in solutions spread across various fish jerky. Coils of tentacles, each sucker filled with a distinct and succulent flavored cream. Leathercap soup, with a devilfish head sac filled with a precisely constructed menu of the creature's favorite prey, seasoned to taste. The Flavorfence, with tiny bits of carefully prepared sea creatures held together along the translucent spine of a fish rib, each mouthful standing independent in a row hemmed in with sticky rice and kelp weave. The crew ate deliberately and carefully, their scalpel-like knives and multi-tined forks carefully working around the exquisite feast.

"I knew you weren't here for the girls," Piccolo said at last, leaning back. "Now I get it." He rubbed at his lean torso. "That's amazing."

"I hope you left room for dessert," Trellis said, wry. He gestured to an attentive waiter, who brought a tray of folded fabric pockets of fungus stem walls wrapped around mysterious wax-like interiors. Lighting a long fireplace match, the waiter dipped flame into each cup, and as they burned they opened and fused, creating a strange crisp and creamy goblet. Piccolo laughed aloud before fitting one in his mouth, and his eyes got very wide as the flavors went straight to work on his brain.

"Cavernfire Bites are very relaxing," Trellis chuckled, and he popped one in his mouth, frowning slightly over his smile as he teased the textures and flavors apart, deepening his experience into lasting memory.

As they finished the dessert, a singing saw was resonating a doleful melody through the bell tank. The length of flexible metal quivered under the special bow, singing a throatless croon where air neither entered nor left, a ballad of drowning. Most of the table was cleared away, and the adepts were eating their supper as quiet settled on the crew.

"Well. That's set the mood," Sanction murmured. "You are here because you are willing to risk taking on a dangerous deception for a most gratifying prize." He looked around the table. "We are after the cultivation rights for the High Six gardens. This is the single most award-winning and prestigious radiant garden in all of Silkshore. Only true masters of the craft of radiant splicing could begin to curate such a space, and we've got just such an expert in our midst," Sanction said with a deferential nod to Trellis.

"That's a carefully guarded treasure," Trellis retorted, "not least because there are a hundred protections to keep anyone from forcing their way into authority when it comes to such a civic treasure."

"There will be no force," Sanction shrugged. "We don't try and wrest the gardens from their owner. We accept them as payment. We have something the owner desperately wants."

"And by 'the owner' you mean the Selwythe House," said the Mistress of Tides. "And of course the Selwythe House is twined into the business of the Circle of Flame. And their representative is Lord Mora."

"Oh yes," Sanction smiled, the light from the candles on the table reflecting from his polished teeth. "Lord Mora is a tough man, and he holds a grudge."

"What does he desperately want?" Piccolo asked.

"The Eye of Kotar," Sanction replied. "And thank you for staying on target. Now, Kotar was a sorcerer, or demon, or god, or something, before the Gates of Death cracked. There are some mummified pieces of this monster still at large in the world," he continued. "Legends like to pick out the Eye, the Hand, and the Heart. I happen to know that the Circle of Flame actually had the Eye, and lost it a couple years ago." Sanction leaned back, spreading his hands. "We found it. We sell it back to him."

The table shared a moment of silence.

"I have so many questions," Piccolo said, puzzled and suspicious.

"One question is, what kind of a sorcerer is Lord Mora, that he would want something like this," Sanction said. "The answer is, he's got zero aptitude for the supernatural. The Circle of Flames uses his connections in the government and among certain disreputable organizations, as well as his wealth and his ruthlessness. He helps manage the day to day so the scholars can delve into their mysteries." He paused. "But he won't go to the scholars with this. He'll want to do it himself."

"You seem sure," Trellis observed, eyebrows raised.

"I am," Sanction agreed. "Lord Mora has a soft spot for one of the mystics in the top tier leadership. Her name is Lady Penderyn, and she likes her consorts to have a talent for the supernatural. Lord Mora has nothing like that, but getting the lost Eye of Kotar might elevate him in her esteem." He leaned in close. "She was responsible for safeguarding the Eye, and it hurt her status when it was stolen."

"So what's the plan?" Piccolo asked.

"Four stages, each requiring careful attention," Sanction replied. "First is the approach. We need to get him interested. Second, the transaction. We need to get what we want, and give him the impression he got what he wanted. Third, the spoiler, where it all goes wrong. Carefully, precisely wrong. And fourth, the aftermath, to make sure our illusions are in place and no one has a reason to look closer."

"How do you approach a hard case like this Mora guy?" Piccolo muttered, inspecting his thumbnails.

"Oh, we don't," Sanction said, crossing his arms over his chest. "We don't persuade him or anything. We try to make him go away. We don't want to have anything to do with him, he's trouble."

"So he forces himself in," Trellis nodded. "Takes control of the situation. But we do it his way."

"Right, run the con standard from there, ask for too much and settle for too little. Bumble a bit. And in the end, he gets the Eye."

"And his dissatisfaction?" the Mistress asked. "Where does that displeasure land?"

"With someone bigger than he is, known for lying, with every reason to deprive him of his prize." Sanction looked around the table. "But we soften the blow, because we've got the garden, and we can use that to our advantage."

"Marble? Regards? Dedication?" Trellis mused aloud.

"Yes," Sanction nodded. He turned to the Mistress of Tides. "We'll need a fake Eye capable of some neat tricks," he said quietly.

"I can do that," she said, "if we know what we're after."

"This plan is rickety," Trellis admitted.

"Of course," Sanction nodded. "I didn't bring you on board for your charm." He smiled to take the sting out of the words, and the smile Trellis offered in return was somewhat wintery.

"I can help shore it up," Trellis said. "Address some contingencies. We only get one shot at this." He paused, sucking at his teeth, regarding Sanction. "Maybe run it down for us, bare bones."

"Alright then," Sanction said, leaning in. "We are some purchasers that work for a noble house, and we realized we got something far more valuable than the sellers realize, so we try to sell it on the side without letting our patron know. But we're clumsy enough that word gets to Mora, and he comes to us, pushes the other buyers out."

"So far so good," said the Mistress of Tides.

"We set up a buy, but first we want him to start the process to sign over stewardship of the High Six; we're taking a terrible risk, after all. Then the meet, and he brings a servant so we can install the Eye; it must travel in a living host. Just then, the authorities break in and in the confusion the Eye is taken, but we help Mora and his servant escape."

"Which authorities exactly?" Trellis asked, dry.

"We have options," Sanction shrugged. "The point is, it's got to be somebody who would lie to protect the secret of the Eye, but might have their own reasons to lock it up or try to use it themselves."

"Why do I get the feeling that end of the operation will lie with me?" Trellis mused.

"Because you're astute," Sanction grinned. "Anyway, we want to make sure Mora doesn't stop the transfer of stewardship; the Eye must be in his possession before it's rudely snatched away. And we must assure, so far as we are able, that there are no hard feelings."

"Homework time," Piccolo said without enthusiasm.

"Trellis," Sanction said, "Work out our interrupters. Who do you choose?"

"Spirit Wardens," Trellis replied distantly.

"Good choice," Sanction nodded. "Mistress of Tides, we need a fake Eye, and I've got some specifications. Remote communication, a sensation avalanche, radiant power burst through it, and so on."

"I'm sure we can work it out," the Mistress of Tides nodded.

"I'll also need one of your adepts, to carry the Eye. And we'll need a pickpocket handy for all this, who can look convincingly like a bodyguard," Sanction said as he looked to Piccolo.

"My silent menace is pretty good," Piccolo shrugged.

"We do this right," Sanction said, looking around the table seriously, "nobody dies. We don't need that kind of attention. Games are one thing, but once people of name die, or their favorite pets, everything is more serious."

"What will you be doing?" Piccolo asked.

Sanction leaned back. "I've got to backstop an identity as a buyer for an aristocratic house, I'm thinking I'll be based out of Six Towers, an impoverished noble who has just enough savvy to realize he's got his hands on something..." He gazed into the middle distance. "Something priceless." He sipped his wine. "A small man on the edge of something so much bigger than him that he knows it will make or break him."

Piccolo rolled his eyes. "I'm sorry I asked."

"Cheer up," the Mistress of Tides said, her lips pursed to contain a smile beneath her veil. "We'll all need a dose of theater to pull this off."

"I gotta admit, I thought there would be more stabbing," Piccolo admitted.

"We'll see," Trellis said, looking Sanction in the eye.

Sanction let a smile work its way into his features as he held his uncle's gaze. "Two days," he murmured, "and we'll reconvene to get the final details nailed down. And we'll set a date for the exchange." He looked at the others. "You know your tasks. Let's get to it."

## NIGHTMARKET. THE VEIL, SOCIAL CLUB. 59ᵀᴴ SURAN.
### (FOUR DAYS AFTER THE DIVING BELL)

Sanction swigged back the wine in the tiny glass, and squared his shoulders. He looked over to Piccolo, who stood at his side with a stoic unreadability, gripping Slack by the elbow. Slack was bowed over, staggered by a weight, quietly whimpering, a deep hood covering his features.

The long curve of the bar was stone, veined through with green. Where patrons stood near the green veins, the veins began to glow, getting brighter the longer someone living loitered nearby. The ceiling was a series of domes and groined arches that intersected in almost runic patterns, nothing quite square. The floor's composition was uncertain, it looked like a glossy black mirror. Sanction stood at the bar on one side of the crooked and twisting room, taking in its staircases up to private rooms, with shadowed corner tables tucked into the curve of their ascent.

The far side of the second floor common room was filling up fast. Cloaked figures waved away attendants who came to help them shed a few layers. It was raining outside, but these guests chose to be layered deep in the hottest season.

"The Mistress can hear you through the Eye, right?" Sanction muttered to Neap.

"She can," he murmured.

"Turns out," Sanction said with a wince, "Volaris is having a sort of a celebration or event here tonight."

"And we didn't know?" Piccolo retorted, eyes wide.

"The Veil is known for their discretion," Sanction said through his teeth. "That's the point. Now, can we make this work anyway?" His eyes darted around.

"Let's do it," Piccolo said shortly, straightening his dark brocade vest. "I'm itchy to be on the other side of this."

"Poor you," Neath grumbled. They pretended not to hear him.

Sanction looked over at the massive water clock that took up a corner by the bar, watching its various trickles and spinning cogs as the night-black face shifted, only the painted luminescent numbers visible.

"It's time," he murmured. He headed for a side room with a glyph over its doorway; even though the Circle of Flame's glyph had no circle, it was clearly recognizable. Piccolo brought Neap along, his grip somewhere between support and dragging.

A man and a woman wore custom-fitted armor and finery, obviously guarding the door into the opulent private lounge beyond. The woman squinted at the approaching trio, her hand on the pommel of her sword. The robed man extended his staff, his adept ritual gift unfolding over the guests.

At once, the crystal in the head of the staff burst in a shower of bright shards, like a log collapsing in a fire sending up sparks. The man staggered back with a cry, and several security personnel looked over to the doorway.

"It's fine," the woman said quickly, stepping forward. "You're expected," she said with an arched eyebrow to Sanction, Piccolo, and Neap. Aiming an exasperated look at her partner, she hauled the door open, and they descended several shallow steps to the Circle of Flame's private lounge in the Veil as the door soundlessly closed behind them.

Metal inlaid on the floor glowed with energy that flowed from Neap, running away as though he had poured molten iron in a mold. The walls rustled, runes of detection flickering.

A table dominated the center of the modestly sized lounge. A trio waited for Sanction's crew.

One was a man with a tall forehead and deep bulging eyes over a mouth that could not straighten out its sardonic curl. He was by far the most expensively dressed. At his elbow, a woman dressed in the flowing robes of a scholar, ink turning her cuticles gray, her face bearing the imprint of a thousand sleepless nights. And, finally, the towering and solid ex-soldier, dressed nicely, death in his eyes and in the scars that patterned what they could see of his hands.

Sanction took half a step back and lowered himself in an elaborate bow as Lord Mora rose to his feet.

"About time you showed, Crendél," Mora sniffed.

"Apologies," Sanction replied. "There were complications getting through the heightened security tonight without revealing your prize."

"Yes, my prize," Mora said through his teeth, his forehead knotting with displeasure. "You plan to sell me this priceless artifact the same night both Mordis and Volaris are here? In the same building?"

Sanction could not meet his eyes, instead staring at his exquisitely tied cravat. "My Lord," he said in an uneven voice, "I can no longer bear the risk of having that—that thing near me." He risked a flicker of eye contact. "I must be free of it tonight." His eyes slid over to the scholar. "Even if you do not wish to purchase it for my asking price. And who is this?"

"I brought my own expert," Mora replied, his tone dark. "Professor Selvacha. She will verify your claims on the item. She's an expert on the Kotar artifacts."

"Of course," Sanction said with a thin smile. "We have nothing to hide."

## BACK ENTRY TO THE VEIL

The heavy door creaked open, and Trellis (dressed as a bartender) leaned out of the doorway. "Now is the time, gentlemen," he said. He paused, frowning. "What, just initiates? Are there any actual Spirit Wardens with you?"

"You didn't say Volaris would be home," hissed one of the bulky armored figures in the shadow, ignoring the question. He stepped forward enough for the stark lights of the buzzing electroplasmic torch to illuminate some of his half-mask, his mouth and chin exposed, making clear his rank of Initiate rather than full-fledged Warden. He pointed at a rune of hammered copper that was prominent on the club's tower, glowing a dull red. "That symbol means he's in there."

Trellis frowned. "Very few people know Volaris' schedule. This doesn't have to affect our plans, it's unlikely he's anywhere near where the smugglers are selling the cases of unrefined plasm. This is a career-making bust!" he whisper-shouted. "It was only luck I found out about this one!"

Two of the initiates exchanged a glance, then they all looked at Trellis. "Another time," one of them said, emotionless. "We have... an agreement with Volaris." They withdrew deeper in to shadow, leaving the back courtyard of the club.

"Right," Trellis said, his mind whirling. He yanked the door shut, dropping the bar in place, and raced up the stairs to trigger the backup plan.

## CROW'S FOOT. TANGLETOWN, EMPRESS OF GULLS' WORKSHOP SLOOP WRECK. 56ᵀᴴ SURAN. (THREE DAYS AGO)

"Thank you for seeing me," the Mistress of Tides said with a deep and graceful bow. "I have committed to a task that is... beyond my abilities."

"Not beyond mine," croaked the Empress of Gulls. Her gnarled form was carefully arranged on the throne, and a strong young man stood on either side. The throne itself was woven together of driftwood and bone, its "roots" curving down the rough steps, its "branches" connected to the ceiling of the dank chamber. Stripes of spellwork and glyphic wards lay unevenly across every surface, and the only light came from mounds of luminescent chips heaped in palm-sized braziers flanking the throne. The Empress of Gulls was shrouded in a deep veil. "Now, what is the challenge?"

"I am to make a false Eye of Kotar," the Mistress of Tides murmured.

The Empress of Gulls cackled, her gnarled hands clutching at the brocade of her dress. "Oh, delights!" she gasped. "And proper rogues still slither this world." She cocked her skull-like head to the side. "The Trellis of Barrowcleft is behind this, yes?"

"He is involved," the Mistress of Tides confirmed.

"And this is not for the Gondoliers," the Empress of Gulls crooned through a grin.

The Mistress of Tides paused for a moment. "No. I am exploring other options."

"Good for you," the Empress of Gulls breathed. "I need you to grow to be strong. Independent. Vicious. And to understand all loyalties are not created equal." Her nod was curt. "I will need your service before the end."

"And you will have it," the Mistress of Tides said, feeling fully visible behind her veil. "The Eye must be able to maintain contact over distance. We expect to implant it in someone, so that must be a... memorable experience. Also, it should radiate enormous power if checked."

"You need a ritual to create an object of power," the Mistress of Gulls confirmed. "That is not easy or cheap."

"I do not want an object of power," the Mistress of Tides said quickly. "I want a fake that can pass a test. It only has to last maybe an hour upon activation. It need not be totally stable."

"All the same I will require a case of silver bricks," the Empress of Gulls sniffed. "I will also need the ghosts of a family that died together, in significant duress. And a month to put it all together."

"I... I have three days. Maybe less," the Mistress of Tides faltered.

An eyebrow cocked behind the Empress of Gulls' thick veil. "Three cases of silver bricks. And, of course, you owe me one. A big one," she nodded.

The Mistress of Tides nodded, and swallowed hard, knowing that much cash would likely wipe out the reserves of the scoundrels; but without this, they could not proceed.

"Very well." The Empress of Gulls turned to one of her shirtless men. "Bring me the wakefulness brew. Then go to the market and fetch a crooked goat. We'll sacrifice it, use that eye; should be an unnerving base we can render positively horrifying." The man nodded, turned, and left.

The Empress of Gulls used the long, long fingernail on her left hand to dip into an inkwell on the throne, then  scratch a pattern on a bone tile, and she handed it to the man on her other side. "Fetch me this jar. Careful, son." She turned to regard the Mistress of Tides. "I harvested the ghosts of this nice family, the father got in debt with loan sharks and was fed to the hagfish. But Dornas, he needed to make an example, so he took the man's wife, mistress, and five children and locked them in a pit in the sewers before the high tides last spring." She shook her head. "They died screaming, clutching each other, drowning by inches. That's what we'll need for this ritual to work. Energy that can pull back into the center, or be drawn out to burst alone—an instinct to escape, and an instinct to gather." The Mistress of Tides could feel the other woman's glittering eyes fixed on her behind the veil. "Only human will do, for the power we need."

"I am in your debt," the Mistress of Tides said humbly.

"What I need from you," the Empress of Gulls said quietly, "is to hold the baseline reservoir together to fill with seven ghosts. Then

I will make seven pockets so that the ghosts may be drawn out and spent. Each one will allow for an artifact level flash of power. But seven is all you get." Her smiling teeth were wet. "An entire lifetime of energy, dissipated for a moment's selfish illusion."

"One to get past the door guard," the Mistress of Tides calculated. "One for random checks. One for the verification."

"If it's a private lounge, you need to trigger detection there too," the Empress of Gulls added.

"Then one when it goes into the servant's eye socket, to transfer the memory," the Mistress of Tides winced, "and probably one to fuel the communication."

"Right," the Empress of Gulls nodded. "That's six. And if the seventh one is spent, then the Eye loses all appearance of enchantment!" She rubbed her knobbled hands together. "It will be a close one!"

Her cackle filled the shipwreck as the Whispers prepared for their dark work.

## NIGHTMARKET. THE VEIL, SOCIAL CLUB. 59ᵀᴴ SURAN.
### (FOUR DAYS AFTER THE DIVING BELL)

"Let's see it then," the scholar said, trying to sound dispassionate as she flung back the deep cowl covering Neap's face. She took a step back, unable to suppress a gasp as she saw the disfiguring, pulsing Eye rooted in his skull.

The flat pupil twitched and flickered, rolling slightly, unmoored from coordination with the dim and wet human eye on the other side. The flesh around the eye had been altered, both drained and polluted to a leathery purple flap stitched with skin tags that formed in runic shapes in response to the power welling from the horrible yellowish orb. Neap let out a very convincing whimper.

Professor Selvacha drew a silver atheme from her sleeve. "I need to see the roots. That's where the runic proof will be," she said in an unsteady voice.

Piccolo grabbed Neap by the shoulders and forced him to a kneeling position as the Bearer of the Eye whimpered. Then the professor brought the knife to bear on the Eye—

A ripple of force washed out of Neap, sending everyone else

in the room toppling over. Neap was on his feet in a flash, and he sprinted to the door and banged out through it at top speed.

"Don't let him get away!" Mora roared.

The chase was on.

# CHAPTER FOUR

*Who was Kotar? Imperial archeologists plundered his tomb and put its artifacts on display in a museum in the Lost District shortly before it fell, centuries ago. All records referencing Kotar were deliberately hidden by an arcane cabal with distressingly long reach into various records and scholarly circles not unlike our own.*

*Some say he was a god, others say he was a demon, and of course there is the idea that he was an extraordinary human. He had the powers of a sorcerer, that seems sure. His remains were mummified. So to take an element of Kotar's corpse on, to replace your own living flesh with his power-soaked remains, is to connect to a world before this one. A time before the sun shattered to embers, before the dead yielded ghosts. You see, the dream of Kotar is more potent than the facts about him. You need to understand that a broken few believe that the only thing in this world that can fill the emptiness they feel is the corpse-might of an ancient. These people are dangerous.*

*- Lectures on the Ancients,*
*Professor Gelina Vellbacht*

"I've hooked Mora fast," Sanction said as he paced the solarium. "We get this set up for two days from now. We know Mordis is in place, so we've got a backup buyer, that's how we can pressure Morda along." He paused, looking over at Trellis. "Seems like a long shot, getting the Spirit Wardens inside."

"Oh, politically protected sites like the Veil give them an itch they long to scratch," Trellis said with a dark smile. "I'll feed them a cover story about smugglers selling cases of unrefined plasm. That's an overpowering lure for those bastards, enough to overcome most of their reservations."

"And when they find the Eye of Kotar instead?" Sanction asked, eyebrows raised.

"Poor Neap thanks them for the rescue and gives them the Eye," Trellis shrugged.

"How do we get him away from the Spirit Wardens after that?" Sanction pressed.

"He dies, of course," Trellis sighed. "I've got a man on the clean-up crew who will be ready to help spirit him away and pull him back to his senses."

Sanction sucked his teeth for a moment. "What else do we have? Just in case?"

"Mordis is in the building, and he's a big deal," Trellis murmured, watching the rim of his glass as his finger slowly traced it. "He hates the Circle of Flame, some bad blood a ways back. I'm just reluctant to use him, because he's sharp, and it's easy to get on the wrong end of a deal with him."

Sanction's smile was crooked. "How can you improve our odds?" he asked.

Trellis regarded him with a cocked eyebrow. "You are loving this," he said.

"Some people are made to dig in the dirt," Sanction replied, something wild and dark in his eyes. He sipped his drink. "What would you call this? What we're doing? What I was born to do?"

Trellis's answering smile was half hidden in his cup. "We call it twisting fate," he murmured, and he drank deep.

Neap dove forward into a roll, sliding right under the door guard's swipe. Down the stairs and out on the floor he tumbled, then he popped up running, a stagger slowing his steps. The armored woman was right on his trail, and he darted forward, turning to present a slim profile, between two cloaked figures. The guard shoved one out of the way and was immediately countered as a big man shoulder-checked her, standing over her glowering as the cloaked figure was helped to her feet by her other bodyguard.

"What is the meaning of this?!" shouted the bodyguard as the Circle of Flame's guard rolled swiftly to her feet. "You dare not touch the Master!"

"Stop that man!" she yelled in reply, pointing after Neap.

"I said—" the bodyguard roared, but the impatient armored woman punched him in the throat and snatched his wrist, spinning to tug the surprised guard off balance as she pivoted him over her shoulder, laying him out at her feet with a throw that reverberated through the floor with the crashing impact. Of course, that knocked another patron over, and the noise spread fast.

"STOP THAT M—" the guard yelled, only to be bowled over by the other bodyguard.

Mora, Selvacha, Sanction, Piccolo, and the adept guard ran up to a tense scene, where bodyguards were shuffling their charges out of the way as Mora's guard cranked a bodyguard around into a sleeper hold.

"What's going on here?" a peacekeeper (one of the security officers) asked as he sidled up to Mora. "Bad form, this," he added with a nod to the scuffle. "Your guard is causing a scene."

Mora snatched a handful of the man's brocade vest. "A runt escaped my lounge, I need him back, now, no questions," he growled through his teeth.

"No questions," the peacekeeper agreed, tugging himself out of Mora's grasp and smoothing his clothes. "We're on it." He gripped a crystal that hung around his neck, his eyes drifting half closed. Then he frowned.

"I'm afraid there's a complication," he said apologetically.

"What?! No! No complications!" Sanction said desperately. "No, we gotta get him back!"

"Shut up," Mora said, fierce. He turned to the peacekeeper. "What complication, and how much will it cost me to smooth it out?"

"I'm afraid that's going to be a matter between you and Mordis," the peacekeeper said, something very like pity in his eyes.

Mora swore.

## NIGHTMARKET. DUNDRIDGE & SONS TAILOR. 58ᵀᴴ SURAN.
### (THREE DAYS AFTER THE DIVING BELL)

The massive figure stood on a pedestal reflected by three panes of mirrors as the languid tailor flicked at his cuff with chalk.

"These colors do me justice," the big man murmured, his light and high-pitched voice unsettling. He flourished the half cloak.

"Just the thing for your party tomorrow," Trellis said from the doorway. He removed his hat with a practiced aristocratic tug, settling it in the crook of his arm. "I thought you might be interested in a wager."

The big man turned, and the tailor swiveled and bobbed to continue work in spite of his movements. "I thought you retired to become a gardener," the big man said in his fluttering voice.

"Yet the sun's fragments pulse and the seas never stop," Trellis shrugged. "I am considering coming out of retirement. What do you think, Mordis? Does it suit me?" He invited scrutiny with a half-smile, arms wide. His spotless suit did not draw the big man's eye, but instead, Mordis seemed unfocused.

As a Tycherosian, Mordis bore the mark of demon blood. His hair was lank, his skin reddish and harder than human skin, and his thick underslung jaw had a pair of tusks, his canines overenthusiastic. A smile crawled across his ugly features.

"Let's hear it, gardener," he said.

"I've got a bit of mischief planned for tomorrow night. Shouldn't involve you or your people," he said dismissively. Then he looked sideways at Mordis, a glint in his eye. "If it does," he said, "I'll make you a wager that what we cooked up will make your heart skip a beat with surprise."

"A risky bet," Mordis observed. "Stakes?"

"If it does, then you shelter our little surprise. If not," Trellis shrugged, "you eat it."

"That's good as far as it goes," Mordis rumbled. "I want something personal. Some skin in the game for you, as it were." He paused. "You still with the Hive?"

"They cashiered me, you know that," Trellis shrugged, looking away.

"My knowledge may not always be reliable. Suns and seas and all that bullshit," Mordis replied. He squinted at Trellis. "You still deal in radiants?"

"Yes," Trellis nodded, suddenly guarded.

"I want something beautiful. Something for underwater." Mordis's smile stretched his face. "Something by a master."

Serious, Trellis nodded. "You'll have it," he said quietly.

Mordis returned his attention to the mirror. "Then let's see if you can surprise me, old man."

## NIGHTMARKET. THE VEIL, SOCIAL CLUB, OUTSIDE THE MORDIS LOUNGE ROOM. 59ᵀᴴ SURAN.
### (FOUR DAYS AFTER THE DIVING BELL)

Mora stood outside the entry to the private lounge room, flanked by armored guards, his adept and professor behind him, Sanction and Piccolo in easy reach. "You have something that belongs to me," Mora said, struggling to remain calm, facing off with the two armored door guards outside Mordis's lounge.

Six peacekeepers stood against the walls, nearby but not intruding. Most of the guests withdrew to a more or less safe distance, still in earshot. Mora spared them an exasperated glance, then returned his attention to the lounge door. "Mordis! I think we need to talk this through."

The door opened, and the Tycherosian's massive form shouldered out, rising to his impressive height. "This is the wrong night to make demands of me, Lord Mora," he intoned inscrutably, his high-pitched voice slightly hoarse.

"Not a demand, then, but a request." Mora's jaw tightened. "A plea. There was a man who left my accommodations and found his way to yours, and I would very much like to have him back."

Mordis looked him over for a moment, then descended the

short staircase and walked right up to Mora, letting him feel the size difference; the Tycherosian loomed over Mora, whose head came up to his collarbone.

"I have lived a long time under the broken sky and above the ink-black sea," Mordis murmured, his voice carrying with the forcefulness of a yell. "There are precious few things that surprise me. Whether they be jump scares, sudden insights, or turns of the ever-tumbling market, all things follow patterns, and the randomness in those patterns is, if not predictable, unsurprising. When something does surprise me, it is invigorating. I am pushed closer to my instincts." He paused. "It's good for me. And the shock I got tonight was a good one." His grin showed teeth that were humanly impossible. "Shall I consider it a present from my friend Lord Mora?"

"I am in no position to give gifts so dear, that—that surprise is spoken for," Mora said, his voice tight and low as he struggled to keep control of himself.

"For the Circle of Flame, of course," Mordis nodded. A smile tugged his features. "For Lady Penderyn." The smile unfurled across his entire face.

"Yes."

"I am actually the owner," Sanction blurted. "It is my surprise that I was going to sell to Lord Mora, but since you fancy it, maybe we could—"

Mora elbowed Sanction sharply, not just as a signal to quiet him but a blow to take his air. Sanction dropped to one knee, and Mora attempted a frosty smile.

"It's my property," he said. "I've arranged payment, and I want it back."

"That's predictable," Mordis nodded, and as he watched Mora, his other eye wandered the crowd of onlookers to find Trellis, who was smiling towards the back. "And my response must be predictable too," he said agreeably. "Let's play this out. Perhaps inside?"

"Yes," Lord Mora said, relieved. "Inside." He turned to Sanction, disgusted. "And we don't need him."

"It's a party," Mordis shrugged. "Bring him all the same."

Mordis led the way into his party suite, followed by Lord Mora and Sanction. The guards, including Piccolo and the adept and the professor, were left outside.

Glowchips lit up purple and red glass, giving the room an ambiance that defeated the eye's ability to adjust to the darkness while suggesting visual ranges beyond what humans could detect. Sitars and drums wove a driven harmony that seemed to coat the walls like the exotic hangings. Rather than tables and chairs, the entire suite was supplied with deep cushions. There were several hookah pipes, and a whole wing of the lounge was elevated and supplied with low beds as an opium den. At the back, a kitchen faced the well-stocked bar. Servants scurried about the vast suite, preparing it for the guests that would flood in later. Mordis settled on his throne, and regarded the others.

"Welcome to my lounge," he rumbled. "The party has not yet started, so let's take care of business before the night unfolds."

"Where is the Eye of Kotar?" Sanction demanded.

"Please excuse this fool," Lord Mora said, anger flavoring his tone. "He is a nobody purchaser in over his head, he needs someone like me to relieve him of a treasure that is too overwhelming for the market to bear."

"Or someone like me," Mordis agreed, settling back. "The Eye of Kotar. Who would have guessed it would resurface after all these years?"

"It hasn't been lost that long," Lord Mora snapped. He rubbed at his forehead. "You keep it damn hot in here," he said.

"Do I?" Mordis inquired, vague, a smile curling one corner of his mouth. "You are looking for this, I believe." He gestured, and Neap shuffled into view from behind a screen, looking glum. In this lighting, the Eye was far more ghastly, radiating a strange glow and a fog, the pupil lit up.

"Yes."

Mordis cocked his head to the side. "What did you pay for it?" he asked.

"That's—I don't see how that comes into it," Lord Mora replied, rubbing the sweat from his face with the crook of his elbow. "The point is, I have a payment already in process, it will be active unless I stop it before noon tomorrow. I'm invested."

"Humor me," Mordis murmured as he leaned back on his throne.

Lord Mora stared for a long moment. "Stewardship of the High Six," he gritted out. "Something this twit thinks he can move on the side, so he doesn't alert his precious master that he's enriching himself with this sort of extra activity."

"Those cultivation rights are expensive to maintain, aren't they," Mordis sympathized. "It was, what, your grandfather? The last one who gave a damn about the gardens for their beauty. You were in it more in it for the prestige. And it's hard to find good help," he commiserated, shaking his heavy head. "People with a passion for it, and the needed mastery."

"Hey, that garden has won all the awards, and is more prestigious than any other site in Silkshore!" Lord Mora retorted. "Maybe any in the city! It's a goddamn treasure!"

"An inconvenient kind of wealth," Mordis reflected.

"Are we haggling? Is that what this is?" Lord Mora demanded. "You devalue my contribution? Because you know better than to try and pay in coin for something as esoteric as that Eye! It must be energy for energy, for if there is a seam, then a curse will flow forth." He snapped his mouth shut, glaring at the Tycherosian.

"You are satisfied it is genuine?" Mordis asked, arching an eyebrow.

Lord Mora's pause was just for a fraction of a moment. "Yes," he replied. "You?"

"I've got no right answer here," Mordis shrugged. "If I say it is genuine, then you agree, and everything gets expensive. But if I say it is a fake, well, that's self-serving in the extreme."

Lord Mora's features contracted as anger hovered at the edge of his features. "Do you think the Eye of Kotar is genuine?" he asked in a deceptively smooth voice.

"Oh, I believe the Eye of Kotar is genuine, alright," Mordis shrugged. "I also believe it's not something you should have. You or your precious Circle of Flame." He shook his head. "It's too dangerous."

Lord Mora's eyes got a touch of meanness in them. "Now you see here," he began.

"But there are other things normally beyond your reach that could serve," Mordis said as he raised his hand. "I'm only going to offer this once, but how would you like the Crystal of Syzannaran?"

"The—that's the purple crystallization of leviathan glandular secretion?" Lord Mora said. "The one that lets you—that detects demonic energy?"

"The very one," Mordis nodded. "And it lets you do some scrying, once you figure out how it works."

Lord Mora was silent for a long moment.

"Bear in mind," Mordis continued, "you're bartering for something I already have. This negotiation is not about the worth of the Eye. It is about the price to bury any lingering ill-will."

"How much time do I have to decide?" Lord Mora asked slowly.

"I need an answer now," Mordis replied, his teeth shiny in the dim light.

"Of course you do," Lord Mora replied, wiping at his sweaty face.


## SIX TOWERS. THE CENTRALIA CLUB. 56TH SURAN.
### (ONE DAY AFTER THE DIVING BELL)

"Well, is she due back?" Sanction winced at the bartender. "Like, maybe this week?"

"We don't give out schedules and you better stop sniffing around or you're out of here," the barkeep growled at him.

Rain sluiced down the glass wall of the parlor, and a throaty rumble of thunder resonated in the bar and everything on it.

"Right, okay, another firecap and I'll get going," Sanction sighed. He leaned over his narrow ledger, striking out a name, then slammed it and tried to contain his frustration.

A man drifted up to his elbow. "Did I hear you asking after Lady Penderyn?" he asked, his smile correct and precise if not warm.

"Oh, yes, I'm a seller. Rare—you know. Found something," Sanction stumbled. "I'm sorry, my name is Crendél. I am an appraiser and buyer."

"And you're out of your depth, but you heard the Circle of Flame was a good customer. For any kind of flim flam scheme," the man said through his teeth. He gripped Sanction's elbow, squeezing hard.

"What? No!" Sanction protested. "I know dozens of aristocratic—ninnies," he protested. "I came here because you know your stuff!" He yanked his arm free and stood, squaring off with his challenger.

"Really."

"Well not you," Sanction shrugged. "The Circle of Flame. Real adepts. Scholars. What, are you a peacekeeper here? Not very smooth," he said down his nose.

"Boy, I am Lord Mora, of the House of Selwythe, and I've got all the credentials I need. Including access to this club. Including access to members of the Circle of Flame."

Sanction looked him over. "If you say so," he shrugged. "Even if you get me ejected here, there are plenty of other ways to get to buyers who will know what I'm talking about."

Lord Mora turned to the barkeep. "Who else has he talked to."

"Sir Lysan, The Marguarite, Baron Ellis's people, and Danforth," the bartender said as Sanction pointed a surprised and insulted look at him.

"You're done," Lord Mora said to Sanction, snatching his elbow again. He looked to the bartender. "What's he trying to sell?"

"He didn't say," the bartender replied, "but I checked his ledger when he stepped away. Something called the Eye."

Lord Mora stared at Sanction for a long moment, then dragged him down the hall and threw him into a storage room, joining him inside and locking the door.

"The Eye," Lord Mora clarified. He drew a silver athame from a concealed belt sheath, and the dim light of the storage room played along its cold edge.

"The Eye of Kotar," Sanction clarified, a tremor in his voice. "We captured a thief who was living homeless in the sewers for years, nobody knows how long, surviving by channeling demonic power through his deformed eye. I realized it wasn't just a mutation."

"You are going to sell it to me. How about 500 slugs, hey?" he growled.

"No!" Sanction protested, eyes wide. "You can't sell things infected with demon energy, it's got to be energy for energy, or you release a curse into the world." He paused. "And I need something I can move on the side. What do you have that's energy? And I can't manage slave trade," he warned.

Lord Mora thought for a moment. "My family has cultivation rights on a radiant garden," he said.

"We're done here," Sanction shrugged.

"The High Six, you idiot," Lord Mora said through his teeth. "The crown jewel of Silkshore." His jaw was set. "Know any master radiant cultivators?"

"I—I actually do," Sanction said, breathless. Then he shook his head. "This is all too high profile, and I don't like your knife. I can find another buyer."

"I can make sure you don't," Lord Mora muttered, dead serious, staring Sanction in the eye.

Sanction let the moment stand, then he sighed, frowning. "How much time do I have to decide?"

"I need an answer now," Lord Mora growled. "The bearer of the Eye could escape from whatever setup you have. I need to provide security."

"I need to have the cultivation rights for High Six set up to transfer, and you can stop the transfer if you're not satisfied. That protects us both," Sanction said.

"I can arrange that, and we can do the transfer at the Veil. It's a club, I have a stake there, they are very discreet."

Sanction looked queasy. "I don't know, this doesn't sit right."

Lord Mora raised his eyebrows.

"A week?" Sanction offered.

"I can have the paperwork done and a site prepared to receive the Eye of Kotar in three days," Lord Mora growled. "We will meet in two days to finalize the transfer process, and the next night you will come with your prize to the Veil. We will meet at the Hour of Silver. Got it?"

Sanction nodded, somewhat numb.

"And hear this," Lord Mora said, leaning close. "Anything happens so the Eye escapes? I'll kill you slow. That Eye is mine," he snarled. "You cut the hands and feet off that host body if you must. Get me?"

"I—I'll do as you say," Sanction replied, defeated.

Lord Mora leaned back, pleased. "See you here in two days," he said, and he unlocked the door and left the shaken man alone with his thoughts.

## NIGHTMARKET. THE VEIL, SOCIAL CLUB, THE MORDIS LOUNGE ROOM. 59TH SURAN.
### (FOUR DAYS AFTER THE DIVING BELL)

"I'll take the Crystal," Lord Mora said through his teeth. "Thank you."

"It will be delivered to your residence tomorrow," Mordis agreed. He vaguely waved towards Lord Morda. "You may go. My party starts soon." He cocked his head to the side. "You'd bring down the mood."

Lord Mora tried to stretch a smile over the glowering frustration that filled him, then he turned and stalked out of the lounge.

For a long moment, no one else moved, then Mordis rose from his throne. "You with the Eye. Come here. And you, Crendél, or whatever your real name is."

"You can call me Sanction," he replied with a smile as Neap strolled up to the towering Tycherosian.

"So how does this work?" Mordis murmured, examining the eye.

"If removed hard, like with a knife or ripping force, our man here appears to die," Sanction said. "However, we can also push here, here, and here," he said, compressing skin tags, "and it slides right out." With a slurping pop he tugged the fake Eye of Kotar out of Neap's head.

"You gave up an eye for this?" Mordis asked Neap, eyebrow raised.

"Mine's in a jar back at the base," Neap shrugged. "We've got about four hours to put it back in before it goes bad."

Mordis chuckled, a fluttering unpleasant sound. "That's a whopper," he said, shaking his head. "Of course that poor dumb bastard would do anything for the Eye of Kotar. The High Six is the end game here?"

"One of the end games," Sanction shrugged modestly. Mordis threw his head back and let out a proper laugh at that, clapping Sanction on the shoulder.

"Well played, son!" he cried. "Why would the Circle of Flame or Lord Mora be upset with you? The victim in all this?"

"Just in case, we've got a few more safeguards," Sanction shrugged.

"I'm sure you do," Mordis chuckled. "Now, you should leave while I'm feeling this rosy mood."

Sanction hesitated. "You will send him the Crystal, right?"

Mordis cocked his head to the side. "I will, yes."

"But that's demonic energy, and if he doesn't trade any energy for it, won't that—won't there be a curse?"

Mordis regarded him for a long moment. "That is probably superstition," he murmured. "And even if it isn't, I may have reasons of my own for passing something as dangerous as the Crystal to the Circle of Flame." He paused, then grinned. It was almost a grimace. "You've used me to your ends, don't waver if I use you to mine."

"Fair enough," Sanction shrugged. "We'll be on our way."

"My regards to the gardener," Mordis said as they headed for the door. Then he threw back his head and laughed again.


## SILKSHORE. HIGH SIX. 60ᵀᴴ SURAN

The tolling of the noonbell resonated as Trellis approached the lone figure standing in the glowshade of the clearing.

"I'm surprised you aren't with my agent. To make sure there are no last-minute problems," Lord Mora said bitterly, not bothering to turn.

"I have people doing that for me," Trellis replied, his voice startling Lord Mora, who pivoted. "Expecting someone else?" he asked, arching an eyebrow.

"Lord Belderan!" Mora replied, eyes wide. "Unexpected! But perhaps inevitable," he conceded as his mind raced.

"You know how long I've wanted to be the curator here," Trellis shrugged. "We've spoken of it numerous times." His smile widened. "You insisted it was part of some Hive plot."

"Is it?" Mora asked, arching an eyebrow.

"No," Trellis replied. "Just an old man's lifetime dream. Look at it," he said, slowly turning as he took in the secluded corner of the High Six gardens.

They stood in the glowshade of a massive oak whose skin shone with an almond sheen, peeking out between shingles of bark, brightening where the skin touched on the leaves and light seeped through their veins. A mounded cascade of rose bushes flowed down a backdrop cliff, each rose emitting a yellow breath of light tinged crimson along the edges, the vines themselves thick and waxy black over the native granite of northern Akoros. Radiant bees hummed like wind-up jewels, drifting lazily around the light and life of the plants around them, and a long row of lilies nodded in the wind, stamen glowing brighter in a breeze, fading in calm.

The path came from above, and looped around the broken cliffs to continue downward, occasionally hiccupping into steps. From here, all of the Ease lay out for review, the lanterns and fog and silk presenting a color-mottled lightscape not unlike the more chaotic beds in the High Six.

"This tree, the oak. My great-grandad planted it when he was a youngster. Called it the Rooted Delta. And every one of us was dragged up here at some time or another for a life lesson in the glowshade. Honor. Persistence. Family. Debt. You know," Mora said dismissively.

"All too well," Trellis nodded. "I've a family of my own, and I too carry the heavy burden of trying to leave it more honorable and prosperous than I found it." He paused. "You are welcome here, Lord Mora," he added quietly. "Any time you need this glowshade for your own thoughts, or to share them, this garden remains open to you."

Lord Mora turned to look at him, squinting against his feelings. "Really."

Trellis nodded, serious. "The welcoming garden, right near the front. I was thinking about shifting the centerpiece to a marble statue of the Weeping Lady." He looked Lord Mora in the eye. "I was thinking of having a dedication to the generosity of Lady Penderyn."

Lord Mora cocked his head to the side. "I'm sure she'd like that. I don't understand why you'd do it."

"I don't know how we got here," Trellis lied smoothly, "but I appreciate this opportunity, and I want you to feel that you've gained help more than suffered a loss."

Lord Mora replied with a curt nod, then turned to look out over the Ease. Trellis stood by his side, and for a long and peaceful moment, both men were alone with their own thoughts.

## BARROWCLEFT. BELDERAN ESTATE. 60TH SURAN

"What happened here?" Piccolo said, his voice hushed with awe. He looked around the massive attic space that had been overflowing with radiant plants. Now it stood empty except for a few chairs, tables, and lanterns; the fairyland had become a dark, echoing cave.

"Sanction's plan called for a very, very expensive toy on short notice," Trellis replied, following Piccolo up the stairs. "I had what you might call a fire sale to cover the bill."

"And it worked like a charm," Sanction said as he too emerged from the stairwell. "That was a smooth operation."

"I need four days of sleep," the Mistress of Tides muttered as she entered the attic. "The ritual was exhausting, and then keeping Neap's eye fresh while communication was open to the fake Eye of Kotar? I'm spent," she sighed.

"We all need some time off," Sanction agreed, leading the others to the table with the lantern in the center. There were enough seats for the four scoundrels, with two more off to the side for the adepts. "But first maybe a few marching orders."

"Marching orders?" Piccolo scoffed. "I don't know about you all, but I didn't even get paid this time out."

"You were with the River Stallions," Sanction said quietly. "Their best job that I ever heard about pulled in maybe 4,000 slugs. Right? Okay, so fix this picture in your mind. Counting upgrades, paying all the staff, general expenses, and putting some aside for a rainy day, the High Six clears 2,000 slugs profit every month. Sometimes more." He leaned back. "We're looking to establish ourselves not just through one off smash and grabs or confidence games, but also through getting ahold of some territory that can bolster our income stream and prestige. This is a big picture kind of crew."

"What does that big picture look like?" Piccolo asked. "Because if this is going to be, like, all gardening heists, then I might start my own crew."

Sanction and Trellis exchanged a long look, then Sanction let a grin grow on his face.

"We're taking on the Fairpole Grotto Council of Gondoliers," he said quietly. "We are going to reorganize the crime of Silkshore."

"That's—really ambitious," the Mistress of Tides said, hesitant.

"We'll follow the two rules of eating a live hagfish," Trellis shrugged. "One bite at a time, and start with the tail." His smile was somewhat unsettling.

"What's this about marching orders?" Piccolo demanded, trying not to sound sullen.

"We need a hideout," Sanction said. "We'll also need a name, some identifier. But we can't make it up ourselves, it has to be given to us. So, keep your eyes open. We'll do supper here, spend the night if you like, and tomorrow we return to Silkshore."

"Victorious," Piccolo noted.

"Victorious," Sanction agreed with a wide smile. "And we're just getting started."

# CHAPTER FIVE

*When the Skovlanders clashed with Akorosian ships in the Void Sea, cooler heads prevailed and authored the Hunter's Compact, to govern the protocols for how the rivals would treat each other upon meeting in open water. When Akoros bolstered their technology to create the mighty leviathan hunting ships we have today, with their iron hulls and starving engines, the Skovlanders could not compete, not with their wooden craft and ancient traditions. As if that was not hard enough on Skovlander pride, the Imperium moved its toxic leviathan blood processing to factories in Lockport, poisoning Skovlan for Doskvol's benefit. That's how you get a thirty six year war, grinding a savage race of hunters out of their mountains and bays.*

*The truth, at the bottom of it all, is both peoples were shaped by their lands. The Skovlanders learned to force nature back enough for them to survive. They clung to the sea, and knots of family. The Akorosians made city prisons, and within them cannibalized each other like crabs in a bucket; they used violence and cunning as a way of life from the top to the bottom, and they clung to exploitation of others as the only way to survive. You put those people next to each other, and of course they find each other intolerable.*

*- From "Memoirs on the Unity War,"*
*by Col. Fester Nordbaddel*

The stink of a slowly rotting cellar soaked into everything. The slow slap and swallow of wavelets in an uneven canal current shrugged under all other sounds. There were shuffling sounds sometimes, or the dull screech of a chair pushed one way or the other. Sometimes the clatter of coins. The dunking swish of a ladle in a water bucket. A shudder of swollen wood, the door dragging on the flagstones. Days crumpled to ash as she passed with exquisite slowness.

The always pain was a view from the bed of embers, a pulsing heat that pained the skin and turned strength to water. The sometimes pain was changing bandages; tolerable agony for the slashes, but for the deep gut stab, a sour darkness ringed with lava.

"You reported her dead," she heard at one point, in the hard cadence of her native tongue. "Now are you worried she'll survive?'

"Worried?" scoffed the other voice. "Look at her."

"I'm looking," the other voice said. She struggled to make her eyelids open, but they may as well have been painted on her glassy sightless eyes. "I see iron in that meat."

"Just a matter of time," the other voice said, dismissive. "When she dies, and the carillon at the Bellweather Seminary rings its mournful tone to mark her passing, and the deathseeker crow soars out to find her remains, we'll be nowhere near Grinder operations."

"Oh, I get all that," the other voice retorted, "but I think they're likely to start wondering where we're spending all our time."

"I told Hven you got a new girlfriend," the first voice said with an audible grin.

"Bastard."

Darkness swelled up around the embers, pulling her down into her private furnace.

In the world of dreams, she felt her heated bones as a long-ship. She stood at the aft of the ship gripping its tiller, hazy shapes bustling with the oars and ropes and sails. Waves piled high, towering, inching towards oblivion in the glow of a lightning strike that lingered for several minutes, rendering everything sharp and translucent. The ship navigated along the crooked trench at the wave's foot. Above the surface, her ship plowed through the hallucinating far fringe of the waking world. But should she fall any further, she would drop through the Veil into the Ghost Field itself. Death yawned beneath the planks at her feet. And yet, she bared her teeth at the needles of rain that shot through everything, and leaned hard on the tiller, carving up the glassy slope to starboard.

## SILKSHORE. THE EASE. ANOTHER GRINDER SAFEHOUSE. 57TH SURAN.
### (SIX DAYS AFTER THE RIVER STALLION RAID ON THE GRINDERS)

The pain dragged her up into the world around her body, by the roots of her hair, if her hair was marionette strings attached to every fibrous bone joint and trained reflex. Her tongue was swollen, and she could not speak, but she felt the rocking of the gondola; a neutered, aberrant stumble compared to the trustworthy sweep of a longship on the ocean swell. They passed an offal cart, and she struggled to shift position, only to feel the black pit in her gut unfold under her, depthless, a secret tunnel to the other side of the Mirror.

But! She could peel her eyes open, though they felt like sandpaper on glass lenses. Staring up, she saw the cruft of moss under a bridge, then the boat drifted clear, and she stared up through the broken sky at the cracked image of the sun. It hung red and crooked, dim, and she felt the whole world as a trembling drop of water suspended from that spigot far above, carrying traces of the cosmic flow now long shut off, but not yet fallen away from its source, with life and time teeming away in the droplet lacking any sense of perspective. She shivered with chill as darkness claimed her once again.

On the ink-black sea at the edge of the Mirror, the mast of her ship creaked as the vessel shuddered down the marbled wall of the wave, and shadows of crew fell from the deck as it was driven against the merciless sea by a sail bellied out by wind. She braced her legs, leaning against the tiller of the ship, her entire slim body pointing its might in a singular direction. She felt the oozing cuts, her arms tied to the tiller with her sinew; to be torn loose was to die, but she would not surrender. A wake of bloody foam sprayed behind the longboat's descent as she drove it across the face of the wave, above the dark abyss and below the shattered sky. Defiant, she cried out the names of her ancestors, from Brovold who stood against the Long Dark in ages past, through to her father Roinestad, who stood against the Akorosian Aggression; in this place, she called to them, and they glimmered indistinct beneath the lightless waves, their arrival pushing her hull further from death. "Not yet!" she cried. "Not yet!"

## SILKSHORE. THE EASE. ANOTHER GRINDER SAFEHOUSE. 59TH SURAN.
### (EIGHT DAYS AFTER THE RIVER STALLION RAID ON THE GRINDERS)

The click and rasp of looms intruded, like carpenter spiders hard at work. She felt the dipper at her mouth, and struggled to swallow the water that tilted out, runnels darting down her jaws and neck, soaking into her bedding. Her eyes cracked open to see the shining pommel of a dagger, fashioned for a broken sun. Some part of her mind remembered her uncle's man, Knut, who had such a knife. Adrift, she let the calm be with her, and it was as though a breeze fanned the embers of her fever.

"She's not going to make it," one voice said, low and insistent. "Knut, this has gone far enough. She has to be dealt with." A pause. "She can't come home," the voice said, almost horrified. "Not now."

"You listen here," Knut responded, anger gilding his tone. "They have ways of making sure what you say is absolutely true, and I will not be the one to admit that I helped the little miss here along through the Mirror. That won't be me!" A pause. "Ingvald, I can't believe you're even thinking about—about putting an end to her."

"I'm a doctor," Ingvald growled, "and my official diagnosis is that her mind is burned out from fever, and her body is slowly shutting down, but that some part of her is still able to feel pain. It is a mercy to end it for her. A mercy I delegate to you."

A harsh curse tore from Knut, followed by: "I won't do it. I will not, and it isn't right, and you know that, and you cannot make me!"

"Suit yourself," Ingvald muttered, sullen. "For now."

And the shuttering clatter of the looms stood in for heartbeats, seconds, anything relentless and predictable, as she faded once more.

As her ship climbed up from the abyss, riding the wave, she saw a light burning in the broken sky above. The Maiden Star. She knew she could follow it to safety.

But behind her, an impossibly massive wave built, touching the sky itself, and the darkness within that wave was illuminated by a tree of lightning that rooted and branched behind the wave, forking all over the sky for an everlasting instant that bled out to minutes.

Within that impossible shape was the shadow of a leviathan silhouette. A demon of the deep, too vast to grasp with the eyes alone, threatened to pull her under forever.

Deny me, a voice whispered in her mind, with enough force to rattle her teeth and buckle some hull boards.

"I deny you!" she cried out, her voice a scrap of paper in the wind.

Then survive, the impossible shape breathed, and she suddenly felt her lungs buck for air, the pillow pushed down on her face.

A cold calculation slid through her veins, and she knew she could not overpower her attacker. So she swung her arm around to where his belt would be, and fumbled—the knife, its pommel insignia the broken sun, its warm wooden grip in her hand. She yanked at the knife, unsheathing it with a rasping slither, and tilted her shoulder, lowering the knife. She felt the pressure on her face abruptly slack as Knut realized his danger, and she flexed to drive the blade up towards her attacker's gut.

Knut let out a strangled grunt as the steel jabbed his flesh, and he staggered back as she hauled herself up on one elbow, the pillow falling off her face.

Her world tilted and wobbled as she focused on Knut, and his hands splayed over his knife wound.

"Now what?" Knut demanded. "You will not make it ten steps. You don't know where you are." He paused. "You should just let this happen," he said through his teeth. "You're done." He winced with a fresh wave of pain from his stab wound.

All she could do was breathe, deep and raspy, like a pouncer wolf regarding its prey. Her eyes glittered with as much steel as the knife she held, and the tremors in her limbs were not a sure enough sign she was helpless.

Knut looked her up and down, gauging his chances, then he sprang to the door and hurled it open, dashing up the stairs as fast as he could while holding his stab wound.

She wasted no time rolling off the bed and landing in a crouch, staggering to the other door across the room, and fumbling to open it. Of course it opened to a walk along the canal.

She staggered out, supporting herself with one hand on the wall as the other trailed the long knife. Her bare feet slapped on the stone as she followed the walkway under the bridge for what seemed like forever before coming out to an intersection.

A shallow gondola was casually tied up to the quay, and the pilot looked up from his pipe to see her loom from the shadows like a ghost with knotted hair and a bloody knife. He adjusted his broad-brimmed flat hat, and stood up, tugging the mooring rope off.

"I can't pay," she said in a hoarse whisper.

"We have traditions here in Doskvol," the pilot replied quietly. "For the victims, passage across the way for free. And we need not speak of it," he added, "for we all have debts from when we were helpless."

She did not hesitate, but toppled into the gondola, and the pilot cast off as the door under the bridge banged open and bootfalls reverberated along the quay. The pilot's boat nosed in among other light traffic, drifting in the tangle of the Ease, paper lanterns jaunty in the dimness of the canal surrounded by stone embankments and buildings.

She regained consciousness as the gondola bumped against stone once more. Her eyes fluttered, and she slowly sat up, feeling the trickle of blood from several of her bandages.

"This stranger thanks you," she slurred.

The pilot smiled to himself. "You know something of our traditions," he said. He paused, something like pity in his eyes as he watched her climb out of the boat and onto the stone quay. "Is there anything further you would ask?"

She could barely shake her head, and when she managed to get up on all fours and look around, the boat was gone.

"I'll confess a bit of surprise finding you out here," the portly man said, a smile smeared across his features with unflattering asymmetry. He adjusted his dark coat with a tug to the lapels, and squared off with Kreeger.

"I hope it is not an unpleasant surprise," Kreeger said, rising from his chair and crossing the study to shake the newcomer's hand. "It's good to see you, Marcus."

"Glad to hear it, glad to hear it," Marcus murmured. "Quite a bit of nastiness, with your house fire. I heard Rutherford was shot!"

"Yes," Kreeger confirmed after a fractional hesitation. "Shall we sit down?" He escorted Marcus over to the game table and settled opposite him. "I can tell you've got something on your mind."

"You, actually," Marcus confirmed. "It's been eight days. I wanted to get a sense of how long you'd need before we could expect you back." He shifted in the chair. "The Department of Roughage misses you, my good son. It's a chaotic distribution node, managing Silkshore's roughage, and you're like an artist when it comes to maneuvering everyone into place." He shook his head. "We need your steady hand back at the reins." Marcus looked him in the eye. "I'd rather have you at the desk than cover for your absence."

"I understand," Kreeger nodded. "I will confess that this attack on my home and my family stirred up—well, feelings. I must replace this chaos with order of a sort, you know how it is, to regain my balance," he said reflectively. "I need more time. I'd rather give my work my undivided attention, and for now this is my work. Once it's finished," he said, a slight crease on his forehead, "we'll have to see."

Marcus looked him over. "I've always enjoyed supervising you, Kreeger," he said. "Some find it galling that you fail to display the proper signs of respect and perhaps awe when speaking with your superiors. They find it cheeky and disrespectful. I've found it refreshing, and the challenge you bring is the challenge to do it better. Nothing personal. It's about the best path forward."

Kreeger nodded, waiting for the rest.

"That's why I'm here. About the best path forward. You have... opportunities in the Ministry, Kreeger. There are wheels in motion that you cannot see, and your future is enmeshed in them. But you have to return for that to matter. I can only cover for you so long before you are cited for abandonment. And, as you know, there's a long queue of candidates who would love to have your post at the Ministry."

Kreeger cocked his head to the side. "Perhaps managing rough-age schedules has lost its appeal," he said.

Marcus slapped his knees. "Indeed! Of course it is boring, on the surface. It's the intricate little personal dealings and selective applications of city codes that always kept your interest, until you could move to the next step in the path. There are many roles you could play that would benefit from your past dealings with every goatherd, stable, and workhouse supervisor in Silkshore. Plus, of course the gondoliers alone," Marcus shrugged. "The Ministry can find a role for you that requires everything you've ever done to be needed in the now."

"I'm not sure what you mean," Kreeger said.

"And I've strayed from my script," Marcus replied. "The point is, we want you back. This show of instability is worrying. More people are watching you than you realize, my young friend, and I don't want them to lose confidence in your future." Marcus squared his shoulders. "So. When are you back at your desk?"

Kreeger watched his supervisor, and the weight of silence grew until it seemed unsure whether he would answer at all. "I can't be certain," Kreeger said quietly.

Marcus rose to his feet. "Three days," he said. "Or I report abandonment."

Kreeger nodded, expressionless. "That sounds fair."

Marcus frowned. "Your uncle had a great career, but he's retired. He cannot afford you a way to advance through the world. This path you're on, it deposits you below us. Among those who are just people," he said quietly.

"I realize that," Kreeger nodded, standing. "I wish I could explain so you would understand."

"I don't want to understand," Marcus shrugged. "I want you back, unraveling our knotty logistics problems, with an eye to the future. A real future." His mouth closed to a thin line. "Don't disappoint me. Not this time."

"Nobody is supposed to starve to death in Doskvol," Kreeger replied abruptly, a peculiar light in his eyes. "That's part of the mandate of the Department of Roughage. Kelp and weed harvested from the canals and bay, treated and processed for the animals and the lowest poor." He shrugged. "Soups. Algae leather. Powder. Several forms. But about ten percent of the people are allergic to it." He cocked his head to the side. "For them, they have to either go out and pursue some kind of gainful employment if they are able, or starve to death while food is waved under their noses."

Marcus's gaze was distant. "I'd heard that you were getting restless."

"I can't live on paperwork," Kreeger said with a gesture. "These last few days... showed me I was starving to death at my desk, and unwilling to go after real food. Better food."

"I'll choose not to be offended by you comparing the basest charity with your executive function within the Ministry," Marcus muttered. "You don't need to abandon your post. You want variety, be patient, it's coming."

"It's already here," Kreeger replied quietly, looking Marcus in the eye.

Marcus looked him over. "Three days," he said with a shrug. Then he turned and left.


## CROW'S FOOT. CANDLE STREET BUTCHERS. 1ˢᵀ ULSIVET.
### (TEN DAYS AFTER THE RIVER STALLION RAID ON THE GRINDERS)

She watched the old woman work, hypnotized. The old woman hefted up the three foot long eel corpse, flopping it on the workbench, matter-of-factly jabbing a shiny hook under its chin so the corpse was tethered to the table. The butcher woman whipped out a knife and cut the skin around the back of the gills, flipping the corpse to cut all the way around. Then she put the knife aside and picked up massive pliers, clamping on the skin. Her muscles bulged all through her forearm and bicep and shoulder, tendon and sinew standing out as she tugged the skin down the corpse with a squish.

Trying not to stumble as she crossed the filthy street, the injured young woman leaned her elbows on the butcher counter. "Aunt Ryha," she said as loud as she could.

The butcher woman looked up, eyes unreadable as she saw the injured young woman at the counter. The butcher shouted over her shoulder, "Mayda, customer."

Part of the back wall of the shop tilted on a pivot, and a woman stepped through, breathing out a plume of smoke as she left what must be a break area in the back. She reached the counter, looking the "customer" up and down, something like contempt in her one eye. The other was lost behind an eyepatch that was flanked by scar tissue. "What'll it be?" Mayda demanded, her Akorosian accent rough. "You come for leavings?"

"I don't have a garden," the injured girl replied sharply in Skovish. "Social call, I'm here for Ryha."

Meanwhile the butcher woman had prodded the guts to one side of the spine, and with a single expert slit she cut the membrane holding it all together, gushing the offal into a bucket. She rubbed at her nose with the back of her wrist, then put her knife on the cutting board, turning to the counter.

"Arright arright," the butcher woman said, "come on back. I have minutes." The butcher woman stiffly limped to the back of the butcher shop and through a door.

Mayda frowned, and hauled at a lever under the counter, opening a side entrance. The injured girl managed to squeeze through it, pale and on the edge of consciousness, then she stumbled back and through the door after Ryha.

The door opened to a narrow muddy alley choked with trash, and the injured girl saw Ryha enter the wooden building across the way. She followed, just in time to see the old woman descending a staircase. Still a few steps behind, she headed down the stairs and saw an arch knocked through the bricks of the building foundation; following the hole, she was in the basement of a nearby building, thoroughly disoriented. A table stood in the middle of the room, and Ryha sat at the table, watching her.

"Do you recognize me?" the injured girl asked, a tremor in her voice.

"Oh yes," the butcher nodded. "Asdis. Welcome to Doskvol." Her Skovish accent had more charm than her Akorosian tone.

That almost got a laugh out of Asdis, who lowered herself onto the rough chair across the table from her great-aunt. "I was afraid you didn't know me," she confessed.

"This is a rough town," Ryha shrugged. "Not good for people to know your business." She paused. "It was wise of you to come to me instead of going to your uncle."

"Why do they want me dead?" Asdis whispered.

"They don't like the between," Ryha said, settling back and tugging her pipe and weedpouch out of her sling bag. She didn't look up as she began packing the bowl. "They leave a hostile place, and come to a hostile place, and there's not enough for everyone, and they have to fight all the time. Fight people who have what they need, who want what they want. Brothers against brothers, strangers pushing everyone down. And the wise voices say to wait, to be patient, that things will get better, but nothing is getting better, and there are more and more mouths to feed, and more and more killings, and more and more scars." She shrugged. "Seems after a certain point the patience is gone, the waiting is suffocating, and maybe some violence will lead to respect and spoils of victory." She glanced up at Asdis. "Can it be worse, they wonder? Better to fall with steel in hand than carrying a rich man's work."

Asdis leaned back in the chair, saying nothing. She watched the slabs of Ryha's arms shift as the old woman lit her pipe and puffed its embers to life.

"You would be a convenient flashpoint," Ryha explained. "Winsome girl like you, popular, newcomer. Stabbed by an Akorosian dog during a vicious robbery. A step too far from the oppressors, to be answered with steel and fire." She chuckled, an unpleasant and gravelly sound. "The problem is they assumed you'd die. Played the odds. You've been declared dead." Ryha cocked an eyebrow at Asdis. "So your ongoing survival is a time bomb waiting to go off. Showing them for liars and cowards and falsetellers to the powerful. Not reporting facts, but trying to propel the Grinders into war."

"I am hurt," Asdis said softly. "Hurt and tired. But when I get life back in me, I will be so angry."

For the first time, Ryha smiled, revealing more gaps than teeth. "That's my girl," she said. "Let's get those bandages changed, and some food in you. Death is still closer than life."

Asdis could only nod.

The house creaked and leaned as the chill wind rubbed along its walls. The first paleness had touched the plants outside as their trunks and stems began to drink all color back inside, locking it away from the coming coldness. Still, Kreeger heard the creak of floorboards in the hallway separate from the settling of the ancient estate.

"I'm glad you're up and around," he said, almost to himself. "Are you sure you're ready to be up?"

"I'm sure," Rutherford said, his wry smile fixed in place like the line of concentration on his brow. He shuffled into the room with a cane, comfortably wrapped in the hooded smoking jacket. "I see you're up to no good."

"Mm," Kreeger agreed, the various books and folios of information on the Ministry and Silkshore covering the desk before him. "You know how a little light reading helps me think."

"And you've got two days to get through all that thinking," Rutherford agreed, wincing as he lowered himself into a chair opposite the desk from Kreeger. Kreeger looked up, worry marring his features.

"Did the doctors check you out for wandering about unescorted?" he asked.

"That's a hell of a thing for you to ask me," Rutherford pointed out. "I understand you've not been in a frame of mind to pay much attention to rules or counsel lately." He shook his head. "People aren't telling me things, which is most of what I need to know," he said as he looked over Kreeger's shoulder out into the twilight of mid-day.

Kreeger paused, then leaned back from the desk. "What have you heard?" he asked.

"You have two days to decide whether or not to abandon your position at the Ministry," Rutherford replied.

Kreeger arched an eyebrow. "You're upset that I didn't consult you?"

Rutherford shrugged. "That is among my concerns," he said.

"I already know what you'd say," Kreeger shrugged.

"Maybe," Rutherford conceded. "It's a conversation I'd like to have all the same."

Kreeger flipped a heavy book shut. "Let's have it then."

Rutherford slowly eased back into the chair. "I need you to know this," he said. "Whatever you do, whatever direction you take, I'll support you." He looked Kreeger in the eye. "I've lived through wealth and privation, and I have never for one day taken our life together for granted. Watching you these last few months... I know you've been unhappy, but I have not been able to think of what we could do about it." His crooked smile stretched. "It did not occur to me to discard our lives and start over. But..." he shook his head. "You look good," he confessed with a slight arch in one eyebrow. "Almost happy."

"Huh," Kreeger said after a moment. "Rutherford, you surprise me."

"Since the day we met, if you'll recall," Rutherford agreed.

Kreeger looked back down at the desk. "I try to imagine going back to my desk, back to what I did for the Ministry. Like putting on wet clothes that have soured overnight. And... I know it's the smart thing to do," he said through his teeth, "but my bones rebel against it."

"The way I see it," Rutherford said quietly, "you played it smart and safe. And that was in the process of very slowly not working out." He caught Kreeger's eye, and held his gaze. "So maybe do the crazy thing. You mad beast."

"I don't know how you do it," Kreeger murmured, holding Rutherford's gaze. "How are you the only one who can make sense when it's chaos all around?"

"Good upbringing," Rutherford teased solemnly, "and excellent cheekbone structure." He paused. "Kreeger, there's more to this, more than I can see, and you need to suss it out."

"What do you mean?" Kreeger asked.

"You want out of the Ministry, fine," Rutherford said. "But there's something else you want. Something you want very badly. And you don't know what it is." He frowned. "Yet it is one step behind you, guiding you all the same. You need to know what it is before it drives you mad."

Standing, Kreeger rounded the desk and knelt by Rutherford's chair, taking his hand and clasping it with both of his, looking up in to the injured man's eyes. "Help me figure it out," he breathed.

"Let me in, and we'll look together," Rutherford agreed, solemn eyes fixed on his husband's face. He leaned forward, ever so gingerly, and they kissed.

Rutherford wondered if Kreeger could taste the trace of bitterness in the sweetness of the moment.

## CROW'S FOOT. CANDLE STREET BUTCHERS SAFEHOUSE.
## 2ᴺᴰ ULSIVET.
### (ELEVEN DAYS AFTER THE RIVER STALLION RAID ON THE GRINDERS)

Asdis ravenously finished the bowl of noodles with a slurp. She clattered the wooden bowl on the other empties, and grinned at Ryha. "You do amazing food," she said in Skovish.

"It's not the same, you can't get the same ingredients here," Ryha shrugged, puffing on her clay pipe. "Some of these dishes are better with Akorosian foods, hey?" She squinted at Asdis. "We should probably talk."

Ryha noticed the increased color in Asdis' cheeks, energy in her movements, and she marveled at the recuperative power of teenagers. A smile threatened as a cascade of decades unfurled behind her, full of old stories, but she shook her head.

"Go," Asdis said around a mouthful of crusty bread.

Ryha hissed out a breath as she lowered herself into the chair opposite Asdis, who still hunched over the remains of her lunch as though prepared to fend off food thieves. "You are in a new place," she said. "This is not Skovlan. Now you are in Akoros, in Doskvol. The Dusk," she said with a gesture, half serious about the city's nickname. She paused.            "Is this your home?"

"Is it my home?" Asdis asked, arching her eyebrows.

"Simple question," Ryha said defensively, puffing at her pipe.

"No it isn't," Asdis protested. "Not simple, I mean. I was born in Hveglaad, but that village was burned in the war. It doesn't even exist," she insisted. "And I more or less grew up in Lockport." She hesitated. "That isn't home. That will never be home." She squinted at Ryha. "What about you? Is this your home?"

"Smart girl, asking questions instead of having all the answers," Ryha said with a slightly wistful smile stretching her pouchy features. She took a long draw on her pipe, and breathed out like the mythic dragon, watching nothing in the middle distance. "Home is powerful," she murmured.

Asdis resisted the urge to push the silence out of the way, and let it simmer between them.

"I was born on Yagled," Ryha said quietly. "A little island. I knew every rock and tree, every family and their ancestors and children. It was my world. I expected to mingle my bones with the rock of the isle, as had my ancestors, as would my children." She sucked her teeth and shook her head. "My world got bigger, little one," she mused. "So much bigger." She looked Asdis in the eye. "I let my world grow. You must let your world grow too." She drew her favorite knife from the leather sheath at her side, holding it up so the smoke curled around the spotless blade in the lamplight. "I was the priest's daughter. Now I am a butcher. If you can imagine it." She turned to Asdis. "You will need your imagination," she said with quiet intensity. "No one, and I mean no one, can tell you who you are going to be."

Asdis looked at her for a long moment. "I don't understand," she confessed. "What's the lesson here?"

"No lesson," Ryha sighed. "And if you want all this boiled down to advice..." she looked the teen in the eye. "Advice from one butcher to another. Be sure before you place the knife."

Her smile was mirthless.

# CHAPTER SIX

*A novelty of training in the Bluecoat regiments is how they scrub the value of words out of their recruits. The whole time they train, Bluecoats hear words like justice, rule of law, integrity, honor, courage, nobility, and so on. Recruits who listen to those words inevitably fail out. The truth of the Bluecoats is a mandate to protect those who are already powerful, and keep the city quiet. Suppress violence, keep the poor in their place, and make sure nothing interrupts the flow of money upwards. If the truth, or honor, or law, or crime, or justice interrupt that flow then a successful Bluecoat will stamp that nonsense out and protect the wealth of the wealthy. Remember that when you go to talk to a Bluecoat. Don't use pretty words, they don't even listen anymore. Instead, point out the path of the money, where it is threatened, and what they can do about it. They know their duty. You want action from Bluecoats, show them how they can visibly protect a noble's cash flow, and you've got them on your side in no time.*

*- From "Treatise on Governance and Stability" by Hon. Judge Wilhelmina Gavros*

## SILKSHORE. LOTUS GARDEN. 52ᴺᴰ SURAN.
### (DAY AFTER THE GRINDER RAID WENT BAD)

The hiss and slap of rain outside was somehow soothing in the lounge. Four sunken pits filled with cushions arrayed around a hookah were evenly spaced in the floor, and no rain could flow up to get into the well-built patios surrounding the main chamber. Potted ferns added life to the art painted on the stone and the glittering mosaics in the floor. Several mirrors bounced the surrounding views through the space, making it even airier against the oppressiveness of the lowering sky and its rain. Shuttered walls were folded back out of the way.

A bow-legged man stumbled in from the rain, shaking his mop of lanky hair. He leaned against the bar, squinting at the immaculately dressed barkeep.

"I'm already a little drunk," he slurred, "so I need more companionship," he mouthed, the word difficult. He peered around, bleary. "Where're the ladies?" he asked.

The barkeep frowned at him. "You would be more comfortable at Dumphy's, next door," he said with a nod towards the ancient heap of a building, an eyesore screened off from the lounge by a row of ferns.

"I don wanna be comfortable," the drunk frowned. "I wanna get laid." He examined the barkeep, noting his embroidered robe, tidy turban, and waxed moustache goatee combination. "Ladies," he added, blinking for emphasis.

The barkeep deliberately looked over to the row of round tables down a side gallery. A man who had been sitting unobtrusively out of the way rose to his feet, striding out into the chamber. His loose shirt was wrapped in place by a red sash, and a cruelly beautiful saber hung at his side. He did not yet reach for it as he approached the drunk.

"Kickn me out?" demanded the drunk, gathering up some righteous protest. "Imma customer, got eels here," he jingled his sling bag "and here!" he grabbed at his crotch.

The bouncer snatched him by the nape of the neck and the back of an elbow, steering him around towards the street, taking big steps so the drunk could barely stagger to stay on his feet. His hands were both full of the drunk, who took up all his attention, so he did not notice the big man standing with his back to the pillar—until the gun butt cracked into the bridge of his nose.

As he let out a yelp, the drunk snatched his wrist with both hands, spinning in place, pulling the bouncer forward as he drove his forehead into the bouncer's face. The bouncer staggered, trying to gasp, spraying blood and teeth.

"Hands up," the man behind the pillar said as he rounded the other side and pointed his gun directly at the barkeep, whose hands flipped up and to the sides. Meanwhile the drunk stepped by a low stone bench and yanked hard on the bouncer, who tripped over the bench and smashed down on the ground; the drunk threw a couple savage kicks into him, and the bouncer was done.

The gunman had a simple mask on his nose and mouth, and a hat pulled low. The drunk was not disguised at all, and he turned with a wide smile that showed off several missing teeth. "Let's start over," he said, sounding less drunk.

"Do you know who I work for?" the barkeep asked, eyes wide. "You are so dead."

"That's kind of why we're here," the drunk winced, slinging himself up on a barstool. "The Red Sashes aren't welcome in Silkshore. This little expansion you're working on?" he gestured around the room. "I have a feeling it's not going to work out," he admitted with a conspiratorial tone.

"But they'll keep coming back to defend their business," the masked gunman pointed out.

"That's a good point," the drunk nodded. "Which is why we're going to burn it down."

"What?" the barkeep said, eyes even wider. "You'd be a fool—there's money hidden here—a floor safe, drug stashes, papers—you wouldn't!" He took a step forward. "I can make you rich!"

"So far you've offered to make me rich and dead," the drunk clarified, "and I believe you on both counts. So, I'm gonna stick to the script." He looked around. "Tough to burn this place, though. All this tile and stone and such. I mean, burning pillows won't do much good."

"Well, it's been burning for a while now," the masked gunman pointed out. The barkeep looked up, alarmed, and caught the whiff of smoke in the wind.

"Why did we come here to bother with the lobby then?" the

drunk protested, turning to the masked gunman.

"We wanted to carry out the idol before the building collapsed," the gunman replied, nodding towards the gleaming torso-sized statue studded with gems.

"Aaah," the drunk said. He turned to the barkeep. "You better run," he shrugged.

"You'll pay for this!" the barkeep shouted, his face reddening. He pivoted, and ran to the end of the bar, pushing open the counter slab, racing away.

The drunk looked over at the masked gunman. "How about we get that statue," he said conversationally.

"Yeah, let's get this over with," the big man agreed. They heaved at the statue, hefted it as best they could, and staggered out into the rain towards where the wagon waited for their ill-gotten goods.


## SILKSHORE. RIVER STALLION TOWER. 52ND SURAN

"This is it?" Saint asked, surveying the table.

"Yeah, it's pretty good," Gapjaw retorted. "That statue may be hollow, but it's plenty valuable. A moneybox, some jewelry and various trinkets from the upper floors." He shrugged. "A solid score."

Saint turned to Red Silver. "Any trouble with the upstairs arson?"

"No," she replied, her feet up on the table as she toyed with the head of her cane. "Once the fire started there was plenty of time for the whores to get clear. I stayed to make sure nobody showed up who was actually able to fight the fire. Safety handled anything requiring light feet," she grimaced, looking at her bandaged leg. "Knocked some pimps around. Nothing he couldn't handle."

"That was the plan," Saint agreed. "Any trouble downstairs?" he asked the shadowed figure seated across the room.

"None," she murmured. "The Red Sashes were lazy in preparing against supernatural threats. Probably because they were so new to the building, they just bought it." She paused. "I also detonated the plasm casks by the loadbearing pillars. When I left, the Lotus Garden was a crater."

"Thank you, Inkletta. Anybody seen the Hammer?" Saint asked.

"He's on his way, he thought he'd verify with the Bluecoats that there were no casualties from our little stunt," Gapjaw replied.

"Well it's about time something went right," Saint sighed. "On that note, time to get ready for my meet with Tarjan." He looked over the table, and picked up a broach, squinting at it in the light. Pocketing it, he prodded at the rings on the table with the tip of his finger, and picked two of those up. "That should do for our monthly fee," he muttered, something dark in his tone.

"I'll go along," Gapjaw said. "You need some backup." He looked over at Red Silver. "And you, missy, need to give your leg some time to heal."

"You aren't wrong, gramps," she said through her teeth. "I may have overestimated myself," she said, flexing her injured leg. "Inkletta, you need to go. The Gondoliers don't take any crew seriously unless they've got a proper Whisper."

Inkletta nodded.

"Where's Safety?" Saint asked, looking around.

"Oh, that," Red Silver said. "He was going to talk to some Blue-coat buddies, try to draw off the heat while we lay low." She paused. "Then I think he was planning to get totally wrecked for a few days."

Saint frowned. "He didn't check in with me," he said.

"Of course not," Red Silver sighed. "He knew you'd tell him this was the wrong time to do it, and that's not what he wanted to hear."

"He misses Piccolo, I think," Gapjaw said with a wry grin.

"About that," Saint said through his teeth. "Inkletta and I can make the meet just the two of us. You find that little shit so we can take some steps to make sure he doesn't cause any more problems."

"I'm on it," Gapjaw nodded.

"Okay, we have our assignments," Saint said. "Let's go."


## SILKSHORE. THE EASE, CENTRAL LANDING. 52$^{ND}$ SURAN. THE HOUR OF SONG

The two workmen at the top of the stairs stood by an open grating. They glanced briefly at Saint and Inkletta, and let them pass. Saint went down the worn stone steps first, holding a hand lantern. Inkletta, shrouded in a deeply cowled cloak, followed.

The stairs led down to the quay. Lisping wavelets in the canal slid along the stone. Several fishermen were mending their gear by the water, humming work songs, immune to the stench of their nets. They paid no mind to Saint and Inkletta; expected, the pair penetrated several layers of the gondolier security until they reached the recessed traffic station and gondola drydock where Tarjan waited for them.

Tarjan smiled, his skin stretching back so the points of his teeth, nose, and chin formed a predatory landscape. His eyes were as bright as his slicked back hair. He stepped forward, sliding his palms down his coveralls.

"Saint, Inkletta, so good to see you," he said in his measured Akorosian accent. "Good job with the Lotus Garden, I hear it burned to the ground."

"Lower," Saint shrugged. "We could not have done it without your plasm bombs."

"We all get what we want, that's the smoothest way the world goes," Tarjan smiled.

"Here's our monthly tithe," Saint said, putting the handful of jewelry on the work bench. "On time and everything." He was not smiling.

"Glad to see that," Tarjan said, nodding at the glittering jewels. "I heard your crew was slipping, what with the Grinders raid getting botched."

"We're better than ever," Saint said, his smile forced wider, "and it's time you gave us a seat on the Fairpole Grotto Council." He straightened. "I'm local, and Akorosian, and this Skovlan threat is just gonna grow if we let it." He stared right into Tarjan's eye, defiant. "You need us, both for muscle and for experience."

Tarjan's smile was peculiar and small as he looked at the jewels, as though he was embarrassed for Saint. "Saint, friend, you know that's not how it works."

"Well the way it works now," Saint retorted, "is you give us the occasional job and we pay you for the privilege of operating in Silkshore. And that's not good enough. Not by a long shot!"

Tarjan slowly shifted to meet Saint's eyes. "You don't have to give us gifts, if you're so unhappy," he said quietly.

"I want us to be friends!" Saint insisted. "I just feel like it's time the Council gave me voice and vote. We've been on the same side of a lot of fights, and there's a big one coming up."

"Saint, don't worry about the big picture, we've got it handled."
Tarjan paused. "I've heard you out," Tarjan said, serious. "We'll be
in touch."

A long moment passed. Then Saint shrugged. "Good to see you,
Tarjan," he said.

"Always a pleasure," Tarjan agreed easily.

Saint turned and left the overhung drydock a different way
than he had entered. Inkletta followed him out, exchanging a long
glance with Tarjan as she left. They followed the stone walkway
down the other side of the drydock peninsula, passing an undercut
set of apartments right on the water. A dry, painful cough wrung
the chest of someone inside, and a dull moan came from another
apartment.

Inkletta knelt by the wall, putting her fingertips on it, her eyes
drifting half closed as Saint stood by her side, glancing both ways.
A moment passed, then she rose to her feet, and the two of them
retreated back up to the streets.

"Are there more of them in the clinic?" Saint asked under his
breath as they sheltered by a looming roughage wagon.

"More than ever," Inkletta agreed. "Whatever this sickness is, it
is spreading among the gondoliers." She shrugged uneasily in her
deep cloak. "This sickness is dragging the life out of them, and it's
tied to the Mirror somehow. I'd have to spend some time with it to
figure out more."

"Time seems to be the thing everybody's running out of," Saint
said through his teeth. Then the pair vanished into the crowds of
the Ease.


**SILKSHORE. RIVER STALLION TOWER. 53ᴿᴰ SURAN**

"So it's about time for me to go to the meet with the Grinders,"
Saint said without enthusiasm, corralling his hair into a ponytail.
"I had hoped I could report we were part of the Council, but that
angle isn't going to work out." He grimaced. "I'm basically trying to
avoid going to war here."

"Goddamn Piccolo," Red Silver muttered under her breath.

The door creaked open and Gapjaw stumbled in, breathing
heavily. His face was covered in bandages, and he was wearing

loose hospital clothes. He staggered to a chair and sat heavily, then winced, shifting the angle of all his bandages.

"What happened to you?" Saint demanded.

"Last night I was tracking down Piccolo, found out he was talking to some relative, so I went to the relative's house to ask nicely about how I could get in touch with the wayward lad." He made a real production of shifting position. "Well, they were a wee bit hostile, turned it into a shooting thing, and I got one of them, then Piccolo showed up and blindsided me. A little flaming liquor, some throwing knives. I jumped off the balcony. Had to go into the canal," he grimaced.

"This is the second time Piccolo slipped through your fingers," Saint said, forcing the anger down to a simmer in his tone.

"You going to be alright?" asked the Hammer, forehead creased. "Looks like you made it to the Weeping Lady clinic."

"Yeah, I did," Gapjaw said. "If none of this mess gets infected, I'll be fine."

"I'll be sure to send them a donation," the Hammer said with a nod.

"Inkletta," Saint said, "you find Safety and put him on tracking down Piccolo. I want eyes on that snot. If Safety has a chance to take him out clean, do it. Also, you don't come to the meet. You, Safety, and Gapjaw can mount a rescue if the Grinders decide to take us alive."

"Understood," Inkletta nodded, still wearing her hood and cloak inside.

Saint grimaced, then set his jaw. "Let's go, Hammer," he muttered. "Get this over with."

## SILKSHORE. GRINDER HALL. 53ᴿᴰ SURAN

Saint, Red Silver, and the Hammer approached the rough-cut palisade with their hands out to the sides. As two ash-smudged Skovlanders approached them suspiciously and checked for weapons, the River Stallions looked over the fortification. Unlike a traditional palisade, the fence was formed by beams that had been sharpened to a point and sunk in place; worked lumber, rather than trees and limbs. Welcome to civilization, indeed. Several neighboring buildings showed signs of scavenging, where they involuntarily donated wood to the wall.

The Stallions were escorted through the open gate, into the courtyard of sorts, where people dressed in filthy layers huddled around cookfires. The main attraction was the deep-beamed Skov trading ship that was planted upside-down, a ready-made hall for a foreign king. A slot had been cut in the hull and given a curtain door of hides, and they pushed through to enter the Grinders' seat of power. First, they were hit by the overpowering stench of wet dog with a little gamy twist to it. They blinked, looking around.

Most of the interior was shadow, but the throne on a dais was brightly lit, so it drew the eye. A massive Skovlander sat on the throne, erect and majestic, his cornsilk hair flowing down over his shoulders.

The throne was flanked by pouncer wolves, who resembled bats more than canines. Their forelegs were naked hide, down to massive knuckles they could run on, then long claws swept back up their forelegs. The membrane of their wings was stretched between those claws. The bodies were whip-thin, the small eyes were beady black, and they had leaf-shaped noses. Red tongues lolled out between their teeth. The end of their tails had a flexible flap that could be used to help steer. The pouncer wolves could not fly, but they could leap tremendous distances, and get up into high places. Currently, the wolves were bored, flopped over to the side and panting lazily.

"Timeliness is good," said a voice from the shadows. A moment later, the nearby watch station's bell tower let out the first of four chimes. "That's a sign you take your time seriously, and ours." A man walked out of the shadows, a pouncer wolf hide on his shoulders, wearing the traditional rough and colorful fabrics of the Skovlanders. "I am Ingvald, and I will be speaking for Hutton. You may address your remarks to him, and I will reply."

As their eyes adjusted, the Stallions saw there were over a dozen Skovlanders in the makeshift court, possibly more in the back half by the water, where there was a pen for the pouncers. The hall could fit dozens of people in it, if needed, but currently there was room to fight.

"Times are hard," Saint said with a smile, spreading his hands, looking Hutton in the eye. "Some competition is inevitable. It is true that we were after some of your goods," he said, "but we had a plan that didn't kill anyone." He paused. "One of our junior members on probation forgot about the plan, and improvised. He is the one who killed Asdis. We didn't mean to do it, her death was an accident."

"We have all the reasons we need to go to war with you, three times over," Ingvald replied. "But we admire the courage it took for you to walk in here, and admit your stupidity. As you say, times are hard. Maybe we can find a way forward," he said.

"I am open to your proposal," Saint said to Hutton, who smiled slightly, inscrutable.

"How about this," Ingvald continued. "An apology for your mistake in attempting to rob us, and an apology for killing Asdis, Hutton's niece," Ingvald said. "Then, some action, to make things right. You will take on Captain Hutch, leader of the Silkshore Gray Cloaks. He is based in the Master Market. You cleanse Silkshore of his filth, and we'll be even. Fail?" He shrugged. "War remains an option."

"I don't want a war," Saint said. "Thank you for your generous offer. We will look it over and see what we can come up with."

"Be diligent, but not lazy," Ingvald replied. "We will not put you on a deadline, but our patience has its limits. Go forth and make this peace real." His smile showed more teeth than mirth.

"Just a moment," Saint said. He squared off with Hutton. "Apologies I can do right now. On behalf of the River Stallions, I apologize for our effort to rob you. It was foolish, and we will not repeat it. Thank you for your grace and nobility in letting that aggression be forgotten." He bowed. "Furthermore," he said, "on behalf of the River Stallions, I apologize for the accidental death of your niece, Asdis. We know what would happen if business involved targeting family members, and we'd like to think we're better than that here in Silkshore. It was the foolish action of a rogue member who has since been removed from our fellowship." He paused.

"I accept your apologies," Hutton said directly, startling Ingvald. Hutton smiled. "Now go."

Saint smiled, and there was perhaps a touch of self-satisfaction in his expression. He nodded to Hutton, not even looking at Ingvald, then he turned and led the Stallions out.

"Well that was embarrassing," Red Silver said through her teeth as she limped along with the cane, struggling to keep up.

"We just traded some pride for time," Saint replied under his breath. "Looks like we need a meet with Captain Hutch."

## SILKSHORE. BUSKER'S COURT. 54ᵀᴴ SURAN

Saint leaned against the low wall, munching away, holding a paper bag of cap dots. The Hammer sat on a stone bench, using a cheap disposable two-tine fork to get into noodles deep enough to slurp them down. They watched the busker set up against the apron of one of the plaza fountains.

"Mysteries of the Mirror!" the magician cried out. "See this chain? Forged of the fire and metal of our world, and yet, it can connect to the Other!" He twirled a thin golden chain, attracting a few passers-by. "You, miss! You hold this for me, and make sure it is all in the hollow of your hand! Your other hand on top, just so. It is impossible that I could affect your hands! You know what you feel! Certain in your connection to this world and its weights and measures and motions! Yet observe as I pull the chain from my sleeve—and open your hands!" They gasped. "It—is—gone!" the magician intoned.

"He's good," the Hammer shrugged. "Maybe we should hire him."

"I'm pretending we've got some dignity left," Saint retorted, and he tossed some more cap dots into his mouth. "You see any Gray Cloaks?"

"No, but we're early," the Hammer shrugged as the magician proceeded to make coins spin in the air. "How do you figure he does that?" he asked, squinting.

"Part of my childhood was spent with magicians," Saint said. "I learned a few tricks. Destroyed my faith in humanity." He shook his head. "We fool each other for fun, and the whole purpose of the Bluecoats and aristocrats is to rob the whole city without them even realizing it happened."

"Hell of a jump," the Hammer shrugged, and he fed himself another stream of noodles.

"You hear from Safety?" Saint asked.

"Yeah, he followed the trail to a point, sounds like Piccolo took this guy Kreeger, and his husband, and headed out to Barrowcleft.

They got an uncle or something out there, Belderan. Holed up in his estate. Safety figured there was a little too much open ground there, with the radiant farms, so he's keeping a low profile."

"Piccolo," Saint spat, like he was swearing. "He's only worth it if we can keep him pointed at making chaos for the targets, not for us." He shook his head.

"You think he's worth it?" the Hammer asked mildly. "Because you told Safety to kill him, so if you want him back, maybe rethink that."

"He's too dangerous," Saint shrugged. "I can never trust him again. So yeah, it's a shame, but you know."

The Hammer sighed. "Yes," he agreed, "I know."

Saint finished off the cap dots. "What's the word on this Captain Hutch?"

"He doesn't like Skovlanders," the Hammer shrugged. "Lost his commission with the Bluecoats when he barred up a tenement house and torched it with dozens of them inside. The neighborhood was pretty explosive after that, but the Bluecoats weren't going to do anything until the Spirit Wardens stepped in. Apparently his little stunt caused a ruckus on the other side of the Mirror, and the ghost problems angered the Wardens to the point where they leaned on the Bluecoats and got him kicked out." The Hammer sighed. "He feels Doskvol is not protecting itself against the Skovlander infection. It is his house, as an Akorosian, and he doesn't care for the guests."

Saint shook his head. "There's nothing in the world more dangerous than a zealot," he sighed. "Trying to reshape the world to look the way they want it to look." He glanced at the Hammer. "We ride the waves, we don't make them."

The Hammer just worked on his noodles, acquiescing. Finishing the cup, he tossed it to the side. "There you are," he said, pointing into the crowd. "Gray Cloaks."

Saint balled up the paper pouch and dropped it. "Let's go have a word," he said, his jaw set.

The two big men moved through the thin crowd to where four people dressed in the distinctive greatcoat cut of the Gray Cloaks stood by a puppet show, watching the naughty Scurlock bop Captain Bluecoat on the head most unexpectedly.

One of the Gray Cloaks spotted the incoming Stallions, and approached with a smile. "Hello, friends," he said, showing his teeth. "Blades only. Show me."

They held their hands out to the sides, then tugged their coats back to reveal flanks and back, in a series of practiced motions. Of course they could both still be quite well armed, but appearances matter, and there was a certain ceremony to these things.

"This way," the Gray Cloak said, leading them away from the plaza down a side street. They stepped into a paved alleyway that had been converted into an outdoor café. Seated at a wrought iron table towards the back, Captain Hutch waited for them, pistol on the table in front of him.

"You wanted to see me," Hutch said, squinting at them, his sparse ginger hair underscoring the paleness of his face.

"Thank you for the audience," Saint agreed, seating himself at the table, the Hammer settling in next to him. "Your name came up recently and I thought you should know about it."

"So tell me," Hutch demanded.

Saint watched him for a moment. "You know of the Grinders, and their chief, Hutton."

"Dirty Skovs," Hutch agreed and swore all at once.

"Hutton said he'd give us a pass and not go to war against the River Stallions, on the condition we get the Gray Cloaks out of Silkshore."

Four Gray Cloaks came in with the Stallions, and besides Hutch, there were two more unobtrusively waiting in the courtyard. All of them put their hands on weapons, ready to act at the speed of thought.

"I'm not here to threaten you," Saint clarified. "Still, you should know you're on the agenda for these intruders. They clock you as a threat." Saint smiled. "That's why we should be friends."

Hutch regarded him for a long moment. "I am unimpressed," he said, "by the strawhead threat of war. They think their mountain steel and fancy dogs will push native sons out of this territory. We earned Silkshore, by our breath and our blood, and it is tied into both. I will burn down their wooden hall, I will put their pets and their whelps to the sword, sell their women, and break their men." He trembled, and spittle gathered at one corner of his mouth. "They think to move against me? Against me? I will feel the crack of their bones. We'll color the roughage they feed their beggars with the blood of their warriors, the canals will be thick with corpses." Hutch paused, then locked eyes with Saint. "Where do you stand?" he demanded.

"With you, obviously," Saint replied. "Hutton offers me war, you offer me alliance."

An unflattering smile spread across Hutch's face like a stain. "Of course," he agreed. "Drinks all around," he barked at one of the Gray Cloaks, who brought over a bottle and cups, pouring the wine.

"Doskvol of Akoros," Hutch toasted.

"Doskvol of Akoros," the Stallions echoed, raising their cups, and they all drank.

*

"Just you and me, Nails," Red Silver murmured to herself as she scritched under the giant bat's jaw. The bat hung from the gable, two feet long from nose to claw, its seven foot wingspan tucked in tight against its fur. It regarded her, one eye a silver marble and the other beady black. The erratic wind helped some of the spongy wood tiles on the roof dry a bit, but overall the rot had set in and the roof didn't have long before it would collapse under its own weight. For now, Red Silver perched on it, almost entirely out of sight, with her giant hunting bat.

She perked up as Saint and the Hammer left, and Saint paused to put his cowl up.

"That's the sign," she said to Nails. "Do your thing."

The bat pivoted and twisted, snapping wings out and lunging up into the night air. One muscular flip sent Nails sailing into the dark.

She pulled a pair of silvered round glasses from her coat, and slid them on. With her eyes half closed, she touched her perceptions, and flexed them so they did not have to rely upon the rules on this side of the Mirror. The vision that drifted into focus on the inside of the glasses was the view of the silver marble in one of Nails' eye sockets.

Nails was perched on a roof, his knuckles on the peak as he peered down at the Gray Cloaks following a weed-choked back alleyway. He scrabbled back into the air in a lazy circle, black against the black of the night sky, his silver eye a lone drifting pinpoint of reflected light. Red Silver let herself enjoy the mild euphoria of flight, nudging Nails to stay interested in the retreating Gray Cloaks.

They approached the service entrance at the base of the Boldway Canal street bridge. Looking all around, they pulled out a key and let themselves through the civic grating, and disappeared into the massive structure.

"You go hunt," Red Silver whispered to Nails, a smile on her face. "You good, furry furry boy." She took off the glasses, tucking them away. No need to watch her bat spend a satisfying evening digging through roof tiles for the grubs and beetles and other things that infested the chimneys and rooftops of the filthy city.

"As for you," she whispered to the Gray Cloaks, "now I know where you are."

She vanished into the night.

# — CHAPTER SEVEN —

*Dawn and twilight are often wreathed in fog. Locals call this the "blind hour" as it is the most difficult time to light the shadows; even the deep of night can hold a light better than the fog-choked transition points, with enough light in the air to ruin night vision and enough fog to smear your light around, making it useless. Decent people tend to pause the day for tea during the blind hour. If you're out in it, you're desperate. Half of all muggings happen in a blind hour.*

*- From "Wisdom Afloat: Travel in the Dusk"*
*by Anton Murlachi*

## SILKSHORE. BOLDWAY CANAL STREET BRIDGE. 54TH SURAN

Red Silver limped along the uneven cobbled way, close enough to grab the wrought iron fence for support if necessary. She brandished her cane as though it was fashionable and not providing necessary support; the pouncer bites still ached up and down her leg. Fog rolled off the river, providing a surreal atmosphere that toyed with light and sound to render both unreliable.

She paused by the civic entry grate, pulling out her slender bone pipe and making a production of packing it with ground-up weed.

Holding her plasmic sparker to the bowl, she flared it to life while drawing air through the stem, lighting the pipe at once. Slipping the sparker back in one of her many pockets, she puffed on the pipe and took in her surroundings, including the fantastic view of the restless river below.

Her stiletto key dropped from its forearm sheath to her palm as she twitched her wrist, and she held the quicksilver blade as she glanced both ways one more time. Then she slid the stiletto into the civic access grate, and paused to attune herself to its slippery essence. She relaxed its shape, then withdrew so it stiffened again, and the metal flexed just enough to fill available space. It formed a rudimentary key, and she turned it, clicking the lock open. She focused on the stiletto again, and it resumed its spike shape, easily rasping out of the keyhole and vanishing up her sleeve.

Gravity pulled at the unevenly hung gate so it clicked shut behind her as she moved low and fast, crossing the distance between the gate and the doorway into the massive piling of the bridge. The heavy iron door had the same rudimentary lock, so she used her stiletto key again, focusing to adjust its shape to a key and back to a blade when the lock opened. She was inside.

Red Silver paused in the blackness of the room's interior, her mind busily sorting the smells. Open water, with all the basement smells that accompanied it, and vermin smell. Nothing unmanageable. She pulled a breath through her pipe, letting the smoke out with her exhalation, and she dipped her hand into another pocket and produced a glass algaeball. Shaking it, she excited the luminescence within, and the ball glowed just enough for her to get her bearings.

The entry room had a basic table and some elbow space, for consultation between experts and decision makers at the edge of the bridgeworks. Stairs led down into the interior, and that's the way the Gray Cloaks went. She followed, instinct softening her steps to silence in spite of the ache in her leg.

Down the stairs, past doors that did not look disturbed, she followed the tracks on the scuffed stone. The hallway opened up to a round room, and Red Silver got one glimpse of the far side of the room before she tucked her algaeball into the fold of her coat and pressed against the wall, hardly daring to breathe.

Across the room, something big stirred in the darkness. Light glowed into the baleful lamps of eyes, and something massive shifted position slightly where it stood in front of the door, blocking further progress. It seemed to listen, looking through the shadows. By the time it relaxed to its inert state again, it was quite alone.

## SILKSHORE. RIVER STALLIONS TOWER. 54TH SURAN

"They have a hull," Red Silver said as she rammed her cane down in the umbrella stand. "I found the back door into their lair in the Boldway Canal street bridge, and it's guarded by a hull."

"Well that's not ideal," Saint said, not turning from where he was fussing with a number of heavy scrolls and cloths along the meeting chamber's side board.

"Did you get a detailed look?" Inkletta asked, arching an eyebrow. "Do you think it was outfitted for war, or some labor hull they refurbished?"

"Multiple eyes, self-rousing mode, looked intentionally crafted. And we know the Gray Cloaks have contacts, especially Hutch. Lots of blue-bloods don't like the idea of Skovs muddying the breeding pool." Red Silver shrugged. "But no, I didn't get a good look at it. I didn't want to start something I couldn't finish, and my leg is slowing me down," she said through her teeth.

"I know the feeling," Gapjaw muttered as he scratched a filthy square nail against his fresh bandages. "What's going on over there, Saint? Smells fantastic."

"I ordered the menu at Wingdae's," Saint said, turning with a crooked smile so they could see the gleaming stacks of tubes. "One of everything, and two of a few of my favorites." He started handing the scrolls over to Safety and Hammer, who pushed them down the table. "There's no reason we should be both busy and hungry," Saint said. "You've been working so you get to eat."

"I refuse to let Silver's bad news wreck my meal," Safety said with a grin.

"That's the spirit," the Hammer nodded, snipping the ties that held the rolled mushroom stem tubes tight. They flattened into plate-like squares already loaded with various nuggets, sauces, vegetables, and fungus. "Noodles?"

"Over here," Gapjaw said, passing one plate and trading for another. The crew started sorting out their favorites, and Safety was the first one to draw a knife to work it out. Seconds later the whole crew was staking claim with knives, rolling some of a dish off one plate and onto another, and generally making the most of the chaos to get their favorite morsels.

Only Inkletta sat back from the melee; three tubes had found their way to her, and her name was scrawled along their sides in charcoal. She opened the first at her own leisure, undisturbed by the rowdy table manners of the rest of the crew.

The next few minutes were unusually quiet as the crew set to the feast. An unused chair off to the side started accumulating discards. Saint sat at the head of the table, opposite Iinkletta. Safety and Red Silver were on one side, the Hammer and Gapjaw on the other.

"Well then," the Hammer sighed. "It's been, what, three months since we last ordered Wingdae's whole menu?"

"Don't ruin a prosperous moment," Gapjaw grunted around a mouthful of food.

"Seems a good moment to celebrate," Saint said, leaning back, "as we've got rocky waters ahead. What with the Gray Cloaks and the Grinders and the Gondoliers and all."

"How are we going to play this?" Safety asked, his narrow and shadowed features especially broody in the dim light.

"It's going to come to a head, and I think we might be in a position to control where and when," Saint replied, "if we handle this just right. I'm thinking we set it up so they end up confronting each other. And we get out of the way." He looked around the table. "Any thoughts as to where?"

"Somewhere public, but with some elbow space; we don't want lots of collateral damage," Red Silver said. She reflectively sucked on a tooth.

"Eightbridge," Hammer nodded. "The Bluecoats don't like going down there, and if there was a scrap they'd be even less likely to get involved until they'd amassed a force for a proper raid."

"The Calcified Steps," Gapjaw said. "You've got the added fun of crumbling stone falling into rat pits or eel nests. That's comedy," he said, his grin bunching up the bandages on his burned face.

"We don't want anyone disappearing," Safety pointed out. "So after the fight it should be easy for the Bluecoats to mop up the winners and losers alike. We don't want anybody to walk out of this in good shape." He paused. "Except us."

"That's why we use the Bluecoats' power against them," Saint murmured, a gleam in his eye. "We use the impound lot. We stage this confrontation at Whipwater Point."

The others looked at him for a long moment.

"Because it's built out over the river," Red Silver said with a nod, "and that's the only way out besides the razorwire fence."

"But how do we get people in?" Gapjaw asked, squinting as he worked it out.

"Both sides already pay off the Bluecoats," Saint shrugged, "so they ask for a quiet meet away from prying eyes. We sell it to the Gray Cloaks and the Grinders by telling them the Bluecoats are in charge of security—no surprises."

"No surprises," the Hammer echoed, eyes glinting.

"And of course we think up all the surprises," Saint clarified.

"Yes I know," the Hammer replied, testy. "Just thinking through the possibilities."

"Like for example we have a chance to get some choice items impounded by the Bluecoats," Saint grinned, "stored away so we can get at them when we need them."

"This plan is dangerous," the Hammer shrugged, "but in a daring sort of way. We could catch both sides off guard."

"And it involves running water, so that's always high stakes," Red Silver pointed out.

"There are a lot of questions to work out," Inkletta said thoughtfully.

"Good thing I got dessert," Saint grinned. He looked at the sideboard, then the table. "Did you already eat the dessert?"

"Pretty much," Red Silver shrugged.

"I got the puffinpaste cone. The bean chip cream?"

Blank stares.

"Animals," Saint muttered. "Okay anyway, forget about dessert. Who has a pal at the impound yard?" He fronted an unpleasant smile. "More to the point, who is about to?"

"How do you propose to make it their idea to meet here?" Saint asked Gapjaw, squinting as he thought it through.

"Push at 'em with a different idea, see who speaks out against us. Who they listen to. Give them the idea through a proxy, then propose somewhere else, and they've already thought of a better idea." Gapjaw raised his eyebrows. "Foolproof."

"And if that doesn't work?"

"Some really quick-thinking softshoe, I don't know," Gapjaw snapped irritably. "I'm bored with planning."

"Sounds like somebody needs to go coffin scouting," Safety grinned at the older man across the table. He looked down at the rough map of Whipwater Point that covered the table. "Remember, over in the smuggling sheds. So we'll need them good and water-tight, no sense starting the festivities early."

"I remember," Gapjaw said, sullen. He pulled on his hat and coat. "Like shopping is so much better than planning," he groused.

"Well you're more scavenging and stealing than shopping," Saint pointed out.

Gapjaw muttered his response too low to share, pushing up the stairs out of the tower basement and passing Red Silver as she returned.

"Well?" Saint demanded, turning to face her.

"I played the part of a young widow, deeply grateful to the Bluecoats of the district for their role in finding justice for my husband's killer," she said, batting her eyes. "Threw a little party for them, wrote a glowing recommendation to the watch commander. I'll be headed back to my home in Severos, but in the meantime, that particular garrison is most interested in repaying me for my kindness." She dropped her simpering smile, and spat in the corner. "And that costly party puts us on hard times until we do some real business. For coin, you understand." She flopped into a chair and hoisted her leg, grimacing as she rubbed at the outside of her boot.

"How's that bite healing up?" Hammer asked.

"Too damn slow," Red Silver growled. "Now it itches."

"We should get a leech to look at that. Or at least a physiker," Hammer suggested.

"It's fine," Red Silver replied. "Speaking of my mauled leg, what's the news on Piccolo?" she asked Safety.

"He's sticking with family," Safety shrugged. "Had a big fancy supper with them last night at the Diving Bell."

"And you didn't take a shot?" Red Silver demanded. "I guess you don't want to risk taking him on in Barrowcleft for some reason, but he was back in Silkshore." She frowned at Safety. "What are you waiting for? What will it take?"

"Now Red," Saint said, "we already lost one crew member because Piccolo was an idiot. Then Gapjaw got all burned and stabbed too. We keep an eye out, we wait for our moment."

"If you say so," Red Silver muttered, grimacing as she rubbed her leg.

Safety regarded her for a long moment, then rose to his feet and headed for the stairs. "Better check and make sure he's staying put," he growled as he brushed past Saint. The Hammer quickly stood and followed him, catching up to Safety at the main chamber at the top of the stairs.

"Hey, don't let her rile you," the Hammer said. "It's the pain, makes her grouchy. We gotta handle this Piccolo thing carefully. You're doing it right," he said earnestly, looking the younger man in the eye.

"Thanks, Hammer," Safety said. He turned to go, then paused, the Hammer's hand was still on his arm. Safety raised his eyebrows.

"There's more," the Hammer said quietly. "You've been ducking out a lot lately. This is a bad time to be a loner. You want some good advice?" He glanced back down the stairs. "Arrange your reasons so they keep you closer to the crew for a while."

"Why, you think my loyalty is in doubt?" Safety asked, frowning.

"Call it a feeling I have," the Hammer replied with a shrug. "Losing Piccolo has everybody on edge. Loyalty needs to be... visible. Easy to see, right now," the Hammer said. "Just until we sort out this next heist. Okay?" His broad face was tugged up by the question in his voice, leaving him oddly peaked as he looked Safety in the eye.

"Okay," Safety agreed. "Thank you, Hammer."

The Hammer's face twisted into half a grin. "Be careful out there. Stay—safe," he said.

"Safety," the rogue said, gesturing to the sides. "It's what I'm all about." He clapped the Hammer on the shoulder, then hauled the tower door open and vanished into the foot traffic of the streets.

Behind him, the Hammer was thoughtful as he shouldered the door shut and barred it.


## SILKSHORE. ANKHAYAT PARK. 58ᵀᴴ SURAN

"This seems... elaborate," Saint muttered to Inkletta.

She did not reply. Wrapped in her deep-cowled cloak, she took in the dimly-lit sights of the park from the shadows by a closed cap stand, Saint standing next to her in his least rumpled and stained outfit. "There," she said, pointing. A doctor stepped out of the pale structure by the river, his shapeless hat and long-wristed sleeves distinctive.

The fancy girl seated on the park bench jumped to her feet and scurried over to the doctor, who looked around in alarm, then let her whisper in his ear. He blinked a couple times, then raced after the fancy girl into the public restroom.

"He thinks his friend bought him an extra tumble," Inkletta explained. "The girl, Tyna, she's his favorite."

"Yes, I get it, let's just—get on with it," Saint said, his forehead creased with his distaste.

They crossed the space to the white building, and as they stepped in the back, Saint snatched a hat and long-wristed coat, tugging them on and doing his best to look like a doctor. Inkletta shed her cloak, revealing a nurse outfit that covered all the tattoos but the ones on her face. Confident, they strode into the convalescence chamber overlooking the dark waters of the river.

Orderlies were preparing a light lunch along the back wall, and a dozen wicker chairs pointed towards the glass wall and the river beyond. This was the moment of the day where the patients were the least supervised, and the River Stallions knew it.

Saint confidently picked up a clipboard that had jotted notes about food intake and waste disposal, looking down the times and quantities, nodding sagely. He mostly blocked line of sight to Inkletta, who knelt before an old woman who nodded in her chair, insensible.

The Whisper let her eyes drift half-shut, and she tuned her spirit to match the half-alive rhythm of the old woman. "I need to know," she murmured. And she reached into the malaise coiled around the old woman's life force.

Meanwhile Saint consulted the second page on the clipboard, and then the first page again, and nodded politely to an orderly with the sort of distant distaste that discouraged small talk. He walked over to another patient and pressed his thumb and fingers against a wrist, nodding to himself, and stalked back into position as though he was reviewing a military parade for out-of-place uniform errors.

"Excuse me doctor, is it alright if they eat?" an orderly asked hesitantly.

"Of course," Saint said, and he half turned. "Mrs. Turlough is deep in prayer at the moment, however, and not to be disturbed."

The orderly opened her mouth, and Saint raised one eyebrow in anticipation; the orderly just nodded instead, and turned to getting the other patients over to the food.

Mrs. Turlough, the patient Inkletta knelt beside, coughed. The orderlies all turned, in time to see the cough turn to a sputter, with water pouring out of the old woman's mouth as though she was drowning. Inkletta sprang to her feet, wild-eyed, and bolted for the door.

"You there! Stop!" Saint yelled at her, and he gave chase convincingly enough until both of them were far enough out in front that another burst of speed put them beyond pursuit.

Stripping off the medical garb and leaving it in a trash can, they strolled on in the normal shabby mid-week best of a couple hard-working citizens, out for an afternoon stroll.

"Was all that drama necessary?" Saint asked.

"I'm going to pretend you of all people did not just ask me that," Inkletta said, shaking her head. "This thing that's got them; it's bad."

"We're hoping for more detail," Saint reminded her. "We already knew that."

"As you know, the slum garrets and clinics are not helpful for finding out more. The risk of being observed or contracting the illness myself is too high," Inkletta reminded Saint.

"Right, which is why we're targeting a few of the upper crust who came down with it," Saint agreed. "And now you've found out more."

"Yes," she said, subdued. "Physikers are calling it 'the Slip' and it's mainly hitting gondoliers and their families."

"That's odd," Saint shrugged.

"But not altogether surprising," Inkletta said. "Everything I can find out from checking with my contacts is that those most vulnerable to this are those most attuned to the Mirror," she added. "The sensitive ones. And the Slip is about slipping beneath the surface; as you know, the surface of the canals and all water really is very symbolic of the surface of the Mirror, between the living and the dead."

"They slip beneath it, right," Saint said. "They get weak and die. Drown."

"Right," Inkletta said. "I have heard of something the gondoliers used to call 'losing the land,' where their mystics pulled too much power through the Mirror until that power pulled them back through it." She paused. "I think something has gone wrong and the gondoliers are living too close to the water. Pulling too much power to protect their position. It's killing them."

Saint was quiet for a long moment as they kept walking. "There's got to be a way to use this," he muttered.

"I know there are ways," Inkletta agreed. "Remember, though, we don't have the whole story yet. Something had to go wrong. Somewhere, there's a cyst of energy that's gone rotten that's affecting all these people. That's my best guess."

Saint let another minute pass in quiet. "The gondoliers aren't going to be able to handle the Skovs," he said quietly.

Inkletta walked along at his side, her silence all the agreement he needed.


## SILKSHORE. SILVER STAG CASINO. 1ˢᵀ ULSIVET

Safety dropped down from the back of the carriage, and it rattled on obliviously. Crossing the more or less evenly paved street, Safety stood before the magnificence of the Silver Stag Casino, a former college or museum of some kind if rumors could be trusted. Now the ancient stone mansion fortress hosted the most complex and high-stakes gambling in Silkshore, possibly in all of Doskvol.

Passing the broad stairs leading up to the grand entrance, Safety passed through the servant entrance to the grounds buildings, crossing a courtyard and forcing his way through the bustle of the crowded barracks-style rooms where the servants of nobles waited upon the pleasure of their employers to wrap up inside.

Pushing his way through the back door, Safety crossed the side yard gallery, moving quickly, head down. He approached the gazebo built up in the shadow of the dead oak, glaring at the two men that were waiting for him.

"Not like you to be late," the first man said.

"People are suspicious these days," Safety replied, "so I doubled back a few more times than usual. If Red Silver suspects me, I have to watch the skies and rooflines too." His chin jutted out with his defiance.

"Settle down, just an observation," the second man said, mockery casual and loaded with threat. "Look how nervous you are."

"Maybe you'd be more comfortable back in Ironhook, where it's all safe," the first man said, his smile ugly.

"Maybe I would," Safety snapped. "Why don't you pull me out?"

"Because you're brave, and useful, and handsome," the first man soothed sarcastically, pressing at Safety's lapels. "Now, what do you have for me?"

Safety paused. "The River Stallions are caught between the Gray Cloaks and the Grinders. Each one has tasked them with helping take the other one out."

"Good boy," the second man said, arching his eyebrows. "We'll let you know how we want it to go."

"There's more," Safety shrugged. "The plan is for it to go down at Whipwater Point."

"The impound yard?"

"That's right," Safety nodded. "Bluecoats sweep up the winners and the losers." He paused. "Preparations are underway to make this work. Redundancies put in place. Make all this sure-fire."

"Hilarious," the second man said. "Nothing the 'River Stallions' do is sure-fire."

"We done here?" Safety demanded.

"What, you got somewhere to be?" the first man asked, raising an eyebrow.

Safety looked him in the eye. "I'm bored," he said.

"Look at that," the first man said to the second. "Guess we're not up to this guy's standards."

"That might hurt my feelings," the second man responded,

pressing his hand to his chest.

"I guess we're done here," the first man said. "I'd say, give my regards to the Stallions, but," he shrugged, "if you did we'd have to kill you."

"Run along," the second man said.

Safety paused for a long moment. "Just curious. One question before I go."

"This ought to be rich," the first man said.

"Does this information go to the Inspectors first?" Safety asked. "Or the Hive?"

The silence landed gracelessly, and that put a smile on Safety's face. He turned, walking away from them.

"We'll be in touch," the first man called after him.

That itchy feeling of a target between his shoulderblades settled like a mantle, but it was worth it to Safety just to smile again.

## SILKSHORE. CROWNWIND COURT. 4ᵀᴴ ULSIVET

The door latch clicked, and the door creaked open. "Hello?" Safety called out. "Red Silver?"

"Get out," came the response from the other room. Her voice was weak, reedy.

"I was kind of hoping I'd open the door and you'd be set up in a chair, a pair of pistols aimed at my head, a no-nonsense menace in your cocked hat and frown," Safety said as he slowly pushed the door open and stepped into the tiny rickety space.

"Go," Red Silver replied.

The entire countertop was buried in unwashed crockery, mostly cups. The table overflowed with dirty clothes and papers that bore scrawl over every inch. A mouse scrabbled across the floor, startled by the intruder. A gust of wind rushed against the tower, and the whole building seemed to sway slightly.

"Red?" Safety rounded the narrow table, peering into the gloom of the only other room in the garret.

The bed pallet was in the middle of the floor, piled deep with blankets that didn't match. A trail of clothes led to the bed, and various weapons and tools of the trade were discarded to the sides on the path. Safety still could not see a woman in the mass of bedding.

"You in there?"

"No," she replied, hoarse.

"I hear you," he shrugged, "but you're a tricky hunter. So maybe it's a trap."

"Go away," she murmured, exhaustion heavy in her breath.

"It's been three days since you were last spotted, and Saint wants to make sure you're getting your homework done," Safety said. "We're getting close. He's about to set all these wheels in motion."

No response.

Safety edged into the darkened room. "I'm starting to feel some worry here," Safety confessed.

The mass of bedding shifted, Red Silver rolled over, and strained towards her pistol. It was discarded on the rough floorboards, and her trembling hand didn't even get close to it.

Safety picked it up and snapped open the breech. "It's unloaded anyway," he observed.

Red Silver lay still, so still for a moment Safety wondered if she had died. Then she stirred slightly, a pale and elegant shape against the dark mass of blankets. "Get out," she whispered.

Safety reached out and took her wrist between his fingers and thumb; her skin was chilled, her pulse far too slow.

"What have you been doing, Red?" Safety murmured.

"That will never be your business," she hissed softly, unable to manage more.

Safety rose, and went into her kitchen, firing up her tiny cylinder stove and finding some runoff rainwater in a dish. He heated it up, scrounging for grounds, and he managed to get a hot drink together along with half a roll and some jerky from his pocket. Then he returned to the bedroom, fending off Red's ineffectual clawing and stabbing attacks. He noticed the long purple bruises on one side of her body, including a black eye and a fat lip, but he said nothing as he managed to pull her naked body into a robe and belt it, leading her in to slump at the table, putting the leftover nibbles and hot drink in front of her.

"I just want to sleep," Red Silver said through her teeth, her bruised eyes closed.

"Eat and drink something, and I'll leave you to it," Safety shrugged. "Humor me."

Scowling, she managed to tear at the roll and jerky, but moments later she retched on the floor. Neither of them spoke as she sat trembling in the chair.

Red Silver managed to lock an unsteady eye on Safety. "I want to kill you right now," she whispered.

"I know," he nodded.

Time passed.

Twilight was buried in fog.

"The Blind Hour," Safety said quietly. "Fog, full of light."

"Now is when you go," she whispered, "and come back."

Safety nodded, and rose to his feet. He pushed through the rickety and poorly hung door, and vanished down the crooked stairs.

Then, later, he ascended those stairs, and returned through the door. Red Silver had not moved.

He gave her broth, and small sour fruits, and soft bread, and he stoked up the cylinder stove and boiled water, and made her something hot to drink. She moved slowly, as though she was remembering how, but once the broth was gone, the other food disappeared much faster, and after the first cup of hot drink, she returned to the bedroom. A few minutes later she came back dressed.

Red Silver looked out the window. "The Blind Hour has passed," she murmured. "It is night."

"Yes," Safety agreed. He paused for a moment. "Saint wants to see you."

Red Silver watched Safety for a long, long moment. She said nothing. He returned her gaze at first, then looked down at the table and waited. She rose, returning to her room, and there were clatters and rustles as she prepared to go out. She pulled on her heavy boots, her leather harnesses, weighed down with guns and bullets and blades, all under a cloak.

She returned to the doorway to the back room, and stared at Safety. "Anything you want to say before we leave here? Before we leave everything here?" she said.

He looked her in the eye. "No."

She nodded, and rounded the rickety table, and pushed her way out into the hall, taking her time navigating the stairs down.

Safety took a deep breath, then released it. He stood, and followed her into the crooked darkness.

They emerged from the elevated door, down the stairs to the

half-paved street. Behind them, a number of tightly stacked tenements leaned on each other for support. The rogues pushed on, into the shadows, then down some sturdier steps to the canal below to hail passage.

Up in Red Silver's room, the candle burned low and wisped out. Then the door slowly creaked open. A knife entered first, held by a sure hand, and a stealthy figure followed. It only took a moment to take inventory of Red Silver's ramshackle place. Then the mysterious figure drew a chair back from the table, and sat down.

She pushed the hood back from her face, and put the knife on the table in front of her.

Asdis settled in to wait.

# ━━ CHAPTER EIGHT ━━

*Akoros has a winter, spring, and fall. They exported all the summer we could ever use to the Dagger Isles. I'm happy to keep their summers; wet and dry are the only seasons we need. There are only a few hot days here in Doskvol, sometimes up to a couple weeks, in the whole year. Only the wealthy have outfits tailored for that sort of weather. Everyone else gives the impression they're wearing their underwear as outerwear. The end of Suran is the height of the growing season, when the docks are emptiest as most leviathan hunting ships are out. It is a time of intense expectation; all this heat and bustle must lead to something, yes? Something in these pale characters longs for the cold, and in this haunted world, that is an impulse I will never understand.*

*- Lady Muli Arana, Personal Correspondence*

**BARROWCLEFT. BELDERAN ESTATE. 5ᵀᴴ ULSIVET. THE SIXTH HOUR**

Ledgers, scrolls, and books were carelessly piled on half the long table of the study. A few lucky sources had been pulled out for closer inspection on the other half, where Sanction sat opposite Trellis, reviewing documents.

"It's got to be three pieces," Trellis said quietly, "and I've got one of them identified. Zhavo. He's trusted, he's grieving, and we can get him revenge."

"My version has five, so two can go wrong and we can still pull this off." Sanction shifted in his seat. "You're sure it's wise to tip our hand before we even get everything in place?" Sanction squinted at the older man.

"Wise?" Trellis echoed. "It's a trade-off. When we pull off this magic trick, we need our misdirection to be in place so they can't see how we could possibly do it until after it's done. But we need them to be watching the trick, using their expectations to hold their attention steady."

"Like the drink under a hat," Sanction murmured.

"Just so," Trellis smiled. "We need enough of the operation to be in plain sight that they accept the misdirection as finesse and not exploitation. We'll need their support."

"Okay so getting Zhavo on board for his piece means checking into the Cult of Starshine, and the Hierophant Ludocian. You said you got a sealed Inspector file on that?" Sanction muttered as he thumbed through a green folio from the Inspector record center.

The door to the study burst open, commanding the attention of the planners. The butler tried to announce the woman who shoved him aside; "Sir, it's—your sister Nebs!" he managed as he stumbled.

"Nebs," Trellis said, rising and spreading his arms for a welcoming embrace as he smiled at the furious woman who closed the distance between them at a rapid pace.

She slapped him heartily, the sound sharp and deep in the live acoustics of the study. She redirected her furious stare at Sanction as she hurled a leather folder of papers down on the table.

"You fools," she growled.

"What did we do?" Sanction protested.

"I don't know!" Nebs shouted, "but it was stupid! And for no reason other than my account being reviewed, I got a visit from the Ministry's executor for Fogcrest. Where I live. Or rather where I lived until this morning, when I was notified that my retirement support from the Ministry was flagged as suspect and temporarily frozen." Squaring off with her nephew, she radiated fury from her slight form. "I don't care what you did. Fix this. Fix it now." Her eyes seemed to bore into him.

"Yesterday was day three, by my count," Trellis said to Sanction. "You may have disappointed Marcus." Trellis raised his eyebrows. "Maybe hurt his feelings."

"That son of a bitch," Sanction said, his eyes icy as his fists clenched. "This is about me, Aunt Nebs," he admitted.

"I tried to talk sense into you," she replied. "I tried to encourage you to be patient. I may as well have read love poems to a fish," she spat.

"So why slap me?" Trellis asked, rubbing the side of his face.

"We're all supposed to discourage him," Nebs said, rounding on Trellis. "You set a price. Gave him a pathway forward. I blame you for this just as much as I blame Kreeger." Her eyes narrowed. "He's an impressionable youth, dammit."

"And you were closer," Sanction said to Trellis.

"Don't make light," Nebs hissed, rounding on him. "I'm still deciding whether you get a loaded fist, just the knuckles, or a slap like the old man. Or whether I get creative. Because you deserve some pain for this." She paused, staring him in the eye. "Don't you dare cost me what I spent a lifetime building," she breathed.

Sanction nodded. "I will make this right," he promised. "One way or another."

Nebs stared at him for a moment. "You have a plan?" she demanded.

"I've got two, the old man's got a couple also," Sanction replied quietly without looking over at Trellis. "I will take care of this for you. You might even come out ahead." He paused. "You like the Chime Era, right? That bookstore across from the Ministry offices in Silkshore?"

"You know I do," she replied heatedly.

"I just need one day," Sanction said. "Do you have your things packed? Are they here?"

"They are," Nebs nodded. "The nice man from the ministry brought a packing crew that tossed my belongings and put them in containers. My home is an empty shell right now." She set her jaw.

Sanction rounded the end of the table, and took Nebs' hand. "This time tomorrow," he said, his conviction clear. "I swear we'll take care of you."

She looked him in the eye for a long moment, then twitched her hand out of his, pivoting and striding the length of the study. When she reached the door, she paused, turning her head but not her shoulders, regarding them indirectly.

"You do this right, you have my support," she said quietly. "Botch it, and you will catch endless waves of grief. From the rest of the family. You understand."

"Better than what we deserve," Trellis responded, subdued.

She nodded, then slammed out.

"That was a good hit," Sanction grinned to Trellis. "Forceful. Meaty, even."

"Glad you think it's funny," Trellis replied, arching his eyebrows, unsmiling.

"We can handle this. It's just asset shuffling," Sanction replied with a wave of his hand. "When I was in the game I had to play carefully. Get the safety harness all set up and inspected before stepping out over the abyss, in case things go wrong. Play with an eye to the long game and political supporters." A smile curled across his face. "Now I'm free to jump. No buckles, straps, or knots. Just the objective and my native skill against a backdrop of story problems and grifting." His smile was unsettling.

"You know you're oversimplifying," Trellis sighed. "You had better be oversimplifying. We've got a long game too."

"It's not the same," Sanction shrugged, almost fussy. "Let me have my moment."

"You can have your moment when Nebs is sorted out," Trellis said through his teeth. "This needs to be tight, I don't want you getting cocky and making unforced errors."

Sanction sighed. "I wondered if we would wait to act on the Ministry until some of my knowledge aged out," he said quietly, "and I hoped we wouldn't. This is just the sort of chance we need to give them something to think about. A reason to hesitate when someone suggests they simplify their problems by having me dealt with."

Trellis looked him in the eye. "Nobody dies," he said. "We don't need that kind of heat."

"Nobody dies," Sanction agreed. "But we might break some things that can't be fixed."

Trellis nodded. "How do we play this from here?"

Sanction rubbed his chin. "I need the crew to make the point. I know it's short notice." He glanced at the water clock on the sideboard. "Sixth hour now, almost lunchtime. I will head into town now, send some messages, get some appointments on calendars. If you can find them all, get them to the Chime Era bookstore before the hour of Honor, that's when I'm going to set the meet. That gives us six more hours before the rendezvous, and we can have supper afterwards." He paused. "Do your best. It would be useful to have everyone."

Trellis smiled, a peculiar expression. "I'll do my best."

## SILKSHORE. THE EASE, CARMEL DOWNS CLUB. 5TH ULSIVET. THE NINTH HOUR

Slender and angular in his greatcoat, Trellis cast a long shadow as he stood before the sputtering arc of the buzzing electroplasmic lamp. He leaned on the doorway into the club, and knocked three times. Momentarily, a view slot shot back, and eyes squinted at him from inside. "We're closed!" someone said gruffly in the darkness beyond.

"It's me, Trellis," he replied. "We have an arrangement."

There was only fractional hesitation, and the viewport snapped shut. Moments later the door rattled open, and Trellis ducked inside.

"I hear my boy Piccolo is here," Trellis murmured as he stepped into the stale thickness of the closed club's atmosphere.

"He made a bet he could pair every kind of sporecap wine we have with every table shroom," the heavyset club employee shrugged. "You know, the squeaker shrooms, you tap 'em and they put out some spores, like dust. Help you get into the mood," he shrugged.

Trellis watched a couple of the wait staff with a cart, trading out the low iron planters that were set in the center of every table. Old shrooms for fresh ones. Trays with chewy shrooms on the side.

"How did he do?" Trellis asked, eyes wandering the room.

"I don't know," the other man shrugged. "They had more spores than record keeping. He's still sleeping it off in the back." The man squinted at Trellis. "How do you know he ended up here? You spy on your own people?"

"Best not to think about it," Trellis replied agreeably enough, and he made his own way back between the tables, homing in on a stream of erratic snores.

Piccolo was twisted, one elbow up the back of the bar seat and the other resting its tip on the table, both his hands back to grip his head, which lolled at an improbable angle.

Trellis kicked the sole of Piccolo's boot, and the scoundrel snorted and rolled over, face-first into the cushions at the back of the shadowy booth.

"Skovlanders!" Trellis shouted. Piccolo snorted, contracted like an inchworm, then flexed to flip over in the seat, coming up with a bloody nose and a knife, his eyes totally bloodshot.

"I can see your pulse in your pupils," Trellis observed.

"Oh hey Trellis," Piccolo said in a wavering voice, dabbling at his nose and mouth with the back of his hand. "This is not a good time to talk. What time is it?"

"Ninth hour."

"I was supposed to sleep all this crap off by the time they opened and start serving supper," Piccolo said in a thin, almost child-like voice. He fumbled at a napkin on the table and blew his nose, unloading a distressing amount of spores. "Oh, my head," He muttered. He snorted. "All is not lost! You can go away and I can sleep about another four hours and rise a folk hero." He coughed.

"We've got somewhere to be in four hours. The Chime Era, a bookstore and public house. You know the place?" Trellis looked down at the scoundrel who fumbled to rise from the booth.

"I know it," Piccolo agreed. "What's my role?"

"Stay flexible, sharp lookout, and don't kill anyone."

Piccolo shivered as an aftershock of the shrooms mixed with wine rippled through his nervous system. "That sounds—so fun," he said through his teeth. "I'm good at the first two, but man, that third one; people just jump on my knife," he said, almost morose.

Trellis hesitated for just a moment, then scrawled a couple notes on a napkin. "Don't be late." He turned and strode out, leaving the napkin for the addled thief to reference.


## SILKSHORE. THE EASE, WEST SHELLS. 5TH ULSIVET. THE TENTH HOUR

The Mistress of Tides hung in the water, almost weightless, her hair drifting around her head like seaweed. On all sides, darkness; only the thinnest rays of light could slip through the layers to reach her depth. She sought balance and buoyancy. Breathing out flat silver bubbles, she reached over to the tube and drew some air into her lungs.

Her eyes flicked open. She could almost see the mesh of the cage that surrounded her; she was one with the water, but separated from any mishaps from eels, warped fish things, or other dangers in the water. Arguably, ghosts posed a hell of a danger, but she was prepared for that.

She was in the water, and the water was in her; she was made of the water, and it was interlaced with her energies. The thinnest borders of skin and blood and meat held life and death apart with the keen interdimensional complexities of the Mirror between the living and the dead. Close to death, fully alive, she felt like an avatar of the Mirror. She let that thought race around in her skull and dart away, focusing instead on the stillness that always followed.

That night the water was only peaceful at this depth. The strain of her pounding heart echoed the howl of wind-lashed surf that tore at those on the small boat when the storm blew up out of nowhere. The lights of shore were visible, but too far away.

Her whole family swam for them. Only she arrived.

The chill of the water drained her heat, cooling her bones.

She unfolded her senses into the darkness. Further, then further.

There were no echoes.

Trellis let his bootfalls echo as he walked along the dilapidated pier. Neap and Slack waited at the end; Slack held on to some cables, and Neap slowly worked a bellows, pressing air down through the tube to where the Mistress could breathe it.

"I didn't know you were aware of the Mistress's recreation," Neap said by way of greeting as Trellis approached.

"I'm invested in understanding my crew as much as possible," Trellis shrugged as he approached. "How long has she been down there?"

"Almost two hours, this time," Neap replied.

Trellis stopped a respectful distance away. "I'm not sure what she's hoping to achieve," he admitted.

"People who drown in or near Doskvol," Neap shrugged. "They trigger a deathseeker crow to find them, as usual, but it's harder if the body is underwater. What interests the Mistress is that sometimes, now and then, there are ghosts that come to this side of the

Mirror, but can't push up past the surface of the water. Like it's a mirror within a mirror."

"It's a question of echoing," Slack explained. "What if drowning souls drift in the world in a different way than the ghosts of those who die on land? There's a reason the canals are haunted, a reason the gondoliers were the foremost primitive authorities on managing ghosts."

Neap watched Trellis closely. "Her family drowned just offshore. She almost did. Dumb luck that she survived to get close enough to be rescued and revived."

Trellis shrugged his coat to a more comfortable fit on his shoulders. "I imagine everyone who hears about this has their own theory."

"Without exception," Neap agreed.

Trellis offered him a wintery smile. "Then I'll keep mine to myself," he said. "Do you think you could get her tidied up and over to the Chime Era bookstore by the hour of Honor?"

Neap hesitated. "I expect she'll be up in less than an hour," he answered, leaving the rest to hang between them.

"You'll give her the message," Trellis said, and he nodded. "Thank you." He turned, following the pier back towards land, moving with the natural grace of a predator through the abandoned drydock. The experiment receded behind him, its questions intact, and he disappeared into the gathering dusk.


## SILKSHORE. FOGCREST, CHIME ERA BOOKSTORE. 5TH ULSIVET. THE HOUR OF HONOR

The plump and grandmotherly woman shrugged out of her greatcoat, and a servant took it over to the curated coatroom. The woman patted at her silver hair as she looked into the smoked mirror by the door of the bookstore, then she squared her shoulders and passed the public seating area, headed for the more private booths in the back. Glancing at the note in her hand, she chose booth four. Standing right outside the curtained booth, she steeled herself for a moment, then put on a bright smile and pushed the curtain back.

"Good evening, Inspector, I did not—expect..." Her features shifted as she regarded the lone man sitting in the booth, waiting for her. "And you are most certainly not the Inspector General," she said, a sharpness in her tone even as her smile did not waver.

Sanction smiled at her. "I needed to get on your calendar today," he explained. "Please join me."

"Deceiving me will have consequences," she said through her teeth. Still, curiosity tugged at her, and she ended up in the booth with Sanction.

"Strictly business," Sanction promised. "But where are my manners? Good evening, Director Talitha Welker. I am so glad you could make it."

"And what's your name?" she demanded.

"My name is Kreeger," Sanction replied. "I brought paperwork." He smiled his most charming smile as he hefted a leather portfolio up on the table; it was several inches thick.

"You must be the Kreeger that was robbed, his husband shot. Sent him off balance, from what I heard," Welker said, leaning back and looking at Sanction down her nose.

"Triggered a chain reaction of imbalance," Sanction agreed. "Sometime in the next few weeks you'll get a review of Nelytha Bel's pension. Questions of impropriety came up," Sanction said with a very serious face as he slid the first packet of paper over to Welker. "You pulled the file to the top of the list and agree that there are irregularities."

"There are?" Welker demanded, eyebrows raised.

"Yes," Sanction continued, "because her record is so much more aligned with desired behavior from agents than anyone gave her credit for. It would be inappropriate to simply reinstate her pension and lodging license. She deserves more." A certain coldness entered Sanction's voice as he looked Welker in the eye.

Welker frowned at the document. "This is the Council sponsorship for designating the steward of—of the Chime Era," she said as her eyes traced the cramped writing.

"A little-known discretionary power of the Director of Commercial Distribution in Silkshore," Sanction agreed. "The Council owns many properties that can be designated the stewardship of individuals. Now, the first document transfers stewardship of the Chime Era bookstore to public option, and the second places it in the care of Nelytha Bel, who will thereby enjoy its profits, in addition to her reinstated pension. And she can even live in the apartment upstairs."

"Who is in that apartment now?" Welker asked, almost a growl.

"Tyla Barrsly," Sanction said, eyes clear and steady.

"That's—isn't that—isn't that Marcus Barrsly's mother?" Welker protested.

"Marcus is well connected and can find her another location," Sanction said evenly.

The truth dawned behind Welker's eyes. "Because Barrsly is the one who initiated the review," she said. "Got Nelytha Bel evicted."

"Brought a crew to pack up her things," Sanction said, letting the slightest flavor of anger color his tone.

"Well!" Welker said, tidying up the corners of the paperwork so far and slapping the top page, "this is a truly amazing bureaucratic feat, organizing all this and navigating the back waters of our by-laws to lay out this single course of action." She paused. "But why would I sign any of it?"

"That's the wrong question," Sanction said, shaking his head. "You are going to sign. That's a sure thing, a fact. The question is why you sign," he said. "If you sign because you agree that one of your underlings overreached and you want to correct that behavior out of compassion and honor, then the matter ends here." He paused, looking her in the eye. "If you sign because you were forced to do so, then all your decisions come under review. Your authority must be evaluated, to see if you've been compromised and forced to act in the best interest of someone besides the Ministry."

"Now I'm curious," Welker said, a sneer creeping into her voice. "How you can be so sure you can make me sign. What do you have. Blackmail? Fear of death?" she made a rude noise. "This is a strange place for amateur hour to emerge in your little shakedown," she said with a contemptuous gesture.

Sanction waited for a long moment. "I hoped we could avoid this," he admitted. Then the curtain whipped aside even though no one touched it. The Mistress of Tides stood less than an arm's length away, in full mask and regalia, flanked by her adepts. Cold air breathed into the booth.

"I'm protected," Welker said through her teeth, clutching at the spirit bane charm worked into her Ministry broach.

"From an adept, or a random loose ghost, maybe," Sanction shrugged. "This is a Whisper. She can tear your spirit out of your body and put in a ghost that's ready to cooperate with what I want." He paused. "I don't want to do that to you. I'm not sure you'd ever recover. I will tell you, though, one way or another your body will sign these papers." He looked her in the eye. "Now."

Welker's grandmotherly image was compromised as she scowled, a snarl showing the yellow of her teeth. "You will regret making me your enemy," she muttered.

"I'm not your enemy," Sanction replied in a flinty voice. "Not yet. That's your choice. You are with the Ministry, with deep resources, so you can handle conflict by attrition. I don't have that kind of depth in my resources. So if I feel threatened, defense is not an option." He slammed his fists in to the table as he rose, and Welker flinched. "When I'm attacked," Sanction growled under his breath, "my only viable option is counter-attack. If you attack me and leave me alive," he said through his teeth, "you don't know where I'll hit you back. And if I take a shot at the Ministry and misjudge my target?" He raised his eyebrows. "I'm done for."

"So it's best," Welker said slowly, "if we leave each other alone."

"I think so," Sanction agreed quietly.

Welker signed the forms.

## BARROWCLEFT. BELDERAN ESTATE. 6TH ULSIVET. THE FOURTH HOUR

"Wasted a perfectly good fallow crash," grumbled Piccolo, poking at his breakfast caps and egg.

"Never complain that things went too smoothly," Sanction said.

"Just saying that right now I could be completely immersed in an out-of-body experience," Piccolo groused.

"I could hit you in the forehead really hard," Sanction offered.

"I tried that, it's just not the same," Piccolo sighed.

"Here she comes," Trellis said, unable to entirely hide his grin.

The glass-lined dining room fell silent as the door opened and Nebs strolled in. She cocked an eyebrow as she looked at Trellis, Sanction, and Piccolo enjoying their brunch, waiting for her.

"Shouldn't you be busy reconstructing a life for me?" she said, arch.

"It's done," Sanction shrugged. "In a stroke of luck, the same day your account is flagged for review, it is determined that you do not get enough compensation. You'll be installed as the steward of the Chime Era bookstore, and live upstairs, with your full pension reinstated." He grinned.

Nebs blinked fast. "Oh, Kreeger," she said. "I'm speechless."

"We're going to be okay," Sanction said quietly.

Nebs crossed the room and pulled Sanction into a hug. "Well, if we can't keep you safe," she murmured into his shoulder as she squeezed him tight. She let him go, and looked up at him. "Go get 'em," she said, a wry smile tugging at her features.

Downstairs, the moving wagons arrived.


## SILKSHORE. THE EASE, CENTRAL LANDING. 6ᵗʰ ULSIVET

The park had one radiant fountain, with delicately etched signs in three languages warning "Do Not Drink." The mid-day twilight was thick with shadows, and the fountain sharpened their edges. Four game tables were spaced around the fountain to use its light, by day or night. The trees added atmosphere and motion, stroking the wind as it slid through the leaves, whispering half-remembered dreams and secrets in their dim heights.

Trellis walked past the two gondolier guards who were pretending to be relaxing citizens tossing a ball back and forth. He slipped past three food carts selling savory or sweet bounties of fungus. One harmless old man among many, he sat down at the game table opposite a gondolier.

"Good afternoon, Khyro," Trellis said with half a smile. He looked down at the swirling board and the glass drop game pieces.

"Well, as I live and breathe," Khyro replied. "It's the Barrowcleft Trellis." He grinned broadly, showing off his flat yellow teeth as he squinted through thick lenses. His hair was slicked back to his neck, and he had enough loose skin to have an almost reptilian appearance. "I thought you retired."

"I did, for a while. Didn't like the scoreboard," Trellis replied. He paused, regarding Khyro. "Things change."

"They do," Khyro agreed.

"My nephew is putting together a crew," Trellis continued. "We even have a legit Whisper. You've heard of the Mistress of Tides."

"Mm," Khyro grunted, leaning back and sucking his teeth, crossing his arms over his chest.

"You and me, we're ballast," Trellis murmured. "We bring continuity. Stability. We've made all the best mistakes, so if the youngsters listen to us, they don't have to make the same ones." Trellis offered a wry smile. "There are plenty of exciting new mistakes for them to make."

"This better end with you telling me they want to work under the gondoliers," Khyro said in an unfriendly rasp.

"No, Khyro," Trellis replied. "We're going to take over the gondolier Council. Reorganize the crime around here. Strike a new balance."

"You can try," Khyro said, expressionless.

"Now don't be like that," Trellis said with a wry smile. "We have lived long enough to know that power is always in flux, waxing or waning. And with Skovlanders pushing in and the Slip that you've got to deal with—"

"What do you know about the Slip?" Khyro demanded.

"It's sapping your people," Trellis replied gently. "I wanted to tell you that my crew is going to step in and make sure nothing gets unraveled too far before we can have some more exciting power struggles."

"Why would you give up the element of surprise?" Khyro demanded.

"One, because I'm pretty confident. The gondoliers are unlikely to send a hit squad after us based on our ambitions alone," Trellis shrugged. "Also, you've got grandchildren in positions of authority now." He paused. "You can remember a time when all of this was a bit more... civilized. Not such a game of domination and scorched earth."

"What is all that supposed to mean?" Khyro growled.

Trellis looked him in the eye. "We're coming for you, and you can't stop us. But once the gondoliers answer to us, no hard feelings. That's just the smart play. The best way forward for everyone."

"May you just get sucked through the next crack in the Mirror," Khyro cursed. "You got some balls, coming to me like this, in my place of power, all alone."

"Just think about it," Trellis said, rising.

"Oh, I will," Khyro snapped. "The gondoliers, they are dragons of the canals. And you? Your pathetic crew? You're just worms. Worms that the birds eat." He spat off to the side.

"In time," Trellis murmured, "you'll see what these 'worms' can do." He pivoted, striding away from the game tables.

In his mind's eye, he saw the uncertainty that infected Khyro. Trellis smiled.

# ━━┓ Chapter Nine ┏━━

*The world beyond easy reach of sight and sound and touch is closer than it has ever been in the history of humanity. Science suggests the Veil separates the Ghost Field from the Real that we all experience. The occultists and mystics call it the Mirror. While the main focus of the common person is the danger posed by lingering ghosts on the other side, industry has focused instead on how to mine energy through the barrier.*

*My own research takes a different approach. I believe the problem of ghosts and the opportunity of energy are both limited fields, and ultimately what we will see as the greatest promise of this Veil, of passing through the Mirror, is how our other senses may be opened and redirected. This alteration of perception may well change what it means to be human.*

*- From "Diary of Plasmic Studies Vol: 8"*
*by Doctor Tyrial Daas*

## SILKSHORE. CROWNWIND COURT. ULSIVET 5

The dull glow of wakefulness spread beneath the early fog of morning in Silkshore. Candles, lamps, and plasmic illumination bled together as the shadows shrank. Veins and arteries pushed darkness back into the city's meat of walls and alleys, and the restless heartbeat of the city sped up, driving its people about their business.

Red Silver dragged herself up yet another flight of stairs, and paused, rubbing at her forehead. The persistent ache was intensifying, and she recognized this flavor of headache; it was an intrusion. Leaning back into a urine-scented corner of the stairwell, she pulled out her mirrored glasses and slipped them on, keeping her eyes closed and adjusting her mind around the dull pain center, pulling it to center stage, surrounding and regarding it.

The pain peeled back like stage curtains, revealing the depth beyond. She sensed Nails' agitation, the clatter of loamy shingles beneath his claws.

"I'm really not in the mood," she murmured.

The pain sharpened, her bat pushing an idea at her that she did not know how to receive. She pressed at her own senses, widening the space around the bat's thoughts that moved into her own, giving more room to Nails.

A combination formed; noise, smell, motion. One central idea emerged.

Someone was in her apartment.

"You good furry boy," she whispered. She tugged her glasses off and put them back in her lapel pocket, and she unsheathed a pistol, snapping it open with a practiced flick of the wrist. Loaded. She folded the breach loader shut, and squinted up the stairs.

One more round up the stairs, then she opened a rickety shutter and stepped out on the ledge, feeling it flex under her slight weight. A couple steps took her to the adjoining wall. The drainpipe had fallen generations ago, but she had reinforced the old brackets to hold her weight, and she slowly climbed up, breathing through her open mouth, willing herself to be lighter and soundless. She reached the ledge around the waist of her apartment, and crept to the window that looked into the main room.

Red Silver drew her quicksilver stiletto, and slowly eased it upward, looking into the narrow reflective band to see into her apartment. She saw dim light painting the ceiling, flowing up from below, and in the faint glow she made out the young woman sitting at the table, a knife in front of her, motionless.

She crept back along the ledge, around to the back, skipping the planks she had sabotaged. Kneeling to reach under the ledge, she folded the supports out so she could reach the window without being pitched down four stories to the cobbles below. She reached up to move the clicker wire that would make noise as the window opened or closed, and slid it noiselessly out of the way, so she could quietly enter the bedroom.

As she climbed in, she gasped as pain fired through her leg; it was stiff, and she kept forgetting how much tender care it still required. She managed to roll down to the floor very quietly, but as she rose to her feet she saw the woman from the main room silhouetted in the doorway.

The woman struck a match, casually lighting the candle she held in her other hand. "Not how I planned this," she said, her accent thick, "but I suppose it is what I should expect." Underlit by the candle, her face was young, freckled, trim, framed by cropped blonde hair.

Frowning, Red Silver raised her pistol to line up on the intruder. "What do you want."

The other woman shook out the flame on the match, scenting the air with sulfur, watching Red Silver. "We need to talk," she said.

Red Silver shuffled back and lowered herself on the only chair in the room, her pistol pointed unerringly at the intruder. "Let's hear it."

"I'm a stranger here, and this city is too crowded to take in a stranger," the intruder continued. "Nobody is going to make it without friends. Advocates. That's what I want."

"Takes some nerve for a Skovlander to come in to my home and expect me to be, what, her patron," Red Silver said. "The whole asking part is a refreshing change of pace from you people, but I gotta say—"

"Besides," the intruder interrupted, "you owe me."

"Oh, so I owe you?" Red Silver retorted, eyebrows raised, gun steady.

The intruder cocked her head to the side. "My name is Asdis," she replied.

Red Silver blinked. "Dead Asdis?"

"Well," Asdis shrugged, "not entirely."

"Like, the one Piccolo stabbed?" Red Silver pressed.

Asdis raised her shirt enough to reveal the bandage on her torso.

Squinting, Red Silver shook her head. "So why come to me? I mean, if you survived, the Grinders—"

"I can't go back there," Asdis interrupted, calm. "I was hurt, bad, and an eager messenger reported my death. That triggered all the politics." She paused. "I go back to my people, and that embarrasses some dangerous people who took big chances and can't afford to lose."

"There are other Skov gangs," Red Silver pointed out.

"Resurrection is a card I can only play once," Asdis replied. "I want it to matter."

Red Silver watched Asdis, her mind sifting through the variables, context, and facts. "Huh."

"Can we sit at the table?" Asdis asked. "I don't like being held at gunpoint."

Red Silver reluctantly holstered her pistol. "Sure, the table is fine," she said. "So, is revenge the thing here? Towards the Grinders?"

Asdis turned her back and walked into the main room, seating herself at the table out of Red Silver's eyeshot. "Revenge has nothing to do with this," she said. "I need to move forward. I can't look back until I've got some kind of security, ongoing."

Red Silver wavered, her pain and weakness washing over her. She closed her eyes and bit back the nausea, waiting for it to pass.

"So what do you think?" Asdis asked, nerves in her voice.

For a moment Red Silver's frailty towered over her, and the only safe and reasonable course of action was to execute the intruder. Then the cowardice faded, and she was left with the cold assurance that if Asdis was telling the truth, it was too good an opportunity to pass up. Still, it was almost too good to be true—so it was almost certainly a trap. But only almost.

"Why did you pick me?" Red Silver demanded.

Asdis chuckled. "A number of local tavern boys figured out where you live, more or less. Once it was down to a few buildings, it wasn't hard. You stand out," she smiled. "Based on your rep, you'd like a perch. Something with a view." She paused. "Are you going to stay in there?"

"I'm thinking things over," Red Silver snapped. "You stay put."

Quietness settled in the rooms, light and loose over the bedrock of tension.

"Okay the thing is loyalty," Red Silver said at last. "If you want help from the River Stallions, I'll support your bid to join, on one condition," she said.

"Name it."

"I need a strong signal from you that you're willing to make this change, long term, not just a convenient move. You give that signal, it helps me feel your loyalty, and makes it easier for me to persuade the others to accept you."

"What do you have in mind?" Asdis asked.

"Ink," Red Silver said, grim.

Asdis only hesitated a moment. "Let's do it," she replied.

## SILKSHORE. STITCHERY ALLEYS. 5TH ULSIVET

The buildings were four to six stories tall, on uncertain footing. They leaned together, and were connected by clotheslines, guy wires, and catwalks. For these few blocks, at the lower levels light only ever moved up, never filtering all the way down. The two women navigated the press of people and the mounds of debris, skirting the pools and fending off the buskers and pickpockets. They wore cloaks and hoods; the crowd had a studied sense of incuriosity, but information could be one of the more valuable commodities that quietly changed hands in the shadows.

"Here," Red Silver nodded, shifting the creaky gate and descending the steps to a basement entrance. Asdis followed, glancing around, and a moment later Red Silver hauled the crimson door open and moved into the swirling haze of the low-beamed basement.

The smoldering incense was only part of the atmosphere; the scent of cooking meat simmered in the air itself, and the heavy breathing scent of human musk seemed wrapped in onion smells. Red Silver crossed to a mass of cushions, pulling one from the pile and lowering herself to sit on it. Asdis followed her example, looking around for where the tapping noise was coming from.

A woman sat with her back to them, hair up in a bun, perched on a paving stone. Her back was wreathed in tattoos; some were patterns, other designs were more representational, some text in various languages. She wore a top that had a strap around the back of her neck, leaving her whole back and arms bare, and her blousy pants were sheer enough to suggest her legs had their share of ink as well. She held a stick with a nail through it, and tapped it with another stick so it bounced on the skin of her human canvas. She paused to scrape the nail on her finger, which had a deposit of ink, and then the stick was poised again, another stick tapping it, embedding ink below the surface.

Red Silver leaned back on another cushion, and her eyelids eased down. Her breathing evened out, slowing, dipping still further to a dreamless snore.

Time passed. Maybe an hour. The stick tapped on the other stick, the man stoically endured art, the artist fleshed out an image on skin. The rhythm of the tapping began sinking into Asdis' will to remain awake; it wasn't totally even, it sounded almost like a heartbeat, pausing and repositioning the way a human heart never could.

Asdis woke with a start, looking at the tattoo artist who sat cross-legged, regarding her. "Time's it?" she slurred, blinking.

"Doesn't matter," the tattoo artist shrugged. She had tattoos on her face, and something about her eyes was deeply distressing. "How do you know Red Silver?" She nodded at where the other woman had rolled over and was sleeping deeply.

"She said she would sponsor me if I would get a River Stallions tattoo," Asdis said in a small voice, shrinking from the artist for reasons she could not articulate.

The tattoo artist regarded her shrewdly for a few seconds. "So joining was your idea, and the tattoo was hers."

"Yes ma'am," Asdis replied, despising the servility in her tone.

Red Silver's breathing shifted, and she took in a deep breath, then sat up stretching. She blinked at the other two women.

"So you've met," she smiled.

"No exchange of names, though," the tattoo artist said.

"Inkletta, this is Asdis. Piccolo's friend," Red Silver said with a meaningful look.

"Charmed," Asdis said, extending her hand.

"You're looking spry," Inkletta observed, coolly clasping her hand. "Considering." She looked over at Red Silver. "You're sure you want her to get River Stallion ink?"

"She says she wants in," Red Silver shrugged. "She gets the ink, that's a lot more convincing. And if it doesn't work out, it may not matter what is on her skin."

Inkletta turned to Asdis. "You want this tattoo?"

"Sure," Asdis nodded. "Things don't work out, maybe I wipe all of you out and start my new crew with your name and colors." Her smile was mostly kidding.

Inkletta shook her head. "I guess I'll have to make your colors flagship cool," she sighed. "I only do work by recommendation, so consider yourself lucky. Where do you think?" she asked Red Silver.

"Right arm, shoulder," Red Silver shrugged. "Palm size, you figure?"

"At least," Inkletta replied with a wry grin. "You get a black one," she said to Asdis, "and we'll add colors if you're with us long enough." She held the stick with a nail over a lamp, so the nail lingered in the flame. "You can use one of these tops." She nodded towards a rack with a number of shirts like hers, designed to make flesh accessible to the artist while preserving some modesty.

Asdis winced as she shrugged out of her shirt and pulled the other one on, then she sat before Inkletta. "So do we have chit chat, or is this quiet time?" she asked nervously.

"Chit chat is fine, I like chit chat," Inkletta said absently as she scraped some of the gluey pigment onto the nail.

"So, what happened to the kid who stabbed me?" Asdis asked casually. Inkletta started tapping, the nail puncturing Asdis' skin over and over. Asdis flexed down hard to suppress a flinch.

"It hurts less if you relax," Red Silver drawled. "Piccolo is being dealt with."

"What does that mean?" Asdis asked.

"He's got a death mark," Red Silver clarified. "Sooner or later he'll cross our path and pay for it."

"Because he stabbed me?" she asked.

"And damn near started a war," Red Silver agreed. "We're still paying for his rash action."

"Okay please stop," Asdis said to Inkletta, an edge to her voice. "That—is very painful," she explained, her face pale. She looked at the narrow line on her upper arm. "How long will this take?"

"Hours. All day. And it depends on you," Inkletta shrugged.

"Fine. That's—fine," Asdis gritted out. She closed her eyes, and Inkletta started tapping again, injecting the ink. "You'd think—I wouldn't mind the pain," she said as a tear leaked out of one eye.

"So did Piccolo actually stab you? I mean, what's the story there?" Red Silver asked.

"I got stitches barely holding me together," Asdis replied through gritted teeth. "As soon as I could get on my feet I came looking for you."

The tapping stick paused, and Inkletta cocked her head to the side. "Let me see the injury," she said. "We can patch you back up."

Reluctantly, Asdis shrugged out of the loose shirt. She tugged at the adhesive holding her bandage in place, and gingerly lifted the half-soaked wad away from the stab wound.

The other two women looked at the bulging and ugly-colored stab wound for a long moment.

"You are looking spry indeed," Inkletta murmured, sober.

"What kind of healer attention did you get for this?" Red Silver asked, eyes locked on the grievous wound. "This doesn't look like a physiker or even a nurse had a look." She met Asdis' eyes. "What, just battlefield dressing and herbal remedies?" she demanded.

"Far as I know," Asdis replied in a small voice.

Inkletta rose to her feet, reaching for her cloak and pulling it on. "I have a few people to see. I'll be back in about an hour." She paused. "With help," she clarified.

Red Silver nodded. "If you're getting a physiker, my leg," she added.

"Yes," Inkletta said, heading for the door. "That too. Get all of you patched up," she said, and she was out the door.

Asdis leaned back, her breathing shallow. "Like I said," she managed. "Strangers won't make it. Need friends."

Red Silver had nothing to add.

## SILKSHORE. BUSKER'S COURT. 6TH ULSIVET

"We can do most of the heavy lifting," Saint said, squinting at the reddish smear of color that pushed through the crooked sky. "You need to know the plan, though. Be prepared to take responsibility."

"Easy," Hutch barked. "As long as your people can stay out of sight." He cocked his head to the side. "And why are we doing the elaborate pantomime?

"Well, to start at the beginning," Saint said, "we want to make it look like the Gray Cloaks had a falling out with the River Stallions and attacked their base, wiping them all out. Except me," he added.

"Then you go crying to the Grinders," Hutch nodded.

"Right. And you send a messenger to beg for peace, have a meet to head off any more unpleasantness," Saint prompted. "Something small, just leaders. So we're looking at Hutton himself and a handful of his best. And on your side, just you and a handful of your best."

"Because the River Stallions will be resurrected and come out of hiding on our side," Hutch said, "and our combined forces will wipe out Hutton's Grinders."

"Bluecoats get Hutton's corpse, pin a bunch of crimes on it, and everyone wins," Saint added. "We make sure Ingvald gets it, he's second in command. We tell any Bluecoats who care that it was an internal power struggle, and we help them clean up."

"With number one and number two down, a power struggle follows," Hutch considered. "They are weakened and we buy a few key voices to keep them that way." He smiled broadly.

"You're really good at this," Saint said with what resembled admiration.

Hutch shrugged modestly. "Bluecoats don't last long if they think keeping the peace is about force. No, it's about understanding the criminal mind," he said, tapping his temple and squinting. "Doubly so when dealing with foreigners." He shook his head. "You see the same behavior among rats." He sniffed, staring across the paved square, rigid on the stone bench.

Saint sat back, taking in the same view. "I expect you're right," he said. "Once they set the location for the meet, we'll finalize our plans for a clean getaway." He let a bleak smile shine through. "The Grinders are just about done here on Silkshore."

"I'll drink to that," Hutch said, his face twisted by a sneer of disgust. He pulled out a flask, spinning the cap off to dangle on its chain, and he took a swig before passing it on to Saint, who also took a swig. "We will attack at the Hour of Flame. Stage this to look good."

"We'll be ready to play our part. You come in to attack, we go out through the escape hatch in the basement of the tower," Saint muttered. "You said you have some captives you can execute to trigger the deathseeker crows, and the bells on the seminary?"

"Yes," Hutch nodded. "One for that girl you've got, and the uppity Whisper, and the three fighting men." Hutch turned to look Saint in the eye. "Everyone but you."

Saint rose to his feet, nodding to Hutch. "See you tonight." He sauntered into the courtyard, blending with the idling morning traffic, ignoring the buskers.

Hutch leaned back, his face stretched with a most unpleasant smile. "And that will be the end for the Grinders," he murmured to himself, then he chuckled and took another swig.

## SILKSHORE. STITCHERY ALLEYS. 6TH ULSIVET

Red Silver felt her sleep thin out, the waking world pressing in, and one of the first impressions she got was the smell of frying sausage. A faint smile touched her lips, and she opened her eyes to find herself in a nest of bedding in the corner of Inkletta's back room.

She looked down at her leg, and saw the tight bandages. She could still smell the minty harsh tang of the gel the physicker had spread on her injuries, and she experimentally pointed her toes, feeling the stretch and pull along the length of her wound—but little pain.

With a little effort, Red Silver leveraged herself out of bed. She looked over at where Asdis was still passed out in her nest of blankets, her eyes appearing bruised with weariness. Red Silver padded into the main room where Inkletta was frying up food. "What, you're making breakfast nowadays?" she teased.

"No, this is supper," Inkletta said without turning. "Sleepyhead."

"Huh," Red Silver muttered, and she gingerly lowered herself down onto a cushion. "Thanks for getting a physicker for us," she added.

"It wasn't cheap," Inkletta muttered, "but I can't have you dying on me. Or this puzzle you brought in." She looked at Red Silver. "I don't think we should tell the others until after we get past the

Grinder job."

"I don't disagree," Red Silver said as delicately as she could, "but we also aren't likely to keep her locked up."

"I figure we persuade her to wear a mask," Inkletta shrugged.

"Perfect," Red Silver agreed, and she started in on the hard biscuits.

"Don't you want the sausage gravy?"

"That too," Red Silver said around a mouthful of food. "I don't need them together. All goes to the same place."

Inkletta heaved a sigh. "Heathens. All of them." She looked over at Red Silver. "Safety came by. Tonight we're doing the battle at the tower."

"Ugh," Red Silver groused.

"I know," Inkletta shrugged. "But that's how it's got to be for the plan."

"I don't like pretending to lose a fight. I don't want to suppress the resistance instinct."

Inkletta smiled. "I don't think she does either," she said with a nod towards the back room. "She's a survivor."

"Apparently," Red Silver agreed. "Now let's see if we can get through this next patch of pretend bad luck and see what kind of luck Asdis will bring."

## SILKSHORE. RIVER STALLIONS TOWER. 7ᵀᴴ ULSIVET

Two hard-eyed Skovlanders led the way into the modest cobbled courtyard. A smudge of smoke still rose from the tower that flanked the courtyard, and there were signs of ferocious battle; sprays of dry blood, craters blown in plaster and wood and stone from a gun battle. The door to the tower was gone altogether, the frame lined with blast exhaust.

A Skovlander dressed in muted finery escorted Saint into the courtyard, and two more Skovs brought up the rear. "Last night, you say?" the important Skovlander asked Saint.

"We were working out our next job in the basement when they blew the door with some kind of plasmic charge," Saint agreed. "We managed to get up there and wipe out their first wave, but they had snipers." He paused, his lip trembling. "Safety dropped first, then

Gapjaw. We pulled back to the basement, but they knew about the back door. Threw in poison gas."

They approached the tower, and Ingvald leaned in, frowning at the burning sensation in his sinuses as he sniffed the air. "The bodies?"

"They took them as trophies," Saint said, barely holding his composure. "To—to taunt any would-be adversaries." He turned his reddened eyes to Ingvald. "They took our women, Ingvald." Checking himself, Saint looked down at the ground, his jaw working. "My women..."

"Not anymore, hey?" Ingvald retorted, clapping Saint on the shoulder. "My my, what a mess. Looks like we asked too much of your crew."

"You wanted them to hit us instead of you," shrugged Saint. "We bought you time. With the lives of my crew." His forehead contracted in a frown. "That is worth something. It has to be."

"They've contacted us, you know," Ingvald said, almost jovial. "They want peace, now that they've sorted out one of our allies."

"Well then this is your chance," Saint said immediately. "We had a plan to take them on, but they hit us first. You could—you could make something of it," he said as excitement grew in him.

"Oh?" Ingvald said, arching an eyebrow.

"They pay off the Bluecoats at the impound at Whipwater Point. So they'd feel safe, just their leaders. Just you. But..." Saint gestured.

"But if we're prepared, we take their leaders and finish them off," Ingvald said. He shook his head. "You have no honor at all, have you."

"Honor?" Saint scoffed. "These dogs poisoned my friends, who choked on their own foaming blood as they writhed and burned in a basement! What is honor to such monsters?"

"It's about who we are, not about our adversaries," Ingvald sniffed. "Now, where can you be reached?"

"I—I want to come back with you. Join the Grinders. I have nothing left," Saint said, forlorn.

"That's not going to happen, Akorosian," Ingvald sneered. "We may have some work for you, a place in our organization, but let's not rush to any conclusions." He paused. "So, where?"

Saint squinted into the middle distance, mastering himself. "For now, leave a message with the barkeep at the Barkskin. It can reach me while I'm deep underground. I don't want to be an afterthought of those murderous thieves the Gray Cloaks." He pointed his most mournful look at Ingvald. "You're... sure?"

"I'll be in touch," Ingvald said airily, and he pivoted and strode away, four guards in tow.

"Maybe I'll see you first," Saint muttered into his forearm as he wiped his nose.

## SILKSHORE. BARKSKIN TAVERN ADJACENT BASEMENT. 8TH ULSIVET

Red Silver scowled at the coil of tough wire as she tugged on it, heavy gloves gripping its shining length. "This is terrible," she muttered.

Beside her, Safety chuckled. "Yes it is. But somebody has to do it. And we're eating the crew's food, so," he shrugged, "we make caltrops out of the crew's wire." He started snipping off finger-length segments.

"You prefer the two twined wires for the caltrops, don't you," Red Silver demanded, her wire twanging as she snapped off a length with the cutters. "I like the elegance of the single strand."

"Whatever," Safety shrugged. He hissed as the wire slithered through the gloves, slitting one of them.

"Are you alright?" Red Silver demanded. "Let me see if you need stiches!"

"I sometimes forget what people know," Safety replied, his tone wry. He tugged off the work glove, and revealed a gleaming metal hand. Intricately crafted plates protected inner workings like cables and nested gleaming steel pipes. "Whole arm is metal. Gift from the Deadlands route, when I was a rail jack."

Red Silver leaned back, her languid expression almost a smile. "So that's where you learned those snappy hand to hand moves?"

"Part of the training," he shrugged, "mainly to deal with ghosts that got into people. Joint locks have limited use on incorporeal foes, but sometimes a possessed human's more than enough to settle things in a very corporeal way." He returned his attention to the wire.

"So how did you lose it?" Red Silver asked, showing little interest in returning to her wire cutting.

Safety paused for a moment, choosing his words. "Look, I appreciate the interest, but... that was then. A long time ago now. Not something I care to dredge up."

"Fair enough," Red Silver said lightly, catching at the wire and measuring off a length. "We all have our secrets."

"You make it sound a lot more dramatic than it is," Safety scoffed. "It's not a secret. It's just—irrelevant." He glanced over at her. "Where are you from? Your folks?"

She looked him in the eye. "It's irrelevant," she shrugged.

"Nice," he winced. "Efficient. No energy wasted. A clean takedown."

"You already know a damn sight more about me than I want you to," Red Silver pointed out.

The door at the top of the stairs banged open, and heavy boots clomped down the stairs as Saint rejoined the crew. "They went for it," he said. "Hutch and Hutton will be meeting tomorrow night at the Whipwater Point impound lot. And neither one plans to play fair." He clapped his hands together, rubbing them gleefully. "Tell me we're ready."

"Coffins, check; locked and loaded," Gapjaw said from across the room where he was loading explosives into pipes.

"Fixed the boats," the Hammer volunteered, looking up from his stolen books.

"I'm as ready as I'll be," Inkletta said.

"We'll have the caltrops done," Safety volunteered.

Saint closed in on the caltrop station in the busy basement. "Maybe I'll help move this along," he said, sitting down and rubbing his hands together. "You cut, I'll twist."

"Good man," Safety said with a nod.

Saint aimed a shrewd glance at each of them. "So Red," he said casually. "I hear Inkletta got a physicker for your leg."

"She did, and I'll pay her back as soon as you get us some lucrative work," Red Silver replied lightly.

"We'll do alright from ripping off a few points in the impound yard," Saint shrugged. "We can even blame whoever wins, to keep the Bluecoats off our backs."

"I hope that's how it works out," Red Silver replied with a tight smile. "At least Piccolo won't screw up this job." She turned to Safety. "Where is he these days, anyway?"

Safety blinked, surprised, then frowned. "Mostly out in Barrowcleft, comes into town now and then, but I've been involved in prepping for the job. He's a luxury. This is our livelihood."

"And you're cool with that?" Red Silver said to Saint.

"Safety's right, we prioritize, and right now we need to get out of the mess Piccolo got us into. Then maybe we figure out what to do with him."

"Or rather when and where. The what is settled, right?" Red Silver demanded.

Saint smiled in spite of himself. "Remind me never to get on your bad side," he said.

"I thought I reminded you every day," she replied.

"Now that you mention it, you do," Saint agreed. He glanced at them again. "Tomorrow we'll be flipping a pretty big rock," he said. "That's when the bugs start scurrying, and everything is all confused. We can't know which way everything will bounce. So... be ready, okay?"

"If we can't handle a few surprises, we're in the wrong line of work," Red Silver shrugged.

"I love your confidence," Safety said with half a grin. He looked to Saint. "No worries, boss." His smile broadened. "Worrying is your job."

"That, and making adorable caltrops," Saint murmured, regarding his work as he put the pliers aside. "Look at that savage pointy thing."

"Beautiful," Red Silver agreed.

Safety grinned. "Tomorrow is going to be a day for watching your step."

Saint thoughtfully tapped the sharp up-swept point of cut wire on the caltrop, and kept his thoughts to himself.

# —⊷ CHAPTER TEN ⊶—

*Charterhall predates most of Duskwall, it was built before the Cataclysm broke the sky and unleashed the tide of ghosts. The Bellweather Crematorium was repurposed in those early days of slaughter and confusion. No one but maybe the Spirit Wardens knows what the massive structure was before it became the Crematorium, but now it is the nerve center wired through the whole city.*

*I don't understand how it works, and I suspect those among the Spirit Wardens who once understood are gone, but the Crematorium senses death in the city. Never stare at the top of that damned tower for too long, because it has been overbuilt on both sides of the Mirror. When anyone dies in this city, a bell rings on the Crematorium, audible near the death if you can attune to the Mirror, and a death-seeker crow launches to find the crack where the life slipped out. After all, if a body lays for over a day, a ghost can pull together out of what energy is left.*

*Once upon a time, the Spirit Wardens were tasked with finding the corpse and putting it to proper flame, rest in peace and all. Now that's just one of their duties. Nights like this, with the flickering lightning that backlights that tower, I suspect the Bellweather Crematorium is a lot more complicated than we realize.*

*- From "Heretical Confessions of a Scholar, Vol: 4" by Hans Zarantia*

A bluster of rain sprayed across the round stained glass in the windows. The building creaked as the wind settled against it. The bartender glanced over at the door as shadows passed by on the street outside.

The bar itself was shaped like the side of a Skovlander long-boat, with trays hanging in front of the stools, like shields from the hull. Only one tray had been pulled up and put on the counter. The rest of the tavern was empty; even the booths with stylized waves carved on them that lined the opposite wall.

"Papa, I gotta open in a few minutes," the barkeep said with a friendly shrug.

"I know it, I know," the old man grumbled, pushing at the lumps in his lunch stew with his fork.

One of the shadows outside halted in the alcove of the door-way, waiting, expectant. The barkeep stepped out from the ship bar, crossing to the door and snapping the bolts out of the way, opening the way for his second customer of the day.

"Good morning," Trellis said as he strolled in, tugging his hat off and shrugging at his overcoat. He draped the coat over a barstool and slapped his hat on top, then sat down, smiling at the barkeep. "You serving lunch yet?"

"Not yet," the bartender said, once again behind the tray shields and countertop. Neither Trellis nor the barkeep looked at the man at the end of the bar finishing up his lunch.

"No problem," Trellis said with an easy smile, shrugging. "I'm not here for lunch." He strolled down the bar and deliberately sat next to the old man finishing his stew. "A word?" he asked quietly.

"They said you were sniffing around the Council's business," the old man replied. "Leave me be. We have nothing to discuss."

"Nonsense," Trellis replied quietly, looking away. "I'm willing to have the Hierophant Ludocian killed for you. And you have something I want in return."

The old man jumped as though stung, and stared at Trellis, trembling. "The Council says that beast is off limits," he spat.

"I'm not with the Council," Trellis replied, his voice even. He looked the old man in the eye. "This is your one chance, Zhavo."

Zhavo paused, his jaw working. He looked at the barkeep, who did not meet his eyes but instead turned and headed back into the kitchen. "Don't you jerk me around, Trellis," Zhavo growled, his teeth stained and crooked and a certain madness in his eyes.

"I'll do it in less than two days," Trellis shrugged. "I've got a knife man ready for the job. A Whisper, too."

"You must want something pretty bad to cross the Council like this," Zhavo muttered, eyeing Trellis.

"I want you to get my crew into the catacombs in the Mistyard," Trellis replied.

"The—you're mad," Zhavo managed, breathless. "It will do you no good, even if I did open them!"

"That's all I ask," Trellis replied calmly. "No coin. Just access."

"Mad," Zhavo repeated. "Only a handful of the most skilled gondoliers alive can navigate those sunken catacombs, and you sure as hell aren't one. And if it's loot you're after," he said with a shake of his head, "you'll find nothing there you can sell faster than hawking your own body parts."

Trellis sucked his teeth for a moment. "Zhavo," he said quietly, "the Fairpole Grotto Council of Gondoliers has put your child's killer off limits to you. They've told you they'll handle that, just like they'll handle everything else that's going wrong. But you've got the years to know when they're working, and when they're stalling." Zhavo tried to look away, but Trellis's gaze held him. "On the other hand," Trellis said softly, "I'm offering you justice."

For a long minute, it was quiet except for the sounds drifting in from the storm outside. The building's sinews and bone resisted the wind's push.

"One condition," Zhavo growled, breaking free of eye contact and staring down into his stew. "I deal the final blow. I kill that monster. And he knows it's me." Zhavo looked back up at Trellis, the haze of alcohol burned off. "Promise me that."

"We have a deal," Trellis replied, rising. "I'll be in touch with the details."

## CHARTERHALL. CLERK STREET, ELLIOTT CARTOGRAPHER & LAW. 7TH ULSIVET. THE EIGHTH HOUR

Trellis relaxed in the leathery over-stuffed chair, and considered the magnificent oil painting of a leviathan hunting ship steaming back to port, riding low with its sloshing and undying load of demon blood. A man joined him, unobtrusively standing by his chair.

"Lovely, yes?" the man said.

"Something in the quality of the light," Trellis murmured. He glanced up at the man. "Hello, Elliott."

Elliott crossed to sit in the chair opposite Trellis. "Good afternoon, you old scoundrel," he said with half a smile. "I know we didn't summon you here for business, and I'm confident any attempt at a social life has atrophied beyond reach for us both, so why don't you fill me in on the mysterious motive force that drives you into my firm's harbor this afternoon." His smile was crooked and unsafe, contrasting his impeccable suit and well-coiffed hair.

"I know one of your clients is Hierophant Ludocian," Trellis said quietly. "I need to know what you've got on him."

Elliott paused for a long moment, then settled back in the chair so his eyes disappeared behind the round lenses of his reading glasses. "It cannot be that you've forgotten the basics of how blackmailing works," he murmured. "The whole point is he pays me not to tell you." Elliot gestured vaguely. "Or anyone."

"I already know too much, if I know you're the one who's got the hold," Trellis countered. "And right now you're wondering how I know. The answer is worse than you thought; I know because I found out from an Inspector report." He paused to let that sink in. "You see, Ludocian is about to have a bad time. He's going to die. When the Inspectors consult the file, they'll see that you were under scrutiny as a possible blackmailing influence. Now that's bad for business," Trellis shrugged.

"You've got a counter, of course," Elliott said through his teeth.

"I can make it look like his bodyguard killed him," Trellis said quietly. "Or I can have his corpse found with one of your dead enforcers."

Elliott's expression hardened. "You've killed one of my people?" he said, barely audible.

"No," Trellis replied. "Must I?"

"You cocky son of a bitch," Elliott replied, almost soundless. "You offer assurances?"

"I don't need any of this to blow back on you," Trellis said. "Give me what I want and I was never here." He paused. "Kill me, or take aim at me in any way, and remember I've got my crew. They know I'm here. And one of them is outside."

"Threats?" Elliott said, eyebrows raised.

"Good business," Trellis shrugged.

Elliott sighed. He tried on a crooked smile. "Wait here." He disappeared into the back office.

Trellis rose to his feet and paced a few times, unwilling to face possible death sitting down and complacent. After a number of minutes ground by, Elliott returned, and thrust an envelope at Trellis.

"Here is that bastard's dirty secret," he said through his teeth.

Trellis took hold of the envelope's opposite corner, but Elliott was not ready to release it. Trellis waited a moment.

"I do this because of what you were," Elliott said. "Before you retired. That's quite a secret, hey?" He let go of the envelope.

Trellis shrugged. "Maybe don't try to put a price tag on that tidbit," he said quietly. "I like you, Elliott. But I don't want to have to come back here." He looked Elliott in the eye, and there was something in that stare that had not been there before. Then Trellis turned, and walked out the front door.

It took Elliott an hour to rebuild his composure.


## BARROWCLEFT. BELDERAN ESTATE. 7TH ULSIVET. THE TENTH HOUR

Sullen echoes of stained light forced their way through the broken sky and the tatters of clouds that hung above the city like a ghost freeing itself from a corpse. The day's twilight slid towards night. Meanwhile, in the library of the Belderan estate, Trellis and Sanction planned their next move.

"You're mad," Sanction scoffed. "Tonight? That's too soon. We need to lay the groundwork, clock the guards, check for surprises, scout the exits, all that," he said with aimless gestures. "You don't just walk into something like this face first."

"I thought you liked the improvisational nature of your new life," Trellis said drily.

"To a point," Sanction agreed. "But this? This is chaos waiting to unfurl, if we get one detail wrong."

"You never have all the details," Trellis shrugged.

"Why do you think we need to do this so fast?"

"Once we make our move, the Fairpole Grotto Council of Gondoliers will be on the alert for a pattern to our activities that reveals our plan," Trellis explained. "We keep them off balance by striking faster than they expect, and while they're scrambling, we sit back and wait."

"Oh, so waiting comes in here somewhere?" Sanction said with a cocked eyebrow.

"Right. Wait for the event that gives them a reason to convene the Council." Trellis let himself smile.

"And if no event presents itself, we make one." Sanction finished the thought matter-of-factly.

"Once we're ready," Trellis amended. "So we have to be ready."

"Sounds ominous," Sanction observed. "What's pushing the timetable?"

Trellis slid an envelope over to Sanction, who opened it. "A train?" he said, skeptical.

"Read on," Trellis said with an almost curious smile.

Sanction paused, then reread with a puzzled brow, then his eyes widened. "Is this real? This happens on the ninth?"

"And we'll be there," Trellis said with a sage nod. A bit of mischief turned his mouth up in a grin. "Unless you want us to get you some accounting position. All predictable and safe."

Sanction ignored that. "So we'll have two of the three pieces we need." He paused. "Do you really think we can pull this off?" he asked.

"Absolutely," Trellis shrugged. "The real question is, will we regret it?"

"I've already chosen not to," Sanction replied loftily. "Now, let's see this secret dirt you've got on the Hierophant." Trellis slid the envelope over, and Sanction peeled it open, reading the paper inside. His eyebrows raised. "Hm, yes, that should draw him out," he said. He looked Trellis in the eye. "This should do nicely."

The spectacular eastern view was alive with light. Looming lightning wall towers anchored sheets of fitful iridescent energy that swirled and tugged like sails made of flame. The river drifted by, sliding along the shores that supported the towers, the surface of the water reflecting back the blaring energy in a distorted and fragmented light show.

"Magnificent," Sanction breathed, gazing into the turmoil of energy. It tightened his skin.

"You been here before?" Piccolo asked, glancing around.

"Never made the time," Sanction shrugged. "Blood and bones, it's beautiful."

"Pretty neat," Piccolo agreed shortly. "I'm going to get in position. You sure Zhavo's up for this?"

"I'm sure," Sanction nodded.

Piccolo hesitated. "And the Mistress of Tides?"

"She's in position too. Don't worry about it," Sanction said, his tone almost dreamy.

Piccolo turned from the lights, facing the city. The view was substantially different. The park, once spacious and luxurious, was now overgrown and dark. Trash piled up in corners, and several buildings had deteriorated past the point of use. The thick leftover brush and greenery that had once been topiaries and gardens was now shaggy and unchecked. Piccolo ducked past a mass of brush and followed broken stairs, creeping along an engraved wall, keeping to the shadows until he reached the gallery of columns, sound echoing up to lose itself in the dome above the open-air space.

Time passed. Traffic didn't.

Piccolo felt alertness flood over him as the distinctive clack of a goat drawing a carriage reverberated through the echoing space. He saw the driver come into view, with the two seater carriage sporting a buckboard, drawn by a single heavily-muscled shaggy goat. The driver dismounted and tethered the goat to a post, then cautiously approached, peering into the shadows. He wore a top hat, and he pulled a pistol from the shadows within the heavy fur coat that rounded his shoulders.

Behind him, a cloaked figure struggled out of the carriage, inconvenienced by a hundred or so extra pounds of flesh. Once free of the carriage, the figure smoothed his cloak, and reached back in to pull out an ornate staff. Both headed into the shadows of the deep arcade.

"Well, I'm here," boomed the oratorically-trained voice, racing through the shadows and toppling echoes to spill from all the stone surfaces. "What would you have of me?" His oiled and scented flesh seemed rancid at the end of a long night of worship and effort; the light pained his eyes, and he focused in on the shadows. His bodyguard settled behind him to the right, warily scanning the surroundings, tightly gripping the gun.

"After this I can make up any conversation I want," said a faint, barely audible voice that raced around the shadows, teasing, coming from everywhere and nowhere.

"You wanted to discuss my connection to the Hive," the Hierophant said. "I want to get this over with, I have a busy day."

"You have no idea," the voice almost whispered.

Piccolo sprang from behind a pillar, slapping the bodyguard's wrist to the side, and jamming his shoulder into the base of the guard's ribs, driving out his air. They slammed into a pillar, and Piccolo was ready; his knees flexed as he dragged the bodyguard over him to flip through the air and crash down on the stone. Piccolo knelt on his neck, bone pushing veins and muscle and airways to spread and jostle for position. The bodyguard's eyes bulged as he slapped at Piccolo ineffectually.

The Hierophant pivoted, raising his staff for a mighty blow—a pistol butt cracked against his pate. He staggered, clutching at his head with a pained grunt, and Sanction kicked him in the hip, sending the corpulent priest toppling down. The Hierophant dropped his staff with a clatter.

"Thank you," Piccolo said, snatching the ornate staff, rising to his feet. He slashed with it, and the ornate headpiece tore skin on the bodyguard's face as the staff whacked across his head. Another swing, and the bone gave way with a sickening crunch.

"Look there what you did," Sanction said, towering over the prone priest, his eyes bright and terrible. "And look what he did." Piccolo scooped up the bodyguard's pistol and discharged it right into the priest's bulk. The priest was too shocked to scream.

"W-why?" the Hierophant managed to gasp, halfway to a sob.

Sanction leaned back against a pillar, inscrutable. Piccolo tossed the bodyguard's gun down by his hand as the bodyguard's last gurgle turned to a rattling hiss. The faraway seminary bell tolled once for a death. The shaky breaths of the Hierophant were in lockstep with the ebb and flow of pain as blood drained from the massive puncture in his gut. Footsteps echoed from the shadows, and Zhavo emerged in the faint light.

The Hierophant squinted, bunching the meat on his face in an unflattering wad. "Who—you!" he managed.

"Maybe your god favors you now," Zhavo growled, slowing drawing a long knife. "Maybe all those sacrifices over the years have bought you a miracle."

"You really need a miracle," Sanction observed, neutral.

"My girl, my Sazyana," Zhavo said with an unsteady voice. "You lure her away with talk of cosmic harmonies. With peace. As if such a thing could survive being lowered into this world," he spat. "And you used her. You used them all. Until she started with—with the questions," Zhavo hissed. "Questions I put in her head, trying to get her back. Questions about what the one-ness of flesh could possibly mean. And you sacrificed her."

"Eventually," the Hierophant leered. "Eventually." He managed a sputtering giggle. His hand wrapped around an amulet that hung from his neck. "Should have killed me—"

Zhavo hurled himself at the Hierophant and slashed at his head, then stabbed, again and again, burying the long knife in the twitching gurgling bulk of the priest.

Sanction looked into the shadows of the arcade, and saw a cloaked figure. He approached cautiously. "Mistress of Tides," he said. "Is the body still connected to—something? Else?" he said.

"Yes," she whispered, her hand trembling in front of her, half closed into a fist. Then her eyes flared, and her hand snapped shut into a fist. "No." A bleak smile shifted her features.

The distant seminary bell tolled once more.

Sanction returned his attention to the grunting, stabbing gondolier. He waited. The bloody knife rose and fell, then once more, then a final time. Kneeling, sobbing, Zhavo mourned his daughter.

Sanction made eye contact with Piccolo and offered a head gesture. Piccolo nodded and retreated. The Mistress of Tides was already gone. Sanction lowered himself to a seated position, and time passed as Zhavo's ugly chest-wringing sobs continued. Eventually he quieted.

"Did you find what you sought?" Sanction asked quietly.

"Such—a thing—does not exist," Zhavo managed. "But you gave—me what was promised." He nodded, weary and exhausted.

Sanction rose to his feet, and nodded, then took Zhavo's hand and helped him up.

"When it is time, we will call upon you."

Zhavo nodded, and there was nothing else to say.

The living were long gone by the time the deathseeker crows found the corpses.


## SILKSHORE. THE EASE, FLAG'S END. 8TH ULSIVET. THE FIFTH HOUR

"Sir Belderan of Barrowcleft," the servant said, "and companions." The servant bowed and sidestepped to the door. Trellis strolled in, looking fine in a pressed suit, flanked by Neap and Slack. They were dressed in the sashes and pantsuits of fashionable adepts, sporting a wealth of varied and intriguing jewelry that could have occult purpose.

The aristocrat in the wing chair set his book aside, cocking his head to take in the visitors. "And to what do I owe the pleasure?" he asked, sardonic.

"Lord Skora," Trellis said with a deep bow. "I have come to offer my help with your current research project."

Skora narrowed his eyes. "I hear you are quite the scholar yourself, with your radiant studies."

"You are too kind," Trellis said with a warm smile and a nod. "My interests are of course focused in radiant plant splicing and breeding, but that is not why I have come to you today, and it is not what I offer."

"Enlighten me," Skora said, no trace of amusement in his expression or tone as he studied Trellis.

"The whole of Doskvol mourns your wife's condition," Trellis began.

"Careful," Skora said under his breath, one hand tightening to a fist.

"You have applied your fortune and your intellect to finding some way to protect her from the Slip," Trellis continued, "without success. Because some of the most...interactive materials that we know of are not easily available here in Doskvol." He hesitated. "Or in Akoros, really," he shrugged. "Even for those who have discretion to bend some of the sillier laws."

"Enough of my business," Skora said through his teeth. "What is yours?"

"Doctor Varia comes in from his expedition to Huraal, in the Dagger Isles, tonight," Trellis said. "He will have a train car loaded with specimens, rare ingredients, materials that he has special imperial dispensation to bring in to Doskvol for his exclusive study due to his standing as Lord Physiker of the Imperial Court. Things he won't and can't share with others who could benefit from the rare materials."

"And you are his friend, I suppose?" Skora growled. "You want to put in a good word for me?"

"Not at all," Trellis replied. "I am part of a crew of accomplished thieves. We got the manifest and we want to be your personal shoppers." He produced a neatly folded page from his lapel and handed it to Skora, who took it with some reluctance.

"That's bold," Skora said.

"The best time to hit the train is third hour tomorrow," Trellis said, matter-of-fact. "We don't have a lot of time for games. I am going to hit that shipment, and I want to do it on your behalf. Of course, if you're not interested," he said with an almost imperceptible shrug.

"Slow down," Skora said, brow furrowed as he examined the manifest. "How did you get this?"

"I have contacts, who have contacts. You know how it is. Money, leverage, connections." He offered a vague wave. "Skullduggery. That's the boring part, and I've handled it for you. The question is, do you want in?"

"Tinctures, unguents, salves, powders, crystals, roots," Skora said as he looked over the manifest. "This is a dizzying haul."

"Normal thieves would not even know what was what," Trellis agreed. "Which is where my scholarly background comes in particularly handy, as an expert in radiants. And really, the format is secondary to the properties. How they interact with the Veil, whether they can push or pull. How poisonous they are, and how to mix them to get the benefit without painful death."

"I see you took the liberty of marking the items you know I've been looking for," Skora said. He paused, looking Trellis over. "How long have you been researching me?"

"Just a few weeks," Trellis shrugged. "I've been looking for a way to help you."

"Here it comes," Skova frowned.

"Your family is Old Guard," Trellis said quietly. "I know your particular lineage passes on the secrets of how to navigate the Mistyard catacombs. I need you to take me and one other person through those guarded and haunted passages to get to the First Barrow."

Skova stared at Trellis for a long moment. "You think I know my way through the Mistyard catacombs," he said at last.

"I know you do," Trellis replied, sure.

"That catacomb is off limits to outsiders," Skova began.

"I have permission to enter, I do not need that from you," Trellis shrugged.

"Even assuming that's true, no one knows the layout of the Barrows," Skova said, almost shouting, eyes wide.

"That's not your problem," Trellis said. "I am offering you anything on that train that you want, in exchange for passage through the Mistyard catacombs. It's that simple."

Skova thought for a long moment. "Word came down from the Fairpole Grotto Council, not to have any business dealings with you or your crew. I hear you threatened them. I begin to see the shape of your plan."

"My crew wants to help the gondoliers," Trellis said quietly. "They've been paralyzed by indecision, struck down by illness, invaded by Skovlanders, and they cannot respond." He paused. "Win or lose, my efforts will revitalize the gondolier leadership."

"And your old contacts?" Skova demanded. "I know who you used to work for, I've looked into you as well."

"The Hive is not going to be happy with how this goes," Trellis shrugged. "It's past time to renegotiate some deals."

Skova frowned. "I don't care about any of that," he muttered. "I do care about my wife Phin. I don't think she has long," he said, "and that is a prospect I cannot bear." He looked at the manifest.

"Bring me fresh ferngristlee, the roots will be packed in a skull. Judging by the size of the samples we're looking at, I recommend looking for a long crocodilian skull." He shook his head. "No one can know about this," he warned.

"Tell me about it," Trellis said sardonically. He offered Skova a deep bow, echoed by the adepts, and then they took their leave.

As they headed down the opulent paneled hallway, Trellis chuckled to himself.

"We're going to hit Gaddoc Rail Station."

## NIGHTMARKET. GADDOC RAIL STATION, PLATFORM 9.
## 9ᵀᴴ ULSIVET. THE THIRD HOUR (AFTER DAWN)

The glass globe hung from the ceiling, mounted on a brass stem, refracting the light as it slowly twisted. Below, the metal-clad corridors rebounded all noise, making every sound restless. The crowds shifted as though they were tides pulled by the broken moon. One side of the ample corridor had an Iruvian coffee shop abutted against a basement access to a rug shop, with a watch station built above it. The other side of the corridor had "Employees Only" in four languages on the metal doors, next to a seating area with a ticket counter nested at the back. A handful of Bluecoats stood off to the far side peoplewatching, and a busker bawled out his hoarse routine as he juggled balls and rings.

The stench of plasmic discharge flowed off the catchercage bolted to the front of the mighty engine housed in the bay adjoining Platform 9, but by the time the odor made it out to the corridor it was mixed with coffee, body odor, rust, grease, six kinds of fried food, bleach, and wet stone.

Three harried porters pushed handcarts overloaded with metal boxes, staggering with the weight and balance as they shuffled along as quickly as they could. An Initiate in Spirit Warden regalia strode behind them, shouting orders that could not be heard in the din of the station. One of the handcarts dumped over as they passed the Bluecoats, who laughed and enjoyed the show as the porters tried to drag the cart back upright and fix the metal box on it once more.

As the handcarts approached Platform 9, they stopped to rest in front of the employee only area as a number of Spirit Warden Initiates walked by, their bronze half-masks revealing a their smug amusement at the porters' misfortune. The Initiate shepherding the porters shrugged at them, and they nodded back; porters, right? Ugh.

One of the porters had to sit down, have something to drink, while the Initiate waited impatiently. A few minutes later, the shift change for Platform 9 was complete, and a number of Initiates left Platform 9, splitting up to go their various ways. A group of them walked by the porters and their carts, and the Initiate with the porters waved to them.

"These boxes are to move Dr. Veria's collection. That's today, right?" the Initiate yelled hoarsely.

"This afternoon. You're early, if you can believe it," one of the Initiates replied.

"You there! Produce the orders!" the Initiate yelled at one of the porters, who fumbled at his jumpsuit and pulled out some papers, moving to the light directly over the "employee only" door to better read. Three of the passing Initiates joined him there.

"Those aren't orders," one realized, but by then it was too late.

One porter jammed a knife up under his jaw, sending the Initiate reeling back choking and clawing at the air. The other porters and the fake Initiate rushed the remaining two, ramming them right through the door, tripping over their stabbed companion, out of easy viewing of the crowd. The attack was swift, but before they could know if it was swift enough, they'd have to finish the fight.

A porter slashed at an Initiate, who easily deflected her blow, but was distracted; another porter chopped three knife wounds into the Initiate's lower back, tugging a scream of agony from the victim.

The fake Initiate had a mace shaped like a scepter, and he let it slide down so he gripped the haft down near the pommel. He swept it up and caught an Initiate right in the gut, sending the unfortunate stumbling back; the mace swept around and was parried this time, but the fake Initiate kicked the real one in the side of the knee, and a dull crunch was clearly audible under the scream. The mace swiped at the center of the chest, knocking the Initiate's air out and bouncing the victim off the wall to collapse on the floor, slowly curling and clutching at his chest.

Only then did the scoundrels feel the visceral chime of the seminary bell as the supernatural tower registered the death of the Initiate who had been stabbed in the head. Far away, a deathseeker crow launched to find the victim.

Moving with ruthless efficiency, the "porters" pulled knives and cut the straps holding the bronze masks on the Initiates. The fake Initiate drizzled a little powder between his fingers, down on the faces of the two that were not yet dead; their struggles eased, and they took on a glazed expression, disconnected from their circumstances.

The "porters" lined the three hand carts along the sides of the "employee only" corridor, out of the immediate way and out of sight of the main corridor to Platform 9. Then they joined the fake Initiate in stripping the Initiate uniforms.

"What about this one?" Sanction demanded, pointing at the one with the stab wounds in his back.

"He'll die slow enough it won't show up with the other kill as a cluster, won't attract as much attention," Trellis shrugged, pulling the Initiate mask into place.

"This guy?" Piccolo demanded, brandishing his bloody knife at the winded and trance powdered Initiate.

"He doesn't know anything. Leave him alive, if he doesn't suffocate," Trellis said impatiently. "Let's go!" He clapped his hands impatiently, then blocked the "employee only" door with his back as Piccolo, Sanction, and the Mistress of Tides clambered into the used Initiate uniforms.

The Initiates were dumped into the metal boxes on the hand carts, along with the porter clothes, and the boxes were locked. Then the crew strode out into the corridor as though they ruled all they surveyed. They headed for Platform 9.

"Wait!" the Mistress of Tides called out, clutching at Trellis's arm. She stepped over to the side, and the others surrounded her.

"What is it?" Sanction demanded.

"Your intelligence," the Mistress of Tides said, low and urgent. "Did it mention anything about Dagger Isle Claimed?"

"It did not," Trellis replied. "Are you saying—"

"We can feel each other," the Mistress of Tides clarified. "They have their own ritualist tradition, their own supernatural abilities. This is gonna get bloody," she said through her teeth, and she tilted her head so her vertebrae cracked. She paused. "Unless anybody wants to turn back."

"Let's do it," Sanction said grimly.

# ── Chapter Eleven ──

*We sharpen the knives we find at our throats. Threats may loom in the future always, but the blades that find their way between bones, the ones that introduce the end, are familiar blades we've handled before. Your kin, your friend, your dream; these will bring your end. Don't try to outsmart this truth, but instead accept it. Get as far as you can, then when it's your turn, do your best to meet your end with some class.*

*- Whisper Mortalis, Private Correspondence*

## SILKSHORE. WHIPWATER POINT. 9TH ULSIVET

The carriage ground to a halt at the cross street near the Whipwater Point Seawall Impound. Doors opened, and tough Skovlanders emerged; first Ingvald, then Hutton, then his two bodyguards, and finally Saint. Doors slammed, and the goats pulled the carriage away down the cobbled street as the small group approached the razorwire-crowned gate. A Bluecoat stepped out of his guard house, smiling at them.

"Can I help you?" he asked.

"We just came to finish up some paperwork," Ingvald replied, passing him an envelope and a small bag of coins.

"Oh, very good," the Bluecoat said. "Let me fill out these forms while you inspect your goods."

"Thank you ever so much," Ingvald replied with a wintery smile. The massive gate creaked open, and the Grinders headed in, Saint at their heels.

The Impound was laid out in a series of overlapping massive timber platforms, seasoned against weather and tides. Vast containers added a layer of complexity, and old hand-crank cranes dotted the landscape, surrounded by mounds of what had been evidence at some point in some investigation. Confident, the Grinders headed down the path between stacked cargo, following the turns, headed towards the central platform of the Impound. They kept the massive seawall to their left.

Rounding a wall of stacked barrels, they came to a clearing where a coach had been parked diagonally, no animal hitched to its bulk. Captain Hutch, leader of the Gray Cloaks, hunched inside. One of his bodyguards stood by the door, the other sat up on the buckboard, keeping an alert lookout for threats.

"Good morning," Ingvald said conversationally. "So glad you could make it."

"I'm always up for hearing Skovs grovel for peace, all things considered," Hutch sniffed. "And there's Saint! I heard one of the River Stallions got away." He shared an unpleasant laugh with his guards. "I do love tidying up loose ends."

"But you came to parlay," Ingvald reminded him, cocking an eyebrow. "You don't get to murder our guest as we negotiate peace."

"Unless that's part of the terms, of course," Hutch shrugged, still somewhat masked by the shadows in the coach. "But let's be honest. Skovs don't understand peace. They don't understand treaties. They just fight, and claw, and scrabble, until you've put a heavy enough boot on their neck." His smile widened. "Just like in the homeland, am I right?" he sneered.

"If you believe that, why come here today?" Ingvald demanded, still playing along. Hutton scanned the sea wall, and saw the pounce wolf trainer's head pop up for just a moment.

"The same reason you came, I wager," Hutch replied as he narrowed his eyes. "We both want to see to it that our rivals are decapitated."

"Looks to me like you're outnumbered," Ingvald growled, glancing over the two Gray Cloak bodyguards.

Then a Skov guard snatched at the hatchet on his belt, and chaos erupted.

## SILKSHORE. BARKSKIN TAVERN ADJACENT BASEMENT. 56ᵀᴴ SURAN.
### (THIRTEEN DAYS AGO)

"History time," Saint said to the assembled River Stallions. "Here is the Whipwater Point Seawall," he continued, drawing a curved line with chalk on the stone wall. "Here's the shore," he added, drawing more or less perpendicular to it. "Why stop at blunting the force of the ocean's bluster when it threatens your port? Instead, that wasted space was put to good use," he said, drawing a quay area out along the land, continuing along much of the wall. "Now you could nuzzle your ship alongside to tie up here. But that's not terribly safe, being on the wrong side of the seawall." He began sketching in the area on the lee of the seawall, by the curve of the coast.

"That's when the city engineers put in a series of platforms on the other side of the wall," the Hammer continued helpfully. "The idea was that small boats could go under the platforms, which would open trapdoors and use small cranes to help unload the boats, then put the goods on these roller tracks that had doors so they could go through the sea wall, right out to where the sea-worthy craft waited."

"Sounds very lucrative," Saint said to the Hammer.

"Indeed," the Hammer nodded sagely. "Too profitable to leave alone."

"So who had this sweet setup," Safety demanded, containing his impatience.

"Lord Bytain, actually," Saint replied. "And his use of this customs point for loading and unloading was protected by an Imperial charter, which irritated the stevedores and the gondoliers to no end." Saint regarded his diagram. "Lord Bytain used his own workers to move cargo, and kept all the profits for himself. So it was no surprise when Lord Bytain's flagship, the Golden Aura, got its engines crosswise and had a massive explosion that sunk it and took out much of the quay." He slashed a line across the quay. "But what to do with the platforms on the other side?" he asked reflectively. "Hammer?"

"The Bluecoats inherited it," continued the Hammer. "Its limited access points to the rest of the city made it a good spot to store a large amount of material where it was more secure than in most warehouses and so forth. A combination of wide-open spaces and no history of prior ownership by various city factions made it attractive as a spot for keeping contraband."

"But wouldn't various rogues use the trapdoors to go up into the platform and steal valuables?" Saint asked.

"Well, the trapdoors were all sealed, but naturally some rogues can work around that," the Hammer replied. "More effective was a combination of tactics. The Fairpole Grotto Gondolier Council was engaged so the gondoliers would offer a level of protection, discouraging people from bringing boats over here and forbidding their own from that kind of heist. Second, Bluecoats mostly store high bulk low value items that are more trouble than they're worth to steal. Third, the inventory organization is poor; you have to find something valuable to steal it, and you may not have the time, as the Point is patrolled. Fourth, everybody needs in at some point or another, so it's an ongoing moneymaker for the Bluecoats as various crews offer bribes. And fifth, they wrapped the whole thing in hundreds of miles of razorwire. Sure, you can get through it, but it takes time and makes every part of the operation harder."

"The real advantage here is that not many crews have put much thought into Whipwater Point," Saint added, "and if they have their focus was on theft and not battle."

"What's our focus?" Safety asked.

Saint looked him in the eye. "We're going to burn it down."

## SILKSHORE. WHIPWATER POINT. 9ᵀᴴ ULSIVET

The Gray Cloak on the buckboard of the carriage was just raising the barrel of his rifle to fire as the Skov tugged his hatchet out and hurled it in a smooth, practiced motion. The hatchet whacked into the Gray Cloak with enough force to carry him off the carriage, his rifle discharging into the air. Meanwhile the other bodyguard pushed Ingvald back by Saint, and took up a position in front of Hutton. The axe-thrower flung a knife with an underhand flick of the wrist before charging the coach.

Hutch's bodyguard managed to get a shot off with his pistol, and it narrowly missed the charging Skov; the hurled knife smacked into the bodyguard's upper leg, and his reaction was too slow as the Skov's rush slammed him against the wall of the carriage with a knife in his chest.

Keen survival instincts galvanized Hutch to open the far door of the carriage and spring out on the other side, pivoting with a pistol in one hand as he drew his blade with the other. "Now!" The Gray Cloak commander cried, and a pile of impounded goods that bounded the clearing burst, the hull that had hidden inside lunging out in a show of depthless might.

The first seminary bell reverberated through the Veil as the guard with the hatchet in his chest expired.

Ingvald lowered his center of gravity with a wide stance; "This is our opportunity, my chieftain," he growled in his native tongue. Then Saint's knife jammed in between his ribs, and Saint's fist snatched his collar, pulling him back and up, cloth tight around his throat as the blade sunk deep and true.

For just a moment, Saint and Hutton made eye contact, and many of Hutton's questions were answered.

The Skov bodyguard shoved Hutton aside, and the two big men sprinted for cover as Ingvald gurgled in startlement and rage, eyes bulging.

The hull crashed through the carriage, and the Veil resonated with another tolling bell as the injured Gray Cloak perished; the attacking Skov managed to hurl himself back so his injuries were relatively minor, but the hull was now revealed in its awful majesty as it blasted a gout of steam and hunched over them.

The shoulders were fashioned to resemble gondola prows, and its massive helm was reminiscent of the lantern cages that hung from the prows. The body itself had similar trim to the fancier gondolas, and the forearms and shins were designed to shift position. The massive hull sported bladed appendages, like claws, and profound strength. Slats opened over the armored core, and electroplasmic light beamed forth as a high-pitched squeal climaxed. Projector nodes on the shoulders and hips flared, and a swirling curtain of energy surrounded the war machine.

Saint twisted his blade and yanked it out of Ingvald, who convulsed as he fell. Pivoting, Saint sprinted for cover, haunted by another reverberating bell.

The light show was the signal for Inkletta, after all.

## CROW'S FOOT. TANGLETOWN, VARIOUS STREET. 6ᵀᴴ ULSIVET. (THREE DAYS AGO)

Inkletta's eyes roved the spiritbane charms, the demonbane charms, the wards and protections. She entered the store, cutting through the haze of incense, observing the various candles, taking it all in.

The young man behind the counter glanced up at her approach, then paused to examine her. "Greetings," he said. He had a number of occult tattoos on his face.

She looked him in the eye. "Why do you have the Basic Five Precepts marked on your face?" she asked, blunt.

"I was once a poor student, and I lack the talent to ever be more," he replied. "Who are you?"

"Inkletta," she said. "I understand you've got pre-made rituals here."

"Maybe," he shrugged. He glanced at the six spiritbane charms worked into the doorframe behind him. "Can you?"

She tilted her jaw just slightly, and snapped all six to attune to her presence on both sides of the Veil. They all clicked, glowing slightly.

"That'll do it," the young man said respectfully. "Please, come back."

She followed him through the curtain to the cramped quarters in the back of the shop. He turned to face her. "Anything in particular?"

"Leviathan's Shrug," she murmured, eyes traveling the shelves. "I need to simulate a breach. I need a wave."

"That's a fairly popular ritual among those on the hunting ships," the young man nodded. "Also smugglers." He glanced at her. "I don't get either vibe from you."

She looked him in the eye. "You want to carry my secrets?" she asked.

He looked down. "No." Glancing to the side, he stepped away from her. "This glass orb. Within, a space to fill with leviathan blood, and then you'll need to add an egg within that. There are anchoring sigils to chalk in place, usually on buoys, or fired out on arrowheads at the same time, to define the area."

"You have documentation?"

"Oh yes." He looked up at her once more. "These materials aren't cheap, of course."

For the first time, she smiled.

## SILKSHORE. WHIPWATER POINT. 9TH ULSIVET

Four longboats were secured to the pylons beneath strategic points under the Impound. The razor wire had been cleared away enough for them to tie up, and as the screaming resounded and chiming of distant bells tolled, Gray Cloaks climbed up the pylons, preparing to shove the trapdoors open and engage the Grinders.

The water level dipped suddenly, dropping half a dozen feet; compacted, it rushed upward, as though something far below was charging the surface. The boats carried the Gray Cloaks right up to the underside of the boardwalk, smashing apart, the merciless water driving up inexorably to spray between the boards in tall, shimmering barriers; any survivors of the pressure were ground against the razorwire.

An entire carillon of bells rippled in the Veil, a surreal and directionless noise as pressured water gushed up and turned to mist, the floorboards creaking and splintering, some pylons giving way.

A rainbow of lethal energy snarled and twisted as the pressurized water blasted across the hull's energy shielding, the multi-directional pressure overloading it; with a crackle, the system shut down, and the torso slats snapped shut. The hull took three steps towards cover when the boards buckled upward, a jet of water pounding into the hull. It was too heavy to be propelled upward, and it flailed at the wooden supports as the water receded as fast as it had risen, dragging the hull down through the busted floorboards.

From where he clung to a slightly tilted pylon, Hutton could see Saint. Hutton jerked his head to the side so his soaked hair flicked out of the way, and he pointed at Saint. "You think you can kill Ingvald?" he roared. "This is war!"

Across the Impound, on a higher platform, a number of cargo containers had been impounded the day before. As the water swirled against the pylons and drained back down, Skovs opened the hiding places and cautiously ventured out to see the situation.

Saint hunkered down low behind cover, squinting, and Hutton copied his example without understanding why.

The Skov strike force raced down the ramp towards the soaked and crooked platforms, ignoring the creak of the overstressed wood and the lack of obvious targets.

Then the explosion tore them apart.

Bells, bells, bells.


## SILKSHORE. WHIPWATER POINT. 7ᵀᴴ ULSIVET.
### (TWO DAYS AGO)

"So what is all this, anyway?" the Bluecoat frowned, looking at the wagon.

"Oh, just shipping the pieces home to Severos," Gapjaw shrugged. "You know, the pieces that maybe she doesn't want to share with customs," he said, eyebrows high as he nodded to the Bluecoat.

"Ah," the Bluecoat said. "Don't fret, we'll look after her shipment. Such a shame; she's lovely to be widowed so young." He shook his head. "Mighty upstanding of her to throw such an event for the whole guardhouse. The rest of the city could learn something from her generosity."

"Indeed," Gapjaw agreed, passing him a small bag of coin. "She's loading these on the 9th, but you don't mind if I arrange them so they're out of the sun, do you? Just... because," he shrugged.

"How many coffins do you have here?" the Bluecoat asked, peering at the two wagons.

"Eighteen. The family had hard times here, but we all wish there was more to take home sometimes," he said, "if you take my meaning." His grin was wide.

The Bluecoat nodded. "Take your time," he said. "On you go."

With that, Gapjaw drove one wagon into the Impound, and the

Hammer drove the other. The great gates slid shut behind them, and they immediately headed for the fault line between the highest ground and the rest of the impound.

The wagons pulled to a halt, and Gapjaw slid down as the Hammer pulled the folded parchment from his pocket, opening up the diagram.

"This is going to take all night," he grimaced, looking at the "x" placements. "Where did you even get this much explosive?"

"Leechcore Avenue," Gapjaw replied. "I've got friends there. Short on fingers, common sense, and eardrums, but they love to make things go boom," he shrugged. "They always have a supply of 'waste material' that doesn't blow up fast enough for portable bombs."

The Hammer stared at him for a long moment. "It cannot have been pleasant harvesting that flammable and explosive material for a load this big," he murmured.

"Oh, but it will be worth it," Gapjaw said, showcasing his smile in spite of its missing teeth.

"Think so?" the Hammer said, skeptical.

Gapjaw planted his fists on his hips, taking in the darkened scenery. "Trust me," he muttered. "It's going to be spectacular."


## SILKSHORE. WHIPWATER POINT. 9TH ULSIVET

With a ripple of dull cracks and snaps, the last connecting tissue gave way, and the upper platform collapsed. It tore down towards the water, undercutting the platform next to it; as the neighboring platform buckled under the strain, it bowed along its length splintering in a messy line, sending impounded goods flying everywhere as the added torsion dragged it away from the coast. In moments, the entire interconnected structure of the Impound shuddered, compromised.

Hutton and his bodyguard clung to a cluster of pylons as the skirt beside them tore off, crunching into the structure abutting the seawall. To one side, churning and frothing water, leaden in the morning light, filled with obstructions and unpredictable currents. To the other side, the wavering dissolution of the Impound.

Meanwhile Saint scrambled to the edge of the Impound, along

the seawall. He hauled open one of the old hatches that the rolling tracks used to use for moving cargo through the wall. Then he tossed in a bundle of pipe bombs, and recoiled as far as he safely could. With an explosion, the channel through the wall was widened sufficiently for him to fit through.

Saint scrambled through the broken stone, ignoring the shallow cuts and bruises he collected along the way. As he shouldered through the gap on the far side of the stone wall, a shadow flicked overhead. He squinted up to see three of the pouncer wolves gliding down, picking up speed.

A gun report, and one of them twirled in midair, going strangely slack as a long ribbon of blood streaked away from its chest. The other two course corrected, pulling up, scanning for the threat.

As they did, another winged shape swooped around the seawall, coming in low and tight, battering into the back of a pouncer wolf. The surprised wolf adjusted its wings, but the attacker was too persistent, and wouldn't be shaken; the attacking bat launched off the unbalanced pouncer right before the airborne wolf flew into a post, rebounding with a meaty crack.

On the seawall, the pouncer trainer stood up and blew a whistle briefly, before another gunshot rang out and sent him flying back off the wall; another chime trembled the Veil.

The last of the pouncers oriented on Saint, and dove into a monstrous signature attack that few mortals could survive. Another gunshot, and the pouncer was driven off course by the impact, rebounding from the unforgiving paving of the broken quay with pulping force. With a scrabble, it slid off the broken stone and fell into the restless inky sea.

"Let's go!" Safety yelled, seated on the narrow carriage that he had carefully navigated out on the broken quay and turned around. Saint ran over and scrambled in, and Safety flicked the reins so the goat sprang ahead, dragging the fishtailing wagon along the ribbon of stone that was still somewhat secure.

"Where are they?" Saint yelled.

"Under the seat!" Safety shouted. Moments later Saint had the canvas sack in his hands.

As they closed in on the end of the quay and the entry back into the twisting labyrinth of the city and its safety, a few proactive Bluecoats ran to stop them at the land side of the sea wall.

Safety snapped the reins, and the furious goat needed no further encouragement; the Bluecoats wisely leaped out of the way, and the carriage barreled past them.

"Don't you do it!" Safety bawled out. "They can't catch us! Don't waste it!"

Saint looked at his back, a smile tugging at his features. Then he looked backwards along their path, and did not see Bluecoats. He stowed the sack of caltrops under the seat, and finally allowed himself to breathe easier.

Far behind them, a profound wrenching crackle broke the last load-bearing pylons, tearing the central platform down so it collapsed into the flaming, frothing wreck piled along the seawall.

## SILKSHORE. BARKSKIN TAVERN ADJACENT BASEMENT. 8TH ULSIVET.
### (YESTERDAY)

"I squeezed my snitch," the Hammer said, leaning back in the half-broken chair.

"Oh," Red Silver replied, not looking up from where she was cleaning her rifle.

"He said that the Gray Cloaks will have their people on boats, under the platform, as we expected."

"That's good," Red Silver replied, attention absorbed.

The Hammer paused. "Where's Saint?" he asked.

"Saint is with the Grinders," she replied. "They used my influence to get permission from the Bluecoats to have a private Skovlander funeral with flaming boats for some of their warriors they just lost, from the privacy of the Impound. Basically two thirds of those who go in will stay, hidden, at the top platform. The rest will leave, but that way they've got people in place for the assault tomorrow." She blew a bit of debris out of the sighting mechanism.

"Any word on the hull? Where they might stash it? My snitch didn't know," the Hammer shrugged.

"Hardly matters," Red Silver said absently. "It will emerge, and it is up to Inkletta to deal with it." She shrugged. "Or I do what I can from the rooftop. Or we just avoid it until we have what we need."

"You seem pretty calm," the Hammer observed, looking her over.

"Killing fools is the easiest part of this gig," she shrugged. Then she flicked the linen cloth over her gun, and rose to stretch. "Good luck with your part," she said.

"Don't you worry about my part," the Hammer replied with a crooked grin. "I've got Gapjaw to cover my back. Should go smooth."

She shook her head, just slightly, then hefted her rifle.

"I hope so," she said quietly.

## SILKSHORE. BOLDWAY CANAL STREET BRIDGE PILING. 9ᵀᴴ ULSIVET

Gapjaw heard the fumbling of the key in the lock, and he smiled from where he stood in deep shadow. The door swung open, and a couple men staggered in, unsteady. One hissed at the other, pointing. A dead Gray Cloak had been dragged to the side, out of the way. Both the men drew pistols, peering into the shadows, their eyes ruined by light from the lamp post outside.

"Let's go," one whispered, and they continued into the shadow far enough to pick up hand lamps; Gapjaw shrank behind a pillar, waiting for them to move along. Sure enough they did, and they found where two more guards had met a sudden and messy end in the hallway. The two Gray Cloaks continued as though they were the hunters, and Gapjaw eased out of hiding to ghost along behind them. The good part was coming up.

The returning Gray Cloaks saw the reinforced door ahead was hanging half open, and there was light beyond. One commanded the other to check it out, and he did; peering in, he paused, then retreated.

"There's a man in there sitting at the table," he growled to the other man.

"Who is it?" the other man hissed back.

"I think it is one of the River Stallions."

"Breath and bone," the other man swore. "Alright. I'll handle this. Cover the rear."

Gapjaw was out of the way as the weak palm light swept the back trail, but he was in easy charge range. He just listened as the bolder of the Gray Cloaks pushed the door open and entered their planning chamber.

"Good evening," the Hammer said to the Gray Cloak. "Good to see you face to face at last, Captain Hutch." He regarded his pistol. "I knew you'd make it back."

"You're awfully relaxed for a man who broke into my base and killed my men," Hutch said through his teeth.

"That's because I have the upper hand," the Hammer said. He rose to his feet, crossing the room to an alcove, and he tugged the curtain down. A short man with pale features and a broad forehead scowled at him, bound and gagged, strapped to a ladder that was leaned against the wall. "See?" the Hammer said, gesturing to his captive.

"No, what is this supposed to mean to me?" Captain Hutch snapped.

"This is Marsden," the Hammer said. "He is a spy, he works for the Hive, and he's your contact directing your moves from behind the scenes. In exchange, he protects your operation, and your position in it, or some nonsense like that," the Hammer shrugged. "I didn't really want answers enough to interrogate him in earnest."

"I guess that's one theory," Captain Hutch said, pale.

"Oh, I knew it before I came here," the Hammer retorted. "I had a snitch in your outfit. I just wanted to know how you were planning to screw over the Grinders, but he wanted to buy his freedom with one last secret, and it was a doozy." The Hammer shook his head. "Maybe your people weren't supposed to know you sold out to the Hive, but some of them did, and more suspected."

"So what now? You want in? Is that it?" Hutch sneered.

"It's like you don't even know me," the Hammer sighed, pulling his knife and turning to Marsden.

"I don't," Hutch replied, raising his pistol, "but if you cut that man you're dead."

"Relax," the Hammer said, his back to Hutch. "I'm going to cut off his gag." He moved slowly, deliberately, and cut the gag. With some effort, Marsden pushed the gag out of his mouth, stretching his face almost comically.

"What do you want," Marsden said, as soon as he could talk.

"I like your priorities," the Hammer admitted. "Focus on what I want; I like that. Me, on the other hand, I just want to be clear. Crystal clear. Unmistakable," he shrugged, looking Marsden in the eye. The spy said nothing.

"So be clear," Hutch said loudly.

"I speak for the River Stallions in this," the Hammer said, easing back down into a chair, gun in one hand and knife in the other. "We don't want the Hive increasing its presence in Silkshore."

"You want a cut, is that it?" Marsden asked, cautious.

"I'm not clear yet, apparently," the Hammer sighed. He looked over at Hutch, then leveled his pistol at him. Hutch quickly pointed his pistol at the Hammer in return.

A wet crunch echoed in the darkness of the corridor, and Hutch glanced back—

The Hammer pulled the trigger, and the pistol roared in the confined space, gusting smoke. The bullet caught Hutch right under the cheekbone, blasting half his head to jelly as his body was forcibly hurled against the doorframe to rebound and clatter to the floor.

Two bells tolled, each one unspeakably lonely in the Veil.

"Sorry, got bored," Gaptooth said with a wide grin as he loomed into view in the doorway. "Does Marsden get it?" He looked at the prisoner. "Do we need to write a note for you to take home to your masters?" His smile was ugly.

The Hammer looked Marsden in the eye. "Convince me you'll be more persuasive and clear in getting the Hive to back off than a note, and I'll let you do the talking instead of your corpse." He paused. "You won't get a better offer."

"I can carry the message," Marsden shrugged. "But I have to ask, do you think you can contain the influx of Skovs without the Hive's influence? We're working the bigger picture, you don't want to disadvantage your piece because it's isolated, do you?"

"We are absolutely willing to give up that advantage," the Hammer said. "We don't need it to win, and we won't bend the knee to your sort anywhere; not back in Skovlan, and sure as hell not here."

"I want to be clear, like you," Marsden said. "You are doing your best to make the Hive your enemy." He paused. "You don't really want to do that, do you?"

"That is certainly one way to look at it," the Hammer conceded. "Try this one on: the Hive has a chance not to make enemies of the River Stallions." He nodded curtly. "How about that?"

"Wow," Marsden said, shaking his head, "that's bold alright. I feel like you might act differently if you understood the scope of our involvement—"

The Hammer's pistol roared, blasting into Marsden's face, killing him instantly as a tolling bell filtered into the end of the gun's smoking report.

For a moment, all was silent.

"I feel like we can do this with a really strongly worded note," Gapjaw agreed.

"Maybe," the Hammer said, rubbing his mouth. "But I feel like this is going to get a lot worse before it gets better."

For a long moment it was quiet, the gun discharge slowly drifting in the air.

"I guess we better get started loading all the Gray Cloak supplies and wealth into the longboat," Gapjaw said at last.

The Hammer felt himself smile, and a tension eased. "This is one hell of a score," he agreed. He hauled himself to his feet, looking around. "Want to bet Captain Hutch has the key to the treasure room?"

Of course he did.

# ━━ CHAPTER TWELVE ━━

*Building a train network between major cities cost two centuries of resources. The process of laying out routes, handling the surveying, bringing materials to the sites, protecting workers and machines, and eventually creating a route that was impervious to weather and attack was a superhuman feat. In every way, the rail system protected the needs of the living against the weight of the past and its lusts.*

*Politics, debts, and feuds threatened the project as much as tides of ghosts and poison sands. Only the Immortal Emperor's resolute will and unfailing focus could provide the lighthouse beacon that united the builders enough to create the impossible. Because of that Imperial focus and mandate, those who would build tread over the corpses of those who would not. The rail line reshaped the aristocracy of the empire, weeding out those who openly defied the Immortal Emperor. Of course, that was almost four centuries ago. It's past time for the Immortal Emperor to choose a new project.*

*- From "Cost Uncounted: Leadership After the Crisis" by*
*Professor Claire Redalia*

"Well how many are there?" Trellis demanded, his teeth visible under the Initiate half-mask.

"Three," the Mistress of Tides replied. "The Dagger Isle Claimed are preparing for us now."

"Right," Trellis growled. "Mistress of Tides, you hold their attention. Piccolo, hit them where they aren't. Sanction, you stay with me no matter what; we're getting into that train car and getting our prize. Right?"

"That's what we'd do if we didn't have a plan," Piccolo observed.

"Get on with it," Trellis snapped, gesturing at him.

Still disguised as Spirit Warden Initiates, the four rogues approached the entry to Platform Nine. It was closed and locked, two Initiates standing guard.

"What's your—" one started to say, but Piccolo pounced and drove his dagger into the Initiate's throat. They clattered back as the other Initiate, startled, dragged his pistol from its holster.

The rogues were too close, it was too late. Sanction was on him at once, snatching his forearm and pressing it to his chest, bodily hurling the Initiate back against the pillar. As one death registered with a doleful chime in the Ghost Field, Sanction drove his forehead into the brassy mask of the Initiate, smashing the other mask crooked; that much harder to resist. Leaning back unexpectedly, he tugged on the Initiate's arm, pivoting the startled unfortunate, and thrust him forward into the pillar as the gun was wrung from his nerveless grasp.

Piccolo jammed his knife into the side of the Initiate's neck, sending a shiver through his whole frame; a moment later another tolling of the spirit bell resonated, and they heard the bootfalls of approaching reinforcements.

"Change of plan!" Sanction hissed. "I'll deflect them; get in there!"

"No time," Trellis said shortly, snatching his arm and dragging him past the gate the Initiates guarded. Leaving the corpses, they ran thirty feet towards where the hulking mass of the engine quietly seethed, motionless but still connected to the cars it drew to Doskvol.

The Mistress of Tides stretched her hand forth towards the vast engine, and felt its fuel and pressures, pent up for use. Narrowing her eyes, she closed her hand to a fist, and pressure surged in the steam chamber, bursting gaskets and sending plumes of steam out the sides between wheels—enough to blanket the platform. Piccolo ran alongside the train, while Sanction and Trellis swarmed up the ladder on the side of the engine, the better to move along the roof.

Instead of moving out, the Mistress of Tides stood before the engine and turned, watching the entry. She drew her Initiate mask off, and tossed it disdainfully to the side as she raised the delicate filigree bone and shell spirit mask to cover her features. Enemies approached.

In the lead, a Dagger Isles Claimed dressed in a tail coat with waxen lapels, pages of mystical texts pressed and sealed to the cloth. He was crowned by a top hat that also had pages waxed and sealed to it, along with brim decorations made of scrimshaw bones, and a glory of gray mane flowed out over his shoulders. He moved with confidence, even though he was barefoot, and he brandished a short spear that was half blade with a long haft. He had a full-fledged Spirit Warden at his side, and a handful of imperial soldiers behind them.

The Claimed twirled his spear with a curt nod, and the Mistress of Tides flexed her hands forward, sending the steam roiling all around her gushing at the newcomers. It flowed around them, and the soldiers looked down in sudden horror. The steam blew away the illusion, and their new reality was that they were hanging over an endless abyss; something in them began to fall, and their consciousness flickered out under the strain. The soldiers toppled over.

Wasting no time, the Claimed tugged the spear down through one hand's grip, cutting his palm. He waved violently towards the Mistress of Tides. Where the blood droplets fell, they became holes, and tiny venomous snakes squirmed up out of the floor, closing in on her as the Claimed's trembling hand helped him focus on controlling them.

Even as a dozen tiny snakes oozed up into the real side of the Mirror, the Mistress of Tides prepared a counter; drawing her pistol forth, she lined it up and pulled the trigger as the Claimed realized his danger. Her aim was true, the bullet smashing into his face and hurling him back, shattered.

The Mistress of Tides withdrew into the steam, and the Spirit Warden dashed in after her.

Meanwhile, Trellis and Sanction scrambled the length of the engine roof, leaped down on the contained fuel car as a shot rang out from the front of the train, and clambered onto the heavily armored specimen car as two soldiers guarding the roof hatch frowned at them.

"Who goes!" one shouted.

"Wardens!" Sanction replied. "Here to make sure the lock is good!"

"The hell you are," the other soldier retorted as Sanction and Trellis jogged towards them. He raised his pistol. "Stop where you are!"

Sanction and Trellis stopped, and Sanction crossed his arms over his chest. "Name and number, right now," he said coldly.

"I believe you to be an intruder, and do not comply with your request!" the soldier shouted.

"I'll be sure to note that in my report," Sanction snapped. "Now, name and number, mister!" He cocked his head to the side. "Or pull the goddamn trigger, if you're so sure."

The soldier's confidence wavered, and the gun barrel lowered. Sanction glanced at Trellis, and the two men approached the soldiers.

Close enough for the blood stains on their armor to shine in the sideways lights of the station.

The soldier's eyes widened, the gun barrel swept up—

With a crack, the hold-out pistol in Trellis's hand snapped a shot into the soldier's forehead, a distressingly neat round hole. The soldier staggered, taking a step back, gun discharging into the traincar roof as Sanction sprang at the other soldier.

The pistol fired, slamming into Sanction's angled chest as he reached for the shooter. The force drove him back to slap down on the train roof, and Trellis squeezed at his hold-out pistol again. It fired its second shot, catching the soldier somewhere in the side of the neck. The target staggered back, slapping at his neck, and he gracelessly fell as a chime tolled in the Ghost Field. Trellis took a few steps and slammed a savage kick into the injured soldier, who slid to the side and rolled off the top of the car with a yelp, dropping into the mist and thudding on the ground. Trellis turned to Sanction.

"Well?" he demanded.

"I'll live," Sanction said, hoarse as he snapped the strap that held the ruined chestplate on. Shrugging the armor off, he coughed. Then he took Trellis's offered hand, levering himself up. "Let's get in here," he said, eyeing the armored roof access to the train car.

Piccolo absent-mindedly twirled the stiletto in his gloved grip, peering through the mist with his goggles. They were tuned to pick out anything living in the artificial fog. His step was silent as he followed the flank of the train, spotting two guards up ahead by the door to the armored traincar.

He squatted, considering the level of paranoia the two soldiers would have, how the interplay of fear and exhaustion would work out, how careful he had to be. Then he hesitated, stiffening, his trust in his instincts absolute. He uncoiled to the side, noiselessly rolling and pivoting to rise in the steam, stiletto in hand. The steam behind him roiled under the sweep of an intangible blade; he saw the flickers of life in his goggles, and his free hand clutched at his spirit charm, snapping his perceptions into its frequency, willing it to life.

Not a ghost, but a Dagger Isles Claimed, discorporated to blend with the mist! The ritualist brandished a blade made of an impossibly thin fold in the Mirror, capable of cutting through anything. Piccolo brandished his spirit bane charm, and it did push at the incorporeal energies comprising the Claimed in his altered form. Piccolo lunged, slashing with his knife, possibly tracing cuts on the not-fully-formed shape of the ritualist.

The unreal blade thrust at him, and Piccolo sidestepped, whipping his face forward and counting on the attunement of his goggles to possibly draw the intangible space together with his life force. He felt a snap, and a single crack raced down one lens, but the ghostly figure staggered back in the mist.

Piccolo jabbed his knife forward repeatedly, gripping his spirit bane charm and trying to focus on the flickering outline of the ritualist, using his perceptions to pull the elusive Claimed and his ruthless blade into the same plane. Then he paused, breathing as soundlessly as he could through his slack open mouth, staring around. His foe was dead, or driven away. Enough for now.

He nodded to himself, and stealthed towards the door guards.

## SILKSHORE. RIVER STALLIONS TOWER. 8 SURAN, 845.
### (TWO YEARS AGO)

"I brought you a signing bonus," Inkletta said with a wry smile.

"I thought the ink was the signing bonus," Piccolo replied, touching at his arm's new tattoo.

"This is enchanted gear, for real, little man," Inkletta replied. "Look here." She swept her arm out, unfurling a night-black fabric that made no friction noise and gave back no light. "It's an Iruvian silk shadow cloak, just the thing for a brand new lurk in Silkshore." Her smile widened.

"Sweet!" Piccolo yelled, pulling it on. "I'm gonna sleep in this thing!"

"Now, hang on," Inkletta said. "I'll warn you right now, don't let the supernatural drive your tactics. The basics are strongest. Save this sort of things for special occasions. Same with those goggles Saint gave you, and those bottles you got at the leech's table during your 'welcome to crime' pub crawl."

"So... why?" Piccolo asked, just his nose and mouth visible in the shadow of his new hood.

She cocked her head. "You never know when you'll lose gear. But you do know that you'll be called to go above and beyond what you can do, over and over. Work on raising your baseline. Save this stuff," she said, gently slugging his cloaked shoulder, "for when you have to go above and beyond."

"Special occasions. Got it," Piccolo grinned. "Now, a serious question. Is it magic?"

Inkletta rolled her eyes. "Sure it's magic," she said, and she left him to it.

Piccolo tugged the fabric around himself, and very nearly disappeared.

## NIGHTMARKET. GADDOC RAIL STATION, PLATFORM 9.
### 9TH ULSIVET

"Hurry," Trellis hissed at Sanction.

"You probably think this is easy," Sanction muttered, then he abandoned the lockpicks. "We knew the locks would probably be too tough for this nonsense," he said, pulling a vial of acid from his belt pouch, pouring it over the keyhole.

Trellis looked up and down the roof of the train. It was a clear corridor, a long island in a sea of mist. "We're too exposed up here," he muttered.

"Did you reload your tiny gun?" Sanction demanded through his teeth.

Exasperated, Trellis popped the small gun's breach open, ejecting the two spent casings. By the time he reloaded, Sanction hauled up on the door, and it opened reluctantly with a screech.

"What was that?" came a voice down by the side door to the train, the other side from where the body fell.

Without further precaution, Sanction pivoted around, gripping the edge of the hole, and dropped into the humid stench of the specimen car.

It was jam packed, but the odd shape of the reinforced shelving and the masses of greenery confused the eye as to what else might be in the train car.

"Well?" Trellis whispered urgently, his head a silhouette in the roof hatch.

Sanction turned, squinting up. "Just give me—" he began, and something hit him with great force from behind, sending him flying out of view.

Trellis leaped up to his feet, and drew the full-size pistol from its holster, pointing it at the hole.

Below, something growled, and Trellis felt his blood freeze.

One of the soldiers by the side door struggled to unlock it while the other soldier looked around warily, pistol out. Piccolo crept along the side of the car, approaching them, able to see them through his goggles though they could not see him in the mist. He paused, seeing the figure of a spirit warden further out in the mist. Grinning, he palmed a throwing knife, gauged the toss, and hurled it. The knife thudded into the Spirit Warden's shoulder, and with a gasp, the Warden pivoted towards the train car, pistol raised.

"Did you hear that?" one soldier demanded of the other.

"Desist your doings!" the Spirit Warden shouted. "I deny you access! That car is the property of the Immortal Emperor!"

"Yes, and we guard it!" retorted one of the solders. "Better come in closer," he added, a threat in his tone.

"So you can throw another knife at me?" the Warden demanded.

"We did no such thing," retorted the soldier. "We'd shoot you, if it came to that."

Grinning, Piccolo silently drew another knife, and fired it off at the Warden, hitting him in the leg. The Warden swore passionately, gun wavering as it pointed towards the train, jerking back and forth.

"Another knife!" the Warden snapped. "Enough!" He flexed down, a string of spirit bane charms glittering along where they were stitched into the chestplate of his uniform, and the mist blew away.

The two soldiers looked at the magnificence of the Spirit Warden where he stood in the cleared air, eyes wide.

"Sorry sir," one said. "We got no knives, as you see," he added, gesturing at his outfit.

"Life is—there," the Spirit Warden muttered, flexing his fist towards where Piccolo lurked.

Piccolo was yanked out of the mist, a plume in his wake as though he was a comet. He felt the grip of the Spirit Warden on his shoulders and lower back, but his arms were free enough. He squeezed the trigger, blasting a shot into the Warden's foot.

The Warden swore, and Piccolo was suddenly released. He bounced up in a wheel kick that slammed into the back of the doubled-over Warden's neck, knocking him down even as warding defenses jolted pain up his leg.

"Halt!" one of the soldiers cried out, leveling his rifle at Piccolo. The scoundrel ignored him, dropping to one knee and snatching the Warden's boot, jamming his knife up into the back of the Warden's knee. He rebounded away from the injured Warden as a plasmic defense crackled, and white-hot runes were momentarily visible stitched across the Warden's back.

"I've got this," the Warden snarled, hauling himself up to his feet and favoring the leg with the bullet and knife wounds. He reached into a belt pouch and pulled forth a glittering set of metal knuckles etched with runes that spilled light and stung the eye. "Come here, you gutter snipe," the Warden growled.

Piccolo pivoted on the ground, spinning up to his feet as he pulled a cloak from its sling bag; it unfurled around him, and he reversed direction so it bloomed in front of the Spirit Warden, its fabric impossibly dark as light fell into it. Piccolo sprang at the cloak, slamming into the Warden on the other side, the cloak fouling the Warden's movements so they both crashed down.

On the ground at point blank range, Piccolo jammed his knife through the enchanted fabric again, again, again, and the countermeasures crisped and battered the formless cloth but did not pass through to the rogue. The soldiers stared in awe, shocked, as Piccolo murdered the Spirit Warden.

The Warden weakly swiped up at Piccolo with the knuckles, and Piccolo slashed at the forearm, cutting tendon with his razor-sharp blade. The smoldering enchanted cloak had stopped all the defenses it could, and Piccolo could look down through the mask's eye hole to see the desperation in the anonymous Spirit Warden's eye as death loomed.

He jammed the blade down through the eye slit, and shoved himself back and up to his feet, leaving the burning cloak and killing blade with the corpse.

"You—you are under arrest," one of the soldiers yelled.

The train car door behind him rattled and unlatched, and both soldiers reflexively glanced towards it—

That's all the opening Piccolo needed. He sprang forward, his forearm knocking the rifle barrel aside, then he was too close for the rifle to be useful. He head-butted one soldier, and pivoted, dragging the soldier around as the other fired at him. The soldier Piccolo used for cover died immediately as the bullet crunched between his lungs, his choked gurgle echoing the dirge-like ringing in the Ghost Field. Piccolo pulled his own pistol, aiming it from beside the dead soldier's ribs.

"Bye," Piccolo said dispassionately, pulling the trigger at close range, pulping the last soldier's face. Piccolo could almost hear the flurry of feathers as a deathseeker crow launched to find the source of the death that provoked such a string of bells tolling.

Behind his stolen Initiate mask, he smiled. Then he turned as Trellis slid the door open.

"Careful!" Trellis said with a frown. "Something in there took out Sanction!"

"Yeah, like that's a challenge," Piccolo muttered under his breath, and he climbed the few steps up into the pungent humidity of the specimen car. "Alright, what's in here? You a specimen, or a ritualist? Or something else?" One hand was free, the other held his blade; it was too close quarters to trust a gun's speed.

He took a knee, and looked around carefully. "I found Sanction," he said. "Looks like claw marks, from behind."

"Is he alive?" Trellis dared to ask, pulling back to the other aisle of the cramped car.

"Probably, he shows up on the goggles," Piccolo shrugged. "Alright." He pulled the door shut behind himself. "Let's hunt this thing. You in, or am I doing this on my own?" he demanded. Snapping his gun open, he reloaded it.

Trellis muttered a reply under his breath, too low for Piccolo's sharp ears to make out. Then the old man raised his knife, ready to proceed.

"Good man," Piccolo nodded. "I'll take this side, you take the other. Don't forget to look up. Everybody forgets to look up," he explained.

"Wisdom," Trellis agreed through his teeth, nerves high.

"This is why people like you need people like me," Piccolo explained, scanning the train car as he followed the aisle. "You plan things out all careful like, but when they go sideways, that's when you gotta stab your way into and or out of it." He nodded. "That's where I live, baby," he said with half a grin.

"It's one thing to look at the manifest," Trellis breathed. "But to see it, here in person?" He shook his head. "That moss could be packed around the roots of a radiant plant and increase the wood's energy thirst by thirty percent or more. In a plant that could normally have glowing leaves, it could absorb so much plasmic infusion that the bark itself would—would glitter," he said, his voice strangely warm. "And over here. The croquaamos spike snake. If properly milked of its cartilaginous marrow, it can be the gift that keeps on giving. They have—they have a breeding pair," he breathed.

"Eyes up, something with claws," Piccolo said tonelessly.

"Right, yes," Trellis frowned, and he prodded a bundle of greenery hanging from the roof. He also cut a generous sample and stuffed it in his pocket. "Blood and bone," he muttered, gazing around the train car.

"Okay, I don't like this, we're running out of hiding places," Piccolo said, approaching the back third of the car. He blinked. "Oh, hey, look—there's the crocodile skull," he said, pointing with the knife.

Weight slammed into him from behind, laying him out in the narrow aisle, three-inch claws puncturing the back plastron of his body armor. He slammed down, winded and bloodied, the weight of his attacker trapping him neatly in the confined space—he felt hot breath on the back of his head, and tried to thrash with panic.

A wet splatting sound turned to a hiss and a scream, and Piccolo felt a rib give as the thing on his back launched off of him, clattering and thrashing backwards. Trellis threw something with a cry of anger, and glass shattered, dragging a fresh hellish scream from Piccolo's attacker. The winded rogue managed to drag himself up enough to tilt sideways, looking down the aisle into a cloud of rancid boiling smoke—he saw green eyes and teeth flare bright in the darkness, and Trellis threw another container that shattered, spraying some liquid all over the creature, rendering its pelt glowing with luminescent spots immediately buried in smoke as its flesh dissolved.

Wincing, Piccolo reached for his gun, dragging it out of its holster with a trembling hand, lining up and between wobbles squeezing the trigger. The gun roared, its report reverberating from the metal walls, and a plume of smoke further obscured the monster. The wet slap of the bullet was still audible, and with one last spasm the creature lay trembling on the floor.

Piccolo struggled to rise, and Trellis traveled the length of the train car to round the corner and get between Sanction and the fallen attacker. As he once again got eyes on it, he frowned.

"I've heard of these," he said, "brought to Doskvol from time to time to provide defense, or be shown as trophies. It's a great cat of some kind, like a puma, or a panther." His eyes widened. "Or it's a damned ritualist," he said, watching the skull crunch and shift spastically, un-flattening, teeth receding, the body's lean strength surrendered to a human form.

"Ew," Piccolo said sharply, and he fired the second barrel of the gun, knocking half the ritualist's head off. "What the hell did you throw at it?" he demanded.

"I'm an expert in radiants," Trellis shrugged, "and I've got a pretty good idea what things in here you should touch, and which ones you really shouldn't." He paused. "You sure you want to know?"

"Nope," Piccolo said, turning to limp over to the upside down crocodilian skull packed with moss, with greenery thrusting up out of it. "I got the creepy planter. Is this the thing?"

"Bring it here," Trellis said absently. He turned and kicked at Sanction's boot. "You still with us, lad?"

"This, right here," Sanction managed to wheeze, "why you went into radiants instead of doctoring? Bedside manner?" He coughed painfully.

"You'll be fine," Trellis said. "We got what we came for. All we need now is to rejoin the Mistress of Tides and escape."

"If she's still alive," Sanction said, gingerly hauling himself to his feet, "she should be near the engine." He pointed a look at Trellis. "According to the plan. So who carries the chompy bush?" he asked with a nod to the crocodilian skull planter.

"I like it," Piccolo grinned. "Chompy bush. Makes me want one."

"That's ferngristlee," Trellis said with a touch of exasperation, "and I had best carry it." He took the heavy planter, almost three feet long and thirty pounds. "Gracious."

"That chompy bush has some heft," Piccolo advised with a nod.

"Get on with it," Trellis said through his teeth, and the three of them limped out of the train car and headed for the engine.

Piccolo lowered his goggles. "I'm surprised there's still steam," he muttered, reloading his gun as he limped alongside the train. Fifty feet later, they reached the side of the engine, where the Mistress of Tides was kneeling and focused, her hands in motion, pulling steam out of the engine. They could faintly hear swearing from the engineer's compartment.

"So what's up?" Sanction asked, unsure, not touching the Mistress of Tides.

"The engineer is trying to quell the flow of steam and he does not understand why he cannot," she murmured, half asleep. "The Initiates have called for a hull, and a dozen of them are waiting at the gate. The Chief Administrator of Gaddoc Rail Station has called up a regiment of Imperial troops to lock down every exit and prepare to move in, along with a conscripted unit of rail jacks." She paused. "Sound carries through mist," she murmured, almost inaudible.

"So, now that you're next to this behemoth, you think our desperation escape plan might still work?" Sanction asked with a pained smile.

"I can make it work," she replied, ice in her certainty. "But the engine must be cleared out."

"On it," Sanction said absently, pulling a round device from his jacket and adjusting the nozzle on it. "Hold tight, and reload everything." He hauled himself up on the train skirt, cautiously working his way around to the ladder up to the engineer compartment.

A soldier leaned into view, pointing his pistol right at Sanction's head. "Who goes!" he demanded, wide eyed.

"It's a mess out there," Sanction replied, his Initiate mask still in place. "I'm glad to see you've kept the engine room safe."

"There's a goddamn witch out there," the soldier shouted. "Go deal with that! It's what you people do, right?"

Sanction leaned back, looking the way he came. "A witch, eh," he said, peering into the mist. From the reflection of the metal wall, he saw the soldier fall to the temptation of looking the same direction, straining for clues, his gun barrel wavering.

Sanction raised his arm in one fluid motion and squeezed the dispenser, puffing a five foot stream of powder that was just long enough to dust the soldier's face. Sanction stepped forward, against the side of the metal corridor, out of easy gunshot line of sight, and the soldier stumbled. "What?" he said.

"Stop this!" Sanction shouted. "You are tired. Sleep." He paused, and heard a slide and thump. Then he hauled at the railings flanking the ladder steps, pulling himself up to the engineer compartment.

The engineer fired at close range, and only Sanction's reflexes managed to yank him out of the way in time; regrouping, he crashed into the engineer, banging into the counter, the gun's second shot blasting wide.

Sanction slung a backhand across the engineer's face, sending him staggering, then aimed his unsteady barrel at the man. "Get that soldier off this train, and keep dragging him, or you both die," he said hoarsely.

The engineer pointed a look of blistering hate at him, but gripped the unconscious soldier, and muscled him out of the compartment and down the stairs.

Out of breath, Sanction sagged against the controls, then squinted at them. "Pressure, sealed," he said, twirling the knob. "Auxiliary bypass, not so much," he muttered as he flicked the switches. "Plasmic draw? Oh, let's turn that all the way up."

A minute later he groaned in pain as he lowered himself down the ladder once, then again, down to the ground. The rest of the crew was gone, but they left an unsteady blood trail, dark splotches on the stone. The steam was fading, and there was a new high-pitched whine coming from the engine. Sanction stumbled along until he saw the baggage station, and he rounded the back wall, surprised that no one was there.

"Keep coming!" came a whisper-shout from further back. He looked to where the rest of the crew had climbed down off the platform, behind the solid stone flanking the emergency line track that was lower than the rest of the station.

"How big is this explosion going to be?" Sanction demanded, suddenly alarmed.

"Will you just get over here?!" Trellis ground out, almost all one word.

Sanction obliged, and painfully lowered himself to where the rest of them crouched. The Mistress of Tides had a wide stance, pressing her back against the stone, her fingers cranked at painful angles, her mouth looping a mumble to help her focus, and she was tied into the circulation of the engine.

After a moment, they heard shouts and the chatter of many footfalls as the first wave of reinforcements came out to assess the situation.

"Blood and bone," the Mistress of Tides said suddenly. "Cover!"

The crew crouched against the stone, wincing.

A shattering crash shook the station as though it was the head of a drum, slapped with force. The stone the crew shrank against reverberated, smacking them, and they sprawled in a daze. They did not hear the whistling scream of metal chunks slashing out from the epicenter, but they saw masses the size of dinner plates embed themselves in stone or ricochet off the surface and cut through metal doors. All the artificial lights and plasmic energy on Platform 9 was knocked clean out.

Scrambling up onto the broken stone as best they could, the crew of rogues struggled with balance as they staggered towards the explosion. Their ears were still filled with the tinny ringing echo of the blast, and it was hard to tell if their balance had been affected, or if the ground was actually wavering.

They got close enough to see through the fog of stone dust and steam, and the engine was gone altogether. So was the ten foot block of stone under the tracks. The platform was breached, the engine fallen through, and swirling darkness reigned below.

The Mistress of Tides shook her glow orb, and tossed it down. Moments later, a heavy crossbow bolt tied to a cable zipped across the void below and embedded itself in a pillar. The Mistress of Tides pointed it out to the others, and they gingerly walked around the broken rim of the hole.

Pulling out a canvas sling that fit under the skull, Trellis wrapped it up somewhat as Piccolo climbed down the broken stone to the cable. They handed the precious prize down, and he clipped it to the cable, which now descended at an angle, away from the hole. He let it go.

The canvas package hummed down the zip line about fifty feet before it reached the pair of adepts roped to a more distant support under Platform Nine. Neap unclipped it, lowering it to Slack, who climbed down into the fogged darkness.

The Mistress of Tides drew forth another glow ball and shook it, but she cracked this one. She rubbed luminescence on the pillar, and climbed down half a dozen feet, then marked it again. Down another half dozen feet, another mark.

The pillars were made to be climbed, with built in ladders, but they were also chipped and cracked by the explosion. About fifteen feet down, the Mistress of Tides could see the seven zip lines that her adepts had set up under the platform; it was no sure thing which way the crew would be exiting, so they tied a number in place. She reached the first, climbed down past it, then drew her pully handle out from the belt pouch. Snapping it in place and closing her eyes, she let gravity pull her away from the pillar, the handle whirring in her hands, the drop yawning below.

Piccolo was next, scrambling around like a sailor in rigging. He clipped the pully, and pushed away from the pillar, gazing down into the devastation below; he saw the shell of the engine, its housing shattered, its internal pressure tubing regulators splayed like tentacles in rigor mortis, wreathed in incense-like smoke; he thought of the funeral of a dead god.

Faced with climbing down, Sanction felt his gorge rise and all the pain in his torso and shoulder protest. Self preservation was strong in him. He cracked his neck vertebrae, and frowned.

"This, or a desk," he whispered.

That was just enough to get him down that steaming, broken pit far enough to find the zip line. Breathing light and fast, he squeezed his eyes shut.

"All I have to do is let go," he whispered. He found that he couldn't.

Trellis chuckled sardonically, something flared in Sanction, and then he was zooming down the line, wind blowing his face, his organs clenched into fists, a scream tearing out of him against his will.

Trellis looked down, passionless.

"At worst, suffering, then death," he murmured. A smile creased his face. "Old friends."

He let go, and the zip line thrummed as he passed along it.

Ten minutes later, they scrambled down an embankment of cinders and broken stone to the old construction site supply canal, long since fenced off. They loaded up in the skiff that was tied up and waiting there, and Neap manned the pole, pushing them along the stone-lined canal.

"That went well," Piccolo said loudly.

"What?" Sanction squinted.

"Never mind," Piccolo sighed, glancing around. They drifted through the sabotaged gate as the first squads from the Imperial Regiment started down the slopes that flanked the station. They traveled dark, just another pack of ghosts drifting on the canals.

# ━◄ CHAPTER THIRTEEN ►━

*The aristocrats resisted as best they could, as their blood thinned out and the torrent of money upward was increasingly siphoned into other hands. Over centuries, the aristocracy diminished. Six Towers will always remind the people of Doskvol that the aristocrats once ruled in the light, and still have immense power in the shadows. As the Six Families that once ruled were winnowed out by time and fortune, they lost the ability to keep up their palaces. However, they kept their traditional elbow room in a space-starved city. This is best for everyone. Inside those thick walls are the byproducts and reminders of the corruption that centuries of power and privacy unleash in a bloodline.*

*- From "A Catalogue of Local Perversions of Power" by Sir Gennet Wylderwither*

## SILKSHORE. FALLOWTHRUSH APOTHECARY. 10ᵀᴴ ULSIVET

"I can knit these two fellows back together," the apothecary said, his voice thick and slow, his eyes hidden behind thick lenses. "For your Whisper, I have recombinant salts, I can rebalance her humors, replenish her energies, humph," he said with a gesture tightening and raising his gut. "But to do it in twelve hours? Expensive," he shrugged.

"I know," Trellis murmured, "and when I come back I'll have payment in hand. You get them put back together and shipped to my house."

"Trellis," the apothecary said, expressionless. "No credit."

Trellis stared at him for a long moment, then pulled his sling back up to the counter, opening it. "Here's a cutting of ferngristlee. Four ounces of shadowflight moss. A philter of sannic interstitial resin. I'll bring the rest. And if you can't live with this, then I take my business elsewhere."

"Always happy to help a friend," the apothecary grinned, taking the ingredients. "So, all this; were you involved in Whipwater Point?" he asked, something sly in his expression.

Trellis frowned. "No questions, I thought that was how all this works."

"Payment up front is how it works too," the apothecary shrugged. "Once the rules get bendy, we all watch them bend, like trees in the wind." His hands offered a visual aid.

"We were nowhere near Whipwater Point. Unrelated business," Trellis shrugged.

"Then you may not know this yet, but the Fairpole Grotto Council is meeting to discuss that mess," Fallowthrush said. He held up two thick fingers. "Two days."

"Huh," Trellis said. "Been a while since the Council met," he shrugged.

"Maybe you all were involved in the rail station?" Fallowthrush probed. "Seems like the whole city is blowing up these days."

"You want to carry our secrets?" Trellis asked Fallowthrush directly, looking him in the eye.

"This kind of information is worth money these days. So many angry people. Relatives, investigators, bosses, you know how it is." His wide smile had no hint of apology.

"You're smart enough to figure this out on your own," Trellis said quietly, "and you know that if you sell us out I'll put you on my to-do list." He turned his back on the apothecary and pushed through the heavy door into the early morning rain.

"Hello?" Piccolo called out from where he lay face down on a table in the other room, the claw-marks on his back exposed. "We doing this or what?"

"Patience, my wounded chickadee," crooned the apothecary. "I will fix you up so good. Now hold still."

The iron door screeched open, and Trellis ducked through the narrow portal. The door groaned into the bang of its closure, trailing off with a rattle of keys, leaving Trellis alone with one other man in the rusting stench of the narrow metal cell.

The prisoner stood with his back to the door, leaning on his elbows against the wall, staring up through the barred slot above. "I don't know you," he said tonelessly.

"I know you," Trellis shrugged, raising his eyebrows. "Thank you for seeing me, Faliq."

"I did not agree to see you," Faliq retorted.

"Still, you'll be glad we talked," Trellis shrugged. "I have an offer for you."

"Aie, an offer to a gondolier in Ironhook; this has always ended well," Faliq murmured, his back still to Trellis. "You don't even know why I'm here."

"But I do," Trellis disagreed, "because I've been keeping an eye on you for a while now." He paused. "I'm sorry about your son," he said.

Faliq turned from the wall, fixing Trellis in a terrifying gaze. "Don't you dare," he growled.

"I came to tell you that I'm ready to rescue your son," Trellis replied, not giving an inch of ground.

"Then let's go!" Fariq shouted, stepping forward.

"You stay here. My crew and I will handle it," Trellis said. "As soon as your son is freed, you can get out of here, yes?"

"In hours, or less," Fariq said. "Why would the gondoliers let you rescue my son, when they imprison me for fear I will try it?"

"The guards let me in here because I gave them inspector credentials," Trellis said with a bare smile, "because the gondoliers would never let me near you if they could help it."

Recognition dawned in Fariq's eyes. "Trellis. We were warned not to talk to you."

"Right," Trellis nodded. "Maybe you heard, Zhavo got his revenge."

"I did hear about that," Fariq nodded. "Many members of the Council are furious."

Trellis watched him for a moment. "You are Fariq Ludellem, bard of the canals, and your son Tanuk was taken by the necromancer Cornelius Bowmore. The Council is reluctant to cross Bowmore, as he is among the last of the Bowmore family, one of the six houses of nobility that originally ruled the city." Trellis paused. "I will not hesitate to cross him on your behalf. He has overstepped, and that will temper any consequences."

"You may underestimate him, for all your boldness," Fariq said with a shake of his head. "He is not a Whisper; no, he is a necromancer, from the Old Ways that are forbidden and punishable by death. He uses ghosts as weapons. He is entrenched in the Bowmore House, one of the last of the Six Towers still inhabited by the original family." Fariq looked him in the eye. "The Bowmores got in on the necroseum fad some four centuries ago, and they have permission to keep some of the brightest lights of the family as ghosts in their vaults beneath the house." Fariq studied Trellis. "You think you can get in there, find my boy, and escape? Then fend off the consequences?" He shivered slightly. "What do you want, for even attempting this?"

"I need you to open the sepulcher with the funerary gondola and last resting place of Saramanca Ludellem," Trellis said quietly, "and allow me to retrieve a single item."

Fariq took a couple steps back, his eyes not leaving Trellis, and he leaned back against the wall. "The charter," he murmured.

"Just so," Trellis nodded. "You know what I can do with that."

"And you've been 'helping' others who have granted you access, like Zhavo to open the Mistyard to you, and someone to take you to the last resting place."

"You are the last piece I need," Trellis said softly.

Fariq paused, then looked Trellis in the eye. "He is my only son. I cannot say no." He paused. "But you need to understand about Bowmore. That family is an ancient stain, a broken bone in the city, the infection in them spreading to everything they touch. What makes you think you can survive him?"

Trellis smiled. "He is between me and what I want," Trellis shrugged. "We have a deal." His smile was unsettling.

They shook on it.

"We need more people in this crew," Piccolo groused, hunching as the gondola drifted through a deeper shadow.

"I don't like Trellis going to a meet by himself either," Sanction agreed.

"To hell with Trellis, I'm feeling an itch for more people to outrun." Piccolo paused. "I like all of you, so we need some iffy probationary members," he explained.

The gondola drifted down the wide, empty channel. Neap wore a deep cowl and a cloak, and he stood at the back of the narrow boat, poling it along. The Mistress of Tides, Piccolo, and Sanction sat in the gondola, gazing at the ancient stonework of the banks and the quays, the mighty piles of stone forming watchtowers and ancestral seats, flanking the channel. A cool breeze shuffled through the half-dead brush clinging to a wrought-iron fence. The water plopped not far away as a fish snatched at a resting insect on the surface.

"I feel like we're going in blind," Sanction murmured, his brow furrowed. "We haven't done half the needed prep. This isn't how I thought it was going to be," he confessed.

"This is exactly how I thought it was going to be," Piccolo shrugged, consulting his pocket watch. "Looks like Sir Spooky has had plenty of time to go chase Trellis. Shall we head in?"

"Let's do it," Sanction nodded, and the gondola nosed up to the heavily reinforced water gate where the canal flowed into the foundation of the Bowmore House.

The Mistress of Tides slipped on her bone spirit mask, and extended her fingers, sliding a battered old brassy ring onto one of her slender digits. She closed her hand to a fist, then unfurled her senses, feeling the ancient spark in the ring. She lined up her own breathing with that spark, and like an ember, it pulsed in the Ghost Field along with her breathing. She directed that energy towards the gate and its numerous wards. It recognized the energy signature of House Bowmore, and creaked open. The gondola slid through the gate, and it croaked and groaned as it sloshed shut behind them.

They maneuvered past a gate mechanism more complex than some of the docks controlled by the city heading into a long corridor with a quay along the side and iron rings to tie up cargo craft or yachts. Neap pushed the gondola close, and Piccolo hopped out to secure the rope to a ring, pulling the gondola snug as the others climbed out.

Chill touched them in the deep shadow, over the breathing water, where the dust had turned to a slick of mud, rust coated the metal, and lichen grew crooked and wild on the ancient stone. They were intruders from a present that had become the undreamable future for this abandoned corner of the city's past.

They confronted the back door, a circular portal with deep carving around the door. The signs and seals formed Spirit Warden Warrant of Exception, the legal contract that allowed the family to keep ancestral ghosts under their Great House so long as certain conditions were met. The door was sealed against entry from the living or the dead, and for a long moment it towered over the intruders, impossibly so.

"We'll need some protection from the ghosts once we get inside," the Mistress of Tides said, handing out crystals dangling on string necklaces. "I've made this cloaking ritual, so our life force should be hidden. As long as we don't engage the dead or make any sudden moves, we're likely to get through alright."

"And if they spot us?" Piccolo asked.

"Run, I suppose," the Mistress of Tides replied coolly. "Now, Sanction, you agreed to lead us in the centering ritual?" she said, turning to him.

"Right," Sanction said. "Now, we must synchronize our breathing, and then the Mistress of Tides will help refract us through these amulets." He paused. "Or something. Anyway, breathe with me." He breathed in, raising his hand, then out, lowering it. Seconds stretched out as they worked on breathing together, and eventually they managed it; as one life force, the Mistress of Tides pressed their vital signs into the crystal, which they then hid behind cloth, under their shirts.

The crew faced the door. The Mistress of Tides lifted her hand, and closed it into a fist, brandishing the signet ring. A rumbling rasp resonated through the stone as channels cleared, then the door drifted open and the cold stench of corruption overrunning preservation seeped out.

"In we go," Sanction breathed.

Trellis smiled with something like relief as he saw the bulky figure consult the wait staff, then move through the narrow tea shop towards his table. He stood, and offered a deep bow as Mordis approached. The massive Tycherosian nodded in return and the two men seated themselves at the table.

"Pardon my curiosity, but it overwhelms etiquette," Mordis growled in his high-pitched voice. "Do you actually have one of the four missing signet rings of the Bowmore Line?"

"Yes and no," Trellis said enigmatically with a shrug. "I do have it, and I am willing to sell it to you, but I do not have it here." He sipped his tea. "And it may have belonged to a bastard of the line."

"But still functional for aligning with the defenses of the Bowmore House," Mordis clarified, his tone light and whispery.

"That's what we're finding out right now," Trellis said with a significant eyebrow raise. "You have a spy in your household that sells information about your calendar, you know."

"Really," Mordis said, expressionless. "Who."

"I don't know," Trellis shrugged, "but the information is good, and has helped me access you a couple times. You might want to look into it."

"That's good advice," Mordis growled, "but why would you risk angering me, offering an artifact you're not ready to sell?"

"Ah, here he is, good," Trellis replied, nodding down towards the door at the far end.

A dark figure had emerged, and was hissing something threatening at the wait staff; the staff blanched, and pointed towards Trellis's table.

"We're made," Trellis said.

"Ah," Mordis said, sitting back, his fingers laced over his stomach. "Nobility."

"The ring is yours, we can talk terms and price later," Trellis said under his breath. "Might as well enjoy this." His smile was bleak, and Mordis dipped his horned head, sipping from the comically tiny tea cup at his place setting.

Then a shadow fell over the table, and the stink of decomposition wormed through their senses as Sir Cornelius Bowmore loomed over the table, his stringy mixed gray beard almost down to his waist, his eyes seeming to burn with a touch of green flame. "Gentlemen," he said, frosty.

Trellis pointed the slightest of frowns at him. "Sir Bowmore," he said. "Something you need?"

"That depends," Bowmore rasped, his voice hoarse as though worn through with screaming. "Did you come here to sell a signet ring of House Bowmore?"

Trellis regarded him for a long moment. "Why, are you in the market? Has one surfaced?" He let a little interest show in his eyes.

"I'm to believe this is, what, social?" Bowmore demanded with an abrupt gesture at the table Mordis and Trellis shared.

"One must invest time and treasure to keep friendships fresh," Mordis admonished blandly, and he sipped his teacup once more.

"If you'd like to join us, we were going to try out the Sporecap Garden. It's a whole tray of sporecaps with the most popular flavors of the season," Trellis smiled. "You did come for the sporecaps, yes? They are unparalleled here this season."

"Do not toy with me, merchant," Bowmore sneered at Trellis. "If you seek to bolster your position at the expense of my family's security, then you will learn of new suffering the likes of which you cannot yet imagine." He planted his knuckles on the table and leaned in close. "I can punish you for centuries if you cross me."

"Better get to it," Trellis said mildly. "I'm punishing you right now." Fearless, he met the aristocrat's gaze with his own icy glare.

Bowmore's eyes narrowed. "I had no reason to cross you, and now you've given me one," he said harshly. "You have chosen an out-of the way place to meet, with adequate security to discourage an attack here." He paused. "But you will lose a step, your vigilance will lapse, and I will destroy you."

"I bet you say that to all the pretty girls," Trellis replied quietly, ice in his eyes.

Bowmore stared for a long moment. "Where is the ring. Please."

"Not here," Trellis replied, unmoved.

"Don't look at me, I don't have it," Mordis shrugged.

Bowmore straightened, glaring at the two men, then he pivoted and stalked out of the tea room, down the stairs, vanishing into the streets.

"Was that entirely wise?" Mordis asked Trellis.

"My crew is in his house right now," Trellis shrugged. "Across town. Unless he can fly, they'll be gone before he gets home." Trellis looked Mordis in the eye. "By the end of the week I expect to have the Fairpole Grotto Council under my indirect control, and they've got enough personnel with adept and master level teachings that I think I'm safe for now."

"I've heard from my people that you taunted them that you were going to take over," Mordis nodded, eyes narrowing to slits.

"That's not hubris," Trellis said, his smile sharp. "It's about subverting expectations. I bet them a mass of confidence that I would drink this cup of coffee," he said, putting the cup on the table, "without touching this hat." He put his derby hat over the cup. He waved his hand then snapped his fingers, and grinned. "I've done it," he said.

"Of course you haven't," Mordis scoffed.

"Ah, but how do you know?" Trellis asked, eyebrows arched.

"Simple enough," Mordis said, picking up the hat—

Lightning quick, Trellis scooped up the coffee cup and tossed the drink back. He put the empty cup on the table, crossing his arms over his chest, and he grinned. "Thank you," he said.

Mordis stared at him for a long moment. "It's like you want to get on my bad side today," he reflected.

Trellis grinned. "That trick shows that I've got a big picture, thinking outside the box," he said. "The purpose of the exercise, or riddle, is to keep the audience focused on you and what you're doing. But you can't seal the deal without some audience participation, so you need a few people that are rendered susceptible to influence because they want outcomes, enough to act against their better judgment and try and provoke you to fail." He paused. "My crew is moving on the gondoliers, and they're about to pull the hat off of our operation." He tilted his head. "We told them we're coming, and when we arrive at the end with their help in getting us there, we'll seem inevitable. We'll figure out the rest."

Mordis watched him for a long second, then a smile curved his features, and he chuckled.

"You people are crazy," he clarified. "Picked a name for the crew yet?"

"Worms of Silkshore," Trellis replied. He shrugged. "Silkworms. Busy, busy workers." He flashed a dangerous smile.

Mordis laughed, short and sharp. "Well then, let me congratulate you; as always, a pleasure watching you work."

"That's what I love about you," Trellis replied with a rakish grin. "You appreciate the finer touches."

Trellis rose to his feet, smiling. "I'll get you that ring."

"See that you do," Mordis nodded. "I may rent it back to you to help with this feud you started today."

Then Trellis had disappeared into the crowd.

## SIX TOWERS. BOWMORE HOUSE. 11ᵀᴴ ULSIVET

The necroseum main chamber was lit with ghost lamps, fueled by the Ghost Field to burn cold and motionless forever. The crew noiselessly stepped through the stone chamber, in awe as they looked around at the embroidered doors, slabs, and drawer faces. Dozens of memoriums were visible from here, and the labyrinthine twisting of the tunnels would guarantee more exposure to the restless dead were a curious visitor to explore deeper. One throne at the end of the room had a flickering haze on it, and no one peered closer to see if they could attune to its energy and spot the ghost.

Following the dust path made of flower petals fallen to nothingness, they saw a ghost standing facing a stone frame like a mirror frame, gibbering and yipping to herself as she combed her rotten hair with her skeletal fingers. Giving her a wide berth, they ascended a staircase to reach the landing at the bottom of the entry to the house.

The round portal carved deep with Spirit Warden Warrant of Exception ritual was half open, left in a state of shocking neglect.

"This is a major violation of terms and conditions," the Mistress of Tides whispered. "That's some hackwork bindings to keep the ghosts in; they were reluctant to let the Spirit Wardens know every time they opened their library of ghosts to consult the ancients."

The crew stepped through the breathing crescent into the darkness beyond, leaving the pale and unwavering ghost lamps behind. At some level, they felt like they were walking through cobwebs, their flesh pulling at strands as they moved ahead, but anchored to this world enough to pass through, where ghosts would be repelled back.

Neap took off his backpack and set it against the gap on the door, and give a small wand-like device to the Mistress of Tides. Leaving the pack in the doorway, they continued.

They came to the back of a concealed cellar wall, a secret door left hanging open and choked with neglect. The members of the crew each took out glass spheres and shook them, activating the glowing algae inside so they had a minimum of light for stealthing around. Following the gallery designed for tuns of wine as well as bottles, they ascended into cellars that were converted to catacombs, and from there up to the back pantry of the Great House. Those were the first signs of habitation they encountered, with a feeble fire in the grating and some efforts in the kitchen towards simple, horrible meat dishes.

From there it was easy enough to follow the signs of use, staying away from cobweb-coated floors and near more shiny pathways. Deeper in then up some stairs, to a tower on the east side of the Great Hall. They paused as they detected a couple guards, both human, at the end of a long hallway flanked with stained glass mirrors.

"I expected more security," Piccolo confessed to the Mistress of Tides.

"We're invisible to ghosts, and no one in their right mind would challenge the Bowmore reputation," the Mistress of Tides shrugged.

"Noise," one of the guards at the end of the hall said, looking up, the goggles on his helmet glowing dimly. "Slojo, chekkit."

"Knicknack, six-up," the other replied in a gravelly voice. The crew recognized some outdated slang railjacks used to use, decades ago, as one of the guards warily started down the hallway for them. The guard tugged a collapsible staff from its harness on his back and flexed it, popping out a scythe-shaped lightning hook and a side handle. The weapon crackled in the dimness.

"Let's go boo, flimsies," muttered the railjack guard. He smelled of rot and wet stone. As he approached, there was an almost infected rawness to him, and the crew felt their hair bristle with disgust.

Sanction and Piccolo exchanged a glance, then they burst out of cover around the corner. Sanction jammed his knife into the crackling sweep of the scythe, and let out a yell as the crackling energy hurled him back, tiny fires flickering across his clothes and hair. Still, the scythe was out of the way, and Piccolo shoulder-checked the guard in the chest, sending him hurling back to flop gracelessly on the floor.

"This is too hard," Piccolo muttered as the other guard squared off with them. He pulled out his pistol and fired both rounds into the guard, sending him reeling to slide down leaving a smear on the wall. The other guard clumsily rolled over on all fours, ready to rise, and Piccolo stomped the back of his helmet, snapping the guard's goggles on the stone floor, then driving his stiletto down into the back of the guard's neck.

"Neap, get Sanction, let's go!" the Mistress of Tides called as she ran past Piccolo to the door at the end of the mirrored hall. Neap hauled Sanction up, and as they managed to get their balance and Piccolo reloaded his pistol, the Mistress of Tides waved the etheric alarm on the doorknob away, then opened it.

The room was bare, except for a large mirror on an ornate stand. The room reflected in the mirror did not match its surroundings. As the Mistress of Tides entered the room, a young boy maybe ten years old leaped to his feet in the reflection and ran to the mirror, planting his palms on it, hope in his eyes.

"Whoah," Piccolo said, walking around the mirror. "He's in there? Do we break it?"

"No, we don't," the Mistress of Tides said quietly, examining the frame, the stitching of runes that crossed time and space, the interstitial living energies binding the room in the mirror to the room on the other side of the Mirror. "That is a space in the Ghost Field, bound to this side of the Mirror by powerful magics. Human sacrifice. Unspeakable pacts." She shook her head. "I can free him."

The clatter of bootfalls was filling up the hallway outside fast, so the crew hauled the door shut and barred it, looking breathlessly to the Mistress of Tides.

The Mistress of Tides closed her eyes. In her spirit mask, she was always suspended over the Deep, and now she let it well up through her veins, next to her arteries, her heart providing the interchange between the front and back of the Mirror, between life and death. The surface of the enchanted mirror she touched became a part of her, like an eyelid, and she simply opened it to touch the warm hands of the young man on the other side. She pulled, and then felt his arms around her, gripping her with the desperation of life at the edge of extinguishment.

"Okay then," Sanction said breathlessly, still leaning on Neap. "Piccolo, where are we?"

"This is the lower east tower, so the end of the hallway is over the broken-down chapel. We blow it there, we can climb down and get to the east wall no problem."

Sanction steadied himself, leaning away from Neap. "Okay Neap," he said, "first charge."

Neap lifted the wand that was attached to the package down by the door, and he attuned to it, then nodded. Somewhere far below, a rumbled detonation sprayed chum on both sides of the Mirror. That was sure to wake the ghosts.

"Give it a minute," Sanction said, listening intently.

The guards that had closed in on the end of the hall were realizing something had happened, and the ghosts were going to come pouring through the house.

Before the guards could form a plan, Piccolo led the charge down the hall, flinging a second pack-shaped charge. A dozen glowing goggles pointed towards him, but he was already tuned to the detonator—

The charge blew out the wall and sprayed the corridor with stained glass and mirror shards. The crew ran, Neap dragging Tanuk along. The wall breach was just where Piccolo predicted, and a short drop put the rogues on the roof of the abandoned chapel. Running its length, they could jog down a broken wall, and cross the weed-choked yard to the outer wall.

They saw the rope ladder, already thrown over the wall and ready to climb. Piccolo hit it at a run, flying up over the twenty foot wall and dropping down the other side to join Slack and the goat cart.

"Anybody injured?" Slack asked breathlessly.

"We're good, just be ready," Piccolo panted. "Woo!"

Tanuk was next over the wall, prodded by Neap, who yelled "Go! Go! Go!" Slack whapped the reins on the goat flanks, and the cart lurched forward, pulling Sanction and the Mistress of Tides up over the wall, and breaking the fall on the other side somewhat. The cart creaked to a halt, and Piccolo helped get everyone on it, then jumped on himself, and they made good their escape, cutting the rope ladder loose and leaving it twisted on the cobbled street.

Trellis was in the study enjoying his tea when the crew returned. They staggered in, variously strained or injured, and collapsed more or less on the furniture.

"Tanuk?" Trellis inquired.

"Dropped off with the gondoliers," Sanction said, wincing at his burns.

"Body count?" Trellis continued.

"Higher than we expected," Piccolo admitted without feeling.

"Ghost complications?"

"Nothing I couldn't handle," the Mistress of Tides shrugged.

"How about you?" Sanction asked. "Did you rile up the Sir?"

"He's plenty riled," Trellis said. "And I need to get that ring to Mordis. But it looks like we succeeded. And I'll take Mordis' payment for the ring, and finish paying off Fallowthrush."

"That was a fast and dirty hack," Sanction said, shaking his head. "We got lucky."

"Yes, well, we also have everything we need to get the Emperor's Own charter of the Sinking Sun, so it's all about to come together," Trellis said.

Sanction leaned back with a sigh. Then he paused, and looked at Trellis. "Did Mordis or Bowmore figure out that you are the one that sold Bowmore the appointment on Mordis' calendar?"

"I don't think so," Trellis shrugged. "I just hinted to the anonymous seller that Bowmore would pay to know about that appointment. It seems likely that Mordis will find his mole, and unlikely it will connect back to me."

"Alright then, let's tattle on Bowmore with the Spirit Wardens—" Sanction began.

"Already done," Trellis shrugged. He smiled. "You all look like you could use a nap."

He was too late; Piccolo was already asleep.

# ◄━ CHAPTER FOURTEEN ━►

*Imperial Charters were one of the first tools the Emperor ever used to gain control of the aristocracy. By allowing key allies to operate with reduced or forgiven taxes and a few special powers, the Emperor assured that wealth and power would accrue to his favorites, who would owe their fortunes to the protection of his ongoing goodwill. In one genius stroke, the Emperor rendered his allies resistant to bribery and grateful for his favor.*

*A critical passage in the law did note that the beneficiary of a charter must be able to produce it at any time to demonstrate ownership. Since the charters did not come with names, the ambiguity of possession-based ownership led to an unexpected flurry of assassinations, espionage, and general skullduggery as the charters changed hands with frightful speed. The winners hid their charters well, and did their best to manage the political fallout from targeting the Emperor's favorites.*

*Charters are no longer issued. However, all ancient charters are honored. These days, when a charter changes hands, an entire infrastructure shifts under the strain.*

*- From "A Catalogue of Local Perversions of Power" by Sir Gennet Wylderwither*

Saint and Safety leaned back against the low wall, looking across the morning bustle of the small market on the spur of land over Central Landing. They waited patiently.

One of the guards recognized Saint, and his eyes went wide. He vanished down the stairs to the labyrinth of quays, docks, slips, and boathouses down on the surface of the canals.

"There has got to be a better way to do this," Safety muttered, shaking his head.

"Just be quiet and back me up," Saint replied through his teeth, then he took a deep breath and released it. "Here comes Tarjan."

"Good morning, my friend," Tarjan said with a wide and insincere smile. "I am surprised you show your face in public."

"Good morning to you, Tarjan," said Saint. "I know I'm safe as long as you wish it, this deep in Gondolier territory." He paused. "We are still friends, right?"

"Of course, of course," Tarjan replied easily. "I take it you were behind Whipwater Point?"

"Yes," Saint nodded. "The Gray Cloaks are finished in Silkshore, and now the Grinders will be ready to talk." He paused. "We took out some of their leadership, and I figure about twenty of their toughest. They are vulnerable for now, and this is when the gondoliers have a chance to reason with them." He looked Tarjan in the eye. "I did that. The River Stallions did that. We earned a place on the Council."

"You make it sound pretty impressive," Tarjan shrugged, "but you don't mention the disruption. The damage. The sheer noise of all that," he said. "Anyway, these matters are not mine to decide, as you well know."

"You influence the agenda," Saint retorted.

"And the Council will meet in two days," Tarjan agreed. He paused. "I'll see to it that they have the opportunity to review your request to join the Council." He heaved a deep breath. "Twelfth Ulsivet, midday. Clear your calendar. Meet here." He nodded. "Just you and your crew's Whisper. See you then."

Saint nodded back, then a smile spread across his face as he headed back down the Central Landing streets. "You hear that, Safety? Our work is paying off!"

"Yeah, that's one way it could go," Safety agreed.

They vanished into the maze of alleyways.

## SILKSHORE. BARKSKIN TAVERN ADJACENT BASEMENT. 10ᵀᴴ ULSIVET

The squeezebox wheezed out a merry tune as Safety flexed it in and out, fingers nimble on the buttons. The Hammer had a hand drum between his knees, and he patted and rapped at it. Inkletta and Saint grinned like fools, dancing more or less together in a circle in the half-cleared basement space.

"Hey!" Gapjaw yelled with the others as the song whirled to an end. Inkletta and Saint bowed to each other, and for a breathless moment everyone was clapping and smiling.

"To the Council!" Saint hollered, carried away in the moment and hefting a cloudy bottle of something alcoholic.

"The Council!" the others echoed, and all took a drink.

"To us!" the Hammer bawled, his bottle almost empty.

"Same thing!" Saint yelled, and they all laughed and took another drink.

"We've had to knife a lot of people to get here," Gapjaw said, brandishing his second bottle, "but they were all bastards, and now we're gonna be fancy, so eh," he shrugged.

"Eh!" Safety said, brandishing his bottle, and they all drank again.

"Say, where's Red Silver?" the Hammer asked, blearily taking stock of the room.

"She's like a cat, that one," Saint said with a dismissive wave. "Leery of crowds, loud noises, and other peoples' fun."

"Maybe," said an arch voice from the stairs. "Or maybe I like to keep my wits about me in case something emerges that changes our situation." Red Silver stepped down the rickety stairs, still dressed to skulk about the streets. "Gentlemen, we have an opportunity," she said, crossing her arms over her chest.

"Swimmin in em, apparently," Gapjaw sniffed, philosophical. The others paused, noting the seriousness of her demeanor, the hum of nerves sharpening her reflexes.

"I'm not sure we can handle another opportunity just at the

moment," Saint said mildly, cocking his head to the side.

"This one is too good to pass up," Red Silver retorted, moving down the stairs and into the party, all eyes on her. "What if I told you we had a secret weapon to help deal with the Skovlanders?" she asked, arching an eyebrow.

"Sounds nice," Gapjaw shrugged.

"Let me introduce her then," Red Silver said. She turned to the stairwell, brandishing a gesture at it. A young woman descended the staircase wearing a turban and facemask.

"Okay," the Hammer said tonelessly.

The young woman unwrapped her turban, revealing fresh ruddy-cheeked features and short hair that looked like it had been impatiently hacked off with a dagger. She smiled, almost mischievous.

"May I introduce the resurrected Skov maiden warrior, Asdis!" Red Silver said with a flourish.

"Wait, what?" Gapjaw squinted. "So I guess Piccolo can't do anything right."

"It was close, believe me," Asdis replied. "My kin did not think I would survive, so they reported me dead because that helped the agenda of going to war. I did not die, so after several days they realized they had to kill me, because if I got better after being reported dead, I exposed them as liars and warmongers." She paused. "I escaped, and once I was able, I sought out the River Stallions."

"How does that make sense, though?" Gapjaw asked, troubled. "Since we stabbed you and all."

Asdis descended the rest of the stairs. "I can only play the resurrection card once, so I need a good hand to support it. You challenged the Grinders, but from what I understand, you didn't want a war; I may be the best peace offering you've got." She paused. "And I can clear your names of murder, as I'm not dead." She shrugged. "Your crew is uniquely guilty of that."

"Piccolo stabbed you," Red Silver sighed. "Now he's with some other crew over in Barrowcleft."

"And the Grinders, how do you think they'll react?" Saint asked.

"They'll be confused, off balance, redirected towards some internal housekeeping I expect," Asdis said, looking Saint in the eye. "Depending on who's left after Whipwater Point."

The Hammer cleared his throat. "And how do we know this isn't just a trick to get us back for hurting you?" he growled.

"I've already promised loyalty to the River Stallions, so I hope you'll have me," she said, and she shrugged her shirt down to reveal her upper arm. The rampant horse head of the crew was freshly tattooed on her shoulder, only days old.

"Inkletta?" Saint said, showing surprise for the first time.

The Whisper nodded. "I think she's a great fit," she said quietly. "She may be just what we need. You want to be useful to the Council?" She nodded at Asdis. "We might just have a way to change the tone of some of our Skovlander conversations, right there."

"And what if we decide to wipe out every filthy Skov but you?" Saint asked Asdis, making eye contact. "What then?"

She looked him in the eye. "It's never that easy," she said. "Not ever."

"So you would disobey orders?" Saint said, raising his eyebrows.

"Stupid orders? Maybe," she shrugged. "But if this is a crew that wants soldiers or morons, I don't want any part of it." She thrust her chin out. "I look at Red Silver, and Inkletta, and I see strength and flexibility. An eye for opportunity." She shrugged. "It's what I offer and it's what I want."

"Piccolo's 'eye for opportunity' got us into this mess," Saint frowned.

"He acted foolishly, sure," she agreed, "but if he hadn't, I wouldn't be standing here with you now."

The room was silent for a moment.

"I like her," Gapjaw shrugged. "She's prettier than Piccolo."

The Hammer's thumbs and finger imitated a rimshot on the hand drum.

"This opportunity is a hell of a risk," Saint said, frowning at Asdis. "I'll sleep on it."

Immediately Asdis' eyebrow shot up, and caution backed her expression. "Oh, yeah?" she said.

"Alone!" Saint retorted, irritable. "Make yourself useful in the meanwhile." He turned and headed to the sleeping corner of the basement.

"Huh," Safety said. Then he pulled the squeezebox apart, so it sounded like an anticipatory intake of air, and he started pushing merriment out of it.

Inkletta was at Asdis' elbow. "You're in with us?" she murmured with a head tilt towards Red Silver, "you're in." Her smile was confident. She shrugged. "We'll manage the men."

"Then how about we dance?" Asdis grinned, and she took In-kletta by the hand, and by the waist, and they trotted the tight circle with glee.

## SILKSHORE. SILVER STAG CASINO GROUNDS. 11TH ULSIVET

"What was so important?" the first man said, his expression somewhat bleary under the rim of his hat. "I had important business this morning." He gestured vaguely with the fried stalk he was holding. "This is not convenient."

"So sorry to bother you," Safety replied, the intensity of his frustration palpable.

"What do you have for us," the second man asked, expressionless as he scanned the garden surrounding the gazebo where the men met.

"News about the Grinders," Safety replied. "The leader's niece, Asdis."

"Right, your knife-man took her out some while back," the first man said, wincing towards memories.

"That's what everyone thought," Safety agreed. "She survived, gave the Skovlanders the slip, and showed up with the River Stallions looking to join."

Both men paused, looking at Safety.

"She's a wild card," the second man said, distant.

"We have to have her," the first man declared, eyes on Safety, "and you're going to get her for us."

A frown clenched Safety's face. "Blood and bone," he muttered. "You know that will put me in peril in my group. That kind of disappearance?" he scoffed. "And if she lives through it and identifies me?" He paused. "I mean, what kind of a team are we going to have available to use for extraction?"

"You're resourceful, that's what you kept saying in Ironhook," the first man said with a sneer. He crunched through another fried stalk.

"'Give me a chance,' you begged," the second man murmured. "'I'll show you what I can do,' you said."

"Okay fine," Safety said through his teeth. "I'll need some time."

"That's better," said the first man, mocking. He turned to the other. "I'm out of stalks. Let's go."

"I'll be in touch," Safety said.

They waved him off, following the back path deeper into the casino grounds.

Safety felt his face contracting with worry, so he put a cigarette between his lips and leaned forward to light it. The taste of the smoke reminded him of a time when he felt more invincible. Shaking his head, he left the garden.

## SILKSHORE. GROTTO HILL. 12ᵀᴴ ULSIVET 12. MIDDAY

Saint shrugged at the brocade coat, and scratched at the thread-crusted collar.

"Stop it," Inkletta said absently as her wrist fluttered, fanning herself with the elaborately patterned silk and fishbone hand fan.

"This thing itches," Saint growled. Then he straightened up, and extended his elbow to Inkletta as the gondolier porter approached, smiling and indicating the way to the gondolier.

The pair descended the stairs to the quay by the canal, where the elaborate and narrow-hipped luxury gondola waited. The emblem of the Sinking Sun, an abstract rendering of an upside-down sunset, indicated that this gondola was under the jurisdiction of the Emperor's Own company. The pilot wore the traditional garb, and as soon as they boarded, he poled the gondola away from the quay and along paths at first familiar and then less so.

Grotto Hill loomed over them. The gondola passed into a runoff corridor, then into the lock itself. The water was pumped out to lower the gondola, and glistening life-streaked walls were revealed, caked with residue of algae and barnacles.

"Been a while since the last Council convened," Trellis said over the slosh of the pumping water.

"I suppose," the pilot replied with an easy shrug.

"I've never been in the Grotto itself," Saint confessed.

"Really?" the gondolier replied, arching his eyebrow. "We call it the Mistyard. It used to be so beautiful. And the smell! The water, and the wood shavings, and the paint, and the sacrifices." He shook his lined and weathered face, bemused. "Layers and layers of runes in the laminate, for luck and for blood, for safe passage, all kinds of things," he said.

The lowering water revealed a foaming grate, and when that spun down, the grating itself clattered away. The process was remote controlled, or autonomous, and soon the gondola was in a narrow, dank corridor some level below the water table.

When the boat drifted out, Inkletta could not help but to catch her breath. The soaring chamber inside roughly matched the shape of the big hill above. An island in the center glittered with festive lanterns, streamers, and flame. Colored drapes, some quite ancient, covered the crumbling ruin of the stone that edged ever closer to dissolution under the weight of centuries. Ramps and platforms along the walls sported water channels and pools for several stories up around the central chamber, where powerful families or allies could sit in their gondolas with the creature comforts of food cookers or incense.

The River Stallions gondola joined the dozens of boats aligned with ropes on the water, in easy oratorical range of the giant houseboat tied up in front of the former drydock. It had upon it many iterations of the Emperor's Own Sinking Sun, one done up in what appeared to be jewels.

Even the trappings and colors of past vigor could not disguise the smell of the water rotting, or the general neglect that stole over the once-proud symbols of gondolier might. Inkletta looked away.

"I've solved a mystery," she murmured.

"Yeah?"

"The Slip," she replied. She looked down into the dark water, with its thick skin. "This is a place of power. But it's been so protected, so closed up, it's stagnated." She turned her deep, engaging eyes on Saint. "These people are connected to these waters, and as the waters go..." She shrugged. "This water needs to move," she breathed.

"When we're on the Council, I'll be sure to mention it," he muttered with a grin.

A trumpet blasted out a note, and then those gathering for the Council began to sing a traditional hymn. Startled, Saint and Inkletta looked at the gondolier poling their boat into line as he sang with gusto.

*Come we now*
*On glassy channel*
*Join as sure*
*As rain finds swells*
*Here we meet*
*Our friends and fathers*
*Bound by salt*
*In blood and sea*

There was passion in the singing, but where the chamber must have once rung with voices, now it echoed with their efforts, unmoved.

## SILKSHORE. GROTTO HILL. 12ᵀᴴ ULSIVET 12. MIDDAY

"I'm surprised at you," the Mistress of Tides said to Trellis.

"Oh?" he muttered, puffing as he hefted the cover off the big air exchange.

"You're usually so reserved, but… it's like you've lost twenty years from your age," she said.

"You don't understand what today means to me," he replied, leaning against the pipe. He squinted out across the view, the whole Ease laid out below as they rested on the roof of the building halfway up Grotto Hill. "I've dreamed of this for years."

"I suppose there is a story there," the Mistress of Tides mused.

"Of course," Trellis shrugged. He paused, then regarded the Mistress of Tides. "Why are you here? I mean, before we started this, I sent Sanction to recruit you. I never asked how he did it."

She returned his frank glance, then shrugged. "He said that if we formed a crew, I could have things my own way. And all my life, since I was a small child, I've been groomed to be a Whisper in service of the Gondoliers." She paused. "What Sanction said to me. I realized I never had the breathing space to consider what I wanted. To consider my own goals, independently. To choose a different place." She cocked her head to the side. "What do you think of that?"

"I think we both chose well to form this crew," Trellis replied. He glanced down the pipe as the faint echoes of singing emerged. "They've started," he said with a mischievous grin, and he tugged at the grapple hook already secured by the pipe. With the cover off, a slender person could fit down the pipe. Trellis lowered himself first, and the Mistress of Tides climbed down after him.

He kicked the grating off the vent when the old breezeway leveled out, and he wriggled out and dropped to the floor.

"Not very stealthy," the Mistress of Tides whispered from inside the vent.

"It's an abandoned firehouse," Trellis shrugged. "Used to service a fine museum, up here on Grotto Hill. That was in more prosperous days. The museum closed, its collection parceled out to other public and private collections." He caught the Mistress of Tides as she dropped, gentling her fall. "No more fear of fire," he said, rubbing his hands together as he glanced along the wall. "Ah. Here."

He climbed up on a bench and used a crowbar to lever the grating off the wall. Behind, they smelled stagnant water, and heard faint singing. "You see, when they have the Council, they open up the Grotto to get circulation. There are access points all over Grotto Hill, if you know what to look for. Back in the day, each one was carefully protected." He shook his head, then climbed up and through the missing grating housing, into the tunnel.

They emerged through another grating, and this time Trellis climbed down more carefully. They were in the dim heights of the inner recesses of the Mistyard. Trellis looked around, as though getting his bearings, then followed a shallow staircase back behind the platform. The staircase curved along the wall some distance and leveled out; there was a pool for a gondola, and a water-fed channel for it to ascend or descend.

The stairs he found were not hidden, but they were not obvious either. Less than ten minutes later the pair had reached the floor of the chamber, the apron of land around the pool than anchored it. Trellis cautiously followed the ribbon of land, pulling out his hand lamp and flexing his grip a couple times to send flashes into the dimness. The flashes were answered, and a smile spread across his face.

"Zhavo," he said. "I am glad you decided to honor our agreement." He approached the shadows, and they resolved into a pair of men with haunted eyes, standing next to a narrow gondola that floated in a channel of shallow water, next to a massive iron grating with excessive carvings all around it, resolving into funerary symbols.

"This is the Mistyard Catacombs," Zhavo said hoarsely, "and I beg you to commit no desecration while you are here." His mouth clamped down, invisible under his moustache. "I admit you to this sacred place because I swore I would," he growled. Then he manipulated controls within the ornately carved walls, and the gate dropped six inches and swung open, noiselessly rippling in the water.

The other man stepped into the back of the gondola. "Well, Trellis," he said quietly. "Here we are."

"Good to see you again, Lord Skora," Trellis replied as he stepped into the gondola, the Mistress of Tides right behind him. "How is your wife?"

"Better," the pilot murmured, and his mouth snapped shut as though it would never open again.

Trellis and the Mistress of Tides seated themselves, and looked around. "Where is Faliq?" Trellis asked.

"He had to lead the opening hymns," Zhavo replied. "He'll be along."

Echoes of another song drifted across the water. Trellis cleared his throat. "Things will change after today," he said.

"If you hurt the Gondoliers we will be enemies," Lord Skora said quietly.

"I don't want to hurt them," Trellis replied. "Refocus them, sure. We need to strike a new balance. A better balance."

"Merely brandishing the charter will not cow these people," Zhavo chimed in.

"I have a plan," Trellis shrugged.

The two men had nothing to say to that.

Some time later, another shadowy figure joined them by the unobtrusive gate.

"Is Trellis here?" hissed a voice.

"Ready to go."

Clad in a bright traditional outfit, Faliq clambered into the gondola, filling it with the four people it could hold.

"Before I can change my mind," he said through his teeth, echoing what the other Gondoliers were thinking. The gate was open, and the narrow boat nosed through it, into the mist-shrouded waters of the canal on the other side.

Generations of human use scored the guts of the rock. First, a mine, then a quarry, then the tunnels had been chiseled with shelves for the dead, and half flooded. Just past the gate, a chamber had been converted to a funerary chapel, where guests with boats could pay their respects before remains were placed further in the trackless maze of corridors beyond. Profound neglect and disrepair evidenced that tradition had ended centuries ago. The gondola passed through the chapel, into the maze.

Gliding almost noiselessly, they passed the slots once carved big enough for bodies, but then filled with jars of ashes instead as the reality of ghosts overwhelmed other superstitions. Once fancifully colored and decorated, at least near the mouth of the catacombs, they became more functional and stark further from the entrance.

Almost a millennia of the dead were stored here, and the mist was not from the temperature of the water but instead a ragged coat of breathing protoplasm over the depthless death settled into the still black waters.

Lord Skora hummed, a deep and ancient tune, and then he instinctively modulated his humming; the Mistress of Tides was startled to feel his attunement as he shifted his own sonorous tuneless breath to the rise and fall of undead consciousness. He was draining motivation from the ghosts, a strange and ancient improvisational lullaby technique normally hidden deep in the Gondolier culture.

They risked only a single lamp, but Lord Skora had the catacombs memorized, and his specially shaped pole was almost noiseless as he propelled them through shallows, tight passages, open passages, and once across something that felt like an underground lake where they were a single star in an endless night sky.

Time passed uncounted, and the dead stirred around them from time to time, but Lord Skora had been trained for this from birth. He navigated through the ancient maze, eventually settling the nose of the prow against an ancient and crumbling stone quay.

This is the place," he murmured, his voice rough. "I can take you no further."

Several thickets of radiant bushes glowed dimly, centuries old and untended. They flanked a pathway leading up to a stone door. Faliq led the way, and put his palm flat on the door.

"Here," he murmured. "This is the resting place of Saramanca Ludellem. That's where the Gondoliers put the Emperor's Own, the charter that gives the Council their tax exemptions and special water privileges." He shook his head. "I'm struggling here." He turned his bright eyes on Trellis. "I'm not a traitor," he said through his teeth.

Trellis said nothing, his face in stark light and shadow. He felt the weight teetering in the balance.

"You," Faliq said, pointing at Trellis. "You took advantage of my desperation. I had no real choice. That was duress."

"I saved your son," Trellis replied softly, "and I mean to aid the Gondoliers." He paused, his expression darkening. "Don't cross me."

Faliq stared at the stone for a long moment, then he ran his hand along the surface. "So far from the living," he breathed, his words pluming steam in the chill. "Such decisions we make in the darkness, to again contemplate when darkness folds around us next." He triggered the secret catches.

The throaty grind of stone on stone resonated around them, and the radiant bushes lit up brighter for a moment. Then the tomb was breached.

Inside, a shallow pool with a funerary gondola on it. The walls were decorated with scenes from his life, and the corners had luggage with desiccated and ancient wealth. Three scrolls lay on the torso of the corpse, and any one of them could be the charter. The others were sure to be traps.

The Mistress of Tides ducked the low doorway and stepped into the tomb. She breathed out slowly to let all things equalize, breathing some of her life into the dusty chamber. Then she regarded the three scrolls.

She recognized protections on each, and dimmed those layers in her vision. She felt the heat of enchantment on two of them; two had spirits bound to them, and the third did not. With a smile, she chose the one that had no spirit bound to it, lifting it from its cradle. She slid it open, dust sifting down from it, and saw the gilt letters from the Emperor's own court. A smile tugged her face, and she looked at Trellis, who risked bursting with the excitement he contained in a wry crook on his mouth.

Emerging from the tomb, she carried a coat of dust and the precious charter back to the gondola, Trellis at her heels. Faliq sealed the tomb, and joined them on the gondola, not meeting their eyes.

The journey back to the gate was uneventful and silent, save for the tuneless lullaby of the Gondoliers. Finally they drifted back into the chapel waters, only one gate from the outside.

The gondola drifted to a halt in the center of the deep waters. Lord Skora called out an archaic phrase, and Zhavo was briefly visible as he peered into the chamber. Then, with a rumble, the gate sealed.

"What is the meaning of this?" Trellis demanded.

"I thought I could do it," Lord Skora confessed. "I thought I could go through with what you demanded from me, and return home with clear eyes. A price for a service." He clamped his mouth shut, shook his head. "But I cannot."

They could feel the relief radiate from Faliq. "I too do not know how I would find a way to live with myself," he said. "Thank you, my brother." He looked at Trellis and the Mistress of Tides with something like hate in his eyes. "It is not too late to atone for our folly, here and now."

"Is that so?" snapped Trellis, extending the charter out over the inky black water. "I drop this, and you lose the charter for good."

"Five hundred years, and no one has demanded to see it," Faliq countered. "If they did, we could make something that would serve."

"I'm not sure you know all the details," Trellis warned them.

"I can live with losing the charter more easily than I can live with handing control over the Council to an outsider," Lord Skora said with conviction.

"There's no way out but the gate, and Zhavo controls that," Faliq added. "You cannot win, outsider."

Trellis let that sink in. "Your son?" he said to Faliq. "Your wife?" to Lord Skora.

"Sentimentality," Lord Skora murmured. "Against the greater vows of bloodline and service, they must give way."

Trellis waited for a long moment, then pulled the charter back, placing it on his lap. "I see," he said. "You are absolutely correct; I appealed to your sense of honor on a family scale, and now we risk betrayal at a clan level," he said, leaning back against the prow of the ship, looking back at the Gondoliers. "I have faced that conflict many times myself, and I feel I was most honorable as I chose what you choose now." He looked Lord Sokra in the eye. "So what then? Kill us, replace the charter, and leave?"

"If we can," Lord Sokra replied, his lips barely moving, his hand tensing for rapid action.

"First, a story," Trellis said, crisp. "I feel we can trust each other, here, like this," he said with a gesture at the ancient chapel. "This seems a good place to bury a secret." His smile was lean. "For almost fifteen years, I served as the Unseen Hand of the Hive." He paused, watching their reactions. He was rewarded with predictable surprise and dismay. "That's right," he nodded. "I evaluated the most sensitive intelligence, made impossible decisions, and when secrecy was a dire need," he said as his eyes wandered up to the darkness above, "I took unilateral action."

Faliq drew a pistol, cocking it as he aimed it at Trellis's heart. The Mistress of Tides leaned back out of the way, unable to escape further.

"You know the Hive has... influence with the Council," Trellis continued, not meeting their eyes. "You do not know how much, however." He paused. "You speak now of regrets, and I will say that I've not had a peaceful night of sleep since I was a young man. My greatest work," he added, looking Faliq in the eye, "was bringing the Fairpole Grotto Council under the sway of the Hive." His smile was mirthless. "I learned the details of your people inside and out. Just as I pressed you to get me to this point, I pressed your mentors and parents, your aunts and uncles... your heroes. When the Hive needs something from your Council, a word is whispered in someone's ear and it happens."

"Why then should I not execute you?" Faliq demanded.

"Because I'm not with the Hive now," Trellis replied, almost hypnotic. "I haven't been for years. They felt I was taking certain of my contacts too personally, that my personal loyalties were interfering with their best interests."

Faliq blinked, unsure what to think.

"Now," Trellis murmured, "if I can get that Charter and take control of the Council, I can undo some grave damage, and protect the Council from further incursions from my former masters." He paused. "I made decisions in the darkness, and I choose to contemplate redemption when the darkness folds around me again."

"Why now?" Lord Skora demanded.

Trellis looked him in the eye. "When I was drummed out of the Hive I was alone," he said. "I had years to savor my regrets." A bleak smile touched at his features. "Then my nephew comes to me, wants to start a crew, make a difference." His shrug was subtle. "The Hive does not yet realize what I'm doing. And by the time they do, it will be too late."

"So you're screwing everyone over," Faliq sneered.

"Not my crew," Trellis replied, meeting his gaze. "And for you, if you support me then I'll take care of you and we all get what we want. Look, I get it; your vow to play your roles for the Gondoliers is weightier than a personal promise. All I'm saying is that maybe if you help me, you are helping your clan. There is no contradiction in duties. You can help me set right old wrongs." He stopped abruptly, and cocked his head, considering the gondoliers.

"Looks like you've got a choice," he murmured, his eyes deep and glittering.

# Chapter Fifteen

*The Hive became an open secret almost three hundred years ago, when their assassination plot very nearly took the life of the Immortal Emperor. They were flayed down to bone, their organization stripped and scattered and pulverized as thoroughly as possible. Still, as a cabal of inveterate plotters and schemers, the few survivors soon rebuilt secret networks. They knew there are limits to the Emperor's attention span. And, really, a transgression of that magnitude may be a black mark, but it's also a badge of a certain kind of courage. So, yes, they are a secret network of merchants. But shadows are deep; what else might they be hiding?*

*- From "Behind Public Curtains"*
*by Tradewytch Sydoloron*

## SILKSHORE. GROTTO HILL, MISTYARD. 12TH ULSIVET

"What's this again?" Saint asked as he gestured at the tonal singing of the gondoliers on the top deck of the massive houseboat facing the assembly.

"Invocation of the Dusk, the home of our city, neath the cracked sky," the pilot murmured in a low voice. He chuckled. "We are almost through the opening ceremonies. The Council will begin their meeting soon."

"So we wait out here until they decide whether or not they want to consult us on our application?" Saint winced.

"That's the size of it," the pilot agreed.

Inkletta pointed a look at Saint. "We've had worse days," she said. "You don't like the gondola?"

"I don't like waiting," Saint growled. "Feels like we should be doing something."

"You want to be part of the Council's work, you better get used to waiting," the pilot said with a shrug.

Saint said nothing, grinding the heels of his hands into his eye sockets just for a new sensation.

"Something's happening," Inkletta said under her breath, sitting up straight.

Several robed figures had found their way up to the top level of the houseboat, and guards moved to intercept them. Hoods were pushed back, words exchanged too quietly to cross the water, then at subtle knifepoint the newcomers were ushered inside. The Speaker of the Council addressed the startled assembly.

"There will be some rearrangement of the agenda," she said clearly. "Please be patient." She turned and followed the guards and the intruders into the houseboat.

"Oh, we gotta get closer," Saint said, and he wheeled around to aim a pointed look at the pilot.

"If you insist," the pilot said, curiosity burning in his eyes too. Their gondola drifted out of line.

\*

"I'm surprised at you," the Speaker said coldly, gripping her golden mask in one hand as she pinned the intruders with an icy stare. "Explain. Now."

Zhavo, Lord Skora, and Faliq stood with their backs to the wall trying to avoid eye contact, but Trellis stepped forward. "Good to see you again, Eisele," he said.

"Belderan," she said through her teeth. Then she paused. "Or should I say Trellis?"

"Today, most definitely Trellis," he replied. "I've come to do business."

"What, take over the Council with me standing right here?" she demanded, her tone penetrating.

"Yes," he replied softly. He gestured, and the Mistress of Tides held up the Charter.

For a long moment, the room was shocked into motionless silence.

Then the Mistress of Tides twirled a silken cover over the Charter and hissed a long sibilant syllable, and the cloth collapsed. The Charter vanished.

"I have the Charter bound to my possession in a way you'll find difficult to break," Trellis said quickly, "and it's mine now. I'll allow you to continue operating under its conditions as long as I have a certain level of influence in the Council."

"You're a dead man," breathed the Council Whisper, a tall and imposing man draped in cloth of gold.

"Belay that," the Speaker said, her voice tight. "Let's have the rest."

"If I have a relatively free hand, I can transform your circumstances in a matter of days," Trellis said. "There are a number of issues to address." He looked around at the masked figures in the room, reading their identities in the earned pageantry and symbolism of their outfits. "Khelmaan, unmask," he said, pointing at one of the advisors.

With a shaking hand, the advisor tugged his mask off, revealing a sweaty, waxen face. Trellis squared off with him, expressionless. "You can go," he said.

"Wait," the Speaker said, hand upraised and her brow furrowed. "Khelmaan is a trusted advisor!"

"Run, now," Trellis said to Khelmaan, "and I'll give you a full day's head start before I tell the Council what you've done."

Khelmaan answered with a short nod, then hustled out of the room with surprising speed.

Trellis slowly pivoted, taking in the room. "Also dismissed: Fenwhyle, Arbogast, and Deltan." Without debate, three figures took off as fast as they could go, and several other advisors shrank back against the walls.

"I've had enough of this," the Council Whisper growled, his hands balling into fists.

"Griggs, I know how you succeeded Nyvana to become the Council Whisper." Trellis paused. "You want to do this?" he asked, eyebrows raised.

Griggs stood motionless, then looked away.

"You want the mantle?" the Speaker said through her teeth.

"No, I want you to run things, you're an excellent Speaker in difficult circumstances. I plan to concern myself more with your circumstances, like excising some excessively corrupt and dangerous advisors," Trellis replied. He turned to the table, where a number of scrolls were neatly laid out awaiting consideration. "Now that some votes are missing and some context has shifted, we're going to change some of these resolutions," he said, touching the table. "Jack up the surcharge on everyone operating in your territory by 20% right now," he said with a nod.

"You want to trigger a war?" the Speaker said, startled.

"They'll pay," Trellis shrugged. "Just out of curiosity to see what's going on. In the meantime, ban the Barrowdale Trade Consortium from Silkshore altogether, scorched earth, assume any surviving assets as back payment."

"That will cross the Hive," an advisor pointed out.

"We'll get to that sooner rather than later," Trellis agreed. "What else have we got here. Ah! A membership application from the River Stallions." He glanced at the Speaker. "Send them in please."

The room was still tense as a guard stepped out, then immediately back in with Saint and Inkletta. "River Stallions," the guard said dispassionately.

Saint and Inkletta both dropped into a deep courtly bow before the august body, then back up with great poise. "It is our honor," Saint said.

"Your credentials?" Trellis asked.

"We orchestrated the battle of Whipwater Point, weakening the Grinders and scrubbing out the Gray Cloaks," Saint said. "We've pushed back against Hive interference in Silkshore. More than that, we know how to cure the Slip."

"What?" the Council Whisper murmured, burning with curiosity.

Inkletta stepped forward, not overawed in the least by the important people around her. "This encysted spirit well has been isolated too long. This water must mix with the city canals and the Void Sea, and those suffering from the Slip will begin to recover."

The Speaker glanced at Trellis, who nodded. "It shall be so," she replied, "unless our Council Whisper advises differently." She turned to him.

"Flush the Mistyard," he murmured. "It could be consistent with lore," he admitted.

"Then we shall do it," the Speaker said, her voice crisp. She looked over at Trellis. "Well?"

"One more thing," Trellis said. "I believe the River Stallions have a death mark on Piccolo."

"Yes," Saint said slowly.

Trellis raised his eyebrows.

"But we're happy to erase it," Saint offered.

Trellis looked to the Speaker. "I think the River Stallions would be a fine addition to the Council," he said.

The Speaker turned to Saint. "One seat," she said quietly. "Let's get you sworn in."

"Thank you," Saint said with a broad smile. "We greatly value this honor. But—there's one more thing we have to discuss," he said.

"Can our Whispers handle it?" Trellis asked.

"Yes," Saint nodded.

"Then get yourself sworn in. We've business to attend to," Trellis said as he stepped over next to the Speaker.

"This won't hurt a bit," she said. She raised the golden mask up over her features and drew the ceremonial dagger.


## SILKSHORE. GRINDER HALL. 13ᵀᴴ ULSIVET

Gravel crunched under boots as the entourage left the road, heading down the path towards the Grinder palisade, the hull-hall a bulky shadow behind it. Faliq was in the lead wearing the white sash of truce, followed by Saint and Inkletta, with the rest of the River Stallions in tow. Trellis was unobtrusive in the gang of gondoliers that came along to help keep the peace.

A dozen bedraggled and violent types stood across the open space within the palisade gate. One of them stepped forward with a pronounced limp.

"I'm Sercy, I speak for the Chief," she said in a hoarse voice. "You have some nerve coming here, Stallions. And what's your business?" she almost spat at the Gondoliers.

"You're the new Ingvald?" Saint said, skeptical. "I hope you're sturdier than the last one." His eyes were unkind.

"We didn't come to fight," Inkletta interjected, stepping forward. "We want to talk to Hutton about how our various changes in circumstance affect our relationship going forward."

"And if I tell you to go away?" Sercy demanded, suspicious.

"Then we go," Saint replied. "But not forever. And we may not come under truce in the future." He frowned at the spokeswoman, who bristled.

"I think you all better come in here," Sercy growled.

"Under truce," Inkletta reminded her.

"Yeah, yeah," she muttered, and the thugs parted so the newcomers could enter the compound. As they crossed the muddy stretch of open ground, Saint frowned.

"We knocked off a lot of these guys," he muttered. "You can hardly tell." He looked at the knots of broad-shouldered Skovs standing around cookfires, or draped in blankets, or chopping wood. The anger in the air was palpable.

"They've been recruiting," Inkletta said in a low voice. "I think we pissed them off."

Then they ducked through the opening in the hull, stepping into the echoing darkness of the ship interior. One pouncer wolf lounged by the throne, looking a bit lonely. Hutton sat straight, gripping the arms of the throne, scowling at the peace delegation.

Sercy limped over by the dais and pivoted. "Say your piece," she snapped.

"I got this," Saint said to Inkletta. She frowned at him, warning, and he shrugged it off. "What. I'm a diplomat." He stepped forward. "Chief, it is so good to see you again," he said, "because this time I come with an offer."

"An offer?" Sercy scoffed. "After Whipwater Point you think you can just waltz in here with a deal for us?"

"I'm an excellent dancer," Saint said, ignoring Sercy and looking at Hutton. "I have been inducted into the Fairpole Council, and I asked them if they would make a seat for you too."

Hutton blinked, startled. "What?" he said.

"We don't have to be enemies," Saint continued. "More and more Skovs are going to be coming in, and we can either turn Silkshore into a battleground, or we can manage the process for our mutual benefit." He paused. "The Council doesn't want the Grinders for an enemy."

"That sure as hell changed in a week," Hutton snapped.

"Chief!" Sercy protested.

"I'm gonna talk for myself on this one," Hutton said with a dismissive gesture. He rose, and strode down off the throne, still tall enough to look down at Saint. "What the hell are you up to? I lost a lot of good friends at Whipwater Point, you scumbag."

"Yeah, well some of them weren't good friends to you," Saint shot back. "You got pushed towards war with us—a war that neither of us wants. Maybe you need a gesture of goodwill. Maybe that would help you trust this."

"Maybe it would," Hutton growled. "What do you have in mind?"

"You should meet the newest member of the River Stallions," Saint said, gesturing back at the Gondolier gang that followed them in. One stepped forward, tugging at the turban and face mask. Asdis pulled the disguise off, revealing her features.

For a long moment, Hutton squinted at her. "Asdis?" he murmured, his lips bloodless.

"It's me, uncle," she said, and she walked forward, past the truce line, and pulled him into a hug. Then she stepped back as he stared at her, slack as though he had seen a ghost.

"They said I was dead because I wasn't dying fast enough," she said, studying her uncle. "Ingvald ordered me killed. I got away. I found the Stallions." She paused. "I see a road into war, and a road into peace, and I know what I want for you. What I want for me." She looked Hutton in the eye. "We have to try."

"I'm so sorry," Hutton said, breathless, unable to release her hand.

"The Stallions took me in. They got healers for me," Asdis said. "What you did then, you didn't know. But now you know I'm alive, and you were lied to." She cocked her head. "Now what?"

Hutton shook his head, just slightly, a lost expression in his eyes. "Now what?" he echoed. He looked over her shoulder. "You got the papers? Oath takers? I'm ready to join this Council right now," he said. He looked around the room, his eye settling on Sercy. "These people are our friends."

"Just like that?" Sercy demanded, incredulous.

"Just like that," Hutton grinned, and he pulled Asdis into a muscled and enthusiastic hug.

*

A thin rain sizzled into the various campfires in the Skov enclosure as Asdis finally stepped out. She breathed deep in the night air, stepping aside to clear the doorway. Darkness was full and heavy, a crushing weight on the few fires still lit.

"I'll be damned," Safety said with a crooked smile, leaning against the hull half a dozen yards away. He strolled over to where Asdis stood. "You are the hero of the hour, that's for sure."

"Think so?" she said, cocking her head back to look down her nose at him.

"Oh, I know it," he retorted. "That's why I'm keeping an eye on the exit. Keeping an eye on you, in fact. Saint told me to. Something happens to you, this whole thing blows apart and we're worse off than we were before." His smile skewed. "Look at you. You're a symbol."

"What, of peace?" she said, unamused.

"You found acceptance and compassion, maybe others can too," Safety shrugged. His smile widened. "It doesn't hurt that you're pretty."

"Are you flirting with me?" she demanded, taking a step back as she looked him over.

"No, actually," he shrugged. "Saint put us under orders for the buddy system. Look, I get that it's probably a good idea for you to leave, you've been here for hours and we don't need some enthusiastic nationalist to stick something sharp in you." He paused. "I know a nearby noodle shop. Best in the Dusk."

"Yeah?" she said. "Got eel?"

"Three kinds or none," he shrugged.

Asdis squinted up at the broken night sky, mostly shrouded in an ocean of cloud. "What the hell." She grinned at him. "Let's go check it out."

"It's called 'Ribbons' because of all the noodles, and that's also an archaic word for eel," Safety said, his smile surprisingly charming. "Eels are meat ribbons."

"Probably meant to be clever," Asdis said, rolling her eyes as she pulled her coat close. "Is it far?"

"Just a couple blocks," Safety muttered. They passed through the entry to the palisade, and trudged up to the street. "This way."

"The rain cooled it off," Asdis observed, looking around at the hurrying few that still crossed the streets.

"All that hot Skov blood, you're all set for what passes for winter here," Safety shrugged as he strolled down the street, careless of the rain. "Right down that way."

Asdis paused. "You're sure?"

"Sure," Safety shrugged. "Ask that guy." Asdis turned to where he pointed—

--and Safety whipped his metal arm around her neck, pushing her head forward with his other arm, forming a sleeper hold. Startled, she kicked at the ground, and struggled for a stance, but he took advantage of his height and leaned back, leaving her legs wildly kicking, trying to connect.

His attack was too skillful, surprise too complete, and in moments she went limp in his arms. He hefted her up and strolled to the end of the street, loading her into a carriage and climbing in himself. Wheels clattered on cobbles, and they were gone into the rain-swept night.

*

Asdis was vaguely aware of the swaying sensation of the goat-drawn carriage, and she saw a blurred and dim image of Safety sitting in the carriage watching her.

The carriage jolted to a halt, and the goat let out a resentful bray. The leather springs jostled, and the door opened; Asdis was roughly hauled out of the interior into lamplight, hanging off a thin man, the lantern held by his partner.

"I need to go along," Safety said, earnest.

"Your job was to bring her here, and now your job is to go away," a snide voice said with something meant to sound like patience.

"We can take it from here," the other man replied.

"Cutting me out is a mistake," Safety insisted. "You might need a familiar face before this is over."

"No means no," one of the handlers said, and a pistol cocked.

"You may live to regret pulling a gun on me," Safety growled.

Asdis felt herself hauled around and dragged down a short flight of stone steps, then dumped onto a wooden floor of a gondola.

There was some chuckling, and the gondola was swiftly steered out into the channel, crossing the wide open space under the crumbling sky.

"Is he following?" one asked.

"No, he's fuming," the other replied.

"Like, smoking, or like, crybaby?"

"The second one," the agent said.

"We're getting away with this," grinned the first agent.

"With the bonus we're getting from this one, I think I can just move into the brothel," the other replied.

"Keep it down," the guard growled. "And keep the girl covered." Asdis felt a tarp roughly pushed over her, and she resisted the urge to forcefully let them know she was conscious.

They crossed the entire Central Waterway. Peeking out of the tarp, she saw that they were closing in on the quay walkway that serviced the mansions built along the back of the Silver Stag Casino. The imposing estates were once built by wealthy families, but most sold over the years to cover gambling debts. The boat was tied up and she was hauled up the stone stairs, down the street, and through a side gate in the wrought iron fence line.

Through an overgrown garden and down into a basement they went, and she got a glimpse of a soldier as they walked by. He wore something like a uniform, but it wasn't like the regimental uniforms of the soldiers that attacked Skovlan.

She was dragged down a short hallway, and the first strains of music were audible. The music grew louder when a tough-looking guard opened the big metal door. She stumbled through a dark area as the music sped up and swelled, peaking somewhat as she was prodded up some stairs. Finally she was deposited on a couch. The two agents and their guard stepped away from her, and she blearily looked around.

There was a big metal door on both sides of the cavernous room, and a huge fireplace crackled with burning canal leavings, taking the edge off the underground chill and damp. The room was decorated with finer things, like paintings and sculptures and rickety old furniture. Near the center of the room, a man sat with his back to her, playing a harpsichord with enthusiasm. He had broad shoulders and slicked back hair, she could tell that much from looking, but he also had a passion that unlocked somehow as he played music that touched on a deep human feeling Asdis could not quite identify.

The music slowed to a halt, and the man at the keyboard pivoted on the bench, looking over at Asdis.

"Welcome," he said quietly. "My name is Karth Orris." He shrugged slightly. "And you are Asdis. I am so glad we can meet."

She watched him and said nothing.

He rose to his feet, turning to face her. "I find you somewhat unique, in a city with nothing new in it," he said. "I also find myself in need of agents, and... if we work together you can make your future whatever you want it to be."

Her eyebrows raised. "That's tempting," she said.

"My intent is to tempt you," Orris said, a secret smile like sunlight on the craggy cliff of his face. "You are positioned to deal with three things that currently occupy my thoughts."

She waited for a moment, watching him.

"You think I'm dangerous," he said quietly.

"I know it," she replied.

"I absolutely am," he agreed. "And I admire your restraint. Not many people have the courage to allow silence into a conversation."

"I'm most interested in what you want right now," Asdis replied.

"Three things, as I said. Trellis, the Gondolier Council, and the Grinders. And you are somehow a lynchpin that connects those three things in an extraordinarily unpredictable way."

"I still don't know what you want," she said.

"You have access to Trellis. I could give you a series of commands that would finish him to my satisfaction," Orris shrugged. "You could help undo the damage Trellis inflicted on my Council with his rash action. And you could help me find Skov agents who were useful and pliable for the ongoing work."

"You want the Gondolier Council destroyed?" Asdis asked.

"I'm an efficient man," Orris replied. "I like to use things up before I discard them. I have been incrementally reducing their power, renegotiating our terms, and working through the Gondoliers to keep some semblance of peace in Silkshore for decades," he said. "I think there's another round in there before I transition over to a Skov import structure to keep overall peace. And each one of those Skovlanders," he added, shaking his head. "They are like a mine that you can continue to visit, extracting more and more wealth, until eventually they collapse. Requires a deft hand," he shrugged, "but that's why we practice."

Asdis swallowed hard. "You work with the Hive."

"I run the Hive in Silkshore, and a couple other neighborhoods," Orris said with a shrug. "I design the overall strategy. Choose the risks to accept, and the risks to eliminate." He paused. "I've chosen to accept you," he said, clarifying.

"So... you are not worried about the River Stallions or the Council?" Asdis pressed.

"They don't know where I am. They can't know. I have a number of safehouses, and I'm immune to scrying or detection or spy-work." His grin was crooked. "I'm the boogyman's boss," he said. He paused, watching her rub her tattoo. "That's nice work. Inkletta?"

"A gift, upon joining the River Stallions," Asdis said, her voice almost forlorn.

"Well, we all accumulate scars from unfortunate but needful betrayals," Orris sighed. "Those betrayals are much like love; fall hard when you're young enough to bounce back, and you'll be armored against destruction in your later years." He chuckled.

"Are you the one that recruited Trellis?" Asdis asked, looking him in the eye.

Orris' smile faltered. "Actually yes," he said. "Trellis told you he worked for the Hive?"

"He told me we wouldn't be able to find you," she shrugged. "He said you were the one calling the shots in Silkshore, and if we could get to you then we could make a difference in the whole area."

"If you could 'get to me'? What is that supposed to mean?" Orris demanded, his expression darkening.

"Kind of sweet of them," she murmured. "They wanted to make sure I understood the risks before I agreed to be bait."

Orris stared at her, then snatched a blanket from the back of an armchair and hurled it at her. Reflexively she put her hands up, and as the blanket came on she deflected it—his fist banged into the side of her head, hurling her back on the couch stunned.

She felt his iron grip clamp on her arm, dragging her across the floor. "The hard way it is, then," he growled, and he triggered a secret catch on the stone frame that pivoted the fireplace to the basement next door and its prepared escape route.

Orris stopped abruptly, confronted by Trellis sitting at the narrow table sipping tea, flanked by Whispers, with a number of rough-looking warriors between the fireplace and the stairs.

"Do sit," Trellis said. "I think we need to talk."

"What of my troops," Orris demanded.

"We've got a number of hardened criminal types attached to the Gondoliers surrounding the property," Trellis explained, "and if their spirit bane charms throb three times they move in. Your troops lead two diversionary escapes, the rest fall back to here, come through the fireplace and confront us, and it's bloody bullets and knives all the way down."

"No one wants that," Orris said, forcing a smile.

"Why don't you let Asdis go," Trellis suggested, expressionless. Saint approached him, hands empty, and Orris released the girl to thud down on the floor. Saint reeled her in and retreated to the wall with her.

"How else could this end?" Orris asked.

"No need for fireworks," Trellis said. "First, sign these re-negotiated contracts with the Fairpole Gondolier Council. They get to keep significantly more of the take," he clarified.

Orris looked the documents over with a grimace. "And?"

"And you release Safety's sister from Ironhook. I want to keep him for my work now, so your agents lose their leverage over him."

Orris's frown deepened as he waited a moment. "And?"

"That's all," Trellis shrugged. He paused. "You still get to use your contacts among the Gondoliers for intelligence and action, more important than ever as the Gondliers are revitalized. And you don't care about one Ironhook contact. Not enough to kick up a fuss."

Trellis leaned back. "Here's the thing. If we fight, then we escalate. We strip Hive influence from the Ministry of Preservation. We go after safehouses and agents. We don't stop at the obvious front companies, but we start burning our way through the back channels." He paused. "War."

Orris stared at Trellis. "You know our reserves are deep enough to win war on the scale you're talking."

"True," Trellis nodded. "But I also know your boss. I'm not sure she'd think the expense worthwhile." He paused. "Especially if I recruit Skovlanders citywide. Care to gamble?"

Saint, Inkletta, Safety, and Asdis sat in the snug of the tavern with Trellis and the Mistress of Tides.

"Welcome to the Council," Trellis said sardonically. "Now tell me about this kidnapping."

"I get Asdis, take her to my keepers, but they'll keep her moving because they don't trust me," Safety explained. "They've been getting hit lately, so I think they might take her further up the food chain if she's turned over to them and they understand her importance."

"And you're a double agent for the Hive and Inspectors," Trellis clarified.

"Yes," Safety said, avoiding eye contact. "But this is the first time they asked me to do something I just can't do."

"He brought it to me," Saint said, "and I wasn't sure what we could do. I was going to talk to the Gondoliers, but I suspect this is even better," he confessed.

"The main weakness of the Hive is that they avoid all things occult, arcane, and supernatural," Trellis mused. "They'll have countermeasures, and good ones, but we might be able to make a beacon."

"You're thinking of using Asdis as bait," Saint said, his tone flat. "I won't have it."

"It's not your call," Trellis said, looking him in the eye. "She's got pluck. If she doesn't want to do it, fine, but she decides. Not you." He looked to the Mistress of Tides. "Any ideas for making her a beacon we can track?"

"I have one," Inkletta said. "She has a fresh tattoo. We could pack the ink of that wound with an intense blend of components that would pour into the back of the Mirror as she moved, better than a blood trail. If you had resources mobilized and ready to go, we could track her with minimal danger to her person."

"We'd have to do it fast," Saint frowned. "There's a lot of risk here."

"But the reward is to strike directly at the heart of the Hive in Silkshore," Trellis reminded him. He paused. "Care to gamble?" he asked with a reckless grin.

Saint looked him in the eye. "I won't take those odds," he said.

"But whatever Asdis decides... I back her."

## SILKSHORE. STAG ROW, FIFTH MANSION BASEMENT. 13TH ULSIVET

"I guess we have an agreement," Orris growled. He leaned over the table, signing documents. Then he straightened, and looked Trellis in the eye.

"So if you stood here, and I sat there, do you think you'd have me killed?" Orris murmured. "Just on principle?"

"Oh, probably," Trellis shrugged. "But you know I have a petty streak." He paused. "You're a better leader than that. You're willing to let this be a win all around."

Orris stared at him for a long moment. "Let's hope you're right," he muttered. He triggered the rotating fireplace, vanishing from view.

"We should go," Trellis said, rising quickly as Gapjaw and the Hammer swiftly gathered the contracts. Saint supported Asdis, and the Whispers stayed wary; they all headed for the stairs.

By the time Orris's troops burst through the secret door, there was no one to surprise.

# CHAPTER SIXTEEN

Some critics and artists are in love with the unending. They feel that a properly concluded artistic effort is akin to an affront to the audience, whose shared experience is concluded at the artist's initiative. The Doskvol Academy has an entire course of study on the "fruitful ambiguity" of unfinished work.

That's fine, it's for students. Grownups know that art is all about following a series of endings until you reach the one that fits the work. The storyteller, painter, sculptor, historian, and composer must all share the instinct of knowing when to quit, how to exit, how to bound from the rolling carriage and land with grace. Art does not begin at the beginning, nor does it end at the conclusion. You choose the medium, and you understand that all you've done is provide a psychic vessel for the audience to inhabit for a time.

If you succeed, then you've changed someone. They moved into the space of your art and saw things, felt things that expanded their capacity. If you failed, then they flow in like water, and out like water, unaltered. Art is so human because it reflects that need to make a difference, to matter. You can choose how to end your art. Don't waste the chance to set your own terms. Only the Emperor is immortal. Art lets you muscle through rebirth as many times as you like before you come to the end that fits your life.

*- From "Collected Notes on Sullivan's Plays"*
*by Ennis Loud*

The frame trembled as Rutherford pulled himself up, chinning the bar, then relaxed down, then up again, and down, his bare arms flexing and his breathing even.

"If you're trying to impress me, it's working," Sanction said with a wry grin, wrapped in blankets and tucked up into a wicker chair.

Rutherford's face curved with a small, secret grin, but he continued with his pullups as he looked out through the glass at the fog. Dim sunlight swam in the murk, exploring its edges, ruining all visibility.

"I love the Blind Hour," Sanction murmured, and he snuggled into his blanket. "I used to imagine that the world was deciding what to be. What shape it would hold, when the dust settled." His expression soured from wistful to something else. "I suppose I know," he shrugged. "Turns out, not much changes. Just the faces, the tracks rain follows down a window, that sort of... ephemera."

Rutherford dropped to his feet, and turned to his husband. "Feeling pensive, eh," he observed.

Sanction shifted, uncomfortable. "Today Trellis pursues his grand dream," he said. "We ascend, or we fall." He looked Rutherford in the eye. "Either way, only a handful of people notice." He grinned. "One of them, however, is very important. So I figured I'd keep an eye on you instead of faffing about the Grotto. That makes it likely I survive this coup."

"It's shameless the way you use me," Rutherford observed with a solemn shake of his head, and he pulled on a thick sweater. "I fancy the old man's odds. He's been preparing for this longer than he's let on."

"Apparently my wish fulfillment dovetails with his," Sanction mused. "Who would have guessed."

"I would have," Rutherford said, "because I believe scoundrel urges are in the blood, so of course they would flow through families." He cocked his head to the side. "How are the burns?"

Sanction lifted his arms from under the blankets, revealing the rolled-up flannel sleeves and the white bandages taped around his forearms. "Delightful," he lied cheerfully enough. "If you ever have the opportunity to bang your knife against a lightning hook, I recommend abstention."

"Once again you make the tempting mistake and serve as a caution to the rest of us," Rutherford deadpanned as he lowered himself into the chair next to Sanction, turning his gaze out the window. "Along a similar line, how do you feel about all this? This direction?"

"What, tweaking the Gondoliers and slapping the Hive and generally taking charge of things?" Sanction clarified. He looked up at the glass ceiling and its constellation of droplets. "It's dangerous, and exhilarating, and a little bit mad."

"So, just what you wanted," Rutherford observed.

"Maybe what I needed," Sanction murmured.

Rutherford took Sanction's hand, and they sat together quietly watching the fog drift past the windows, thinning and draining as morning settled in.

## SILKSHORE. HIGH SIX. 12ᵀᴴ ULSIVET

Trellis paced, nervous, not looking at the Mistress of Tides where she sat with her back to the radiant tree. The morning was dim, but unusually well-lit under the glowshade of the old tree.

"Our gambit will work, yes?" he said, eventually unable to help himself.

"Patience," she murmured, eyes concealed in the spirit mask. "I've almost finished."

"Today is the day," Trellis said, tight, resuming his pacing, the city dim and murky before him.

The Mistress of Tides rose to her feet, turned, and put a cloth against the tree bark. She reached through it, shoulder deep, then withdrew her arm. "I've created a ghost door into the heart of this tree," she murmured. "If we get the charter, I can hide it here."

Trellis perceptibly relaxed. "You're a real talent," he said.

"Kind of you to say it," she replied coolly.

"I've left the High Six to you. Should all this go wrong," he said. "And if you double cross me, the prize is, well, it's rich," he said with an ironic and sour grin.

"I—I would never," she protested.

He stopped her with a raised hand. "I'm gambling on my value to you as a planner being superior to the value of the High Six," he said. "I want to elevate you, Mistress of Tides. I want to build you a temple, and fill it with acolytes, and I want you to write scripture and flense ghosts and solve riddles and—everything a Whisper could want," he said with a vague gesture.

She broke the pause reluctantly. "Why? Why me?"

He turned his back to look across the city. "Because this stinking cage rewards obedience and creativity in submission," he said, something hard in his voice. "Merit frightens those who haven't got it, who don't deserve what they get. I've seen into you, Mistress, and I know you've got—you've got untapped reserves. You're going to change this city." He let that stand for a long moment. "I want to be part of that."

"You know something," she said, a chill behind her voice.

"Yes," he replied.

She waited, but he did not move or speak.

"Tell me," she said quietly.

"No," he replied, and his smile was kindly as he turned to face her again. "Now, let's get going. We have an appointment on Grotto Hill."


## SILKSHORE. BOLDWAY CANAL STREET BRIDGE PILING. 14TH ULSIVET

"Not much has changed in five days," Gapjaw shrugged. "Smells a little worse."

"We should not have moved all the loot," the Hammer sighed. "If we're taking this place over, we should have just left it here."

"Things may have taken an unpredictable bounce," Saint said firmly, circling the table in the meeting area, ignoring the bloodstains and looking for the space's potential. "We're on the Council now, and our old base is, you know, eh," he shrugged.

Safety walked in. "I like it," he shrugged. "A bit of a maze out there. Multiple street entrances."

"You're on probation, so don't push it," the Hammer said darkly.

Red Silver followed Safety in. "Bad enough that you were informing on us," she frowned, "but you failed to kill Piccolo when the opportunity was ripe." She shook her head. "I have serious doubts about you."

"I know you're all trying to be funny," Safety said through his teeth, "but you are not funny. Let's move on." He turned deliberately to Red Silver. "I saw a lookout post atop the tower, maybe you could roost your bat up there."

"Or maybe," Red Silver countered, "you could put your sister up there so she won't compromise you again."

"Saint?" Safety said, exasperated.

"I'm sorry, you're probationary," Saint said patiently. "So until you're not, I have no reason to prevent verbal abuse." He paused. "And maybe some slapping and the occasional trip or friendly punch."

"Food tampering," Gapjaw added wisely.

"Sleep interference," the Hammer nodded.

"Demeaning makework," Red Silver said, wrapping her lips around each word as she looked Safety in the eye.

"Well what about Asdis? She's new!" Safety retorted.

"Yes, but we like her," Red Silver explained.

"She's pretty," Gapjaw clarified.

"Spine of steel," the Hammer added. "Smart."

"Safety, the takeaway here is how much we value your contributions," Red Silver said, a chill in her voice. "We feel you're good material, worth a second chance." She paused. "Or you'd be face down in a canal with hagfish stripping your corpse." She looked him in the eye, letting the moment stand.

"Fair," Safety shrugged.

"Oh, Gapjaw!" the Hammer said, suddenly remembering.

"Yes, the Hammer?" Gapjaw replied.

"I just realized someone is going to have to bring in all that stuff that's arriving at the dock downstairs and put it away!" the Hammer said.

"Good idea!" Gapjaw replied. "I will supervise—"

"Dammit," Safety sighed.

"—while Safety does it!" Gapjaw concluded.

Most everyone was laughing, and that was enough for now.


Several floors above, Asdis gazed out over the slow squirm of the river's surface, light laying uneasy on its languid turbulence. She caught her breath as she noticed Inkletta standing an arm's reach away.

"The river moves through the city like veins through flesh, draining its trash away," Inkletta murmured.

"That's deep," Asdis replied, momentarily at a loss. She cleared her throat. "So, do you think maybe I could get colors? For my ink?" she asked. She patted her shoulder, the tattoo invisible under cloth.

"You've earned it," Inkletta nodded. "That was some good work with the Hive." She paused. "If you die today, was it worth it?"

Asdis squared off with her. "Every inch," she said quietly, "because if I turned away from that challenge, the rest of my life would be reliving it until I didn't."

Inkletta's smile grew slowly. "Aren't you the fresh-faced philosopher," she said.

Asdis looked back out over the river. "Where I come from is not so different from here, underneath it all," she said quietly. "You live as hard as you can until life wrecks you and you can't." She shook her head, a wry grin taking over. "If you get old, you regret the smart choices that let you."

"You think someone like Trellis is riddled with regrets?" Inkletta asked, almost humorous.

"Yeah," Asdis said quietly.

"Well, regardless, we'll give it a week or two for the toxins I put in your tattoo as a marker to drain out, then we'll go back in," Inkletta said. "And we might want to keep some extra vigilance for curious ghosts who might be drawn to it."

Asdis looked her in the eye. "None of this would be possible if you didn't take me in, heal me, and ink me," she said. "You put yourself on the line to vouch for me. I won't forget that."

"See that you don't," Inkletta nodded. "Also, you owe me some of that Skov gold that Hutton gave you."

Asdis grinned. "It's yours," she said. "Now that we're on the Council, does that mean we don't get to plan our own scores, that we're beholden?"

"No, it means we're partners," Inkletta said. "The Council only becomes an issue if we hit members or if we draw too much attention." She shook her head. "I'll bet you Saint was talking with some of the Skovs last night to come up with our next heist."

"I guess if they don't go to war they might as well plan crime," Asdis said with a shrug.

"Criminals and spies," Inkletta said. "Grudges are expensive and stupid. The sort of thing aristocrats can afford, but people who work for a living? Hah." She stepped up to a slit in the stone, gazing over the river. "You slip their clutches if they can, or those grudges will kill you. It's all water under the bridge."

Asdis leaned against Inkletta, who tensed for a moment then put her arm around the young Skov. Together, they watched the water drift along its banks, towards the inevitable ocean.

## SILKSHORE. HIGH SIX. 16ᵀᴴ ULSIVET

Trellis sat on the bench, book in hand, basking in the glow-shade of the ancient tree. He looked up as three hooded figures approached.

"Look there," mused the woman in the lead. "A man visiting a place he owns, but controls with a light hand. Ever heard of such a thing?" She looked Trellis in the eye.

He was on his feet in a moment, and he dropped in a deep, courtly bow. "Lady Maha," he said, rising. "I am honored." His pleasant smile was impenetrable.

The woman had some silver hair flowing in her dark mane, coiffed and styled. She seemed ageless, and her dark clothes were expensive and stylish while amplifying her subtle menace. The figures flanking her were also expensively dressed, their faces concealed by fogmasks. A faint mist sifted down from under the cut of their greatcoats, almost unnoticeable.

"You are indeed honored," she agreed, sitting on his bench, the other two shadowy figures stepping a discreet distance away. "Please, join me," she said, patting the seat.

Trellis lowered himself to the opposite end of the bench, closing his book and tucking it into his coat, slowly removing his hand. He waited, a touch of bemusement in his smile.

"Surely you're wondering why I'm here," she pressed, raising her eyebrows.

"I would not intrude into your personal business, but I am entirely at your disposal," he replied, nodding a bow to her.

"So sweet," she said through her teeth, her smile a tense curl as she patted his face. "You've confronted me with a fait accompli in your sweeping assault on the balance of Silkshore," she continued.

"That seemed the least confrontational approach," Trellis agreed.

"You've got the charter," she said, counting on her fingers, "and the Gondoliers have accepted your influence, plus two thirds of my operatives in Silkshore have met gruesome ends of one kind or another. My contracts are renegotiated. Peace has been brokered between the Skov invaders and the Gondoliers." She cocked her head to the side. "My tactical plans need a total overhaul to match these new developments."

"To be fair, the last plans were probably a bit boring, yeah?" Trellis squinted. "You've had them for so many years, after all."

"Strategies are fun," she agreed with a smile, "but I like power more than fun, so I'm miffed with you. Just a bit," she said, indicating with her fingertips that a bit was not very much. "When you left, I let you live. What did I say?"

"Don't make me sorry," Trellis said. He paused. "Are you?"

"So cheeky," she replied, smiling. "You shook up Orris, now he's proving himself to me. I do enjoy that. And you know, maybe you're right; maybe sunsetting the Gondoliers was a rote move, not carefully considered. You haven't broken anything that can't be fixed." She paused. "Still. It is within my power to restore the previous balance, by the end of the day."

"Without the charter?" Trellis asked, raising his eyebrows.

"Please," she scoffed. "If I can't prevent an Imperial functionary from requesting the Charter, my comedy is more of a tragedy, don't you think?"

"Sure," he agreed easily. "So you could restore the balance. Or, strike something close," he amended. "You're here instead."

"Talk me out of it," she shrugged.

He looked down at his hands for a long moment of silence, then nodded. "Alright, let's be persuasive. You know I've got ways information gets distributed upon my death or disappearance," he said, matter of fact. "Ways that you may investigate, but cannot realistically be certain you control."

"Annoying but fair," she agreed.

"I know where the Drowned Library is," he said quietly, glancing furtively at her guards. "Every scrap of blackmail your people have centralized. The backbone of Hive power in all of Akoros, not just Doskvol."

She leaned back, her eyes unreadable. "You think you know where it is," she said.

"I offer you no proof, that knowledge is worth my life," he countered. "But what if I do? What if I pass that information on?" He intentionally eased his grip, the white fading from his knuckles. "Even a modestly successful intrusion could spell the end of the Hive as a group."

She watched him. "That's a hell of a card you haven't played," she observed.

"You're a hell of a player to visit my little table," he retorted, looking her in the eye. "You don't flash a hole card like this at the help." His smile was a touch unsure, he could not stop adrenaline from filtering through every inch of his blood.

"And your crew? Your confidants?" she said. "Anyone else know?"

"Only upon my death or disappearance. Even then, there are... conditions." He shrugged. "It's complicated."

She looked at him for a long moment, then smiled to herself. "The Worms of Silkshore, also known as the Silkworms, will pay double the standard tithe to the Hive's agents in exchange for their free operation," she said. "I think you can spare it," she added, conspiratorial.

"And in exchange for all that fountaining wealth?" Trellis dared.

Lady Maha rose from the bench. "We have a new status quo," she shrugged.

"So you're not sorry?" Trellis pressed.

"What, that I let you go?" Lady Maha replied with an arched eyebrow. "Oh, Trellis of Barrowcleft, the fun we may yet have..." Her smile deepened. "Let's go another round." She glanced at her two guards, and they fell in step with her as she strode away from the ancient radiant tree.

"One more round," Trellis whispered to himself as the shakes overtook his hands. He focused and took a deep breath.

"You knew this was coming, old boy," he muttered. Still, the tremors in his legs kept him from rising off the bench for a few minutes more as his composure slowly returned.

Life, in all its vulnerability, was extra sweet for the whole of that day and the next.

The key turned out to be unnecessary, as the door had been kicked in then nailed shut. Sanction squinted at the crooked front door, his forehead creased. "I didn't bring a prybar," he said, his voice small.

Rutherford took a step forward and lashed out with a practiced kick, knocking the door in with a bang. He shouldered against a plank across the doorframe, splintering it, and stepped into the smoky cave that had once been his home. Sanction followed.

"Bluecoat training at its finest," Sanction mused.

"Looks like we had some squatters over the last month," Rutherford observed, looking around the wreckage. "Little fires there. I doubt upstairs will be a pretty sight."

Sanction walked into the living room, where bars of light filtered in between the boards over the windows. "Blood and bone," he murmured to himself. The burning stench lingered, along with various smells of neglect and despair. Yet some of the pictures were still on the wall, blackened and crooked.

Rutherford unlocked the tool closet, which was untouched, and joined Sanction in the living room. This time he had a prybar.

"I don't know," Sanction said, looking around. "Maybe we start over somewhere."

"Took us a year to get into this place, even with all of your skullduggery," Rutherford said. "I barely care about this," he added, gesturing at the burned living room with the prybar. He attacked the doorway to the balcony, peeling off the boards, then stepped out. Taking a deep breath, he surveyed the river, the far shore, the lights and the darkness of the overbuilt city. "This, right here, is why I wanted this place."

"It's a hell of a view," Sanction agreed softly from inside the living room, looking at his husband framed by the smoke-damaged walls and nail-chewed doorframe, awash in the dying of the light, resolute and armed.

"This place was a lot of things before we moved in, and I pretty much rebuilt it," Rutherford said, squinting at the drowning sun. "I'm happy to do it again."

"You just—you can't give up, can you," Sanction murmured. He stepped out on the balcony. "You can't just let a broken thing be broken."

Rutherford looked at him sharply. "I think you know that I can," he replied. "I'm not going to torture any metaphors here. You are different. I think you were born different. And that was one of the things that—our spark came from me, on the side of law, and you, on the side of mischief. I thought maybe if we both stepped away and found a middle ground, it would work. And for a while it did." He paused. "I think I'm capable of satisfying my need for law and order in my own way, but you? You've got to chase your own madness and power down paths I don't understand." He looked back at the river. "We found our balance once." His resolve steeled his voice and expression. "Stay with me and find it again."

Overcome with emotion, Sanction could only answer with a kiss.

## SILKSHORE. MASTER MARKET, ZEPHYR STREET, MAURO OVERVIEW. 18TH ULSIVET

The Mistress of Tides stood in the broad window and looked down at the sheer drop of five or six stories, and the market bustling below. Beyond that narrow strip of activity, water glittered, and the gondola trade bustled across the surface as the canals accessed the river.

"This place came to mind," Faliq said quietly. "My great-aunt was a powerful Whisper, like you, even as a young woman. This was her place, where she held court." He glanced around. "I didn't realize how bare it was without her."

"So the gallery here, two rooms above, the main floor, and a basement?" the Mistress of Tides clarified.

"Yes, this space should belong to a Whisper with the Gondoliers," Faliq nodded. "You were with us once, before Trellis. Now, we share interests, yes? Work together?" There was something almost anxious in his tone.

The Mistress of Tides put her hand on his shoulder, her flesh cool. "We rise and fall on the same tides," she assured him quietly. "I feel your success as my own."

"Trellis has been good to his word," Faliq shrugged. "You can understand our... you know."

"I know," the Mistress of Tides nodded. "You made the right decision helping us. We will continue to help each other. The Hive is still a very real threat, and others will make their moves as well."

"There's another matter," Faliq said, turning away from the window and crossing to a bench. He sat down. "A number of your former peers are interested in joining your adepts. Learning at your feet. Serving the Silkworms."

The barest of smiles touched her features. "I'll get my disciples and we'll set something up. I've got room for two more. Now that we've got some stature."

Faliq paused. "Do you think this will all work out?" he asked quietly.

"For now," she shrugged. "That's all the guarantee you could hope for."

## SILKSHORE. THE EASE, CARMEL DOWNS CLUB. 18ᵗʰ ULSIVET

The door swept open and Piccolo swaggered in, his new coat and hat still dark and crisp, a squeak in his tall leather boots. He slapped a handful of coins down on the counter, leaning against it conspiratorially.

"Hevden, my dear man, I believe this settles up my tab here," he said with a smug grin.

"Huh," the neckless barkeep said, looking down at the pile before sweeping it off the counter and tucking it in his belt pouch.

"I thought you'd be pleased," Piccolo prompted.

"Eh, you lost me a bet. I figured you'd never pay me back and we'd have to sell your debt to somebody who cuts stuff off dead-beats like you," the barkeep shrugged.

"Got all my digits and wiggly bits right here, and it's time to party," Piccolo grinned.

"Megs is out of Ironhook, came here first. Settled some score, I gotta get that cleaned up. In the meantime, she's over there," he said with a nod to the far end of the bar.

Piccolo squinted. "You sure that's Megs?" he said, skeptical.

"She's been in Ironhook for six months," Hevden shrugged. "She might be hungry enough to want whoever's behind all those shiny brass buttons," he added with a sardonic nod to Piccolo's waistcoat.

"I know, these buttons are awesome," Piccolo grinned. He left the barkeep, strolling around to where Megs sat at the bar with a dusty bottle, half full.

"Well, look at you!" Piccolo said.

Megs glanced up at him, then smiled broadly. "My little Piccolo!" she gleed, and she pulled him into a hug. "Look how fancy you are!" A certain grayness had settled in, touching her hair, her gums, her teeth, the whites of her eyes, her fingernails. It was a common side effect of hard times in Ironhook.

"Yeah, my crew pretty much runs things," Piccolo shrugged.

"You got on with the River Stallions?" Megs said skeptically.

"What? Oh, yeah, but then I left them and they put a death mark on me. So we got this badass family crew going on and took over the Gondoliers, and Skovs, and now we kind of run things."

"Okay, sure," Megs said, not particularly caring whether his boast was true or not. "At least you got money out of it!"

"Yeah, I know, right?" Piccolo agreed. "I figured we'd be doing scores and stealing museum stuff and art, and books, and maybe kidnappings and murder and all that. Making some money. But instead it turns out getting paid by other crews for the privilege of operating has mad money in it." He shrugged. "And we own the High Six, so if you want a pass to visit, you just come to me and we'll get it taken care of." Another broad grin.

"You are so full of it," Megs scoffed. "But you're funny. I like funny. I've missed funny."

"Are you coming on to me?" Piccolo asked with a grin, cocking an eyebrow.

She looked him in the eye and grabbed his crotch.

"Right!" he yelled. "We'll be upstairs!" he informed the barkeep and general surrounds, and then he followed Megs up the rickety stairs to the stained rooms above.

Megs kissed him against a wall, and pulled back with a predatory smile. "You taste good," she breathed.

"That's all the good luck," he agreed. "Believe me, you want in on this."

With a laugh, they tumbled into the room, and the door slammed behind them.

# TIMELINE

| DATE | PLACE | EVENT | CHAPTER |
|------|-------|-------|---------|
| *Suran 51* | Silkshore, Ankhayat Park | Nebs and Kreeger talk in the park. | 1 |
| *Suran 51* | Silkshore, River Stallions Tower | Get back from Grinder raid gone wrong, Piccolo leaves the Stallions. | 1 |
| *Suran 52* | Silkshore, Lotus Vericae | Stallions wreck the Red Sash drug den for the Gondoliers | 6 |
| *Suran 52* | Silkshore, Veyles Tea Shop | Piccolo tries to persuade Kreeger to go into professional crime. | 1 |
| *Suran 52* | Silkshore, Chimewater Close | Gapjaw attacks Kreeger's home, shoots Rutherford, Piccolo starts fire. | 1 |
| *Suran 52* | Silkshore, Master Market, under the Boldway Canal streets | Mistress of Tides uses a ritual to conceal a tunnel entrance for Captain Hutch of the Gray Cloaks, were shortchanged. | 2 |
| *Suran 52* | Barrowcleft, Belderan Estate | Adepts talk to Belderan about Gray Cloaks job as insurance. | 2 |
| *Suran 52* | Barrowcleft, Belderan Estate | Kreeger and Rutherford seek asylum with Belderan, offer payment in the form of doing a heist to get Mistress of Tides on board. | 2 |
| *Suran 52* | Silkshore, The Ease, Central Landing | Stallions ask Tarjan and gondoliers for a seat on the council, get shot down. Inkletta detects more sickness among gondoliers. | 6 |
| *Suran 53* | Silkshore, Master Market, Zephyr Street underbridge stalls | Kreeger meets with Neap to arrange a meeting with Mistress of Tides. | 2 |
| *Suran 53* | Silkshore, Grinder Hall | Stallions meet to get terms to not go to war. | 6 |

| DATE | PLACE | EVENT | CHAPTER |
|---|---|---|---|
| *Suran 53* | Silkshore, Master Market, under the Sluice Den | Kreeger recruits Mistress of Tides to go after the High Six gardens. | 2 |
| *Suran 54* | Silkshore, Busker's Court | Stallions meet with Hutch, form an alliance against the Skovs, Nails leads the way to the back door to the Gray Cloak hideout. Red Silver checks it out. | 6, 7 |
| *Suran 54* | Barrowcleft, Belderan Estate | Kreeger, Rutherford, and Styles get settled in Belderan's estate. | 2 |
| *Suran 54* | Silkshore, River Stallions Tower | River Stallions start planning Whipwater Point while eating Wingdae's menu. | 7 |
| *Suran 55* | Silkshore, the Diving Bell, Hour of Thread | The crew meets for the first time to begin planning the High Six heist. | 3 |
| *Suran 55* | Silkshore, the Ease, Grinder Safehouse | Asdis is feverish but still alive. | 5 |
| *Suran 56* | Six Towers, the Centralia Club | Sanction as Crendél gets Mora's attention as a customer for the Eye. | 4 |
| *Suran 56* | Crow's Foot, Tangletown, Empress of Gulls' Workshop Sloop Wreck | Mistress of Tides goes to her mentor and begins putting together a fake Eye of Kotar. Very expensive. | 3 |
| *Suran 56* | Silkshore, Barkskin Tavern adjacent basement | River Stallions plan to assault Whipwater Point. | 11 |
| *Suran 57* | Barrowcleft, Belderan Estate | Involve Mordis. Twisting fate. | 4 |
| *Suran 57* | Silkshore, the Ease, another Grinder Safehouse | Asdis is feverish but still alive. | 5 |
| *Suran 58* | Nightmarket, Dundridge & Sons Tailor | Trellis recruits Mordis, agrees to give up some radiants. | 4 |

| Date | Place | Event | Chapter |
|------|-------|-------|---------|
| *Suran 58* | Silkshore, Ankhayat Park | Saint and Inkletta pose as doctor and nurse and check Mrs. Turlough's case of the Slip, learning more, suspecting an infected energy cyst. | 7 |
| *Suran 59* | Sillkshore, the Ease, a third Grinder Safehouse | Asdis recovers enough to stab Knut and escape by gondola. | 5 |
| *Suran 59* | Nightmarket, The Veil social club | Pull the heist to get the High Six gardens from Mora with the help of Mordis, who gives Mora the Crystal of Syzannaran as payment. | 3, 4 |
| *Suran 60* | Silkshore. High Six. | Trellis makes peace with Mora and takes possession of the High Six. | 4 |
| *Suran 60* | Barrowcleft, Belderan Estate | The crew forms in the empty attic. | 4 |
| *Ulsivet 1* | Barrowcleft, Belderan Estate | Marcus visits Kreeger, offers him 3 days to get back to work. | 5 |
| *Ulsivet 1* | Crow's Foot, Candle Street Butchers | Asdis finds Ryha's shop and gets help. | 5 |
| *Ulsivet 1* | Silkshore, Silver Stag Casino | Safety meets with his sneering contacts and reveals the Slipshore plan; they represent Inspectors but he knows they answer to the Hive as well. | 7 |
| *Ulsivet 2* | Barrowcleft, Belderan Estate | Kreeger and Rutherford have a heart to heart about the future. | 5 |
| *Ulsivet 2* | Crow's Foot, Candle Street Butchers | Asdis has a heart to heart with Rhya about the future. | 5 |
| *Ulsivet 4* | Silkshore, Crownwind Court | Safety goes to Red Silver's tenement tower and nurses her back to health from the edge of death. After they leave, Asdis waits for her in her apartment. | 7 |
| *Ulsivet 5* | Barrowcleft, Belderan Estate | Discover Nebs has been evicted to punish Kreeger. | 8 |

| DATE | PLACE | EVENT | CHAPTER |
|------|-------|-------|---------|
| *Ulsivet 5* | The Ease, Carmel Downs Club | Trellis retrieves Piccolo from stupor. | 8 |
| *Ulsivet 5* | The Ease, West Shells | Sanction retrieves the Mistress of Tides. | 8 |
| *Ulsivet 5* | Silkshore, Fog Crest, Chime Era Bookstore | Sanction shakes down Director Talithia Walker on behalf of Nelytha Bel's pension, evicting Tyla Barrsly, mother of Marcus Barrsly, Sanction's former boss who got Nebs evicted. | 8 |
| *Ulsivet 5* | Silkshore, Crownwind Court | Asdis makes her case to Red Silver. | 9 |
| *Ulsivet 5* | Silkshore, Stitchery Alley | Red Silver takes Asdis to Inkletta, who gets a surgeon and starts on Asdis' tattoo. | 9 |
| *Ulsivet 6* | Crow's Foot, Tangletown | Inkletta buys pre-made ritual for Leviathan's Shrug. | 11 |
| *Ulsivet 6* | Silkshore, Busker's Court | Saint arranges a mock battle so it looks like the Grinders took out the River Stallions. (The staging is that night, offscreen.) | 9 |
| *Ulsivet 6* | The Ease, Central Landing | Trellis threatens Khyro, telling him they are going to take over the gondolier leadership. | 8 |
| *Ulsivet 7* | Silkshore, Whipwater Point | Gapjaw and the Hammer get into Whipwater Point pretending to have Red Silver the Widow's coffins for transport, place explosives. | 11 |
| *Ulsivet 7* | Silkshore, River Stallions tower | Saint shows Ingvald of the Grinders the scene of the "battle" and convinces him the River Stallions are done. | 9 |
| *Ulsivet 7* | Silkshore, Carven Forest Market | Trellis gets Zhavo to hire him. | 10 |
| *Ulsivet 7* | Charterhall, Clerk Street, Elliott Cartographer & Law | Trellis gets the dirt on the Hierophant from the blackmailer Elliott. | 10 |

| Date | Place | Event | Chapter |
|---|---|---|---|
| *Ulsivet 7* | Barrowcleft, Belderan Estate | Sanction thinks things are going too fast. | 10 |
| *Ulsivet 8* | Six Towers, Mistshore Park | Worms assassinate the Hierophant. | 10 |
| *Ulsivet 8* | Silkshore, Barkskin Tavern adjacent basement | River Stallions prepare for the Whipwater Point meeting the next day. We find out Safety has a metal arm. Saint makes sure the Grinders took the bait, reports such. | 9 |
| *Ulsivet 8* | Silkshore, Barkskin Tavern adjacent basement | Hammer squeezed his snitch, found out a secret, talks to Red Silver. | 11 |
| *Ulsivet 8* | Silkshore, The Ease, Flag's End | Trellis gets Lord Skora to hire him to hit Gaddoc Station. | 10 |
| *Ulsivet 9* | Nightmarket, Gaddoc Rail Station, Platform 9 | Early morning attack on the train just after the spirit warden shift change; encounter Chosen. Steal the ferngristlee, blow up the train, use zip lines to get down under the platform to a service canal and away. | 10, 12 |
| *Ulsivet 9* | Silkshore, Whipwater Point | The big battle, where Ingvald dies, along with lots of Grinders (and pouncers) and Gray Cloaks, and the hull is pulled underwater, the Point destroyed. Captain Hutch of the Gray Cloaks escapes. Hutton, of the Grinders, escapes. Saint, Red Silver, Inkletta, and Safety escape. | 11 |
| *Ulsivet 9* | Boldway Canal Street Bridge Piling | Gapjaw and the Hammer sneak into the base and capture the Hive spy Marsden, then confront Hutch when he returns. They kill Hutch and Marsden as well as all the other Gray Cloaks, then take the treasure room key and loot the base. | 11 |

| Date | Place | Event | Chapter |
|---|---|---|---|
| *Ulsivet 10* | Silkshore, The Ease, Central Landing | Saint and Safety meet Tarjan, get invited to the Council gathering, apply for membership. | 14 |
| *Ulsivet 10* | Dunslough, Ironhook Overflow Incarceration | Trellis used Inspector fake credentials to talk to Faliq Ludellem, Bard of the Canals, to offer to rescue his son Tanuk from Lord Cornelius Bowmore the necromancer in exchange for opening the funerary gondola for Saramanca Ludellem so he can retrieve the charter. | 13 |
| *Ulsivet 10* | Silkshore, Barkskin Tavern adjacent basement | River Stallions are celebrating the invitation, Red Silver introduces Asdis, their secret weapon, and she is accepted by the Stallions. | 14 |
| *Ulsivet 11* | Silkshore, Silver Stag Casino Grounds | Safety reports to his handlers about Asdis and is ordered to capture her. | 14 |
| *Ulsivet 11* | Six Towers, Throughline Canal, Adjacent to the Bowmore House | Sanction, Piccolo, Mistress of Tides, and Neap intrude into the house with the Bowmore signet ring and a cloaking ritual. | 13 |
| *Ulsivet 11* | Fogcrest, Tenwylder's Tea House | Trellis meets with Mordis to sell him the Bowmore signet ring he's using to break in across town, and their meeting is crashed by a furious Bowmore who wants the ring. (Trellis bought information on Mordis' calendar and arranged for it to be sold to Bowmore.) Trellis demonstrates the hat trick and names the crew the Worms. | 13 |

| DATE | PLACE | EVENT | CHAPTER |
|---|---|---|---|
| *Ulsivet 11* | Six Towers, Bowmore House | They sneak past ugly hackwork of unsealed ghost containment, and they kill a couple railjack guards before pulling Tanuk out of the mirror. They blow the door holding the ghosts below, and throw a bomb into the gathering railjack guards that knocks the wall out, and they escape down through the yard and Slack has a ladder over the wall and a goat with a cart so they can all escape. | 13 |
| *Ulsivet 11* | Barrowcleft, Belderan Estate | Debrief. Tanuk returned, Mordis will hunt out his mole selling his schedule, Mordis paying for the ring will pay off Fallowthrush. | 13 |
| *Ulsivet 12* | Barrowcleft, Belderan Estate | Rutherford and Sanction consider the future. | 16 |
| *Ulsivet 12 midday* | Silkshore, Grotto Hill | Saint and Inkletta have a gondolier pilot take them down the locks into the Mistyard. | 14 |
| *Ulsivet 12* | Silkshore, High Six | Trellis and Mistress of Tides prepare the hiding place ghost door for the charter in the oak. Trellis reveals he knows a secret about the Mistress of Tides, and that she is his heir. | 16 |
| *Ulsivet 12* | Silkshore, Grotto Hill, Mistyard | Trellis and the Gondoliers with him interrupt the Council, Trellis lays down the new law, dismissing counselors and raising prices on affiliates. He gives the Stallions a seat on the Council and they lift the death mark on Piccolo, and also Saint tells the Silkworms about the plot to capture Asdis, which they green-light. | 15 |
| *Ulsivet 13* | Silkshore, Grinder Hall | The Silkworms, Stallions, and Gondoliers meet with the new speaker, Sercy, and they apologize and offer a seat on the council and show Asdis back; Hutton is so pleased he agrees. | 15 |

| DATE | PLACE | EVENT | CHAPTER |
|------|-------|-------|---------|
| *Ulsivet 13* | Silkshore, Grinder Hall | The Silkworms, Stallions, and Gondoliers meet with the new speaker, Sercy, and they apologize and offer a seat on the council and show Asdis back; Hutton is so pleased he agrees. | 15 |
| *Ulsivet 13* | Silkshore, Grinder Hall | Asdis steps out, Safety goes with her, kidnaps her for the Hive, is left behind so she is taken to meet with Karth Orris in the mansions behind the Silver Stag casino. He wants to turn her, but her tattoo leaks behind the Mirror, so her back-up is nearby. Orris tries to escape, but Trellis confronts him and gets him to sign agreements that favor the Gondolier Council, and release Safety's sister from Iron Hook, and they all part ways. | 15 |
| *Ulsivet 14* | Boldway Canal Street Bridge Piling | River Stallions move into their new base with general banter, Safety on probation. | 16 |
| *Ulsivet 16* | Silkshore, High Six | Trellis is confronted by Maha, leader of the Hive, who decides to let his antics stand. | 16 |
| *Ulsivet 17* | Silkshore, Chimewater Close | Sanction and Rutherford return to their home. | 16 |
| *Ulsivet 18* | Silkshore, Master Market, Zephyr Street, Mauro Overview | Faliq hands a space over to the Mistress of Tides for living and working, and she will be receiving more adepts to serve her. | 16 |
| *Ulsivet 18* | Silkshore, the Ease, Carmel Downs Club | Piccolo is dressed nicely, pays off his tab with Hevden the owner, and sexes up Megs who is fresh out of Ironhook. | 16 |

# PATREON SPONSORS

Thank you for your support while I was writing. You change what is possible.

Blaze Azelski
David Brock
Jeremy Collins
Noah Crisp
Chuck Dee
Ryan Dunleavy
edchuk
Todd Estabrook
Benjamin Hamdorf
John Harper
Phyllis Hurshman
Kear
Kevin
Eli Kurtz
René Lößner
Nat Lanza
MapForge
Elizabeth Parmeter
miller ramos
RavenRavel
James Robertson
Mark Robison
Max Stevenson
Video Store Cowboy
Logan Waterman

Made in the USA
Las Vegas, NV
01 July 2021

25790690R00156